STORIES FROM CALLAMAR

Maylea and Jonah

A Novel by

BRENT NEUMANN

DEDICATION

This book is dedicated to everyone in the world who is stuggling to live life as a good person and struggling to live life on their own terms.

TABLE OF CONTENTS

PROLOGUE

Pierre Rodin, Professor of History at Callamar University, sat in his office rereading several of his recent correspondence while finishing a small cup of coffee. Hearing a knock on his open office door, he turned to see the department secretary, Martina, silhouetted in the doorway.

"Sorry to bother you, sir, but there is a man at my desk asking for you by name but he doesn't have an appointment. He claims he is from a company called Callamar Recyclers that does demolition work in New Callamar."

Curious, Rodin thought. "Did he say what his business concerned?"

"No, but he did say he had a truck load of documents just outside in the courtyard."

"All right, thank you. If you don't mind, please see him here to my office. We shall find out what he wants." Martina went back to her desk and escorted the man to Professor Rodin's office.

Rodin pondered, *documents*? He was now very curious as he had no reason to believe he knew anyone in the demolition business or the construction business for that matter.

A well-built man in rough work clothes appeared in his doorway holding a hard hat in front of him with both hands. He asked, "Are you Professor Rodin?"

"Yes, I am Rodin. How may I help you?"

The man smiled. "Thank you for seeing me. My name is Gordo and you probably won't recall me as we've never met. But I did notice you and some of your colleagues in the Bardic Echoes Tavern some months ago and overheard you discussing history. That's how I remembered your name."

"Yes, I frequent Bardic Echoes along with my colleagues. I also conduct research on historical topics regarding the history of the northern kingdoms."

Gordo smiled again. "I work for a demolition company, Callamar Recyclers. I apologize for my appearance. My company is currently demolishing several buildings located on the east side of Old Callamar to make way for a new business and commercial complex. The building we have been demolishing has three floors. While dismantling the upper floors, we came across a secret room with a large stash of old books and loose papers. My foreman instructed me to get rid of them. I was going to donate them to one of the libraries but then I remembered you and I thought I would ask you first if you would like to buy them before I donate them."

You sound like a scalper, Rodin thought. "I will have to see the books first before deciding if they are worth anything."

"My truck is parked outside in the courtyard turnaround. I can show them to you right now if it would please you. All of the papers and books appear to be handwritten and I cannot read or understand most of them."

"All right. Lead me to your papers and I'll have a look."

Gordo led Professor Rodin to his truck which held the books and two of his work buddies. Rodin's first impression was of an enormous stash of volumes falling apart and loose papers in great disarray. Gordo grabbed one of the books from the truck and handed it to Rodin. Rodin began thumbing through the pages and recognized that they were handwritten in old suborean. The papers were very tattered and handwritten using feather quills instead of fountain pens. He looked at several of the other loose documents noting some were summaries of information while others contained poetry and literature. It soon dawned on Rodin that he was looking at documents several hundred years old.

Rodin was finding it hard to contain his excitement about the find. "Gordo, what were you hoping to get for these papers?"

Gordo pondered, "Well, I don't know if they are valuable or not but I was hoping to get maybe twenty gold crowns for the lot."

"All right. I will buy them from you for thirty crowns split three ways for you and your two buddies here. If that sounds acceptable, you and your buddies can unload them into my office. There is a small side room where you can stack them." In a short time, the three men unloaded all of the papers into Rodin's office. Rodin retrieved several bank notes he kept stashed in a secret book on one of his office shelves and gave one to each of the three men. "Each of these bank notes will get you ten gold crowns from the Bank of Callamar. I am buying all of your papers and any more you find in the future. Deal?"

"Yes, that sounds like a deal. Thank you, professor. We will bring any more papers we find directly to you."

"Thank you very much for thinking of me. And, oh, here are some silvers for your next round at Bardic Echoes."

The three men thanked Professor Rodin profusely then mounted their truck and drove away. Rodin went over to the stacks of documents and wondered what secrets they contained. Several bound volumes were old diaries while others held loose letters. Some were reports of some kind while others appeared to be ledgers of expenses.

As the months passed, Rodin organized the papers. While many of the documents were reports and diaries useful for academic purposes, they were mostly about ordinary people living extraordinary lives. He began rewriting their stories, giving new life to their long-silent voices.

PART 1

Anya and Maylea

Anya and Maylea fled farm and granger
While living a life of risk and danger.
Maylea was younger
And Anya the stronger.
Both feared neither friend nor stranger.

One day in a bar they were minding their own
When a tipsy man called, of local renown.
He was really a brute
When he tried to get cute
Then kissed up the floor with a groan.

But this cocky man was a noble chap
Who wouldn't stand for a womanly slap.
He challenged her strength
To wrestling arm length
And felt his arm break with a snap.

His buddy drew steel and spat on her ground
When Maylea, now armed, spun quickly around.
She uttered a curse
While swiping his purse
Then knocked him out cold in a round.

"There's nothing here but vermin and mice.
Let's leave this place to these parasites."
Midst shock and uproar
They went for the door
Then out of the village and into the night.

Flight

Along the northern edge of Wesseltown farms, outbuildings, and fields lie covered in newly fallen snow. Near a fenced field of half-eaten grass a barn sleeps quietly in the morning cold. Sporadic snowfall sprinkles two sets of footprints leading in through the barn's rear door. Within, the still air chills the stalls where several animals lie huddled together keeping warm. A nearby haystack fills one corner of the barn creating a cozy cocoon for two girls sleeping within its depths.

Leaning against one wall many farming tools stand arrayed. From the wall, a wooden pitchfork animates then plunges into the haystack poking around. Within the hay, Anya dreams of outrunning pursuers then trips and falls thinking, *oof.* Unexpected pain jolts her awake. Everything around her is dark and prickly when the pitchfork jabs her in the ribs again.

"I know yer en there. Git out," an old woman's voice rasped menacingly.

The haystack shuddered as Anya squirmed away from the pitchfork's wooden tines. Soon they returned, narrowly missing her head and stabbing the floor with a thud. Unable to roll away, Anya bumped up against May, waking her.

"You can't stay here. You have to git," the old woman said.

Anya's muffled voice emerged, "All right, I'm coming out; stop your poking."

May groaned, "Huh?"

"Git out. You can't stay here," the old woman repeated.

Anya and May groggily crawled out from under the haystack and were greeted by a glowering older woman wrapped in dark woolen robes, chiding them, prodding them with a pitchfork.

Anya swatted the pitchfork away. "Stop! We're out. We're just passing through and –"

"I know why yer here and you can't stay. Everyone knows what happened last night. The Baron's son, Willem and his goons and his hounds will all be up soon looking for you twos. And if they find you HERE, I'll git trouble so you have to go now! You twos'll both be in trouble and it'll not be pretty when they drag you down the road to the manor."

Anya and May blearily looked at the older woman then at each other as they slowly got up and brushed off the hay sticking out from their clothes.

"It's too cold to leave now and where can we go? We don't know our way around," May protested.

"I don't care where you twos go but you can't stay here. If you take the road through town, they'll catch you. Yer best chance is to walk the creek through the woods. The hounds won't catch you if yer lucky."

Anya looked at May and saw that she was cold but also concerned that they might get caught and dragged away like animals, maybe even beaten.

"Give us a moment to make a fire and warm up before we leave," May pleaded.

"Look, I'm glad you gave him his due, but there's no time. You have to git now. Follow the creek. It ain't froze over so you might still fool the hounds. The creek is cold but not snow cold. You look strong enough to handle the cold so you might get away."

The old woman reached out for a small burlap sack she had set on a nearby table. "Here, take this and be off." She tossed the bag at Anya pointing a finger towards the rear door, "Out that door so no one sees you. I don't like to sees anyone git into troubles 'cause the Baron and his good-for-nothing son run this town and they hurts people without good reasons."

Anya and May quickly packed up and reluctantly left through the rear door heading north towards the creek. A newly stirring breeze stung their faces. The ground snow did not hamper their progress though it preserved their footprints, confessing their flight. Their clothes were not very warm but the lack of wind made the cold tolerable. The trees thickened a little until at last they reached the creek. The steady gurgling of flowing water gave them some hope. Anya looked at May as she said, "The old woman said to walk in the creek but I don't think that's a good idea. It's cold and our feet'll freeze in no time." May paused then replied, "Let's just walk beside the creek. It doesn't look too hard to follow."

They began following the Creekside, leaving footprints. In the distance, they could hear the howling of dogs – the old woman had been right. They picked up their pace. Their shoes began accumulating snow and the cold slowly crept into their shoes, into their feet. Half a mile became a mile then two as the snow slowly thickened. Their crunching footsteps grew louder and their efforts to continue became more difficult. The barking of dogs still sounded menacing in the distance. The gurgling creek did not help their hearing but the barking did not seem to be fading.

As their exertions increased, they began sweating. Their chilled bodies shivered with each gust of wind. Each step froze their feet further. Wind gusts increased in frequency until there was a howling breeze. After some time, Anya and May felt the pangs of fatigue and sore muscles sneak up on them while the barking did not fade. If anything, it sounded louder and closer. Fortunately, the sound of flowing water was still sufficient to mask the noise of their shoes plodding through the snow. Then the snow got deeper.

"This isn't working. I'm getting tired and the dogs are not going away. If the Baron's son brought horses, they'll catch us for sure no matter how much of a lead we have." Reluctantly Anya said, "I think we should start walking in the creek." Anya stepped into the creek and found it was not deep. Soon, she found her effort was not as bad as crunching through the snow. But also, she could feel the icy cold slowly creeping into every part of her feet and legs. May followed Anya into the water. They were soon making better time though the cold was getting worse. Splashing the creek and trudging the snow took its toll and their feet went from cold to numb.

At long last Anya huffed out, "We can't sustain this pace. We have to lead the dogs away." Catching her breath, she said, "I'll make a false trail then double-back. You keep moving up the creek and I'll catch you soon. If we don't do this now, the dogs'll be on us. Stay in the water as you go and leave no footprints."

Cold and tired May responded, "Yesss."

Anya found a narrow snowless patch of forest floor. She began leaving a trail of obvious footprints away from the creek. After a good distance she took out a leather pouch and spread a few pinches of crushed weeds along her path and footprints then continued a little further up the way. Doubling-back she returned to the creek. But before continuing, she spread a few more pinches of weeds then secured the pouch back in her bag. Briskly she raced to catch up with May.

And then something strange happened. The creek water began to feel warm against Anya's feet. She reached down into the water with her hands and felt the same lukewarm sensation. She found this phenomenon puzzling but did not dwell on it long. She returned to plodding upstream until she finally caught up with May.

May was bent forward with her hands on her knees resting in the creek water when Anya came upon her, saying, "We have to keep moving. We can't slow down now." May nodded reluctantly in agreement. Both girls drew upon their reserves of energy and strong legs to carry them further into the cold evening. They plodded upstream leaving no footprints or scent behind. Gradually, the barking of dogs grew fainter. Anya swore she could hear the yelps of confused dogs but the gurgling creek and wind made it difficult to be sure. "I think we may have lost them, but let's not stop yet," Anya huffed.

May said through chattering teeth, "I'm cccold and tir'd. I cccan't feel any ... I cccan't go on."

"All right, just a little farther and then we'll rest and build a fire. I can't hear the dogs anymore, I think."

Soon, they happened upon a snowless clearing that contained mostly dead grass and needles. Nearby, a few young evergreens formed a small enclosure with a single entrance. Breathing heavily May stopped and nearly collapsed. The wind began picking up again, moaning through the clearing and sapping the last of May's strength. May went to the ground and began shivering. Anya could see that May was in danger of freezing and immediately began collecting dry grass and twigs. Anya pulled out her flint and steel and began to make a fire. Amazingly, the fire was easy to start and sustain. She gathered some rocks and a few larger branches, building up a warm campfire. Anya reached down and dragged May over to the fire and then removed her shoes and socks. She faced May to the fire and began rubbing her back, feet, and hands vigorously.

Much time passed. Anya's careful tending of the fire and monitoring of May slowly brought her hands and feet back to life. Anya also set up a small leeward shelter she kept packed in her bag for just such occasions. Despite the wind, their camp began to achieve a mild coziness in which they both fell asleep together, exhausted.

Decision

May was a big girl who stood almost six feet in height with strong arms and legs. Maylea was her real name but growing up she had always been called May so she thought of herself as May. Her light brunette hair fell to just below her shoulders though she mostly wore it in a ponytail that she could easily tuck underneath her sheepskin cap. Her face was a bit chiseled into a squarish jaw line with some rounding at the corners. Her brown eyes were framed by short dark eyelashes.

Inside May's pack, she kept a flint and steel, a whetstone, a small padlock with a key, a long thin leather rope, an extra tunic with pantaloons, and a few extra underclothes and woolen socks. Nestled with the rope, May kept some spare leather scraps which she frequently used when making traps and snares for catching small game such as rabbits. Tied to the outside of her pack was a homemade water skin and a custom sheath holding her prized skinning knife.

Like May, Anya was big and strong but she was taller at over six feet and stronger. How else could she have broken the Baron's son's arm with a single-swift motion? She was also brown haired with fair skin and lighter hazel eyes. Her cheeks were more rounded than May's. She was strong, fearless, and good-looking all at once. Anya carried a shoulder satchel of sorts holding an extra set of warm clothes, her own flint and steel, several wax candles, and a small leather pouch with many small compartments, each containing several types of herbs and weeds. Tied to her belt was a vicious-looking hunting knife.

Anya and May had been traveling together for some time after running away from home back in Farmston where they both lived. May was an only child living with her father on a farm. May's mother had died not long after she was born, and her father had grieved her for many years. When May was younger, her father taught her how to handle animals like goats and pigs and even to ride their one horse before the horse died. They had a small farmstead where they grew much of their own food, harvested eggs from their coop, and sold some crops in town for a few silvers. However, when May reached her teenage years, her father succumbed to drink and before long, had poured all of their money and miseries into his drinking habit. Overcome with drink, he became abusive and accusatory towards May and that was when May sorrowfully decided that she would have to leave. Nothing she had said or done ever convinced or compelled her father to return to his old happier ways.

Anya had been May's good friend in their younger years and did not live far from May's farm. Anya came from a larger family but was much younger than her siblings. Anya took a liking to May when they first met and they had been friends ever since. Farm work had made the two girls strong and they grew up surprisingly big for their age. May's naivete was always getting her into trouble without really trying and Anya was always there to help bail May out of her troubles. When May decided to run away, she confided in Anya. Anya convinced herself that she needed to go along with May as she did not think May could take care of herself all alone. Anya had always hoped that May would eventually grow homesick and long to return home, ending their wayward adventures. Then one night in a bar changed everything for the worse.

The embers from Anya and May's campfire cooled throughout the night. Anya's leeward shelter and the young trees kept them slightly warmer than the surrounding forest and deflected the wind. Anya held May as they huddled together by the dying embers. May clutched her pack tightly, keeping the cold away from her body core.

Anya slowly opened an eye and peeked about. She heard May sleeping soundly. Anya did not want to wake May but she knew that they had to keep moving lest the dogs return. Anya got up, drank the remaining drops from her water skin then sorely hobbled over to the creek and refilled it. As her hands touched the water, she expected it to be warm like last night but only freezing water splashed against her hands. *Strange,* she thought as she returned to May who was groggily shifting her weight. Anya was getting hungry. She knew May was carrying the food bag the old woman had given to them, but she decided not to bother her just yet.

May was dreaming and arguing with herself, entertaining dual soliloquies. She replayed many events from the past several days over and over again. *Why does it always have to be like this? Why do we keep getting harassed and bothered?* She could not satisfactorily answer those questions with herself. Instead, she asked if there was anything they could have done differently. She seemed unable to resolve any of the dilemmas she pondered.

Anya went about collecting more grass and twigs, attempting to restart last night's fire. She looked over at May just as May was opening an eye. May closed her eye slowly and let out a long sigh of exhaustion. "I can't figure out how everything turned out so badly."

"I don't know either. Everywhere we go seems to turn ugly at some point," Anya said matter-of-factly.

May opened up her pack and pulled out the burlap sack the old woman had given them yesterday. "Here, take it. I'm not hungry right now."

Anya took the bag and opened it to find two small loaves of bread and two small chunks of cheddar cheese. Anya sniffed the bag and thought, *sourdough.* "The old woman is the only person who's shown us any kindness at all, and she shooed us out of her barn."

"I don't blame her," May said. "She would have suffered at the hands of the Baron's goons had they found us in her barn. For all we know, they slapped her around anyway, just for fun."

Anya sat silently for some time, her ears turned towards the creek. "I don't hear any dogs or horses but we still have to keep moving."

"What'll we do?" May asked. "They'll search and cover all the roads. They'll expect us to get tired of the cold and the forest and double back to the road where they'll catch us."

"Then we'll have to stay in the forest and continue following the creek," Anya shrugged.

"I don't want to get my feet wet again. Last night was terrible. I couldn't feel my hands or feet at all but now I can wiggle my toes again. Thank you, Anya."

"I'm happy you feel better. Unfortunately, I don't really know where we are or where this creek is leading us."

May asked, "What are we going to do for food? This bread and cheese won't last us very long. We'll have to go back into town again to buy food or we may have to start trapping rabbits. We could use the cheese to bait a few traps but that will take time."

Anya shot May a puzzled look, "Buy food with what? We've naught but a few coppers left."

May cracked a silly smile as she revealed, "We've got coin now." May pulled out a small leather pouch that jingled as she swung it in front of Anya.

"What is that?" Anya paused then gasped with a worried look, "Oh no."

May giggled, "I took it right off his belt when everyone in the bar was scrambling to catch you after you cracked his arm – emphatically, I might add. I was going to tell you before but the old woman chased us out of the barn in a hurry and we've been running ever since. There are many silvers and some golds, too."

Anya chided May, "Now we're in big trouble. I can't believe you swiped his purse. Now he will continue to hunt us down to get his coin back and … what did you say was in there?"

"Not if we spend it first. Serves him right for what he did to you," May smiled. She tossed the bag to Anya saying, "Count it yourself."

Anya sat down, opened the pouch and started counting the coin. "Thirty-two silvers and five golds and … and this," she stated, surprised. Anya pulled out a small key from the pouch and held it up for May to see. "He won't care a rat's tush about the coin but he will definitely want this back. And you can bet he'll chase us down until he does." There was an awkward silence after which May opened her eyes, then closed them again, trying to keep them warm.

Anya spoke up after a while, "My father used to talk about a place called Northcamp. It lies somewhere along the main road going north, which we were following until last night. I think it's somewhere north of Wesseltown. He told me that some of the supplies he bought came from Northcamp. Maybe if we follow the road while hiding in the forest, we can get there in a few days. I think they buy furs and hides there. Maybe we can sell the rabbit furs. It might be far enough away from this place that no one will know who we are."

"Don't chance on that. The old lady called him Willem. Willem's goons will be there somewhere if they are looking for that key. We'll have to sneak in if we are going to blend. But it may take many days or even weeks before we get there and it will be cold the whole while," May said.

"We can handle the cold if we keep good fires every night, catch a few rabbits, and stay out of the creek," Anya said. "We should leave now and put more distance between us and those dogs."

"All right, but first …" May said as she sighed off to sleep again.

Anya scowled and began packing her things.

Northcamp

Northcamp is one of several towns founded amidst the great northern forests of Borea where furs, pelts, and hides are bought and traded year-round, peaking in the fall and winter. Come the winter, most animals fill out their furry coats making them most valuable to trappers and traders. While dubbed a town, Northcamp is more akin to a village with its main street slicing east-west across the northern portion of town. Several large buildings located within the town's east end are utilized for trading furs, foodstuffs, and services. Local residents possessing no interest in the fur trade prefer patronizing the west end of town.

A steady stream of traders arrive in Northcamp from the large coastal cities of Borea and Callalande hauling carts loaded with grain, vegetables, and salted meats. They sell their goods to merchants then quickly buy up as many furs as possible. When fully laden, the carts are hauled back to the coast. The fur trade is very lucrative with many investors and stakeholders profiting. Thousands of animals and many humans give their lives each year to the trade. Furs, pelts, and hides are crafted into cold weather gear, fashionable apparel, and luxury accessories for the more well-to-do citizens of the coast. Many fur products end up exported to foreign markets far away.

Northcamp is host and residence to many trappers and mountain men, tough burley types who usually travel alone or in small groups. They seek out furs with the hope of cashing in on the Northcamp bonanza and reaping the rewards of wealth and fortune. That is mostly a delusion. Many a trapper perishes in the wilds from the cold or lack of supplies as a result of poor fiscal planning and discipline. Too frequently, a drinking binge or a gambling spree drains a man's hopes and dreams faster than the cold ever can. The financially backed companies and trading houses are the real winners soaking up most of Northcamp's profits.

From the forest's edge, Anya and May observed Northcamp's activity with apprehension. They spied people on foot, on horses, on carts, all moving about with vivacity and purpose. Steady winds conveyed the sounds of hustle bustle, the smells of animals, and the lure of profit. From previous encounters, they knew that the Baron's goons don forest-green cloaks sporting a red emblem, a crest portraying a horse and rider emerging from a rising sun.

"What if the Baron's goons are in town right now and they spot us?" May said.

"Is it the Baron's son or the Baron who is after us? The old lady said the Baron's son but you keep saying the Baron. Which is it?" Anya asked.

"I guess practically, it is the Baron's son but he would be using the Baron's resources unless he has his own. But you heard him yourself in the bar; he was an annoying little tush who probably never had to organize anything in his life. He probably orders the Baron's henchmen around to do his bidding. He's the kind of brat my father warned me about."

Anya replied, "Agreed. We're also out of food, our healing salve is finished, and we can't rely on trapping rabbits all the time; we have to go into town." Anya turned back towards the town counting, "It looks like there are more people down there than houses. That means there must be many mouths to feed."

"Maybe we can find work in one of the taverns or kitchens," May said. "I know how to cook a little and you could do some cleaning and fire tending. "

Anya glared at May, "Tavern work? You DO recall what happened the last time we walked into a tavern?"

May pouted. "All right, let's get a closer look at one of the kitchens."

The two girls slowly worked their way along the forest's edge until they had a good view of a large multilevel building located on the west end of town where people seemed to be entering hungry and leaving satisfied.

Anya pointed, "That building looks more like a kitchen than a tavern. It might even be an inn because it has several upper levels. It does not have any nearby stables, though. It appears to have a supply shed in the back because I can see several people going back and forth from what looks like a kitchen."

May suggested, "Maybe if we sneak around the back of the kitchen, we can talk to someone while they are in the shed."

"All right, but let's wait until it gets darker."

Anya and May waited. As evening arrived, so did the cold. They slowly sneaked their way towards the supply shed. Working their way behind the shed and along its side wall, they found two open doors. Through the shed's doors, they spied a large woodpile and several unmarked barrels lined up against one wall. Many large sacks containing turnips, beets, carrots, and other foodstuffs were stacked against the opposing wall. Towards the rear, they could see a man pulling a bucket of water out of a well. His eyes widened with surprise as he spotted their faces staring at him through the doors.

From behind the two girls, a strong authoritative voice boomed out, "All right! What sort o' mischief ares you two ups ta?"

Surprised, Anya and May quickly turned and reached for their waists. They now faced a burley looking matron wiping her hands on a greasy apron. Her light brown hair was disheveled but secured by a blue head scarf matching her bluish eyes. She was not as tall as May but she did look big, appeared sweaty, and sounded intimidating. She approached Anya and May.

"There ares no free handouts here. You gots ta pays like all the rest." Walking up to Anya and May, the matron was surprised then impressed to see how big the two girls were up close. Eying them suspiciously she said, "You'res a couple o'young'uns. What ares you doings up here in this madness all alone? Cookie! Gets that water inside and starts a new pot! We ain't gots all night!" She returned her attention to Anya and May, crossing her arms.

"My name is Anya. We just arrived in town and need some work. May here can cook a little and I am handy in the kitchen and the shop."

"We ain't gots a shop here. Why would you comes here for work in this forsaken place anyways?" Her question was rhetorical. "So, you wants work, huh!" She reached over to Anya's arm and gave it a good squeeze. Then she reached over to May's arm and did the same. Her eyes widened a little. "You looks young and you feels strong, maybe I can use you, maybe I can't. I'll gives you two a try and if you can handles it, we can talks later. Stows your gear upstairs in the empty bunkroom and claims one o'the footlockers." She turned to Anya and instructed, "You draws some buckets o'water and takes 'em ta Cookie inside the kitchen there." Turning to May she ordered, "You gets a bag o'turnips and starts choppin' 'em up."

Anya began thanking the matron but she had already turned around and was heading back into the kitchen. "What do we call you, ma'am?"

"Everyone calls me Ma!" she said as she disappeared into the kitchen.

Anya and May climbed up the steep stairs behind the kitchen to the second floor and entered a narrow hallway. Several doors lined the hall where they eventually found an empty room with two bunks and a pair of footlockers. They stowed their packs into one locker; then, May took out her padlock and secured it. She placed the key in one of her secret tunic pockets. Then, the two went downstairs to complete their first tasks.

"I hope this works out. We should be careful not to show our faces to anyone else, if possible," May said.

Anya went straight for the well, drew some water, and then took the buckets into the kitchen. May grabbed a heavy bag of turnips and heaved it onto her shoulder then went into the kitchen. The bag was dirty and trailed dust.

"Tooks you long enough. Now gets ta work," Ma instructed.

Anya delivered the water to Karl who then poured it into a small cauldron hanging over a large fire pit in one corner of the kitchen. Karl directed Anya to fetch more water and some firewood from the shed. May found a wooden basin filled with dirty water used for cleaning turnips and other large vegetables. Opening the bag, May poured out all of the turnips into the basin splashing water all over the floor. Ma scowled at the mess May was making but continued her work carving up rabbits. May stirred the turnips before placing several onto a cutting board. She found a cleaver then began slicing the turnips into large chunks, filling several bowls destined for the cauldron.

The kitchen held two other workers, Karl and Berthe. Both turned to see the new girls walk into the kitchen and were surprised at how big they were, handling their heavy loads with seeming ease.

Karl whom Ma called "Cookie," was the cook in the kitchen. Karl stood close to five and a half feet and was a little portly about his waist. He had tanned fair skin with a layer of variegated stubble on his face. He was also much older than everyone except Ma and mostly kept to himself. He was capable of some strenuous work such as hauling water, firewood, and sacks of vegetables but he avoided it whenever possible. His back was not as strong as it used to be. Karl always gave out advanced warning of what ingredients he needed so that those cutting and chopping could fill his requests. Anya and May did not learn much about Karl right away but did learn that he lived in his own place and did not spend much time upstairs at all.

Berthe was the one Ma called "Baker" and was in charge of baking the bread rolls. Currently, Berthe was filling a large flat sheet with dozens of balls of bread dough. Once the sheet was filled, Karl moved aside as Berthe rolled the cauldron off to one side of the fire pit then rolled a separate rack that supported the baking sheet over the fire pit. While the cauldron simmered, Berthe baked the bread rolls until they browned up nice and hot. She rolled the cauldron back over the fire pit and Karl resumed cooking.

Vikki and Sal were Ma's servers and rarely ever entered the kitchen. It was too hot, smelly, and sometimes beneath their station to work in or even be in the kitchen. They thought of themselves more as bartenders rather than servers since they were responsible for pouring the beers from the kegs. They handled dishes only when clearing tables; they never washed dishes. As a result, they never interacted socially with the kitchen crew with the exception of Ma. Ma had a different relationship with the servers, distinct from the kitchen crew. The servers were Ma's customer service representatives, requiring a different skill set, and were primarily responsible for sustaining Ma's customer base. They helped bring in the coin and also made tips on the side but nowhere as much as the servers working the taverns on the east end of town.

Ma frequently gave orders to everyone in the kitchen as well as the servers working the main floor all while cutting up rabbits, chickens, and lamb for the stew. The kitchen was very warm, even uncomfortably hot at times, but Anya and May did not complain one bit especially since they had been camping in the freezing forest for many nights.

Throughout the evening and night, Ma's Kitchen cranked out bread rolls, meat and vegetable stew, and mugs of cheap beer to their customers all for the price of one silver. For an extra two coppers, one could also get a small chunk of cheddar cheese. All night long, May chopped vegetables in quantity. Turnips, carrots, onions, barley, lentils, and beets all found their way into the stew. Anya kept the well water coming, tended the fire pit, washed the dishes, and even replaced the beer kegs when needed. They soon realized that Ma was terse and sassy. But for the most part, she kept an orderly and efficient workplace. There was no doubt who was boss in Ma's Kitchen.

Ma periodically ventured onto the main floor to schmooze up her regulars and deal with signs of disorderly conduct. She preferred nipping problems in the bud before they got out of hand. She also didn't allow anyone to give lip to or harass her servers. She was bossy enough to handle any back talk from trappers and traders. Most of the heavy drinkers and rowdy types did not patronize Ma's Kitchen. They preferred the liquor variety at Keeg's Kegs or The Wolf Pack taverns further down the main street. As a result, Ma rarely dealt with unruly customers. This made for good business and allowed local families to dine more comfortably. She never tapped out more beers than she served up stews. She was running a kitchen, not a tavern, and her customers knew that.

Ma's kitchen was a bulk operation with only one item on the menu: Ma's Stew with bread and cheap local beer – nothing fancy but it satisfied the hunger. Ma's secret was her special blend of salt and herbs that Karl stirred into each pot of stew. Perhaps due to the fact that Karl never emptied the cauldron, Ma's stew developed that distinct, unique, and hard-to-pin-down Northcamp flavor.

At the end of the evening, everyone in the kitchen was exhausted. Ma closed down the kitchen when the town bell rang announcing the middle of night. Kitchen operations were shut down, dishes were washed, and leftover food secured in the cellar. The supply shed was closed and the cauldron left to simmer.

Ma finally addressed Anya and May. "You dids good for a first night; however, there's things you'll have ta learns if you wants ta stay. I'll gives you more time ta decides if you wants ta stay, but this place is busy as you saws and we needs ta keep the food moving all night long. You gets paid every seventh day, and every three days, we hauls up fresh water for the showers in the bunkhouse."

Anya and May climbed up the stairs to their room bringing the smells of the kitchen with them. Their room was pleasantly warm as it was directly above the kitchen where the fire pit had been going all night long. Karl went home and Berthe came up the stairs later. Berthe had her own room, much smaller than the other rooms, across the hallway from the bunkroom. Anya and May claimed one of the bunks in the empty room. As they prepared for bed, they felt good that nothing had gone wrong this day and for the first time in a long while, they slept contented and not cold.

Foray

May awoke at dawn as light streamed in through the small windows of their room. May was already dressed as she rolled out of the upper bunk and straightened up her clothes. She wanted to make her body look more like a man's body so she wrapped some clothes around her torso just below her chest. She put her hair into a ponytail then tucked it neatly under her cap to mimic the appearance of short hair.

Anya cracked an eye open as May prepared to leave the room. "Where are you going?"

"I want to see the town up close. I'll return in a short while. If Ma asks, tell her I went to trap rabbits." And then she left the room. Anya went back to sleep.

May quickly moved down the stairs, turned a corner then into the street. She viewed Ma's Kitchen from the street side for the first time. There was a closed double door with two small paneless windows. A wooden sign next to the door was decorated in colorful but faded paint displaying a likeness of Ma smiling with her mouth open, holding up a steaming bowl of stew. May thought, *does Ma ever smile?*

The morning was cold and the sky a little gray with the sun struggling to break through the clouds. May turned away from the kitchen and walked down the street. The village was already coming to life as many trappers prepared for travel. Some were packing provisions suggesting they might be away for several weeks venturing deep into the northern woods. The main street was very wide and could fit several carts side by side with room to spare.

May aimed to seek out traders of rabbit furs to assess what prices they offered. May had about eight rabbit pelts she had collected while traveling to Northcamp. She was also able to scrape and preserve them and was hoping she could get a good price.

Walking down the street, she spied various shops selling all manner of venturing supplies. Salt, salted meats and vegetables, breads, cheeses, and dried legumes seemed to be popular and in high demand. For trappers with horses or mules, blacksmiths were available to mend and sell harnesses, barding, shodding, and affordable feed.

Along the south side of the main street, May noticed a small shrine dedicated to Artemis, Goddess of the Hunt. Offerings abounded in the form of fur tufts, small food items, and any number of charms and talismans all to ensure a prosperous hunt and a safe return. Continuing on, she came across the first of the east-end taverns, Keeg's Kegs. What looked like the proprietor was wearily sweeping the floors and cleaning the tables in preparation for another busy day. The taverns were where the hard liquors, ales, and wines were sold and consumed. Ma maintained that drunk and unruly customers resulted in broken furniture and utensils. But since she couldn't completely forgo alcohol, she stocked the cheapest local beer which her customers found acceptable though not very satisfying. It was affordability that made her place popular. May did not enter the tavern nor make inquiry but she did wonder what prices they charged for their food and drink.

As May strode further down the east end, she observed what appeared to be the proprietor of The Wolf Pack tavern boarding up a window that had been broken the previous night. A nearby stable bustled with activity as saddled horses snorted their breath into the morning air. Outside another shop, a group of trappers were arguing over how much coin to spend on supplies they would need for their forthcoming foray into the woods. Small groups of children, mostly boys, hid and spied from behind several bushes along the street, looking for an opportunity to collect a dropped coin. On and on, activity crescendoed into a mind-numbing drone when May finally reached the great trading house at the eastern edge of town.

Outside the trading house were cart ports of varying sizes for the loading and unloading of goods. Some were automatically reserved for the large trading houses; others had to be reserved in advance. Approaching the main entrance, May discovered that visitors were required to have goods to trade to enter the house – no goods, no entry, and no spectators. As May was not carrying anything to trade, her attempt to enter was challenged. Looking past the doorman, she began waving at someone inside who wasn't looking her way. She smiled at the doorman, pointed inside at a random person, gave the doorman a nod and wink then swiftly sidestepped past him saying, "Tomas is expecting me inside." She was in. She lost herself in the crowd then began surveying the house before the doorman could react to what had happened.

Inside, the trading house resembled a large rectangle with its longer walls twice the length of its shorter walls. Built into the shorter walls, sets of large double doors allowed the only passage into or out of the trading house. Great crossbeams supported a soaring angled roof. Large ceiling windows allowed a flood of sunlight into the massive hall and a modicum of ventilation. Many ensconced lanterns decorated the walls and support pillars throughout the house but had not been lit. The sounds of haggling, trading, arguing, dealing, coin changing, tall tales, and intelligence sharing all contributed to the confusing din surrounding May. As she browsed, she strained to overhear the many conversations within the house. May sensed an air of desperation in many trappers trying to collect payment for their goods. She thought, *are the shorter days in fall making business more hectic and stressful?*

Against the longer walls, many large cubicles were occupied by traders competing to procure the pelts and hides of larger animals such as deer, elk, bears, wolves, cats, and so forth. Huge piles of stacked pelts and bundled hides awaited transport to markets elsewhere. Some traders amassed antlers, skulls, teeth, tails, and other strange body parts. May noted the absence of hides from domesticated animals such as goats, sheep, and cattle. She knew such animals were considered livestock as they produced other valuable products such as milk, cheese, and wool. Northcamp appeared purposed for the trading of game animals, not livestock.

Clustered within the central floor area, knockdown tents and stalls featured traders that collected furs from smaller animals such as rabbits, weasels, ermine, sable, minks, beavers, foxes, and others May had never heard of before. The putrid atmosphere of blood and decay, rancid must, dirty sweat, and muddy beer penetrated every nook and cranny of the house. The pervasive reek was giving May a headache. In one corner of the house, May spied a makeshift bar with three empty stools where small tankards of beer could be purchased and consumed. May made her way over to the bar and sat down on one of the stools, massaging her head.

"I've not seen you here before. The stench in this place can hit you like an iron skillet if you're not ready for it. I've got a two-copper-fixer-upper for you right here." The bartender spoke to May as he slid a half-full tankard her way.

May plopped two coppers onto the bar then picked up the tankard and took a swig. With her nose stuffed full of trading-house stench, she drank down the worst beer she had ever tasted. She felt like retching but contained herself. She feared looking amateurish, but she had already given the bartender that impression.

The bartender asked, "You feelin' any better?"

"No," May groaned. After a short time, May did start to feel a bit better. She asked the bartender, "I was wondering, do you know which traders buy rabbit furs? Most of the traders make it hard to see what they are buying."

"I can't say for certain. But, you might talk to Gooner over there." The bartender pointed over towards a brown tent. "I think Gooner buys rabbit furs but he is picky and never buys damaged furs. If you ask Rogue over there by the rear door, he might offer a fair price. He sometimes buys things Gooner won't buy but does not pay as much. However, Gooner doesn't pay in coin. He only passes out tickets."

"Thank you for the beer. I'm feeling a little better now. What's a ticket?"

"Now I know you're new here. A ticket is a promise to pay. You can take it to the bank and trade it in for coin when the bank is open." The bartender pulled out a ticket and showed it to May. "You see, this here ticket tells me I can get three silvers from the Northcamp bank against the credit of Callamar

Fur Traders. I will have to go there tomorrow as they don't get their coin until their coach arrives from Callamar."

"I see. How do you know when to go to the bank?"

"You just know. It comes with the trade. Many trappers don't like getting paid with tickets as the bank usually closes before they can cash them in. Most trappers want to get their coin as soon as possible so they can splurge it all on real booze in the nearby taverns and not on this rat piss I have to sell here."

"Is that what you call this stuff?" Both May and the bartender laughed. May put some more coppers on the bar. "By all means, let me have some more."

As May's queasiness wore off, the bartender explained more on the promissory ticket system. "Tickets are promissory payments or credit against the buyer's coin which results from delayed and uncertain deliveries. Boxes of coin are regularly transported via mule trains protected by hired guards; then, they are deposited into the Northcamp bank and finally doled out as needed for purchasing goods and cashing promissory notes, these tickets here. The less coin changing hands, the less pickpockets and thieves can steal. At least that's how they justify using tickets. It's all a bunch of hogwash if you ask me."

May did her best to listen as her head slowly stopped spinning around. She thanked the bartender for his friendliness then wandered off toward Gooner's tent.

In Northcamp's early days, furs, pelts, and hides were abundant and easy pickings. Word-of-mouth soon created several bonanza years which attracted even more trappers than the village could accommodate, and overnight Northcamp became a boomtown, putting many of the original residents and settlers on edge. New buildings seemingly went up overnight, merchant shops, taverns, inns, stables, hostels, a bank, a jail, and even a brothel. As the years passed, great numbers of furs and hides were hauled out of Northcamp emptying the nearby forests of animals and wealth. As a result, trappers had to range longer and farther out just to collect half as many furs, pelts, and hides as they once did.

Small enclaves of residents called Northcamp home for many years. Verily, they disapproved of what their town had become. Many bemoaned the destruction of the surrounding forests while some provided trapper services; others just wanted to be left alone.

After the great trading house was erected – a temple to the trade – the influx of coin transformed the economy. Simple values and morals were replaced by business protocols as the village morphed into an edge-of-anarchy, for-profit hive of primal greed. A small law enforcement presence existed, but most people were left to their own devices for justice and recompense. As a whole, Northcamp evolved into a massive operation designed for one purpose: profit.

May finished her survey of the trading house then quickly sneaked out of the back door before anyone noticed she was gone. She overheard several conversations near the rabbit traders and discovered that only the highest quality furs received the best coin. Present demand dictated that rabbits with solidly colored furs could get a half-silver apiece if they were properly cut and skinned. May knew her furs were not properly prepared and hence not worth much. Armed with this knowledge, she figured she could prepare future furs to the proper specifications.

Once May left the house, she wound her way back to the main street and off toward Ma's but not before taking a quick peek into one of the nearby hostels. A pungent odor assailed her nose as the drone of snoring trappers echoed from most of the beds. May quickly left. She meandered her way back down the street to Ma's without further ado.

Acquaintance

After May left the bunkroom, Anya fell back to sleep.

Anya and May's familiarity with the bunkhouse slowly grew. They found that the hallway doors were kept closed most of the time. The washing room was the one room that everyone used. There were two shower stalls that drew water from a roof-top tank set just above the showers along with two basins for hand and facial cleaning and two stalls for privy use. Laundry had to be done outside. In the shed was a large basin for laundry and also for other things like cleaning vegetables.

The door to Berthe's room slowly opened and Berthe slipped into the hallway. She first went to the washing room and freshened up her face and hair. Anya could hear noise from the washing room next door as she was trying to go back to sleep. *Thin walls*, she thought. From the washing room, Berthe slowly walked down the hall to the bunkroom, cracked the door open, and looked inside. She tiptoed in quietly and sat down on one of the chairs, watching over Anya's bed. Berthe quietly watched Anya sleeping.

Without lifting an eyelid, Anya spoke, "What do you want?"

Berthe smiled as she spoke, "I wanted to see you. I've never seen anyone like you before. All of the girls and women I know are small, except for Ma, but she's not tall. You are the tallest and biggest girl I have ever seen. Last night you were carrying all those heavy water buckets and kegs like they were little toys."

Anya sighed then answered, "Yes, they were heavy and yes, I can lift them but I still get tired and just like you, I need my sleep." She then rolled away from Berthe and faced the wall.

Berthe asked, "Where are you from? You must be from down south since I have never seen you in town before. Actually, everywhere from here is down south," she giggled. "Ma calls me Baker but that's not my real name. My name is Berthe but you can call me Baker if you like. Sometimes it rolls off the tongue better. Berthe, Baker, Berthe, Baker, you see? I grew up in Fallmouth before I came here with my family. Ma can be sassy but she's really nice. I like working here and Ma always takes care of us. The last girl left us because the town got a little rough for her. Are you going to leave us, too, or are you going to stay?"

Anya paused and groaned then reluctantly rolled back over to face Berthe. As she slowly opened her eyes, all she could see was Berthe silhouetted against the windows and all she could hear was Berthe talking. Berthe looked a little bit on the slim side but also older, perhaps twenty-five years. Anya admitted to herself that Berthe had a cute smile. Berthe was fair-skinned with dark brown eyes. Her long hair was braided into two ponytails both tucked behind her ears.

"Ma will be here soon and she'll want us to unload the cart when it arrives. The cart always comes in the morning so we can have food for the day and evening. I don't see the other girl around. Did she step out? Is she your friend? She also looks new in town like you and big like you and I've never seen anyone cut up veggies as quickly as she did last night."

Anya could tell that Berthe wasn't going to stop talking even if she ignored her. Reluctantly, Anya swiveled her legs out of bed and onto the floor as she sat at the edge of her bed, head in her hands. There was a small nip in the air but at least it was not ice cold like the forest. Anya realized that Berthe might have some useful information about Northcamp, if she had lived here for some time.

"Berthe is a nice name. How long have you lived in Northcamp?" Anya asked.

"Thank you. I've been here many years. I came here when I was young and my family moved from Fallmouth. Oh, I already told you that. My family lives at the south edge of town on a small farm, away from all the trappers and traders. Once in a while I go to visit them but I live here mostly. I give most of my money to my mama so she can help my younger siblings grow up. My father tends the farm and animals but sometimes he goes off hunting for furs to help our family. My father wants my younger brother to go off to school in Vassans. He doesn't think this place has a school good enough for him."

Anya interrupted, "Berthe, I need to find out where I can get some medicines. Are there any healers in town? If not, maybe there's someone who specializes in herbs? Do you know where I might find someone like that?"

Berthe frowned, thinking for a moment then she smiled again. "There's a healer in town right next to the Rabbit's Run. For herbs, there's a lady who lives in a small white house with a white fence around it. She might know how to help you. She lives south of the shrine."

Anya looked puzzled, "The what?"

"The shrine. It's in the middle of the main street though I don't go by it much. I don't go to the east end either 'cause it's too rough and dangerous. Bad things happen there. Most of the trappers go there to sell furs and get drunk. My daddy goes there to sell his furs when he has some and he tells me and my sibs never to go there, so I don't. Working in the kitchen, sometimes I overhear bad things about the east end that sound scary like fights and muggings and thieves. It makes me shiver thinking about it. But I bet that kind of stuff doesn't frighten someone like you, all big and strong as you are," Berthe said with a giggle and a smile.

Anya rolled her eyes and then realized that she still smelled like yesterday's kitchen and fire pit. "I need to clean up before I throw up," she said as she stood up and wandered off into the washing room.

Employment

May was just returning to Ma's when she rounded the back corner and nearly plowed straight into a fully-loaded supply cart.

Ma was talking to the cart driver when she spied May coming her way. Ma decided to talk some sense into May but instead scrunched her nose up saying, "Peeww! Where'ds you gets that stink and why'ds you brings it back here? Gets inta the shower and cleans yourself down and don't takes long lest you wants ta hauls it all back up ta the tank yourself. When you're dones, gets down and unloads the cart out inta the shed."

Ma strode off, thundering up the stairs. May followed Ma up the stairs then turned left into the washing room, running right into Anya. When she got a good whiff of May, Anya coughed and gasped then pinched her nose saying, "Where'd you crawl out of, the slaughterhouse?"

May replied, "I went to the trading house to see how much our rabbit furs are worth."

"And are they worth anything?" Anya asked still holding her nose.

"Not much, but if I can prepare them properly, we might stand to make some coin. Larger animals might be worth more if we can find any."

"Sounds great," Anya said. "Now go open up the locker so I can put some clean clothes on."

The shower was cold but no colder than the creek they had been using for weeks. May quickly cleaned up then hurried into their bunkroom and quickly changed into her spare clothes. Anya and May now realized that Northcamp possessed an assortment of putrid smells that clung to you everywhere you went.

Anya and May came down the stairs where behind the kitchen was parked a medium-sized cart loaded with sacks of foodstuff, kegs of beer, crates of coarsely ground wheat or maslin, and two big wheels of cheese. Each of the items weighed around five stones.

Ma came back down the stairs, found May, and scolded her. "The next time you takes off like that, tells me first so I don't haves ta worry about you. Many bad things can happen ta a young girl in Northcamp, even a big girl likes you. The less you needs ta wander, the less you gets in trouble. And if you haves ta go, takes someone with you ta bes safer. Now, there's lots o'work needin' ta be done. We opens the doors near midday. The bread needs ta be ready and that means grindin's the flour and bakin's the bread. Now go helps Baker takes the cheese down ta the cellar."

Anya and May were both strong enough to lift the sacks and crates themselves, but things worked better when they lifted together. The cart was quickly unloaded and the entire inventory neatly stacked against the walls of the shed.

Ma looked over her new inventory. Satisfied, she pulled out a small coin purse tucked into her brassiere and paid the cart driver what he was owed plus an extra coin for his efforts. They parted in agreement as the driver cracked the reins of two draft horses. His cart rolled away and out onto the main street.

Anya and May found Berthe in the kitchen and told her they had the cheese wheels. Berthe lit a lantern then showed them the door leading into the cellar. The wheels were easy to roll into the kitchen but going down the stairs was more challenging. Instead, they carried the wheels together down the narrow stairs but they were bulky and awkward to handle. Progress was slow but they knew Ma would be upset if they dropped or damaged them. The cellar was colder than the upstairs and ideal for storing cheeses and meats.

Preparations for the day included grinding grain into flour using a granite bowl and pestle. Anya and May ground up flour so that Berthe could make the bread rolls. Berthe made several batches of dough before they opened the doors. Then, when the doors opened, she placed her first sheet of rolls onto the fire pit so they could be served hot. Karl was preparing the first cauldron using the remnants of last night's stew. While the two girls were grinding flour, Karl was chopping beets and carrots and Ma was carving up chickens. Ma's servers Vikki and Sal arrived just before opening, ready to take the orders, tap the kegs, and bus the tables. Outside, anticipation was growing as people began arriving to get their midday bowl of stew with a brew.

The doors opened and the people filed in orderly. Ma greeted everyone as they entered. Karl began serving up bowls and Berthe brought the first rolls off the sheet. Several chunks of cheese were readied for anyone wanting them. Vikki and Sal filled several mugs of beer and the day was off to a good start.

The whole day was spent making certain the machine that was Ma's Kitchen operated smoothly and efficiently. After the opening surge waned, Ma began to rotate everyone's afternoon break times and give them their complimentary meal of the day. Each worker was allowed one free meal along with a mug of beer as part of their compensation. Ma knew that full stomachs made good employees and made sure everyone got what she promised them.

Chopping, skinning, baking, stewing, firing, watering, tapping, serving, and schmoozing moved the day along and before they knew it, the sound of the night bell rang. Ma closed the doors and nagged the stragglers to finish. "You can goes down ta the taverns if you wants ta but we are closin'." The kitchen was stowed and cleaned and soon everyone was gone.

Anya and May went up the stairs followed by Berthe and Karl. Karl had his own place elsewhere, but some nights he was too exhausted and used the room Ma had assigned to him. Karl cleaned himself up in the washing room then retired for the night.

By now, all of their clothes reeked. "We will definitely have to do some laundry soon," May said.

"It's your turn. Wake me up tomorrow when you're done."

After using the washing room, Anya and May got to bed and began falling asleep.

Anya spoke first. "Berthe told me this morning that there was a healer in town and an herbal woman somewhere south of a shrine living in a white-fenced house."

"All right, I will go there tomorrow. We need to get another healing salve or we need to stop getting injured."

Anya said, "You have to be careful in town as well. There are many ruffians up to no good and many scuffles out near the east end."

May trailed off to sleep with Anya not far off.

Apothecary

May had already seen most of what the main street had to offer. However, crossing the main street were several smaller north-south streets which featured some interesting buildings and shops. May heard from Anya who heard from Berthe that there may be an herbalist or medicine expert who might be able to help them find a healing salve. That's what May was seeking, a healing salve that could help their wounds heal faster and more cleanly. She also knew that such salves could be expensive but with the golds she now carried from the pilfered coin pouch, she could afford one.

May walked down the main street until she passed the shrine then turned south down the smaller street. Several shops along this street sold domestic goods, not traveling supplies like the ones along the main street. She passed by several government buildings and private residences. Most of the farm residences and barns were located towards the south end of town. She also ended up passing a complex set of buildings featuring both a moon and a sun mounted on their roofs.

Before long, May arrived at a small well-crafted residence surrounded by a whitewashed wooden fence and a closed swinging gate. She stopped and craned her neck. She thought, *this has to be the place*. Opening and closing the gate, she passed through then hesitantly walked up to the front door. A long narrow sign affixed to the door possessed a single word. A smaller sign, also with a single word, hung from a hook pounded into the front door. Two small pictures of a glass phial and a ceramic jar were painted on the door below the two signs. A small brazen bell with a thin string attached dangled beside a small-paned window next to the door. May grabbed the string and gave it a tug. The bell replied with a mouse-like ring.

May waited. When no one appeared, she gave the bell another ring. After what seemed like a long time, she was ready to ring the bell a third time when she noticed a shadow moving beyond the nearby window. A high-pitched, muffled female voice called from beyond the window, "What do you want?"

May replied, "I'm looking for the herbal person in town. Is this the right place?"

A pause ensued. May could see the face of a small girl behind the window saying, "This is Northcamp Apothecary but we are closed. You can come back tomorrow."

"Please don't go. I came to buy a healing salve and I have the coin to pay for one."

"It is Sunday and we are closed on Sundays," the voice squeaked.

May just then realized that she had no idea what day it was. "I'm sorry. I didn't know it was Sunday. Please, I really need to buy a salve. My last one has dried up."

The girl behind the window disappeared. For some time, May stood outside the door staring at the window waiting to see if the girl would return. The longer May waited, the more foolish and fidgety she felt. May was starting to think she would have to return the next day and started to turn towards the gate when she heard the sounds of a lock being turned and the front door creaking open. Behind the door stood a smallish girl gesturing towards a nearby parlor chair, "Please come in and sit down over there. My lady will greet you shortly." May stepped through the door to see a small girl tilting her head upwards, getting a better look at May. The girl did not look much younger than May but was much shorter and dressed in a plain white and yellow dress with a thin white sash wrapped around her waist and bow-tied on her back. The girl wore a bright yellow head scarf over her golden hair as her blue eyes registered her shock at never having beheld a woman quite as tall or as big as May.

The girl scurried off to fetch her lady. May sat down and looked around the room. There were two cushioned chairs and a finely crafted parlor table set in front of a small cushioned sofa. May thought, *this is a really nice chair.* Against the wall were several shelves holding strange curios and a potted plant snaking wildly around the shelves and onto the floor. Within a far wall was another door different from the one May had entered, slightly ajar with light streaming from beyond. Several small-paned windows appeared along the facing wall looking outward towards the front gate. Below one window was a small foot stool.

After a short time, an older lady quietly walked into the room where May was sitting and ogled her for a few moments. A confused look crossed her face as she pondered how such a big girl dressed as a boy who probably couldn't read came to be sitting in her parlor room on a Sunday morning. The lady was wearing what was probably the nicest dress May had ever seen as she began to think how out-of-her-element she was. The lady glided across the room then sat down in the other cushiony chair saying, "Welcome. You must be new in Northcamp as you have no idea what day it is and I have never seen you before. What is it that you want?"

May cleared her throat and then spoke, "I'm seeking to buy a healing salve. I was told that you could be someone who might be able to help me find one."

The lady locked her eyes onto May and said, "Usually, one begins by seeking a healer. Healers and physicians frequently have herbal and medicinal remedies in stock all the time. We have one in town nearby the Rabbit's Run. You look a bit young to be buying a salve. How old are you?"

May responded, "I … I don't know for sure but I think I'm sixteen years. My … my father never told me when I was born. Am I too young to buy a salve?"

"No. Is he with you? Is your family here in town right now?" the lady asked.

May replied, "I don't have any family now. I'm alone in town working in Ma's Kitchen but I can also trap and sell furs. I have several rabbit pelts already and I've been saving my coin to buy a salve."

The lady said, "I see, new in town and alone. And how did you come to be in Northcamp this season?"

May realized that she didn't know anything about this lady and her naiveté was making her reveal more about herself than she wanted to. The lady made a subtle hand gesture and on cue, the yellow-dressed girl entered the parlor from the far door carrying a nice wooden tray with two steaming cups of tea. She stopped in front of May and offered her some tea. May clumsily took a cup leaving the saucer on the tray. The girl came over to her lady who then took a cup and saucer. The lady slowly blew some air across the top of her cup and sipped a little tea. The girl left the room as quietly as she had entered it.

"Please have some tea," the lady said as she continued to lock her eyes onto May's face. May did not drink tea but also did not want to be rude so she took the cup by the rim, raised it to her mouth, and took a gulp. She winced and squirmed as the hot liquid burned down her throat to her stomach. She tried masking the pain by opening her mouth slightly, breathing in and out quickly, cooling off her seared tongue. The lady set down her cup on her saucer then proceeded to talk softly, smoothly interrogating May, subtly eliciting, compelling her to keep talking on and openly. May spun a tale of her travels and arrival in Northcamp, her hometown life, and her chores growing up on a farm with her father. May did her best to edit out the Baron's son escapade. She also tried to keep Anya out of the story but soon realized that was impossible. Eventually May confessed that she was not in Northcamp alone. The lady listened intently the whole time.

Then May stopped her story. The lady slowly took another sip of her tea then set her cup down and began to speak, "At first, I thought you might be a runaway from the brothel but you do not look the part and you certainly do not smell the part. Your sincerity appears genuine and touching with hints of evasion. You possess your own vulnerabilities and passions which do you service and credit but also can be exploited. I might be able to help you."

May gave a long, almost imperceptible exhale as the lady finished speaking.

The lady sipped some tea and continued, "Most of the time I do not carry salves. Healers and physicians tend to buy them up when they run out of their own, usually when their suppliers suffer delayed deliveries." She paused. "Salves are not cheap but I do happen to have a salve I can sell you. You can have it along with several bandages for five golds." The lady stared right into May, gauging her reaction.

May opened her mouth slightly when she heard "five golds." "I … I only have two golds and a few silvers with me now. It might take me several weeks to get the rest but I can get them. Maybe you can sell me half of a salve?"

The lady gave another cue and the yellow-dressed girl reemerged with another tray. The girl approached May but stood temptingly out of arm's reach. The tray held a small ceramic jar with a cute white ribbon bow-tied across the top. "As you can see, my salves come in small ceramic jars, easy to carry and store. They are very hard to cut in half." The lady leaned back in her chair taking a long sip of tea. Her eyes gave May a long penetrating stare, leaning forward, she spoke again, "Maybe I can sell it to you for three golds, but you will owe me a favor." She leaned back again and sipped some more tea.

"I might have the three golds if I put all my silvers together. What kind of favor would you have of me?" asked May. Then her curiosity got the better of her. She inquired, "Also, if I may ask, what do your signs on the front door say?"

"The signs say 'Apothecary' and 'Closed.'" The lady paused again neither frowning nor smiling saying, "I need to visit the forest to the south and forage for elderberries. Return to me in three-day's time and I will let you know exactly what I want you to do. Agreed?"

Deep in thought, May walked back up the street trying to figure out what had just happened. She asked herself, *what am I missing here*? In her pocket snuggled the smooth bow-tied jar along with her remaining coin. May also realized that she had committed herself to owing a favor. In her heart, she knew this could lead to trouble but she also felt good at having cut two golds off the cost of obtaining her precious salve.

Passing the shrine, she turned left towards Ma's and arrived shortly thereafter.

Laundry

The next day, Anya was tired of her clothes smelling all the time. May had forgone the laundry and Anya was getting impatient. She wanted the laundry done now and didn't have anything clean to wear while washing her clothes. So, she took out her leeward shelter and wrapped herself up then took both of their clothes down to the shed. Ma was already there. She turned her head saying, "My, aren'ts you the early bird today?"

Anya asked, "May I use the wash basin to do my laundry?"

Ma said, "Helps yourself. While you'res at it, uses a wee bit o'the white powder in the back ta gets them cleaner." She picked up a sack then walked back into the kitchen.

Anya did not spend too much time scrubbing the clothes, but she did use some of the white powder which she found in a small barrel against the back wall. The smells were mostly gone and a small breeze helped air out the clothes faster. Anya went back up the stairs and put May's clean clothes onto the chair next to the bunk. May was still asleep as Anya slowly left the room and walked down the hallway. Berthe cracked open her door then smiled and whispered, "Where are YOU going all bright and early?"

Anya stopped and turned around to see Berthe smiling coyly from behind her door. "I have to go into town and check something out. I'll be back soon to grind some flour for you before Ma opens the doors."

"All right, have fun and don't get into trouble," she said with a smile and a tiny wave.

Have fun? Anya thought, *what's that supposed to mean?*

Anya went down the stairs, to the edge of the main street then walked toward the east end of town, keeping in the shadows where possible.

Berthe crept down the stairs following Anya as far as the main street. She peeked around the corner and watched Anya disappear down the street into the shadows. Berthe frowned then went back upstairs into the bunkroom and watched May sleeping soundly.

May opened her eyes and found Berthe watching over her and smiling. "I thought you were Anya. Anything happening that I should know about?"

Berthe said, "No, I just wanted to see you. I've never seen anyone like you before, except Anya …"

Anya returned in the late morning and went to work in the kitchen grinding up flour for Berthe. Grinding flour was labor intensive, especially tough on the wrists and forearms. Anya worked efficiently; nevertheless, she did feel a soreness creeping into her wrists. Anya felt that Berthe was watching her every time she did something strenuous in the kitchen.

As Karl tracked Anya's progress grinding the wheat, he insisted that she chop up more turnips and beets. They were the hardest ingredients to chop and he preferred not having to do the chopping. May soon entered the kitchen and began slicing carrots and onions. The onions seemed to give May no bother; everyone else gave May some space and let her slice away. Anya gave Karl the chopped turnips and beets then went back into the shed to haul more firewood for the pit.

Another day of stews and brews ensued and before long, the night bell rang. The kitchen was closed down and everything secured for the night.

In the evening before Anya and May were preparing for bed, May asked, "What's a brothel?"

Anya fell silent staring at her then responded bluntly, "It's a place where women spend time with men in bed for coin."

May looked confused then asked, "Really? Why would a woman do that?"

Anya scowled at May and replied, "'Cause men have selfish personal needs that sometimes only a woman can meet. And there's coin involved. Do we have to talk about this? My mother told me never to go around such places as they were dangerous and people are always getting hurt, women getting hurt the most."

"Well, there is a brothel in town so I guess we should stay away from there," and there May let the conversation end.

Changing the subject, May told Anya about her visit to the apothecary. She revealed the ceramic jar and showed it to Anya. Anya sighed and smiled with some relief that they had finally procured a new healing salve. Then May told her about the favor she owed the lady in the apothecary.

Anya scolded May, "What did you do and how did you let her talk you into that? That's just crazy. I'll have to talk more sense into you before long. Now go to sleep before you talk any more craziness tonight or I won't be able to sleep at all." And with that, she flopped onto her bed trying to fall sleep.

May was confused but finished preparing for bed, then climbed into her bunk and fell asleep.

Forage

Three days working in Ma's Kitchen had passed without incident and three days passed since May's last visit to the apothecary. She was just turning the corner, passing the shrine, and heading south but she wasn't walking alone. Anya was walking beside her.

As if the herbal lady had timed it precisely, the ever-present clouds smothering Northcamp burned and parted. Above, sunlight generously bathed the town in autumn warmth. Birds above sang and chirped from the trees while Anya and May bickered on their way to a visit with the herbal lady.

"Do we really have to go through with this? We've got the salve now and you gave her the gold she asked for. The deal is done. You don't even know what she wants. Maybe she wants us to go into the forest and hunt down a bear and make her a bear-skin rug for her parlor floor," Anya complained sarcastically.

"We're not going to kill a bear. She can make healing salves so why would she want us to kill something. And she has a little girl, too. I don't know. She did say something about elderberries. It can't be that bad, can it? We'll know soon enough," May replied confidently.

"Oh, now you tell me, elderberries. And what else? You don't need four people to hunt for elderberries."

"She might want something else, too. But she didn't mention bears. Of that, I'm sure."

The two girls continued down the street, passing the moon-and-sun-roofed complex which Anya now saw for the first time.

Anya asked, "Do you know what those buildings are for? I've never seen anything like them."

"No," May replied. "Also, when we get there, don't say anything about how we got into Northcamp. I spun a story about how we got here and I don't want the lady knowing about the troubles we've had, all right?"

"All right," Anya agreed.

They finally arrived at the white-fenced house. They opened the gate, approached the front door, and rang the bell. The little girl answered the door. She greeted and welcomed Anya and May into their parlor and said that her lady was almost ready.

The girl was not wearing a dress but rather a small riding outfit or so May thought. May remembered once seeing a riding outfit back in her hometown. They were mostly worn by women who rode horses for pleasure or sport. The girl wore a light brown shirt with long sleeves tucked into tight-fitting pantaloons that reached her knees. The rest of her legs were covered by dark sheeny-leathered-knee-high boots. A thick black belt was held taught by a shiny brass buckle. Her golden locks were neatly tucked into a rounded brown helmet. Once again, May felt strangely out of place. Anya was not sure what to think or say, so she remained silent.

"I'll go find my lady," the girl said as she shuffled off.

Anya stood frozen and agape. "What was that?"

"That is the young girl I told you about, though last time she was wearing a yellowish dress."

They could hear heavier footsteps approaching the parlor room as the lady entered with her boots pounding the cottage floor. The lady was dressed in an almost identical outfit to the one the little girl was wearing. The lady sported a darker shade of golden hair and hazel-colored eyes. Her complexion was fair with a hint of some years etched onto her cheeks and brow line. She carried a small leather tool pouch attached to her belt.

May turned to the lady and said, "We are here and ready to perform your task. My friend Anya thinks you want us to make you a bear-skin rug for your parlor floor. Say it ain't so."

A subtle smile crossed her face as she said, "No, I do not want a rug."

The little girl came skipping, clomping into the parlor as the lady began to explain, "We need to forage for herbs, mushrooms, and elderberries. This time of the year is challenging because of the snow and meltwater but the sunshine and lack of snowfall for the past fortnight may allow us a short window. If we wait longer, the next snowfall may bury everything for the winter. My carriage should be along any moment now to take us out of town and south to the creekside. I understand that the two of you are experienced in woodland travel. We need to be certain that we do not get lost, get hurt, or get stuck. In addition, we may need your assistance in carrying back some of our harvest."

"Ahh, so it's mules we be," Anya said with a smirk.

May shot her a scowl then turned back and said, "We can handle that but we can't stay too long or Ma will get angry at us."

The lady said, "Do not worry, I have already taken care of Ma. You may call me Danae and this is Deanna." Deanna looked up with a smile and waved. "Please do not repeat our names in town as I have a reputation to uphold.

Shall we leave?" May agreed as they all filed out of the front door to a newly arrived carriage waiting in the street. The carriage was uncovered, pulled by two horses, and appeared to seat four in addition to the driver. Deanna was toting two medium-sized baskets while Anya and May were handed several empty brown sacks and a larger-sized basket. May peeked inside the basket and found it was empty but nested with many small compartments.

May could hear the front door lock behind them as they climbed aboard the carriage. As soon as they were seated, the carriage set forth, down the street, onto the main street, and away from town. They rode south for a league or so. Just before they crossed the creek bridge, they turned onto a small dirt road, more like a foot trail, and followed the creek. The trail was dry in some places and soggy in others. Tall trees prevented much of the sunlight from reaching the forest floor but as the sun reached its zenith, the forest lit up enough for them to begin their work in earnest. The driver stopped the carriage and everyone got out. Danae approached the driver and told him to keep the carriage while they went off to their harvest. She also told him there was a sack lunch in the carriage prepared for him as well as a large bottle of ale.

"I thank you, my lady. I won't move a muscle," the driver said.

Danae turned to Anya and May saying, "We are looking for several items. Firstly, I want elderberries. There are a small group of trees around here that could have intact bunches, assuming the birds have not eaten them all. They are not too hard to collect. Secondly, I want mushrooms, mostly oysters and buttons. Nearby are some fallen logs by the creek that frequently host mushroom colonies. Thirdly, I will take any dill weed we can find and with any luck, we may cross some wolf's bane or Saint John's wort."

With the mention of "wolf's bane," Anya's face perked up, as her own precious supply was running low. Maybe this would be her opportunity to resupply?

"May, you take Deanna down by the creek and look for elderberries and buttons. I will go with Anya and seek out wolf's bane and dill weed. Anya, in the back of the carriage is a wood axe. Please retrieve it and follow me." Danae instructed Deanna to be careful, not to get into trouble, and listen to May if she thought something might be too dangerous.

Anya retrieved the axe and set off with Danae to find the fallen logs. They followed the creek a good distance then turned deeper into the woods. Anya asked Danae, "What does wolf's bane look like before it's crushed up?"

"They look like dark blue or purple flowers that resemble a miniature hooded monk's robe but they can also be found in a yellow variety. If you see flowers of that color let me know. Frequently, bees can give away the presence of flowers. Listen for bees buzzing and then follow the sound. If you see any larger black bees, then our fortunes may be better."

Anya asked, "What's a monk?"

Danae replied, "It is a long story but a monk is usually a man who wears a long-hooded robe."

Soon Danae and Anya found a large tree that had fallen long ago. The log was caked in green and shriveled mosses in addition to other plants attempting to take root in the contested bark. Danae could see a few mushrooms near the ground. She examined them but did not collect any. She slowly worked her way around the log. Several old branches were still attached, full of mosses and dead needles. Then, below the branches of the dead log, she spied a small colony of oyster mushrooms. She waved Anya over to where she was then pointed and said, "These look good. See if you can find any more like them on that log over there while I collect these into my basket."

Anya went over to the other log but could not find anything. She sought out a third log when she spied what she thought could be mushrooms. As she rounded the log, there was clearly another colony of oysters huddled together on the stub of a broken branch.

Anya called out, "I found some over here."

Danae had just finished collecting her mushrooms then quickly joined Anya. She spotted the oysters and said, "If you use the axe to chop off the broken branch, we could take the whole lot intact. Do you think you can chop it off without destroying the colony?"

"I can try." Anya took the axe and landed a few well-placed blows; as the stubby branch popped right off of the log, Anya picked up the branch and saw that nearly all of the mushrooms had survived undamaged.

"Good job!" Danae said as she opened one of the brown sacks. "Now gently put it in the sack and then we will take it back when we are finished here.

Over time, Danae and Anya heard and tracked many bees, discovering colorful pockets of dill weed, blooms of wolf's bane, and Saint John's wort. Danae slowly filled up her basket with these and other herbs. She found some button mushrooms and a few others she didn't talk much about. Danae wore some tight-fitting gloves and used a few specialized instruments from her tool pouch when harvesting certain herbs such as yew berries. Danae's boots allowed her to walk easily through the soggier parts of the woods and to wade right into the creek without getting wet. Anya was much impressed with Danae's boots and wondered how she might get a pair like them for herself. Eventually they turned around and headed back when Danae had filled her basket. As Anya was hauling the heavy sacks, she noticed a glow and a subtle smile on Danae's face suggesting she was having fun. Anya had a hard time remembering the last time she had had any fun.

Lady Danae spoke to Anya, "Your friend May tells me that the two of you trap rabbits and collect their furs for selling. Is that true?"

"Yes. But it's mostly May that does the trapping. She sets and baits the traps. I just make sure she doesn't get hurt."

Danae continued, "I recommend that the two of you stay close to Ma's when working in Northcamp. While there is coin to be made skinning animals, many of the other trappers in Northcamp will turn on and steal from each other for no reason other than coin, especially since the animals are now scarcer and harder to find."

"Well, May and I don't trap much other than rabbits so I hardly think we will be much competition to others. But if they threaten us, we can hold our own."

Danae continued, "I believe you and I would expect most trappers to be intimidated by you and May. But do try to avoid some of the meaner and more notorious trappers, such as Nimrod and the Wolf Hunter. They are unscrupulous murderers who care naught for anyone but themselves. The sherrif is powerless to enforce the laws against them. It is best to stay away from them if you leave town to trap rabbits. I like you and May and I would not want to see anything bad happen to either of you."

"Thank you Danae. That means a lot to us. We don't plan to do much trapping as there is more than enough work to do at Ma's to keep us busy."

May and Deanna worked their way towards the creek and the elderberry grove Danae had spoken of. The creek was smaller and narrower this far north but just as cold as before.

"I think the berries are over this way. Follow me," Deanna said.

Deanna appeared excited as she began wading into the creek. May cringed recalling her own experience a few weeks back. However, May noticed that there was something special about Deanna's boots that seemed to leave her unaffected by the cold or the wetness of the creek.

May called out, "Aren't your feet getting wet?"

Deanna replied, "No. These boots stop the water from coming in. I also have wool socks on underneath." *All right*, May thought, *but I'm still not stepping into the creek.*

At one point, Deanna was walking through the water and slipped on a mossy rock, almost falling into the creek. May reacted with cat-like reflexes, grabbing Deanna by the shirt and preventing her from getting wet.

May said, "Be careful. Once you get wet, you get really cold and you have to dry off as fast as possible. Bad things happen if you don't."

Deanna thanked May and off they continued. By the by, they came upon a thicket of elderberries. Many of the trees had grown to nearly eleven feet high. Deanna noticed that the lower berry bunches had already been eaten up by numerous birds and bugs. However, she spied many newer bunches ripening amongst the highest branches, out of their reach. Even May was not tall enough to reach them. They scoured around for some rocks to stand on but the berry bunches were still too high. The trees were not climbable, as the branches were not strong enough to support even Deanna's smaller weight. They tried finding sticks they could use as hooks to pull the branches lower. No success. Finally, May suggested that Deanna sit on her shoulders and try to reach the berries. This helped but Deanna still could not reach the highest branches. May then convinced Deanna to stand on her shoulders while holding onto the tree trunk. This worked well enough and they began to fill their sack with berries.

May discovered that keeping Deanna balanced was not an easy task and at one point, Deanna lost her balance and fell backwards off of May's shoulders. May spun quickly around and caught Deanna in her arms before she hit the ground. Deanna gasped then found herself staring up at May, cradled in her strong arms. Deanna smiled saying, "You are fast."

"I got you," May said and smiled back.

Working together, they collected far more ripe berries this way. Deanna plucked the berries from the upper branches then dropped them down into the sack that May held below. Eventually they succeeded in filling the greater part of their sack with luscious elderberries.

Deanna said to May, "That's the last of them." Deanna paused then asked, "Will you catch me again if I jump off of your shoulders?"

May was not sure that was a good idea. She said, "Yes," anyways. As if fearless, Deanna jumped off May's shoulders as if expecting to land on a pile of leaves. May caught Deanna as before, but this time, Deanna was smiling and laughing. May gently set her down on her feet and off they went looking for button mushrooms.

May asked Deanna, "What do you do with the buttons when you get back home?"

Deanna replied, "We make pickled buttons. We pack and seal them in jars with dill weed and brine and let them sit for a few fortnights. In the winter when it's cold and you sit by the fireplace, they taste really good. They are the only mushrooms my lady lets me pick on my own."

A thought popped into May's head. "Deanna, is Danae your mother?" Deanna paused then smiled saying, "No, she is my mother's oldest sister. I call her 'my lady' as I am living with her right now. I love her like my mother. She does many nice things for me."

May was a bit surprised at the frankness of Deanna's response. She paused then considered another question that had been nagging her. "Deanna, I want to ask, do you know what those buildings are near your house that have the sun and moon pictures on their roofs?"

Deanna responded, "I am not supposed to talk about those things. My lady might get angry at me."

Deanna and May found a small moss-covered log by the creek and found several bunches of button mushrooms which she began to gather into her basket.

Deanna looked up and said to May, "Promise to me that you will not repeat to ANYONE what I say to you now. You must promise me."

May swore to Deanna, "I promise never to tell anyone what you say to me now or I hope to die."

Deanna fell silent for some time picking more mushrooms; then, she began, "The dark building is the Vault of Selunia and the bright one is the Light of Solarus. Selunia and Solarus chase and catch each other across the sky in cycles throughout the year. Selunia possesses many moods that portend good and bad things. I have much to learn before I can read her portents. My lady is a scion and teaches many young novices the ways and moods of Selunia. Solarus is above us now and he guides our paths during the day and the year. The moods of Solarus are more subtle to read but easier to understand. That is what I am learning right now. Solarus brings the seasons, which are his moods and life to the Earth. Selunia brings cycles and life to the Sea. Together, they keep life and death in balance. I don't know much more as I am still very young and learning." Deanna smiled then wandered off to collect more mushrooms on another log further away.

May had never heard anything like that before in her life. She wondered, *what is the sea?*

In time, Deanna filled her basket with button mushrooms while May scouted around. At the edge of a small clearing, she discovered a trove of blackberries glistening in the sunlight. The two girls quickly picked as many berries as they could. They even popped a few berries into their mouths, fresh blackberries at their peak of ripeness. Returning to the carriage, they found the driver waiting and resting. He was not too keen on walking about the soggy forest but was clearly enjoying his ale. Soon enough, Anya and Danae returned with their haul and they all agreed it was time to leave, as the light was waning. Their ride back into town was not eventful except for when a carriage wheel got stuck in the mud. Anya and May had to get out and push, helping the horses unstick the wheel. They arrived back at Danae's apothecary in the afternoon just as the clouds were darkening the sky again.

Danae thanked the two girls. "Our haul today was worth far more than the two extra golds I asked for the healing salve." Danae went inside and brought out a small pouch and handed it to Anya saying, "Here, take this. It is ground-up wolf's bane. It works best when given to dogs or other canines with food. Reexposing dogs to the bane at a later time will keep them away, most of the time. Do not eat it yourself as it can give you severe stomach cramps – not pleasant at all and sometimes very painful."

Deanna gave May a hug before they walked away, up the street, and back to Ma's.

When Anya and May arrived back at Ma's, Ma, Berthe, and Karl were preparing for the evening flood of customers. Anya and May quickly cleaned up and went downstairs to help out in the kitchen. Ma didn't say anything when they arrived. She just gave then a scowl then continued with her cutting. Karl said that he needed several turnips and onions chopped up as soon as possible, preferably now. Berthe was puzzled as to where they had been but did give them both a big smile when they arrived.

The day ended like all the others and business had been good. The kitchen was cleaned, food stowed, and the doors closed. May and Anya were extra tired that day. They went up to their room quickly, cleaned up, and jumped right into bed.

Before they fell asleep, May suggested to Anya, "I think we have enough furs to sell at the trading house. If we go in the morning we could be done before Ma opens the doors."

"All right, let's do it," Anya said. Then she fell asleep.

Brawl

This was the day that Anya and May decided they would sell their furs. May bundled all of her furs together, including the ones she had collected during some mornings before Ma opened the doors. May would set out early, trap a rabbit or two, then skin them and give the meat to Ma for her stews. Ma insisted that May store the skins in the shed as the smell began to stink up the bunkhouse and was seeping into other unseen parts of the building. May counted about fourteen skins in all. If she got even one silver for each, she would walk away with a nice profit. Anya wanted to go along so she could assist May in bargaining, but also to experience the inside of the trading house. May hoisted the skins onto her back then set off towards the trading house with Anya providing escort.

The street was filled with trappers hauling furs to the trading house. As coincidence would have it, many of the traders who had ventured off some weeks ago were all arriving in town at the same time. The main street became flooded with pelts of all types. A large crowd in front of the trading house was yelling and complaining about the long wait to get inside. As large as the trading house was, it could only accommodate so many people at one time. And Anya and May had to wait like everyone else. They waited for most of the early morning, tolerating the loud din, but seemed no closer to entering than they had been before.

Anya said to May, "This isn't working. Maybe we should go back?"

Then as bad luck would have it, Nimrod the Giant arrived in town with his train of fully loaded horses carrying huge stacks of elk, moose, and bear pelts. His six massive horses clomped their way to the trading house cart ports. Without a care, he pulled up to several ports and tied his horses down.

Like his namesake, Nimrod was a giant of a man standing at over seven-and-a-half feet tall and weighing twenty-two stones of pure muscle, bone, and attitude. He shouldered a large club with one hand and tucked a large battle axe under his belt. His person reeked of forest, blood, mud, and sweat. His scraggly red beard was tinged brown from all the dirt caked onto his whiskers. Most people, even law enforcement, did not want anything to do with him. He had the reputation of being the largest, strongest, most intimidating trapper in all of Northcamp and Borea. When trappers spotted him, they gave him a wide berth as he passed by.

Nimrod took one look at the crowd of trappers massed together blocking his way into the trading house. He was not going to have any of this nonsense. His bull-horned voice boomed out over the crowd as he strode towards the door. "Out of my way now or I'll skin the lot of you." Most of the trappers quickly yielded their places, but a few of the burlier ones tried to hold their ground. When they failed to yield, Nimrod began lifting them up and hurling them aside as if they were children's dolls.

May was watching the ensuing chaos as the giant got closer to her and Anya. As people were getting launched into the air, many of their possessions got separated from their persons. Sooner than she liked, May was staring right up at the giant and before she could take a defensive posture, she was lifted and thrown against the side of the trading house. She fell down to the ground and temporarily blacked out from the blow to the back of her head. Seeing May go down, Anya yelled at the top of her lungs, "Stop!" He quickly turned around and barked right back at her, "This is no place for a girly like you!" He drew his long arm up to slap Anya across the face and barely missed her when she dodged the blow. Seeing himself miss, he reached out to grapple her and caught the top of her tunic. His iron grip closed down onto her shoulder pinning her in place. With his other arm he back handed her across the face sending her reeling across the ground for a good ten yards. When she stopped moving, Anya lay blacked out on the ground with blood streaming from her mouth.

May's eyes slowly opened as she found herself lying prone against the trading house wall, her vision blurry and thoughts incoherent. She spent a few moments refocusing and was soon able to get to her knees and stand up. Then she discovered that her furs were missing. She looked around and could not find them anywhere.

The crowd in front of the trading house had mostly dispersed. The giant had thundered in through the main door and could be heard dictating his terms of sale inside.

As May looked around, she spied Anya lying on the ground with blood around her head. May rushed over to her. Anya was unresponsive and bleeding but also breathing. She was too heavy for May to lift, especially in her present condition, so she dragged her out of the street. May noticed a large crowd keeping clear of the main door. Not a single person offered any help to her or Anya. May tried to stop Anya's bleeding and tended her own facial cuts. Anya's face had swollen up where the giant had slapped her. Eventually she did manage to flag down some younger men to help her carry Anya back to Ma's. While carrying Anya through town, May could see off in the distance two figures side by side scanning the remnants of the chaos, talking to people and searching for something or someone. They were both wearing green capes with red crests emblazoned on their backs. May could not be sure of what she was seeing as her head did not feel quite right. May turned her head away pulled, up her collar, and continued carrying Anya to Ma's then up the stairs and into her bunk.

May had difficulty believing what had just happened that morning. She felt fortunate that Anya was alive but was really furious that some vultures had pinched her furs right off from her back while she lay blacked out on the ground. At least Anya was resting in her bed, her wounds cleaned and the bleeding stopped.

Sometime later, Anya opened her eyes. The first thing she saw was Berthe hovering over her with a damp, red-stained cloth wiping down her forehead and mouth. Berthe broke into a smile while wiping a tear off her face. She said, "Don't move. You are strong and you will heal up real soon. You need to rest now. You need to rest." As Berthe nursed and cooed over her, Anya closed her eyes wondering what had happened to her after she blacked out.

For the rest of the day and into the evening, May worked in the kitchen. She chopped, stewed, hauled, cooked, baked, and even cut meat for both herself and Anya. She never said a word to anyone and everything went smoothly in the kitchen and nary a customer had gone hungry or dry. When the kitchen doors closed, May went back up to her bunkroom and sat next to Anya. Anya was asleep and appeared to be in a lot of pain. May was thankful that the healing salve she bought was working on Anya's wounds. The salve did not get rid of the pain but reduced the throbbing quite a bit to make it tolerable. After some time, they both fell into a form of sleep, off and on throughout the night.

Scouting

The next day, May woke up early and checked on Anya. After seeing that Anya was doing well for her condition, she walked outside and headed east, surreptitiously poking her head into each tavern and inn and hostel looking for the green-caped goons. She was attracting many curious stares as she walked down the main street, and once in a while, she crossed a face wearing a hateful scowl. Most of the people didn't notice her at all. She was not having much success until she noticed the two green caped goons appear from the far side of the trading house walking side by side. *There they are*, she thought, *I was not imagining things*. She skulked back into the shadows and watched the two men walk down the side of the main street.

May was preparing to follow the goons when she was startled by a faint voice behind her whispering, "Whats you looking for?" May turned around and hiding in the nearby shadows was a small boy clinging behind an empty barrel watching her intently. He couldn't have been more than eight years.

She said to him, "Mind your own business, boy."

He said, "Those men with the green coats, they beens looking for you."

"And why do you think that, boy? And don't lie to me or I'll twist your arm and snap it," she whispered angrily.

"'Cause I heards them talking abouts you and someone else hiding in town together. They beens talking everywhere in town and means to catch you and your girlfriend and hauls you off to somewhere. I forgets where."

May became alarmed by this revelation. She thought carefully then paused and concluded that the boy couldn't be lying as he could not have known anything about how Anya and May had come into town. May asked, "Do you know where the green coats are staying?"

"No," he said.

"I've got a deal for you. You find out exactly where the green coats are staying and I'll give you a silver."

The boy replied, "Two silvers. One for finding the green coats and one for helping you."

May quickly grabbed his arm and squeezed hard, "I really CAN snap your arm." The boy winced in pain until she let up.

"My mama needs the money to buy food for our family. My papa went hunting one day and never returned. Please stop, it hurts." May relented and said, "All right. Two silvers then. I'll come back to this spot tomorrow and collect my information. That's when you get paid. And how did you know I was a woman?"

"My mama taughts me never to hurts a woman or to helps a woman if I cans. Isn't it obvious?" The boy said as he sneaked away massaging his arm.

May sat there dumbfounded for some time. Eventually, she spotted the green coats again wandering about the main street. She also realized that it would be better to let the boy do his job and hope he did not sell her out. He probably would not sell her out until he at least got paid. After that, anything could happen. She waited for the green coats to wander into a building before returning to Ma's.

May returned to Ma's and went straight upstairs to see how Anya was doing. Anya had woken up but was still lying in her bed. Anya's face was throbbing in pain from her slap. She tried moving her tongue around but more pain instantly erupted. She moved her tongue anyway and could feel a large chunk of her inner cheek missing as well as a tooth. Berthe was using a cold cloth filled with snow from outside the shed to help reduce the swelling and hopefully the pain. When May entered the room, Berthe moved to fetch more clean water and a new cloth. As she left the room, she gave Anya a wink.

"How are you feeling?" May asked.

"Everything hurts," Anya winced. "What happened?"

"I don't know what happened to you, but when I woke up again, you were lying on the street in a pool of blood." She continued telling Anya her story of the brawl and then followed up with her recent sortie into town to locate the green coats. She concluded by whispering that she thought things were getting worse for them in town and that maybe they should consider leaving before too long.

"Tomorrow I will go find the boy and figure out where the green coats are staying." May said.

Anya replied, "Don't go. It could be a trap. What if he goes ratting you out to the green coats for even more coin and they set up an ambush for you? Or worse, he is already working for them."

May said, "I had not thought of that." She paused. "I don't think he would do that. He sounded honest enough to me."

Anya said slowly, "Don't fool yourself May. My father always told me to count the coin. If I've learned anything about this town, it's that the only thing this town cares about or respects is coin. Our furs got pinched and everything is expensive. And no matter how nice Ma is to us and the others, this place takes in lots of silvers every day. She gives some to us and her suppliers, but where does the rest go? Everything in this place is nice and costs something and it all belongs to Ma and whoever else it is I hear at night going up and down a staircase I've never seen."

May absorbed what Anya had said and concluded that either she had had her head knocked crazy or that they were really just fresh meat for the Northcamp grinder.

While Anya's body had mostly recovered from her shock, she still had puffy cheeks. She was able to work a little in the kitchen but did not do any heavy lifting. Berthe was spending time showing her how to make the dinner rolls. Berthe explained that once the bread dough was ready, the bake-prep was relatively easy.

Berthe took a small piece of bread dough from a large bowl nearby. She moved much closer to Anya and gently took Anya's hand and placed the dough into her palm. Anya let Berthe take her hand and turn it over.

Berthe gently moved Anya's hand around and around. "As you roll the dough around, it turns into a ball. Then you take the ball and place it onto the baking sheet like this. You repeat until you fill the row and then you start another row. When the sheet is full, it is ready for the fire. After that, it's just dinner roll, dinner roll, dinner roll all night long."

Berthe gave Anya a special smile then moved away to make another batch of bread dough as Anya was making the dinner rolls that evening. Anya worked for some time into the evening but then excused herself and retired before the doors were closed.

May was working a full shift that day and night. Caught in her own thoughts, she had decided that she would go meet her spy boy in the morning. She figured that while they would meet in the shadows, it would still be broad daylight and no one would run an ambush in plain view on the street, or so she hoped. However, she did not want anyone following her back to Ma's, so she planned to walk a winding route through town designed to detect and evade anyone attempting to follow her.

Karl, who usually kept to himself most of the time, was more talkative that evening and expressed to May his best wishes for a quick recovery for Anya. He told her that Nimrod was a monster that should be exiled but that no one in town had the backbone to stand up to him, not even the sheriff. When Ma stepped down into the cellar, Karl whispered to May what it was that made Ma's stew popular. "Just because there is only one item on the menu doesn't mean that there isn't room for creativity. Ma has a secret blend of salt and herbs that we keep under the counter. She uses a combination of something called basil with pinches of rosemary and oregano. Ma spent several years tweaking the blend to get the flavor just right. The exact blend is her trade secret."

Ma emerged from the cellar carrying several chickens and placed them onto a cutting board before going to the shed. "I used to experiment with Ma's stews by adding thickeners to see whether the customers would complain or compliment the stews. I once asked Ma if she would be willing to use her stew as a filling for pot pies. Ultimately, she rejected every idea I proposed. So then I began experimenting with cheese rolls. I once baked several samples for Ma to taste, but she vetoed every idea as too expensive."

Ma emerged again into the kitchen with some fire wood and then went to her counter and started cutting up the chickens. And with that, the whispering ended.

Karl began peeking onto the main floor every few moments as if he was anxious about something. Eventually, he appeared to find what he was looking for and then politely asked May if she would keep an eye on the stew for him. May said she would and Karl went over to Berthe's counter and pulled out a small hidden cloth concealing something wrapped inside. He then scurried off. May took a quick glance through the open door towards the main floor. She could see Karl visiting a table with two older women and two young children, a boy and a girl. He spoke briefly to the two women and hugged both of the two children. He then took out the secret cloth and slowly opened it to reveal two dinner rolls. The children's eyes lit up as he gave one roll to each child. May could see the children eating and smiling as Karl left the table. May turned briefly toward Berthe and saw a small smile come and go on her face as she went back to work. Soon Karl was back in the kitchen tending the stew pot. He also had what appeared to be a smile on his face as he stirred the pot.

May thanked Karl for sharing his stories and when the night bell rang, she went upstairs to find Anya fast asleep. May prepared herself for bed and went to sleep not long thereafter.

Cleaning Route

May got up early again and told Anya what she intended to do that morning. Anya again emphasized that she should not walk into an ambush. May said that she would be careful and then left.

May took a different route into the east end and also to her rendezvous with her spy boy. She went to the same building and hid in the shadows. Eventually she heard a familiar whisper beckoning her into the bushes behind her. May complied. Behind the bushes, the boy was trying hard not to be seen.

May asked, "What did you find? Did anyone follow you here? Where can I find the green coats?"

The boy said he did not think he was followed but could not be sure. He also said, "Those green-coat guys frightens me. They acts like bullies and don't seems to cares about anything or anyone." He then proceeded, "I followed the green coats into the Bear's Den Inn. They're staying in one of the upstairs rooms. I believes it's room number eight. They drinks a few beers in the tavern at night then goes upstairs. They most likely stays there until dawn."

"What does a number eight look like?" May asked.

The boy looked puzzled. "You don't knows what a number eight looks like?" He found a twig lying on the ground and proceeded to draw a figure eight in the dirt. He said, "This is a number eight, 8. It is posted on the front door of the room the green coats are staying in."

"Thank you." She pulled out of her pocket two silvers and gave them to the boy.

The boy told her, "Don'ts leave until after I'm gone and tries not to shows yourself in the main street when leaving the east end. You never knows who might be watching. Thanks." He held up the silvers then disappeared.

May waited, not sure whether to be scared or not. She thought, *at least I haven't been ambushed yet.* She worked her way through the bushes and shadows to the back streets of Northcamp. Her plan was to duck into many different shops and alleyways while checking to see if she was being followed, a cleaning route. She hurried up and waited many times while making sure not to pass by the apothecary and not to look too suspicious. Her circuitous tour of the south end eventually brought her to a curious building that did not look like any of the others she had seen or expected. The front door of the building was open and inviting. She ducked inside.

The building interior was not very large. The far wall appeared to be a window made up of various shards of colored glass all joined together somehow. In front of the window was a large statue looking like two small logs joined together to form a figure like a "+" perched on a dais directly in front of the colorful window.

May quickly scanned the street from behind the door then moved away from the entrance and sat down on a bench set against the wall. She looked back towards the door, waiting to see if anyone else would follow her in. To her right was a side wall with no doors and to her left was a side wall with a single door ajar not far away. She counted four long benches in the whole room facing the colorful window and the statue together. Along the side walls several small rows of lighted candles sent a flickering glow throughout the room.

May got the feeling that she was being watched. A grey-robed figure opened the side door and slowly stepped into the room, glancing at her. The figure appeared to be a man with a well-trimmed beard that worked around his chin from ear to ear, blending into both ends of a moustache. Both his hands were clasped together in front of his chest holding a small rectangular item.

"Welcome my child to the Chapel of the Holy Cross. Blessed are those who come in the name of the Lord. What brings you here this lovely day?"

May was confused. Looking around the room, she noticed no one else inside. She asked the man, "What is this place?"

He smiled as he opened his arms, reciting, "This is a place of peace and sanctuary; a place where followers of the Lord can feel comforted and experience his presence. You look agitated. Is this your first time in the chapel?"

May sat silently for some time, not sure what to say.

"Many people find their way to this chapel seeking guidance or answers to things bothering them. Everyone has problems. The world and this town have no shortage of problems and troubles. The chapel wants everyone to know that even when life appears sad and hopeless, the Lord comforts them and gives hope to those in need."

May noticed something he was carrying in his hand that was not very large and had a picture on its outside that looked very much like the statue in the room. "What is that in your hands?"

The grey-robed man said with a smile, "This is my prayer book. It has prayers I recite and sing every day and some stories from the Bible I read for comfort. The Bible is the story of the world and the people of the Lord. I have a large Bible in my room over there but it is too heavy for me to carry around, so I carry my prayer book instead."

"Will you tell me a story from your book?" May was stalling for time and did not want to spend any more time talking about herself. No one else walked through or looked in from the outside door.

The grey-robed man placed his book in his palm, opened it up, and began speaking in a story-telling voice, "In the beginning ..."

After a short time, he stopped speaking and closed his book. May smiled and pointed to his book saying, "That was a nice story. You have a nice voice for telling stories. May I see what you were looking at in your book?"

The grey-robed man came over to her, opened his book, and showed her the words he had just read to her. She looked at the marks on the page and did not understand a thing. "The words are all in Latin but I told you the story in Suborean so you could understand. That's why I spoke slowly."

"I guess I never learned how to look at words." She was amazed that everything he had said came from a few marks scratched on a piece of paper. "I have to go now. Thank you for telling me your story."

He explained, "It is not my story. It is everyone's story." He bid her farewell until the next time.

May looked out from the chapel entrance and did not see anyone loitering outside or down the street. She began her hurry-up-and-wait strategy again but did not detect anyone else nearby. Finally, she made it back to Ma's feeling pretty sure that she had not been followed.

While May was walking around town, Anya was working on waking herself up. She could not tell how she looked just by touching her face so she went into the washing room and found the small mirror hanging on the wall. She could see that the swelling was much better though not completely gone. There was still a little pain where her tooth used to be. Sticking her tongue into the vacant spot brought a jolting reminder of how much it still hurt.

In the hallway, Berthe opened her door. She had been waiting for Anya to enter the washing room. Now that Anya was there, she quickly scurried into the washing room and squeezed behind Anya to get to the corner shower. Anya briefly glimpsed Berthe passing behind her. When Berthe got to the shower stall, she started taking off her clothes. Berthe pretended to ignore Anya and made no effort to conceal her body. When she was naked, she neither smiled nor frowned; she just briefly locked eyes with Anya then stepped into the shower.

What is going on? Anya thought. Anya finished washing her face as quickly as she could then zipped back into the bunkroom. The look Berthe had given her was one she had not seen before and she wondered what she should do or say to Berthe, if anything. She went back to her bed hoping May would show up soon so she wouldn't have to be alone with Berthe the rest of the morning.

May returned and went around the back, climbed the stairs, and slipped into the bunkroom to find Anya looking uneasy and confused. "What's going on? Are you all right? Your swelling looks better. You should be feeling better too, I hope."

Anya replied, "I'll be all right. Don't worry. Berthe keeps telling me I am strong and will recover soon. Maybe it's true."

May gave Anya a strange look then changed the subject by telling Anya about what her spy boy had told her. "He told me that the green coats are staying at the Bear's Den Inn on the east end in the upstairs room number eight. What if we were to sneak in, knock them out, and hogtie them quietly in the night then leave right away? We'd have a head start before they realized we were gone."

Anya retorted, "I don't think that's a good idea. If we knock them out then when they wake up, they'll suspect that it was us and it would confirm their suspicions that we've been hiding in town all along. Then everyone in Northcamp who has seen us or had anything to do with us might be interrogated until they talk. We would be putting everyone in danger, Ma and Karl and Berthe and the servers and Danae and Deanna and on and on. I don't think touching the green coats does anyone any good."

"Then what do we do? I don't think we can wait them out. I think they're getting closer to us each day and soon they'll find us here at Ma's. I don't think going to Danae's place any more is wise. Someone might think she is helping us which might get her into trouble. I already have the jitters walking around town now. It seems every eye that looks at me is suspicious and hostile, especially since the brawl. And we're fortunate that lame sheriff hasn't seen either of us.

They pondered their predicament and slowly came to realize that maybe the best way to resolve things without anyone getting hurt was to just leave in the night when no one was looking and hope the green coats never found out where they had stayed and visited during the past fortnight.

May stated, "If we leave then it has to be soon. I would say tonight after the doors close. Everyone will be tired and once everyone falls asleep, we can sneak out to the shed then melt into the woods." May began shedding tears, "I was starting to like this town, even in spite of the brawl."

Anya said, "Yes, me too."

Anya and May worked that day and night but not very hard as they were going to need their strength that night. Business was good. The girls did not talk much and usually only if spoken to. They performed their usual tasks and by the time the night bell rang, they were mentally ready for the task ahead. Berthe gave Anya and May a curious look before heading into her room. Karl headed to his home, and the servers were always gone by the bell. Ma closed things up in the usual way then headed off for her room. The two girls washed up then went quietly to their rooms and packed up. Without the lost furs, it would be easier to pack. They got into their bunks and then waited until they felt it was time to go.

They loaded themselves up, removed their shoes, and slowly walked down the hall. By now they knew where all of the creaky spots on the floorboards were and did not make any large sounds getting to the stairs. The stairs were harder to sneak down but they did move more quietly than they had ever done before. They put their shoes back on then found and moved along the shadowed side of the shed. They waited a few moments then quickly sprinted off into the woods. When they got into the woods a ways, Anya stopped and looked back at Ma's Kitchen with tears in her eyes. Then she cried. After she stopped crying, she took one last look before following May deeper into the woods.

Anya was starting to like Berthe. While Anya suffered in pain, Berthe flattered her with kind attention and caring hands. Her touch was gentle and she had a cute giggle. But presently, Anya realized that to stay in Northcamp was to put her own and Berthe's lives in danger. Anya knew that if she and May were discovered at Ma's, they would probably have to fight their way out of town which meant that either or both of them could get killed. Anya had no money or property to her name and had a friend she'd known since childhood that just couldn't stay out of trouble. Keeping May out of trouble had been her full-time job for a long time. Thinking about herself had never been a priority to Anya, but Berthe had helped Anya see herself differently and become better acquainted with her sensitive emotions. Anya tried not to feel sad for herself, but still she cried until she left the town far behind.

Walking through the woods, Anya had what she could only describe to herself as a vision, a premonition of the future. In her mind's eye, she could see Berthe running up the stairs to her room, slamming the door behind her then falling onto her bed, crying and crying and crying. Anya would never rid herself of that vision.

Bounty Hunter

For the past few nights, a darkly clad figure walked up and down the road leading southwest from Northcamp. He walked the road as far south as the creekside bridge, sometimes beyond, looking for people leaving town in a hurry.

His dark hair was short and he was clean-shaven except for a thin black moustache running across his upper lip. His fair skin and dark eyes, like most people in Northcamp, looked expressionless most of the time. He was bedecked in a dark, flat-colored suit with special shoes that allowed him to make very little sound. On his person, he carried minimal supplies as he always returned to the Bear's Den Inn in the early morning. Circling his waist, a simple black belt held multiple pouches. Three small throwing daggers were tucked into his belt near the small of his back. He was armed with a simple, well-cared-for short sword sheathed in a padded scabbard and a masterfully crafted assassin's bow, a small black crossbow that could be quickly reloaded. Wrapped around his wrist, he carried an ammunition bandolier with multiple sleeves for holding crossbow bolts. Each bolt was specially designed for maiming its victims. Often, he brought back his bounties alive, well enough to collect.

A few days ago, he had met up with two henchmen in the service of Baron Wesselman. They presented him with an edict approved by the Baron for the apprehension and return of two girls traveling together. Reading the edict carefully, he deduced that it had not been approved by the Baron, much less by the Viscount in Vassans. The handwriting was sloppy and the Baron's seal gave him a funny feeling he couldn't quite place. Ultimately, none of that concerned him. All that mattered was getting paid the stated bounty and letting the involved parties resolve their grievances. The girls were described as tall, young runaways. The Baron wanted them alive but delivered into the custody of his son, Willem, for questioning regarding wanton crimes committed against his family.

Two roads led south from Northcamp. One led southeast towards Wesseltown and the other wound its way southwest towards the Rowan River and the ferry to Callalande. He figured that the girls would not leave town the way they entered, so he positioned himself along the southwestern road expecting them to distance themselves from the Baron's men.

A crescent moon illuminated patchy clouds that cast a frosty glow across the forest. While walking the road, he spotted a faint flickering illumination against several distant trees to the west. He left the road and sneaked his way tree by tree, shadow by shadow, until he spied a campfire. His intuition had served him well. From his vantage, he saw two girls huddled near a small campfire eating bread. He thought, *this might be easier than I thought.* One of the girls was bigger than the other and appeared to be staring off into space while the other was drifting off to sleep. He gauged the time to be well before dawn.

He crouched down, scrutinizing the girls, planning how best to approach and capture them. He reasoned that disabling the larger girl would be his first move followed by knocking out the sleeping girl with a quick blow to the head. Returning to the first girl, he would disarm and pummel her until he neutralized her resistance. Finally, he would secure the two girls with several ropes, parade them together into town, and collect his bounty – a challenging plan but simple enough.

He observed Anya carefully and noted that she was armed with a sheathed knife tied around her right leg. Assuming she was right-handed, he slowly nocked a bolt into his crossbow and took aim at her right shoulder joint. He crouched onto his right knee, leaned forward in a two-handed stance, and aimed. As he shifted his weight forward to his final shooting position, he felt a slight backward tug on his right foot. Suddenly, his leg jerked backwards taking his entire body to the ground, prone. He heard the words "Anya" and "take cover" coming from the campfire.

His shot flew errant, nicking Anya's right collar bone. Now on the ground, he rolled over and sprang to a crouched position again when a knife plunged deep into his upper thigh, compromising his mobility. He let out a loud grunt of pain as he scampered away to cover. In one quick motion, he reloaded his crossbow and shot again at an approaching candle light that appeared out of nowhere from the same direction the knife came from. He shot another bolt and heard it whiz away, hitting a far-off tree. As he was reloading a third bolt, he saw a fast-approaching shadow, so he dropped his crossbow and drew his sword.

Then he was hit by the charging shadow, and a knife plunged deep into his shoulder joint. He gasped in pain and dropped his sword. He brought his off hand around and punched back at the shadow, hitting it in the face. A scream of pain erupted from the shadow, but now both of his arms were pinned to the ground in a grapple. In terrible pain, he tried rolling away but the knife stuck in his thigh resisted, sending searing pain through his leg. Pinned and grappled, he found his hands and legs being hogtied. A final blow to his head knocked him out.

May was lying down, warming herself by the fire. Anya sat quietly as she nibbled on one of Berthe's rolls. Suddenly, May sensed that one of her rabbit traps was about to be sprung. She rolled over and drew her skinning knife. As she turned, she was surprised to see a man's face flickering in the firelight. She forcefully threw her knife at the ground where the trap was set just below the man's face. A grunt of pain echoed through the trees as her knife hit its mark. "Anya," she called out, "Take cover!"

Anya was passive and numb when she was startled by May's yelling, followed by a crossbow bolt that nipped the top of her collar bone, cutting cleanly through her upper shoulder. Instantly, she felt a sharp pain as she went down, rolling away from the campfire.

May grabbed one of Anya's candles and lit it. She began crawling towards her rabbit trap, raising the candle above her head. She saw the faint outline of a man scrambling to take cover behind a tree. A crossbow bolt whizzed by her ear and hit a tree behind her. May raised her candle up higher.

Anya unsheathed her hunting knife; taking cover, she tried to spot what had just shot her. As May's candle illuminated the surrounding forest, Anya heard shuffling through the undergrowth and caught a glimpse of a shadowed figure. Once Anya spotted the mysterious figure, she instantly moved to rush her foe. The figure attempted to reload its crossbow but the instant it recognized Anya charging, it dropped the crossbow and drew a sword. Anya slammed her entire weight into the figure, driving her knife deep into its upper chest and clavicle. It dropped its sword. She grabbed its arm as its other fist landed a heavy blow to Anya's face and her jaw erupted in a universe of pain. Screaming loudly, Anya attempted to pin the figure to the ground in a grapple, hoping that May would arrive soon to help her out.

When May arrived, she quickly hogtied the man just as her father taught her. She could feel him writhing in pain as she quickly gave him a blow to the head, knocking him out.

"Are there any more? I saw only him."

"I don't think so. Be quiet and listen," Anya whispered.

Time passed and they heard nothing else moving about the surrounding wood. All they heard was their own heavy breathing. Anya stood up, grabbed the man by the collar, and dragged him over to the campfire. She gagged him and waited for him to wake up. May wandered around picking up his sword and crossbow.

Anya grabbed her shoulder and pointed. "He must have hit me with one of those things he's wearing on his wrist."

May came over to Anya to inspect her wound. The wound was slowly bleeding. May took Anya's hand and put it over the wound and said, "Pressure the wound while I get the healing salve." May took out the salve and a bandage. She opened the tear in Anya's tunic, revealing her wound.

"It looks like a clean cut all the way through. I will apply some salve and wrap it up with a bandage." May took some time but soon, Anya's wound was all wrapped up. "Feel better?"

"Yes. Thank you," Anya said.

May looked up and down the man, saying, "Who is this guy? I never saw him back in town or anyone dressed like him before."

Anya said, "Judging by his outfit and weapons, he might some kind of professional. Maybe he's a bounty hunter? Maybe he works for the Baron, but I don't see a sliver of green on him anywhere. We should search him."

Anya and May spent some time searching the man and found a few items of interest. In addition to his weapons, they found a small bolo with three padded weights, a handful of very small marbles, a long thin rope, three small throwing daggers, and a small folded piece of paper with writing on it. As the two girls continued searching, he slowly began to stir.

"He's waking up. You should be the one to ask him questions. After all, he did shoot you," May said.

The man slowly regained consciousness and winced a few times. A few muffled yells came from his gagged mouth as he struggled to sit up but found himself hogtied. He soon noticed Anya and May staring down at him. As he realized his predicament, he stopped struggling and looked out across the campfire silently.

With steel in her eyes, Anya crouched and asked, "Who are you and why did you shoot me?"

The man remained silent, making no effort to speak.

"Let me try that again. Who are you and why did you shoot me?" Anya repeated.

The man remained silent.

Anya stated, "I guess we can stay here like this all night long and if you bleed out, we won't get any answers from you. Or we can do this!" Anya raised her fist and slammed it into his wounded shoulder. The man yelled out in terrible pain but the sound was muffled by his gag. "We can also do that all night long until you bleed out."

The man began talking through his gag but May and Anya couldn't understand a word he was saying.

Anya said to him, "I will take off the gag. If you want to yell for help, go ahead but no one will hear you this far into the woods." She removed his gag.

The man gasped for air saying, "Release me now and surrender and I will forget all of the grievous pain you have inflicted upon me tonight. If you don't release me, the entire town of Northcamp is set to gather out here at first light, hunt you down like animals, drag you back to town, and turn you two into the sheriff, dead or alive. That's why surrendering to me is important because it can save your lives."

"That's hogwash and you know it," May interjected. "That chicken sheriff doesn't care one copper about what happens to us or to any other trapper in Northcamp. All anyone cares about in that town is coin, just like you. Are you working for the Baron? And what is this?" May shoved the unfolded paper into his face.

The man stated matter-of-factly, "That is an edict issued by the sheriff of Northcamp stating that the two of you are wanted dead or alive for crimes committed in Northcamp and Wesseltown over the past fortnight. As I said before, you should surrender now as I promise to bring you in peaceably to the sheriff or soon these woods will be swarming with the Northcamp posse trying to drag you away to jail. At least I can promise you that you will arrive in Northcamp safely and alive. The posse does not make any promises."

The man caught his breath and continued, "If the posse comes to drag you away, they will also arrest your friends in town for harboring and abetting known fugitives. The sheriff does not take kindly to those kinds of charges. Your friends may be thrown into jail and their property confiscated. Do you want that on your conscience as well? The best way out of your predicament is to surrender peacefully and no one else will get hurt."

That last statement angered Anya tremendously. She buried another fist into his wounded shoulder then unsheathed her knife, placing it across his neck.

With desperation in his voice, the man said, "Killing me would only add an additional charge of murder against you and would result in a death sentence. Do you really want that as well? They will hang you or burn you in the center of town and all your friends will watch you die. You should surrender now and let the sheriff enact his justice on you and he may be lenient. That would be best for everybody."

"I've heard enough," Anya said. "You are a false witness. What did Ma or Karl or Berthe ever do to you? Who are you to threaten innocent people?" And then she yelled into his face, "And Berthe! What did she ever do to you? What did she ever do to hurt anyone? All she wants is to work and help her mama raise her siblings and help her brother go off to school. She wants nothing else but to do good in her world and YOU come along and threaten her here to my face!" And with that she took the knife from his throat and plunged it into his heart. She stared down at his face as darkness fell over his eyes.

May recognized raw emotion when she saw it. She said sarcastically, "I guess we're not going to get any answers from him now, right?"

Anya replied, "He wasn't going to tell us anything. He was a desperate man whose only way of talking to people was to intimidate and threaten them. Every word he said was false and desperate. And there isn't some mob of people coming to get us this morning. If that were true, they would have picked us up during the brawl when we got knocked out. Or surrounded Ma's Kitchen with bear traps demanding we surrender. Or maybe we would even know what that cowardly sheriff looks like."

Anya put her hands on her head and quietly whimpered. May took a long look at Anya then said, "Do you really like Berthe that much?"

Anya sniffed and sighed, "I don't know. She made things confusing for me."

May said, "Sounds to me like she was a little special."

They both sat down staring into the dying fire.

May broke the silence. "It will be light soon and I'm too exhausted to begin moving again. Let's camp here for the day and get some sleep, then decide what to do later tonight. We also have to figure out what to do with his body. We can't just leave it here or a mob really will come to get us."

Callalande

The two girls slept until near midday when they were finally roused by the sounds of creatures moving about nearby. The girls realized that they still had some bread from last night but neither of them was hungry.

Anya said, "I think the man here is starting to attract scavengers. We should get rid of him or clear out."

"We need to bury him somewhere. Do you have a shovel?"

"No." Anya took off to scout around for an appropriate place to bury him. She did not want to have to carry him too far as he was heavy. She discovered lots of undergrowth making the ground squishy to step on; but underneath, the ground was hard from the cold weather. Maybe instead of digging a big hole, she and May could uproot a bush or two, dig into the ground a little, then replant the bushes on top and no one would be the wiser. It sounded good in theory, but would it work?

Anya came back to May with her plan and she thought it was a good idea, too, but also thought it might be difficult to implement.

May suggested, "Maybe we can sharpen some large sticks into spears or pry bars which we can use to loosen the ground and dig at the same time."

Anya replied, "Let's try it."

Anya and May found some sticks then pulled out the man's sword and began sharpening the ends into chisels rather than points. They went off to find some bushes that looked like they had looser ground underneath and began digging. They managed to uproot several small bushes and dig a hole about three feet deep. They were getting very tired.

Anya said, "Remember, we're just digging a hole, not a grave site." They made the hole large enough to fit the man if placed in the fetal position a few feet into the ground.

Before burying him they decided to keep any gear they could find on him with the exception of his bloody outfit. They removed his belt and discovered that it was heavier than they expected. Flipping the belt over, they found several small sewn pockets each holding a gold coin. In total, they counted ten golds.

"He has a coin belt along with all of the pouches and the three daggers. Quite a nice belt, I would say." May said. "And these shoes he's wearing. He must have been able to sneak up on us with them."

After removing everything except his clothing, they put him into the hole. As they were about to cover him up, they both noticed that he had a small tattoo mark below one of his ears on his neck. It was definitely not the Baron's crest. It looked like a blacked-out sun along a horizon either rising or setting. They buried him and then replanted the bushes on top of him. When they were done, the sun was sinking into the west and they were tired again.

May stood over the newly made grave and said, "I know he was hogwash but may he rest in peace and let him be judged as fairly as he deserves. Amen."

"Where did you get that?" Anya said.

May replied, "I visited the Chapel of the Holy Cross in Northcamp before we left. There was a man in there who said 'amen' after he finished telling me a story. It sounded like something appropriate to say."

"Anyway," Anya stated, "we can't go about wearing any of his stuff yet as someone might recognize it and set a mob on us. We'll have to pack all of it into our bags. That crossbow is the bulkiest item and barely fits. Maybe you want to carry it? I also found one of the bolts stuck in a tree nearby."

"Sure."

"But we are dividing this stuff up for carrying purposes. As far as I am concerned, you can have all of it if you want," Anya said.

The two spent the rest of the afternoon packing their bags and by evening had built another fire. They decided to rest a while before leaving later that evening.

Anya said, "At least we have not been attacked by a mob. But sooner or later, the mystery man will be missed and someone is bound to get curious."

"All right; here, have a bread roll." May offered one of their remaining rolls to Anya.

Anya took the roll hesitantly. She sat down, broke it, and savored it slowly.

May watched Anya eat her roll then said, "Someday, when this storm blows over, we will come back to Northcamp and visit Ma's for dinner."

"Yes." Anya curled up by the fire and fell asleep.

After some time, the fire died out and moon glow filled the forest with an ethereal light. The sky cleared and the moon guided them southward. They loaded up their packs, threw some dirt onto the fire, and began moving.

They kept to the woods for some time then moved closer to the road. They didn't see any signs of traffic along the road but with the night visibility, they would know if someone was approaching for some distance. They made good time walking along the road. As the dawn began lighting the east, they moved back into the woods. They broke for the morning. In the distance, they could faintly hear flowing water, the Rowan River.

While resting in the woods, they built a small fire. The girls decided to keep moving later in the afternoon. Not far from the road, they could hear a caravan of carts heading south. The carts were fully loaded with furs and hides and protected by several guards. It would be better for the girls if they were not seen, so they kept quiet and hidden.

Continuing south, they kept to the woods. Soon they came within view of the Rowan River. It was not a broad river, but it was too deep for animals to ford. Two docks and a ferry had been built where the flowing water seemed smoothest. A single punted barge crisscrossed the river several times a day.

Anya suggested, "I think we should wait until evening before crossing. Paying the fare is the easiest way across."

"It's just you and me. What if we hire a local fisherman to ferry us across?" May suggested.

Anya looked about then reported, "I don't see any boats in the river or docked along the shore on either side."

May conceded, "All right. We wait till evening."

The girls waited. As evening neared Anya said, "I don't see anything on either side of the river looking to cross. That caravan we saw earlier must have already crossed. Let's make our move." The girls loaded up and approached what appeared to be the ferryman.

"Hello. We would like to hire your ferry to cross the river. Would that be you?"

The ferryman answered, "Aye, that'd be me but I'm closin' up for the night. Maybe in the mornin' I can take you across."

"How much do you charge for a crossing?"

"A crossin' is one silver a person, two silver a horse, and three silver a cart."

May pulled out one of their gold coins and held it up in front of the ferryman. "How about you take us across tonight?"

The man held out his hand and gently took the gold coin from her hand then put it up to his mouth and bit into it. He looked back at the coin, looked up into the sky, then back at May, shrugged his shoulders and said, "All right, get in." He unsecured the ferry and started punting towards the other dock. As they left their dock, they could see an older woman walk out onto a porch from what passed as a house. She looked at them sternly then put her hands on her hips. "Yeah, you just wait till you get back here and see what I do to you." Then, she strode back into the house.

He slowly pushed the ferry and the girls across the gentle water, and as they neared the far shore, they could see several buildings lining the river. Beyond the dock, a road led away towards a small gate and gatehouse. They did not see any caravan carts moving or waiting. As the ferryman brought the ferry gently to the dock, he secured it and waited for the girls to disembark before returning to the opposite shore.

"Thank you, ferryman," May said.

"No, thank you. You just bought me beer for a month. Come again anytime." The ferryman chortled as he drifted back to the Borean shore.

The two girls walked along the road and soon came upon a closed gate. They approached the gate and found an empty gatehouse. As they looked around, an individual with a lantern emerged from a nearby building and walked towards them. "Aren't you a little on the late side to be traveling?"

May explained, "We are lagging behind the caravan that passed by here earlier and want to purchase a pass."

The official eyed them suspiciously then said, "State your business."

May paused a moment then said, "We are trappers and do business in Northcamp most of the time, but the weather up north has gotten too cold for us so we are headed south to assist fur traders treat and prepare their furs and hides for market until the spring."

The guard gave them another good eying then pointed to their knives, "Are these the only weapons you have to declare?"

May said, "Yes, this is my skinning knife that I use, mostly for rabbits. Right now, rabbit furs are in demand."

The official recognized the knife as a genuine skinning knife. "All right, I can give you two a season's pass which can be renewed by any official working in the Office of Security. You are bound by all laws and edicts of Duke Olan. Trapping and trading require a separate permit signed by an official in the Office of Resources in Callamar. Some animals are protected by edict and if you hunt them, you may be subject to fines and/or imprisonment or both. Do you understand?"

"Yes, we do." May said.

"A season's permit will cost you one gold each. If any official of Callalande challenges you, you must present your permit or risk a fine and/or imprisonment or both. Do you understand?"

"Yes, we do." May said.

The official opened up the gatehouse and began filling out some paperwork. He placed some melted wax on each paper and affixed an official seal of Callalande onto each one. Then, he checked to see that everything had been properly filled out. Then he took out a small bottle of ink and proceeded to ink up Anya's and May's right thumbs; he then affixed their thumbprints to each document in turn. He finally signed each document himself. He presented each permit to Anya and May. May paid the official two golds. He tipped his hat and said, "Welcome to Callalande." As he slowly raised the gate, Anya and May walked through the gate and into the twilight beyond.

PART 2

Monastery

The road running north from Scullsbergen emerges from a vast forest to cross a small coastal lea before reaching the southernmost of the Aerieal Horns. The Aerieal Horns rise as a mountainous barrier to overland travel from Korgynslande to Callalande. The southernmost Horns plunge steeply and deeply into the Sea of Calla. Mighty soaring and kiting birds grant their name to these great looming walls, the Albatross Cliffs. The tip of an undersea spur juts above the monstrous swells to behold the cliffs and crashing waves. Perennially battered, the dark-rocked island houses the loneliest public servant in all Callalande. From a rocky igloo scavenged by skuas, he monitors and relays the light signals using directioned lanterns from Callamar's southernmost gate to the Inn of the Narrows, allowing caravans to brave the road without conflict or collision. Travelers and merchants who cannot pass because of weather or congestion must waylay themselves at the inn or garrison.

Huge breakers pound the rocks below, spraying the road with seawater. Wet and slippery, the road snakes along the cliffside, chiseled out from the looming walls to emerge at the southern tip of Callalande. The narrow road accommodates only carts and foot traffic passing single file. Poorly driven carts and careless footmen sometimes slip, sinking below to abyssal graves. Rounding the last spur, one glimpses the southern gatehouse where patient caravans wait, a detachment of the Duke's Garrison controlling traffic. Nothing into or out of the gate passes unnoticed, unknown. The gate is not large and is the only route through the southern wall. From behind the southern wall rises the bell tower of the Monastery of Saint Dominic, part of a larger complex of buildings extending to the base of the Aerieal Horns. The road continues beyond the monastery and into the sprawl of Callamar.

The monastery comprises four major structures: church, dormitory, stables, and scriptorium. The church and dormitory are bridged by a soaring walkway spanning the grounds beneath. The church cradles the chapel, the bell tower, the abbot's rectory, and the priors' quarters. The dormitory holds the refectory, the kitchen, the cloisters, the privies, and the brethren, as many as eighty monks and scribes living spartan lives. The stables keep the animals that provide milk and cheese and other supplies for transport and storage.

The scriptorium is the shining jewel enclosing the Library of Saint Dominic and work space for its scribes. It is the tallest monastery structure and the most easily recognized from all approaches. The scriptorium has only two doors: one entrance at ground level and one on the roof. Recesses along the outer wall used to be windows but have since been bricked over. The entire building is a cylinder standing five levels high and committed to harboring its texts in a humid-free cocoon. Organized by subject and text type, the most ancient of writings is their collection of scrolls, preserved on the least humidified levels of the library. Atop the roof is a man-sized egress passing into the center of the circular roof and sinking down to all levels below. The shaft provides illumination for all work and library levels by using an ingenious system of solar reflectors and collectors, eliminating the need for torches, candles, and lanterns, though they are still needed during the night.

Presently, the scriptorium is obligated to maintain and restore its extensive collection of new and ancient texts and to acquire new codices and academic works from anywhere they can be obtained. However, recently its scribes have been contracted to fulfill the needs of Callamar's various government offices. Scribes are assigned to provide copies of legal documents, law books, tax codes, and official correspondence.

Traditionally, the city's scriptorial duties have been carried out by the government's own corps of scribes but as their offices became overwhelmed, the scriptorium was contracted to assist. Before long, this contractual arrangement sapped much of the monastery's resources, and with the introduction of deadlines, the meticulous work normally performed became substandard and sloppy. Pressured and overworked, the monastery staff convened and opted to launch a campaign of recruitment and acquisition. Recruitment efforts were cast both within and beyond the borders of Callalande, seeking quality scribes by offering incentives and prestige to families in exchange for services.

Contracts with the Duke's government for copies of legal documents brought an influx of coin to the monastery. Over time, the coffers swelled and the monastery lost some of its ascetic ways by concentrating on the needs of the scriptorium. And without realizing what had been wrought, the coin attracted corruption and unwanted scrutiny from near and far.

In decades past, the monastery was isolated from Callamar but as the city expanded westward, it slowly encroached upon the monastery. Saddened monks who craved the old ascetic traditions witnessed their world change and their numbers declined.

Callamar

Duke Olan of Callalande was the third and youngest son of the late King Edmund II. The first son became King Edmund III after his father's passing while his second son Caleb was ordained into the Church of the Holy Cross before his nineteenth year, becoming Bishop Caleb. Born after a gap of several years, Olan's father expected Olan to rise through the ranks of the military, destined to become a general or even High Protector of Korgynslande. However, to his father's dismay and his mother's secret delight, young Olan demonstrated neither aptitude for nor interest in the military. Instead, Olan liked playing around the royal gardens and riding horses. He preferred spending time with the smiths, craftsmen, and cooks of the castle and shunned the conniving politicians and cronies of the King's Court. He preferred watching the woodsmith carve wood into furniture, the blacksmith pound metal into horseshoes. When Olan could read, he read everything he could get his hands on and thus his journey toward scholarship and discovery began. When the king died, Edmund III ascended the throne and Caleb influenced the church. Olan was thought of by his brothers as unneeded and at best, kept out of their way. So, Olan was awarded the Dukedom of the isolated northern province of Callalande, where he became Duke Olan, servant to the Crown of Scullsbergen Castle.

At the time, Callalande was a backward province in a wilderness. Upon arriving, Duke Olan set about transforming the economy. His policies allowed every resident the opportunity to thrive based on their work ethic and not their birthright. He firmly believed that busy, happy people contributed to the common wealth and institutions of Callalande, empowering them with ownership and a stake in its future. This made the Duke very popular with many citizens but also despised by others.

Callamar is the largest city north of Scullsbergen. Running through the city, the Lycus River provides fresh mountain runoff as drinking water and irrigation for the many orchards found within and beyond the northern districts of the city. Callamar is a self-sufficient city on a coastal plain that produces a variety of abundant crops during the summer and fall and exports products throughout the year. In order to provide resources, the duke established several natural preserves for conservation and regrowth of its overharvested forests. North of Callamar, the Duke's Forest is one such place.

Craftsmen of many trades produce enough goods for both domestic use and export. Callamar is seat to churches and temples of several prominent religious orders, with many smaller orders also finding a niche. It possesses several schools that provide citizens and residents with a basic education and several specialized schools and institutions for more advanced studies. Many government offices provide services to the people and law enforcement for keeping the peace. Crime in Callamar has been low for many years, but gang activity still exists on its fringes. The city of Callamar has been through many cycles of boom and bust but still remains a thriving city because its success is not measured by coin alone.

As a province of the greater Kingdom of Korgynslande, Callalande has a military presence. The province borders two foreign kingdoms which presently do not pose a military threat, Borea and Apollande. The Korgyns' navy uses Callamar as a homeport for a small flotilla of fast sloops capable of keeping piracy at bay and guarding the fishing fleet. Callamar possesses an excellent deep-water port with a long breakwater and large docks capable of accommodating the largest of ships. A thriving maritime tradition has existed for generations, and the fish markets of Callamar have been lauded as second to none.

For some, Callamar represents one of the last bastions of freedom from repression, while others use it as a base to centralize their influence and proselytize outward. Some neighborhoods and districts within Callamar are melting pots while others are cultural ghettos, enclaves of indigenous or foreign peoples. Each day, Duke Olan rides into a different part of his city from his Palisade set against the base of the Aerieal Horns, greeting its residents and learning their thoughts, sampling their cuisines. The Duke takes pride in the accomplishments of all Callamar's residents, and nothing takes place in Callamar that he does not know of, or so he thinks.

Cloister

A tower bell tolled in the foggy morning air telling the brethren of Saint Dominic's, its monks, to awaken and gather for prayers at dawn.

Jonah arose from his cot, put on a warmer robe then went over to a shuttered window and cracked it open. Peeking out from his second-floor window, he glimpsed a foggy, rocky seacoast. While the window was small and shuttered, the cold air still seeped into the room. Jonah thought, *at least the winds died down.* On some autumn evenings, the onshore breezes could be as cold as the devil winds that raced down the ice-capped Aerieals in winter.

"Wake up, Danan," Jonah nudged his roommate. "We don't want to be late or Prior Damien might get angry at us again." Danan stirred but didn't waken.

Within other cloisters drowsy monks donned their robes and took care of privy business before proceeding to the chapel and morning prayers. Jonah stepped out into the dormitory hallway and greeted Pompey as he emerged from his room. Together they chatted quietly while they walked down the long hallway that eventually became the soaring walkway that descends into the chapel.

"It's definitely a foggy morning and cold," Jonah said with a shiver.

"Fog means cold blanket," Pompey replied as they trudged down the hall. "I don't like the cold but the faint sound of the crashing waves calms me down."

Danan arrived a little later and joined Jonah and Pompey standing in the queue leading into the chapel. Danan stood quietly behind Jonah, waiting. Jonah turned around a few times, looking concerned when he finally noticed Danan just standing there behind him. Jonah whispered, "How long have you been standing there? I didn't even hear you coming."

Danan smiled at them as the monks began filing singly into the nave, filling the pews, and facing the altar. A few monks filed into several small nooks evenly spaced along the side walls. Those were the monks that possessed chanting voices that made prayer time a special, hypnotic experience.

With everyone present, the abbot proceeded into the chapel, followed by his priors, and stood before the altar. Abbot Eddo led the brethren in service and prayer and chanting until it was time for their morning meal. The morning meal was simple: day-old bread, water, and cheese. The brothers who worked in the scriptorium were allowed a short morning break before beginning their workday. As Jonah finished his break he joined Danan; then, the two walked over to the scriptorium.

The upper three levels of the scriptorium contained the library itself. The lower two levels housed the main work floors and the archscribe's office. Jonah and Danan sat down at their workstations and prepared to resume their work from yesterday. Jonah was copying a set of tax law codices for the Office of Civic Revenue. Danan was newer to Saint Dominic's and was not as proficient as Jonah, so he had been tasked with organizing transcripts from several recent judicial proceedings, an easy but boring task. Jonah's tasking required greater speed and accuracy in order to complete the requested codices on time. This work earned the monastery much coin from the Office of Civic Revenue.

Jonah had been described as the fastest scribe in the monastery, and according to the archscribe, the fastest scribe ever recruited. Jonah also possessed a high accuracy rating which earned him favor with the scriptorium staff and scribes but also scorn from others with conflicting ambitions. Several scribes viewed Jonah as a clear and present threat to their interests or were simply jealous of Jonah's high favor with the abbot and priors.

As Jonah and Danan finished their work for the day, the sun dipped behind the tallest of the western Aerieals. From the scriptorium, they ambled through one of the ascetic gardens, taking their time. Danan spoke up, "I don't really mind working as a scribe but I don't like the fall or winter months since there is less daylight. It also gets cold and gloomy. I wish we had more time for reading. There is a whole library full of books above our heads and little time for reading them."

"You're right. It does get darker sooner and the workday is shorter. And yes, I would also like to spend more time reading the books." Jonah sighed.

The tower bell began tolling. It was time for vespers in the chapel. The abbot led his priors and the brethren in prayer and mass. When the chanters began their magic, every monk was granted time for introspection in humility, self-improvement, and communal service. When vespers ended, Jonah and Danan headed off to the refectory where they met up with Pompey. Today's evening meal consisted of a salty fish soup with vegetables and dinner rolls.

Pompey asked Jonah, "How is your work on the law codices progressing?"

"I am close to completion, just a day or two more."

Danan added, "If I may, I could use a change from the judicial transcripts I've been organizing. They are very boring and don't have much in the way of interesting conversation to copy."

"All right. If you like, I'll lobby the archscribe to get you a book to copy. Then, you can read as well as write. Perhaps something a little more philosophical would suit your fancy?" Pompey suggested.

"Yes, that would be nice. Thank you Pompey."

After evening meal, Jonah and Danan returned to their room. From the window, Jonah liked watching over the rocky coastline, listening to the breakers pound the shore. Over the years he observed that the waves sometimes hint at what the weather may bring throughout the night.

Danan kept a small diary in his desk drawer which he would take out and read every evening. He usually added a few thoughts before going to sleep.

Pompey endeavored to develop and maintain as many relationships as possible within the monastery, though he spent extra time with Jonah and Danan where possible. So when they took their leave of him for the night, Pompey circulated throughout the refectory and dormitory, socializing with as many monks as he could before returning to his room. He recited a few bedtime prayers before falling asleep.

Sometimes during stormy nights, Jonah lay awake in bed, listening to the waves, howling winds, and thundering skies rattling his shutters. He thought about his present life in the monastery and about where his life was going. He knew he did not want to remain in the scriptorium any longer than he had to. He also had no interest in becoming a scribe working for any of Callamar's government offices, even for salary, though he could do that if he really needed to. He didn't want to return home to his family in Scullsbergen either. He strongly felt that his parents sold him off to this forsaken place. And for years since that day, neither of his parents had ever visited him or written him a letter.

Sometimes he thought about how scribing all those copies of legal codices had made him far more knowledgeable of the legal system in Callamar. He imagined himself working with plaintiffs, representing them as a barrister or assistant. He imagined himself returning to school and becoming a professor of the classics. These thoughts swirled through his mind like crashing waves. And the more he imagined, the more his ideas seemed far away, out of reach. When the weather calmed, he fell asleep and his thoughts scurried off until the morning bells tolled a new day.

Scribe

Jonah was committed to the monastery by his parents when he was fifteen years. He grew up to the south in Scullsbergen, the capital of Korgynslande. When he was attending school, he demonstrated a fantastic aptitude for penmanship and languages. When he was recruited as a scribe, he was expected to live as a monk, learning the ways of piety and service in the name of the Lord. For his recruitment into the monastery, his parents received honors, prestige, and a stipend.

To the monastery, recruitment meant acquiring scriptorial talent by searching both within and beyond the borders of Callamar, offering the parents of school-aged boys reward for committing their sons to service in the scriptorium. A scribe was required to serve until reaching his twenty-first year, whereupon he could be released from his service, ending a contract he had never signed himself. It was hoped that a scribe would choose to remain within the monastery and embrace the life of a monk for years to come. Many times, a boy's age was intentionally misrepresented so that he might serve an extra year or two beyond his twenty-first year. It was a system born of necessity that turned scriptorium monks into indentured servants.

Generally, scribes were assigned to one of several types of projects. One project type involved the copy and conversion of ancient scrolls into modern texts by creating extra copies and preserving the original scrolls in sealed cases. These scrolls were usually written in ancient, sometimes extant languages. If the language was known by the scribe, he might attempt a translation. When Jonah first entered the monastery, he was assigned to making copies of several classics such as Euclid's *Elements*, Plato's *Republic*, and Herodotus' *Histories*. He had studied some Greek before being committed but was better at reading than speaking. The texts he copied were written in Greek with facing pages written in a language called Arabic, which he could not read but could copy easily.

Another project type involved the copying of government documents. Forms, manuals, and codices were needed in bulk for the Offices of the

Judiciary, Civic Revenue, and Administration. Codices of the laws and edicts of Callalande were important for the proper functioning of government services within Callamar.

Another project type involved the organization of documents. Court proceedings and transcripts were frequently recorded by hand and needed to be organized and bound into dockets. A project subtype involved more private needs such as organizing and copying personal letters. For those projects, scribes had to sign Loyalty Oaths and endure a board of inquiry into their character and background. Those that were deemed worthy were granted a clearance to work with confidential documents.

Jonah realized that, at times, being a scribe could be boring and feel like a dead-end profession. He also realized that being a scribe also had its benefits and rewards, especially when compared to other jobs within Callamar such as working in the junkyard or the brick manufactory or scrubbing down the fishing wharfs. Keeping a positive mindset, Jonah copied texts for posterity and read them for knowledge and intelligence. As a result, he became more familiar with many of the western classics. For three years his copied texts bolstered the library's available volumes. Jonah's success and reputation eventually led to his being assigned to more current projects such as producing copies of official government documents.

Copying government documents was a mechanical exercise to Jonah. Once he achieved a certain rhythm, his eyes and hands cranked out copy after copy with little or no cognitive effort. As such, his mind freed up and became available for introspection. He sometimes thought of himself as a victim. He thought about how he had been denied or cheated out of a complete education back home when he was pulled out of school and transplanted into the monastery. His writing skills allowed him to readjust and make some new friends. But he never really got over the move and did not, could not, understand why his family did that to him. Did they want to get rid of him? Was the honor and prestige worth more than his presence within the family home?

Jonah likened monastic life to a spartan boarding school without the studying and with no escape. More than anyone else in the monastery and anyone since his recruitment, Jonah was a prized possession, a golden boy, a fulfiller of lucrative contracts. And he never saw a copper from the monastery for all of those noble efforts. He did receive free room and board, two meals a day, even some cheap homemade beer, and a lonely life by a sounding shore. Many a scribe longed for home and escape from the droning breakers.

Abbot Eddo had been the abbot at Saint Dominic's Monastery for many years. During that time, he corresponded frequently with the Church of the Holy Cross in Scullsbergen and many of its other bishoprics and monasteries. When it came to paperwork, the abbot was continually swamped in letters that cried out for order. Abbot Eddo was well aware of Jonah's reputation for speed and accuracy, so he figured who else but Jonah should organize his office in short order. One day, Abbot Eddo summoned Jonah before his panel of priors and grilled him ceaselessly regarding his background and integrity. When the abbot was satisfied with Jonah's vetting, he was granted a clearance to work with confidential materials and was required to sign a Loyalty Oath. Soon afterward, Jonah began working on the abbot's special project by sorting his letters and papers into categories such as logistics and supplies, activity scheduling, monastic policy, disciplinary issues, and private communiques between the clergy in Callamar, Scullsbergen, and abroad. Abbot Eddo bought three blank codices for Jonah to rewrite all of his letters into so they could easily be referenced by subject and date. This task was to be accomplished secretly in addition to and separately from his normal duties as a scribe. For all of Jonah's efforts, he earned the abbot's favor and some silvers slipped under the scriptorium table (hush hush). And with some silver in his pocket, Jonah's access to Callamar changed.

Although Jonah liked his arrangement with Abbot Eddo, keeping his whereabouts secret from his friends was almost unbearable. Jonah also learned that keeping secrets within the monastery was nearly impossible. Spending many of his free hours, Jonah organized the abbot's letters and meticulously copied each one into an appropriate codex. After many months, he completed the project.

The abbot's project taught him that letters were a very different kind of document. Frequently people wrote things they truly meant. Through letters, one could more readily learn a person's mind and what motivated their actions. Their petty squabbles, idiosyncrasies, peeves, and dislikes were all laid bare. It was their dislikes, even hatreds, that he found most troubling because he understood that the monastery, and by inference the Church, was supposed to cleanse a man's spirit, allowing him to live a life of peace, harmony, and service to others. He did not find much evidence of that when reading their letters. Also, he found the endless brown-nosing and kissing-up-to-the-bishop most difficult to stomach. Jonah had to copy and write and rewrite all of this hyperbole and drivel, letter after letter after letter. He was relieved when the project as last came to an end. And without realizing it, he had taken his first step into the world of intelligence.

And then, without warning, Abbot Eddo was gone, reassigned to another position in Scullsbergen. His last day was never announced; he departed without any ceremonial fare wells. The tower bell tolled and a new abbot arrived like a whirlwind. He walked through the hallways with a holier-than-thou attitude and an overdeveloped sense of entitlement.

Sometime during his eighteenth year, Jonah began to experience twinges of pain in his writing wrist. Over time, the pain slowly got worse. When he had breaks on Sundays, he rested his arm and by Monday it had recovered. But by Friday, the pain returned. After several months, the archscribe noticed that Jonah's production numbers had dropped. When Archscribe Rene called him into his office and confronted Jonah with these facts, he confessed that he had been experiencing wrist problems. The archscribe and his superiors had little sympathy. They accused him of slacking and being distracted by other things and not concentrating on his responsibilities as a scribe. They left Jonah feeling dumbfounded, thinking that maybe his predicament was his own fault. He did not reveal to them his special project with Abbot Eddo.

Skuas

Centuries ago, the mountain range west of Callamar was dubbed the Aerieal Horns. For generations, skuas have made their homes within its myriad inaccessible ledges pocking the icy horns, their aeries. Their dull brown feathers helped them adapt to the extremely cold environs of the Horns, allowing them to thrive for millennia, omnipresent and free. The skuas lived primarily as scavengers and feasted off the leftovers and discards of the human sprawl below. The great port of Callamar harvested fish all year long. When fisherman unloaded their catch, cleaned their catch, and skinned their catch, they invariably dumped the entrails and leftovers for the skuas and other birds to hoist away. From within Callamar, trash and edible leftovers were freely left to rot or were dumped into the Lycus River and carried to the sea. The skuas helped clean up the human mess and brought the food back to their families huddled high in the Horns. Many a skua perched upon the monastery rooftops, scanning for easy pickings below, leaving behind their calling cards. The city below indulged the skuas for many centuries, growing them to epidemic numbers.

The brethren of Saint Dominic's are of three main types: the leadership, the ascetics, and the scribes. The abbot and his priors have the power to make permanent decisions concerning policy and personnel. The ascetics are those who chose monastery life to better themselves and their relationship with the Lord through penitence and service. Many of the ascetics keep to themselves and maintain the various gardens, flower beds, and fruit trees between the church and the scriptorium, quiet areas for meditation and introspection. They also keep and care for the animals that live in the stables that provide some of the cheese they eat every day.

The scribes work in the scriptorium and are managed by an archscribe. Many of the scribes are impatient and eagerly look forward to the day when they are released from their contracts and can start a new life in Callamar or return home. But some scribes have aged beyond their thirtieth year and don't want to leave the monastery. Several of these older scribes have been tasked with becoming role models to the younger scribes. But for some, their discipline has deteriorated much over the years. Now, instead of role models they have become bullies and bum-licks. Four in particular have made it a point to share their company, ingratiate themselves with the priors, and earn the abbot's favor. They call themselves the Skuas.

The Skuas were Ergan, Borse, Lars, and Kraig. Ergan and Borse were scribes that had lived in the monastery for many years but were not recruited like the younger scribes. For years, they methodically copied texts with little recognition. They possessed good accuracy and never rushed their projects to completion. They were loyal to the monastery but not to any particular prior or the abbot. Lars and Kraig have not yet turned twenty-one years and were recruited as scribes. They found it difficult to adapt to monastery life. Like others, they had been waiting for a mentor or role model to emerge and latch onto. And so when Lars and Kraig became toadies to Ergan and Borse, they had found their role models, and their psyches and self-images improved.

When Jonah entered the monastery, the Skuas' resentment of all the attention Jonah received gradually built up. The Skuas thought that their work as scribes should've garnered more attention and favor than it did. They thought they deserved more for all their years of loyalty and for the quality of work they had completed.

Abbot Eddo had been fair for the most part, but he did give favor to anyone who was able to impress him. And that's what Jonah accomplished with his calm demeanor and good penmanship. So when Abbot Eddo suddenly left Saint Dominic's, a power vacuum materialized and everyone's slate of favor and rapport had been wiped clean. All monks and priors would now scramble to establish rapport with the new abbot. Bum-kissing skills were dusted off as the new abbot represented an unknown quantity. The Skuas saw this as a golden opportunity to ingratiate themselves with the new abbot and to begin a campaign to tear apart Jonah's reputation.

Despite their best efforts, the Skuas discovered that Jonah was still Jonah, the fastest and possibly best scribe in all Callamar. So if they wanted to rise above him, they would have to tear him down, smear his character, and disparage him somehow. That is when they began targeting his roommate, Danan, as a means to that end.

Danan was recently recruited as a scribe from Vassans in Borea. His parents had committed him at fifteen years as he possessed the necessary qualifications. Danan was small for a boy of fifteen. He was perceived as weak by many of the brethren though they would not admit it openly. He was intelligent and possessed a different kind of wisdom than the other scribes. His skin was pale and he had a strange way of saying things. In many ways, he gave the impression of being a fish out of water. His size and hesitancy to speak up right away when spoken to led him to become vulnerable to others' more quick and decisive conversational skills. In short, he became easy to pick on.

Danan was assigned as Jonah's roommate and from the start, they got along. Danan was hard to get to know because he didn't talk much. It wasn't that Danan didn't want to talk; it was just difficult finding something to talk about that interested him. Since none of the other brethren were from Vassans, Danan had no one to talk to about home. But over time as Jonah and Danan worked together in the scriptorium, they began to find common subjects to share and discuss. It was not easy but eventually they came to think of themselves as friends.

Pompey

In the early days of the recruitment program at Saint Dominic's, Pompey entered the monastery as a scribe in his sixteenth year. Pompey had grown up in Callamar and represented local talent. From a young age he had been familiar with the monastery and the work that was performed within.

Pompey was the second son of a successful import/export merchant in Callamar and had attended one of the Duke-sponsored schools in one of the more well-to-do neighborhoods of Callamar. At a young age he found he liked reading the books his father had collected from Korgynslande and other foreign lands. His family knew many of the other merchant families in Callamar both socially and as business clients. As a result, Pompey developed friendships and a social persona for conducting business and for succeeding in school. He learned to get along with just about anyone but became frustrated with many of his friends and acquaintances because he couldn't find anyone with interests similar to his. Right or wrong, he perceived that most everyone he knew cared only about rubbing elbows with government officials, other rich families, and the Duke himself. While Pompey never found himself wanting of coin, he also never felt any drive or desire to become part of his father's business. His older brother was more than happy to carry the family banner. As a result, Pompey felt little pressure to take on any responsibilities within the family business.

Then one day in school, Pompey learned that the large cylindrical building to the south contained an extensive collection of ancient tomes and texts. He was amazed that such a collection containing knowledge from many past centuries could be so close by, within his reach. In his dreams, he decided that he wanted to work there and read the books. He also understood that the collection belonged to the Church of the Holy Cross. He concluded that that meant he would have to convert to the beliefs and tenets of the Church if he wanted to work there some day.

As a consequence, he made a conscious decision to do well in school subjects such as reading, languages, and penmanship. He hoped his efforts would be recognized, and he consistently lobbied his family to let him join the Monastery of Saint Dominic's as a scribe. At first, his father was shocked that he would want to leave the family business and convert to the Church of the Holy Cross. His parents had both been members of the Temple of the Embracing Goddess for many years, though they did not attend services regularly. Pompey explained to his parents that his older brother was the one who was keen to carry on the family business. Also, Pompey did not expect to benefit much from his status as a second son, so he thought joining the monastery would allow him the opportunity to pursue his dream of working in the Library of Saint Dominic's. Over time, Pompey's parents came to realize that committing him to the monastery might result in a prestigious recognition for the family and for Pompey himself. Eventually his parents relented, on condition that Pompey finish his schooling up to his sixteenth year. Then, he would receive their blessing to join the monastery.

Pompey entered the monastery as a scribe six months before Jonah was recruited. Pompey's social skills opened doors to him as he began getting to know the minds of the younger brethren. He found it more difficult getting to know the ascetics, but over time he chipped away at their skepticism and gained a modicum of trust. As most of the ascetics did not work in the scriptorium, Pompey found it difficult to share his enthusiasm for the library. However, he did find other topics of interest to them. Pompey spent time researching books within the library that featured prayers and introspections written by monks from various monasteries over the decades. Then, he shared these writings with many of the ascetics. Many monks found Pompey's efforts of interest and of value and so came to accept him as a member of the monastic community. Being the son of a merchant, Pompey also had unique access to the City of Callamar itself and was able to procure highly interesting and sought-after items such as luxury foods and warm blankets. And while the ascetics were ascetic, a warm blanket was a warm blanket in anyone's eyes.

Pompey first met Jonah as a newly recruited scribe when Jonah was preparing to begin work in the scriptorium. Speaking with Jonah, Pompey perceived an aura of confidence about him and a calm can-do attitude when it came to scribing. He perceived in Jonah what he thought was a subtle enthusiasm for scribing, but he could not be sure. Regardless, he took a liking to Jonah right away. And while Jonah did his best to put a positive face forward, Pompey could sense some underlying issues that Jonah did not want to talk about. It was not until later that Pompey discovered Jonah's superior talent. Jonah recognized Pompey as someone who had qualities that he did not possess and so Jonah took a liking to Pompey as well. They spent time together and as they became better acquainted, they began a friendship that would last for many years both inside and outside of the monastery. Over time, Jonah's scribing and accomplishments grew. Through Jonah, Pompey's own reputation for enthusiasm and flair also grew, catapulting him into a position where he began to influence Archscribe Rene.

Archscribe Rene had been the archscribe at Saint Dominic's for many years but was itching for a promotion to become one of the priors. Becoming the abbot was probably beyond his reach, as it required approval from the Church of the Holy Cross in Scullsbergen. Becoming a prior was acceptable to him but he had been waiting a long time for an opportunity. His new scribe Pompey was demonstrating an uncanny desire to work in the scriptorium and even began helping him organize the scribes by their talents in an effort to streamline the productivity of the scriptorium. And for all of his effort, Pompey never showed any interest in taking over Rene's position as archscribe. Nevertheless, Archscribe Rene remained suspicious of Pompey's motives and kept his suspicions in the back of his mind. For years, Pompey never demonstrated anything other than a desire for greater access to the library proper. Archscribe Rene viewed this as a reasonable price to pay for Pompey's enthusiasm, so he granted him special access to the library and reaped a few benefits from Pompey's accomplishments.

Over the years, Jonah and Pompey spent much time together. Like a chicken guarding her brood, Pompey spent time nurturing and maintaining all of his relationships. Pompey discovered that each relationship was fragile, but very much worth the effort to maintain. Pompey also volunteered to do favors for no other purpose than to facilitate better communications between groups and cliques. Pompey also came to know all rumors that were spread and also learned how to draw out information regarding decisions made by the priors. As a result, he was up to date on all happenings within the monastery walls.

Jonah's fast and accurate work built up favor with Abbot Eddo and the priors. Pompey was able to procure for Jonah many a bimonthly pass to spend time within Callamar and to hike up to the shrine. When Saint Dominic's had first been constructed against the walls of the Aerieal Horns, the shrine was built as a place where monks could temporarily leave the monastery, pray outdoors, and experience the fresh mountain air. The path to the shrine was a three-mile roundtrip up and down the mountain to a small perch overlooking Callamar. The hike was good for clearing one's mind from the monotony of daily routine, especially for the scribes. Pompey helped many brethren get time off for a hike to the shrine. He also helped scribes get passes for forays into Callamar.

Jonah and Pompey took the hike up to the shrine several times a year in their early years at the monastery. As time moved on, they spent more of their free time on excursions into Callamar itself. It was on one of these excursions where they discovered The Charging Boar and spent an evening there having dinner and a brew. Over many months, they made this place a regular stop on their walks into Callamar. Once in a while, Pompey was also able to visit his family and show everyone at home how well he was doing and to also acquire rare supplies and exotic foods. His father was able to obtain special shipments of paper, quills, and some inks for the monastery in bulk quantities.

After Abbot August placed new restrictions on weekend passes, Pompey and Jonah escaped the monastery less frequently. The abbot asked that monks travel in groups of two or more for their own protection and to keep an eye on each other as potential witnesses. And in spite of Abbot August's crack down on the lax policies of Abbot Eddo, Pompey was genuinely happy with his decision to join the Monastery and Library of Saint Dominic's.

After about six months, Pompey finally received permission from Prior Lund to take Jonah and Danan up to the shrine in the late summer. During this hike, Danan finally felt comfortable enough to talk about some of his interests.

Pompey asked, "What kinds of things did you like to read in Vassans?"

Danan walked silently for a while as they made their final ascent to the shrine. When they arrived, Danan sat down on a large rock overlooking Callamar. "I liked reading books on philosophy and other religions such as the Vault of Selunia and the Greek Pantheon. I never read the Bible as much as we read it here."

"Oh."

"You can probably imagine what the abbot and the priors would think if they heard me say that in their presence. I would expect to receive only trouble and condescension. As much as I might fear their response, I fear my father's reprisals even more if he ever heard me say that. I don't want to get thrown out of the monastery."

Pompey said, "You are right to be cautious. They might even spend extra time reindoctrinating you with the Church's tenets, but I doubt they would throw you out. The monastery needs good scribes. Danan, you are a good scribe and you do quality work. Don't let anyone tell you otherwise."

"Thank you, Pompey," Danan said as he wiped a tear from his eye.

Pompey declared, "I just love this view of the city. Isn't it magnificent?"

Danan looked down upon Callamar's rooftops and saw many impressive buildings such as the Cathedral and the Duke's Palisade and the other temples and the distant orchards of cherry and apple trees. Danan asked, "Why are there so many birds flying all over the place? No wonder there's so much poop everywhere."

Jonah laughed at Danan's response. "They are called skuas and I guess they live off the refuse of the city and harbor below. I wish our brethren would pay more attention to where they walk and step. They sometimes trail it into the dormitory. During the summer, the odor can get quite rank if no one cleans it up off the floors. Please try not to bring any into our room."

Danan gave Jonah an incredulous look. "Really!? I've been careful since my first day."

Many months passed as Danan grew more comfortable with his duties as a scribe. He was also slowly learning to talk to the other brethren. Many of the monks found Danan's company awkward and did not want to spend time with him so he spent most of his time with Jonah and Pompey.

Pompey spent much time arranging for Jonah and Danan to join him on a foray into Callamar. When the day finally arrived, they decided they would walk all the way to The Charging Boar. They welcomed a break from eating fish stew, cheese, and stale bread for breakfast and dinner.

The Charging Boar

The Charging Boar is a tavern located on the east side of Callamar where the main road runs eastward and crosses the bridge over the Lycus River. The Boar features beer and ale at cheaper prices than taverns closer to the monastery, so it is worth the long walk. Getting an opportunity to visit The Charging Boar is a matter of acquiring a weekend pass for a Saturday night. Passes have to be earned. Good behavior or simply possessing favor with Prior Lund usually does the trick. With luck, a monk can get a pass once every three months while someone with favor can get a pass more often. As luck would have it, Pompey managed to get a pass for himself and his friends for the upcoming Saturday night.

So one Saturday in mid-autumn, Jonah, Danan, and Pompey left the monastery together and began walking to The Charging Boar. They followed the main road passing by the monastery. By chance, they came across a passing cart and hitched a ride in exchange for a blessing from Saint Dominic's. Hitching meant riding which meant less time tolerating the rank smells of the harbor and fish market.

The three soon arrived at The Charging Boar. As they entered the tavern, they found it quite busy with many locals eating, drinking, and singing next to a cozy fireplace. The loud din made it difficult to hear anything clearly. They managed to find an open table next to the wall farthest from the fireplace. Their brown robes made them easily recognizable as monks. However, they were not the only monks in the tavern; they could see at least two other groups dining and drinking. One of the two groups were the Skuas, sitting along the far side of the tavern. At least they were far away, almost out of sight. Many of the tavern's patrons were eating boar from the spit with bread and cheese or a boar and vegetable stew with a choice of four different beers and ales to sample, for the right coin of course.

Pompey started things off. "I want some boar. They just don't carry boar on the monastery menu."

"What menu? But I also agree. We've come this far for ale; we should have our boar as well," Danan seconded.

Jonah closed the deal. "Boar it is."

One of the serving girls squeezed her way over to their table and took their requests. "All right, that's three boar plates and three golden ales. Would you like a bowl of boar rinds to go with that?"

"Sure, why not? Thank you," Jonah said courteously.

Their server flitted off and returned shortly with their plates and mugs. Danan took a sideways peek at her as she walked back to the bar. The three had not had a night out for a while, and this was only Danan's second soiree since joining the monastery. They began with a lot of small talk which somehow evolved into a discussion of quills and which quills were best for scribing. After some debate, they eventually agreed that swan quills were the best under most circumstances and were worth the price if one could find and afford them. A good second choice was goose quills, which were much more common and affordable.

After a few swigs of ale, Jonah began confessing that he was getting tired of the whole scribe routine with the government documents. Jonah speculated that perhaps starting his own private practice might suit him better. Jonah also wondered how he could acquire a copy of Callamar's business laws without having to purchase one.

Jonah lamented, "I spend lots of time making copies of law books and I don't think I can even afford to purchase one that I made." *What a sad irony,* he thought.

Danan and Pompey listened curiously.

"If I had my own supply of quills, ink, and paper, I might be able to scribe my own copy of a law book. I can almost dictate one from memory." Jonah thought, *well, not really.*

"Hold that thought," Pompey said. He was also surprised to hear Jonah's tipsy candor. Pompey enjoyed monastery life, but he was not a super scribe like Jonah and didn't feel the same pressure to produce results that Jonah did.

Danan offered no opinion but also said that getting out of the monastery may be the best way for him to avoid some of the problems he was experiencing.

With surprise Jonah asked, "What kinds of problems are you having?"

Danan hesitated before he spoke. "Ever since Abbot Eddo left, I've heard disgusting rumors circulating about me. Sometimes I overhear brothers talking about me while I'm eating in the refectory. But when I turn to look at them, they hush up and ignore me. I don't know who started those rumors but I wish they would stop." Jonah recalled hearing these rumors but had never paid them much mind. *That must be what Danan is referring to,* he concluded.

Jonah's mind began wandering as he recalled working on Abbot Eddo's project. He recalled being confused by many of the letters he read and copied for the abbot. He thought, *maybe some letters made better sense in the context of rumor.* Then his mind shifted to code words. He concluded that many of the abbot's letters likely contained coded messaging, code words substituted for other words, concealing their true meaning. The abbots and priors seemed to use code words extensively. He pondered this revelation then shook his head and cleared his thoughts. He found Danan and Pompey staring at him while chewing on their boar steaks.

"Are you going to eat your boar? If not, Danan and I would be more than happy to help you finish it." Pompey smiled while nodding.

"Yes, I'm going to eat all of my boar no matter how cold it gets. So there."

In his peripheral vision, Jonah saw what he thought might be two unaccompanied young women sitting off in one corner of the tavern near a window, eating bowls of stew and talking to each other. They both appeared to have short hair and were wearing sheepskin caps. He thought, *they both look big, tall, and attractive.* As he glanced their way, he caught one of them looking back at him with curiosity. The other girl soon turned his way as he looked towards the two of them, both catching each other staring. Jonah turned his attention back towards his company.

But Pompey caught the whole exchange and elbowed Jonah in the ribs saying, "Why don't you go to their table and invite them over here since you're clearly interested (nudge nudge)?"

"What makes you think I am interested? I just noticed them looking this way. That's all."

"Ahh, so then she's interested in you. All the more reason for you to go introduce yourself since why would she walk over here (nudge nudge)? In fact …" Pompey got up and walked over to their table.

Jonah whispered, "Pompey, no!" Jonah thought, *what are you doing? Sheesh, now you've done it.*

As he walked up to the two girls, Pompey got a better look at them as he bowed and introduced himself, "A good evening to you two fair ladies. My name is Pompey, wandering monk of Saint Dominic's. I pray you are enjoying the boar this fine evening."

Somewhat startled, the girls looked at each other and said, "Uh, we are not ladies."

"Perhaps not, but my colleagues and I beseech of you your fair company this evening. We three are all monks of Saint Dominic's out for a nighttime stroll and would enjoy a civil conversation. We all possess a gentlemanly manner and invite you over to join us at our table over yonder." He waved his hand in introduction towards Jonah and Danan who were watching him work his charm.

The two girls had already finished eating their stews. They looked at each other then nodded while picking up their mugs and stepping their way over to Pompey's table.

Pompey commanded everyone to scooch down the bench and make room for the two young women. "I am Pompey, master of pomp. This is Jonah, fastest scribe in all Callalande, and this is Danan, resident philosopher of Saint Dominic's. We have been discussing quills for some time and are in the predicament of being uncompromisingly divided over which quills are best, goose or swan. Jonah here is inclined to swan feathers but Danan is steadfastly opposed and favors goose wings or was it goslings? Would you care to enlighten us with your thoughts?"

Danan smiled slightly as Pompey shifted into a master-of-ceremonies persona. It had been a while since he had smiled.

"Sorry, but we know naught of quills," she said glancing toward her partner seeking help; her partner shook her head side to side. She cracked a smile and introduced herself, "My name is May and this in my friend Anya. Rabbits are more my specialty."

"Ahh, rabbits she says. Do you perhaps represent the Duke's Office of Wildlife Resources?" Pompey took another swig of his ale then orated dramatically, "Ahh, woe are we in Callamar, we who cower in fear of invading rabbits. The Duke's Forest to the north is swarming with rabbits and, alas, they overrun us like invincible hordes." He placed the back of his hand on his forehead and sighed with abandon.

Jonah looked at Danan astonished. "Rabbits? Since when has there been a problem with rabbits? All I see are skuas flying all over the place." Danan shrugged and chomped down on another boar rind while glancing over towards Anya.

May responded. "No, we don't work for the Duke's office of whatever."

Pompey winked at Jonah and Danan, then continued, "Ahh, a pity. I thought you might be our mighty saviors come to rescue us from the rabbit legions pouring into our city like conquering armies."

Jonah and Danan couldn't help but chuckle to themselves as Pompey wove a tall tavern tale.

"You are silly," May said.

"Ahh, but 'tis true. They plot to destroy us now from within and only a true rabbit-trapping hero can save us all. Callamar desperately needs a hero to rise and stem this flood of apocalyptic doom." Pompey spoke with pleading eyes and a big sigh.

Anya spoke to May with her eyes, *don't look at me girl. You brought up the rabbit thing.*

As their conversation, boar rinds, and golden ale carried them into the night, Jonah noticed that one of the Skuas had spotted them from against the far wall. Grabbing his mug, Ergan wandered over to their table with Borse reluctantly tagging along. Ergan clumsily approached their table, a little intoxicated, and began to speak, "Well, well, what have we here? A pair of nighthawks escaped from the convent? Ha, ha, ha!"

Anya rolled her eyes. May whispered under her breath, "Not again."

Jonah and Pompey were confused by his manner but clearly sensed that he was drunk. "We're here enjoying dinner and a brew just like you." Danan looked away.

Ergan announced, "We? What a fine group of hedonists, says I." He glassily looked at both Anya and May then spoke to Anya, "Hey darling, are you all together here? Come to escape the convent for a night? Come to find a big man or two before you return (wink wink)?"

Anya sat up straight then placed her hands on her knees. May looked right at Anya saying, *please don't*!

Jonah interjected, "Come on, Ergan! You're making a scene here and we just want to finish our meals before heading back. That's all."

"Hey Danan, is this what you've been waiting for, a big wench ready to show you how it's done?" As Ergan turned to Anya and pointed at Danan, he slurred his words with beer breath, "Hey, sweetie, maybe you can show this boy here how to be a man, right?"

That was the last straw for Anya. She stood up, "I've had enough of your foolery. It would be best for you to leave this tavern now." Fully standing, she was clearly taller and stronger than Ergan.

In his stupor, Ergan was having a hard time focusing. Incredulously, he raised his voice and sputtered, "Are you telling me to leave? And who are you to tell me anything?" He clumsily spilt some beer and soon, the entire tavern fell quiet, all eyes turned upon him. Borse nervously tried to pat Ergan on the shoulder. Ergan shrugged Borse's hand off.

Then, Ergan drunkenly tried to grab Anya's tunic and as he grasped thin air, he fell forward onto the floor spilling the rest of his beer. Anya had quickly spun away, dodging his outstretched hand. Borse went down and tried to help him up. Ergan was muttering, "She spilt my beer." Borse whispered back to him, "No, you slipped. Let's get you back up. It's time for us to go."

The tavern's bouncer swooped over to Jonah's table. He said, "Okay, you've all hads too much to drink. It's time you all wents home nice and peacefully, yes?" First, he escorted Ergan and Borse to the door. Lars and Kraig came up from their table to help him out. "Don'ts be hurting my customers anymore, right?"

During this time, Anya and May had demonstrated tremendous restraint not wanting a repeat of what had happened several fortnights ago. Anya wanted to wipe up the floor with Ergan but controlled the urge to do so.

After the Skuas left the tavern, the bouncer returned to Jonah's table. "I dids not sees what happened here but I recommends all of you leaves soon. If there's any funny business inside or out, I am going to throws you out to the skuas, right?" Anya and May were not the least bit intimidated by the bouncer but they kept quiet and let Jonah do the talking. It felt strange but good having someone on their side for once.

Pompey explained to the bouncer, "We understand. We were just heading out as well, as we have a late night appointment with the night watch. Thank you for all of your help, sir." The bouncer grunted then walked away. Jonah turned to Anya and May and offered to pay for their meals and apologized for the things his brethren said to them. May accepted his apology but told him that he was not to blame for what his fellow monks said. Jonah took care of their tavern tab. Danan and Pompey also pitched in a few coin. *Wow*, Jonah thought, *everyone has a hidden stash of coin.*

As the three brothers left the tavern, they were greeted outside by Anya and May. May quietly said to Jonah, "If you are interested, I might be able to get you some of those quills you spoke of, maybe even for cheaper than your supplier charges."

Jonah explained, "Quills are not cheap and the Duke does not allow swans to be hunted in Callalande. And goose feathers, they usually have to be imported except during the migration season where they might stop over on their way to … to … to wherever they go."

"I'm not from Callalande, but if I can get you some quills without killing any birds, would you buy them?" May asked. Anya looked at her incredulously.

Jonah looked right into May's eyes and realized that she was serious about what she was saying. "Well, I guess I could but I don't have lots of coin. Everything I spent tonight took me a long time to earn.

"I will return with some quills and if you want them, you can buy them. Otherwise I will sell them to someone else. I will seek you out in town when I return. I will first try The Charging Boar, but if you aren't there, I know where you live. Thank you for an interesting evening." And with that, Anya and May took their leave.

The three brothers slowly walked back to the monastery. Unfortunately, they were not able to hitch a ride.

Jonah turned to Pompey asking, "Are there really rabbit problems in Callamar or were you full of skua spittle back there?" Pompey laughed and said most of it was made up but he did work on the government's complaint files a few times each year. He continued, "Citizens of Callamar are allowed to file petitions and complaints to the Duke's government. They must visit the Office of Requests and Complaints and speak to a magistrate. Usually his assistant takes their statements down. Since most people cannot write, a scribe records their complaints and then files them with the office. These files get sorted by type and then are recorded in the Official Register of Complaints. For whatever reason, there seem to be lots of rabbits in the Duke's Forest slowly spilling out and eating up crops in the nearby farms. So yes, there are rabbits, ha, ha, ha."

The brothers returned to the monastery uneventfully.

Later that night, Jonah was trying to fall asleep. Thoughts passed through his mind about future possibilities. Maybe he could get the supplies he needed to make his own copy of Callamar's law books. He would have to be secretive about it but where could he set himself up without anyone finding out? He pondered the thought. Would his now ailing hand be able to handle the strain of normal duties and secret work? Maybe he should begin by acquiring the necessary materials, quills, ink, paper, then decide how to implement a plan afterward. His thoughts swirled until at last, he fell asleep.

Interrogation

With the tolling of the morning bell, Jonah and Danan awakened and prepared for prayers at dawn. After morning meal they walked to the scriptorium. When they arrived, it began like any other work day; however, Jonah noticed that when the Skuas arrived, they were without their leader, Ergan. Jonah thought that was odd but began his business as usual. The Skuas looked over at him once in a while but then turned away when he caught them staring at him. Morning turned to afternoon, when Jonah was mysteriously summoned to Archscribe Rene's office. Rene informed Jonah that he was to report to the abbot's office immediately. Jonah left the scriptorium, walked over to the chapel, and then found his way to the abbot's office. He knocked on the door and after a short while, he was admitted.

Inside the office were Abbot August, Prior Damien of security and discipline, and Prior Lund. Jonah was not greeted but directed to sit down in a small chair facing the three administrators. To Jonah, it seemed that Prior Lund was there to record the results of whatever this inquiry was about, a scribe so to speak.

They all sat there silently while Abbot August scribbled a few items on a paper he was marking. He put down his quill and began, "As a brother of Saint Dominic's Monastery and under the Lord's watchful eye, you are bound to answer all questions posed to you truthfully. Also enunciate clearly so Prior Lund can hear you clearly. What is your full name and what is your age?"

Jonah responded, "Jonah Bergan, sire. I am eighteen years."

The abbot said, "You may dispense with the titles. Where are you from?"

"I am from Scullsbergen in Korgynslande."

Many more questions ensued regarding his background, recruitment, duties, room location, roommate, and many other things he thought they would have and should have already known about him. Jonah answered every question dryly until they finally got to the core questions he had sensed would eventually come.

The abbot began, "Where were you last night after you left the monastery?"

Jonah responded, "I was walking to a tavern called The Charging Boar in Callamar where I spent the evening with two brothers, Danan and Pompey, having dinner and ale. Then I returned to Saint Dominic's near the midnight."

The abbot continued, "And how were you able to leave the monastery last night?"

Jonah responded, "Pompey requested and received a monastery pass for the Saturday night from Prior Lund. The pass was also valid for me and brother Danan that same night."

The abbot paused, allowing Prior Lund to catch up with his writing. "When you entered into the tavern called The Charging Boar, were you and your two companions the only brothers within the tavern?"

Jonah replied, "No. I recall there were two other tables where brothers were sitting and eating. I did not recognize the brothers from the first table but the brothers sitting at the second table were the Skuas, Brothers Ergan, Borse, Lars, and Kraig."

The abbot asked, "What is this term, 'Skuas'?"

"I believe it is the name the four brothers call themselves. I believe it was Ergan who first came up with the name but I am not sure," Jonah replied.

The abbot queried, "Then you did not give these four brothers that name, The Skuas, yourself?"

"No, I did not," Jonah replied.

The abbot pressed, "Yet you still use this term?"

Jonah paused a moment. "I guess maybe I'm indulging Ergan's vanity."

The abbot paused then continued, "After entering the tavern, what did you do?" Many more questions ensued and Jonah gave a full version of what had happened in the tavern that night and the events that transpired, up to and including the bouncer's activities in the tavern, and their uneventful walk back to the monastery. He did not mention anything about quills.

There was a long pause. Abbot August went silent and Prior Damien began his questions. "Were the two women you accompanied within the tavern last night sisters of the Convent of Saint Lucia?"

Jonah was a little surprised by the question. "I do not believe so but I do not know for sure. My impression was that they did not look like sisters –"

Prior Damien interrupted, "Were the two women you accompanied within the tavern last night sisters of any other convent within Callalande or Korgynslande?"

Again, Jonah was surprised by the question. "I do not believe so but I also do not know for sure."

Prior Damien continued, "Were these two women that you accompanied within the tavern last night prostitutes or night ladies?"

Jonah responded, "The two girls we accompanied never told us who they were or where they came from. Eventually, they did tell us their names, but we ourselves only met them in the tavern that night after we had seated ourselves and had received our dinner plates and ale."

Prior Damien continued, "Did these two women come over to your table and solicit you or your companions for any sexual favors for a later time that same evening and did you or your companions pay for any such services rendered or anticipated by yourself or your companions that evening?"

By now Jonah was getting frustrated and disgusted with the inquiry but he did his best to remain calm. "Neither I nor my companions paid for any illicit activities either before, during, or after our dinner at The Charging Boar tavern. After the bouncer escorted the Skuas out of the tavern, I paid for the two girls' dinners and apologized to them for the conduct of myself, my companions, the Skuas, and all the other brothers that evening. I did so because I believed it was the honorable thing to do."

Prior Damien sat back pondering the answers he had just received from Jonah and gave Prior Lund some time to catch up with his transcript. Prior

Damien continued, "Did you at any time last night during your time away from the monastery, strike or otherwise injure Brother Ergan?"

Jonah replied, "I never laid any hand on him nor did Danan nor did Pompey lay any hand on him last night."

Prior Damien continued, "Did you witness Brother Ergan receiving any injuries last night while you were away from the monastery?"

Jonah replied, "Brother Ergan did receive an injury to his face when he fell to the tavern floor. I did not see what part of his face was injured."

Prior Damien asked, "How did Brother Ergan receive this injury you just described?"

Jonah replied, "Brother Ergan came over to our table, drunk from drink, and tried to put his hand on one of the two girls, but she backed away very quickly and Brother Ergan fell forward onto the floor. Brother Borse tried to help him up but had a difficult time assisting him because Ergan appeared to refuse any help."

Prior Damien asked, "When you saw Brother Ergan hit the ground, did you try to assist him in any way?"

Jonah replied, "No, I did not try to assist him. Brother Borse was already at hand and assisting Brother Ergan as soon as he went down. My path to Ergan was blocked by the girl who backed away from Ergan's attempt to touch her."

A little anger began showing in Prior Damien's voice, "So are you saying that a girl was in your way and you could not squeeze or push yourself past her to get to Brother Ergan and assist him?"

Jonah responded, "Yes, I did not try to get past her to help Brother Ergan. She was standing up and she was big. I have never seen any woman as big and strong before as she. When the bouncer came back to our table to tell us we should leave, he tried to stare her down and she was not the least bit intimidated. In fact, she looked like she was going to fight him right there in the tavern. As you can see, I am not strong, so I did not try to push past her or the bouncer."

Prior Damien sat down, giving Jonah a cold, hard stare. "Where did you get all that coin to pay for all those 'honorable' dinners?"

Jonah explained, "I can only speak for myself. Like most brothers, I did not walk into Saint Dominic's copperless. Also, some of my coin came from Abbot Eddo before he was reassigned. Danan and Pompey chipped in a few coin as well for last night's dinner." On hearing Eddo's name, a small scowl appeared on Abbot August's face as Prior Damien finished. "I have no more questions."

Abbot August began speaking again, "Did either of your companions, Danan or Pompey, conspire with you to answer in concert the questions put before you today?"

Jonah replied, "No, I have not conspired with anyone. I did not know anything about this inquiry until I walked through your door."

Abbot August spoke solemnly, "Do you swear by your Lord and Savior that everything you have answered today is the truth and nothing but the truth?"

Jonah responded, "Yes, I swear it to be the truth."

Abbot August admonished Jonah, "You are obligated to speak to no one about this inquiry under penalty of punishment or expulsion from the monastery. You may be summoned at a future time to answer more questions regarding these matters. Do you understand, Brother Jonah?"

"I understand, sire. Thank you for your admonition." Jonah clasped his hands and bowed his head.

The abbot waved his hand saying, "You are dismissed." Jonah turned around and went out of the door. No one in the room thanked him for his time or acknowledged his departure.

Jonah walked back to his room and stayed there until vespers. He was confused and angered by the inquiry. He felt like he was being accused of soliciting prostitutes. And where did this whole cockamamie story come from anyway? Something did not seem right.

The rest of his day felt surreal as he floated from vespers to dinner then back to his room without really looking at or noticing anyone. He lay down on his bed staring up at the ceiling trying to piece together what he had heard and what he knew for sure had happened last night. And he was not supposed to talk to ANYONE. How was he supposed to refrain from talking, especially to Danan, when he returned to their room? There was a good chance that Danan and Pompey had also been summoned for an inquiry like himself. And wouldn't the Skuas and the mystery brothers from the tavern also be summoned for an inquiry? Why not just summon everyone while they were at it? It was too much for him to think about at one time.

After a long time, Danan came back to their room. He opened the door quietly, entered like a cat, and crept into his bed. It was still earlier than usual for sleep but Jonah did not feel much like doing anything else that evening. He could hear Danan slowly breathing as he lay there in his bed.

Danan said to Jonah, "Let's not talk about anything until tomorrow. I'm exhausted."

"All right," Jonah said to Danan as he closed his eyes and tried to go to sleep.

Speculation

Perhaps a week had passed since Jonah's interrogation and nothing further had been said regarding the events at The Charging Boar. He learned also that nothing had happened further in regards to Danan. Pompey had been disciplined for his part even though Jonah knew that Pompey had done nothing wrong. Pompey had not spoken to him at all since then. The one thing he was most thankful for was that no one had made mention of May's offer to acquire some quills for him. He figured if anyone found out about that, he could have gotten in big trouble because of the Duke's anti-poaching policy.

Over time, Jonah spent considerable energy wondering about what had happened that night at The Charging Boar. Indeed, the only scenario that seemed consistent with all of the facts as he understood them was that Ergan had complained. Jonah recalled that most of the questions he had been asked were based on the drunken drivel Ergan spewed during their conversation that night. Jonah specifically remembered Ergan's insulting everyone by suggesting that the two girls were soliciting sexual favors and using the word "convent" several times. But why did Ergan spin a story so outlandish that Jonah and Danan looked guilty of committing unethical conduct? And what of the two girls, Anya and May? Were they provocateurs planting seeds of chaos or something else? Jonah did not think so but he did not know either.

Two motives seemed most likely to Jonah. One motive suggested that since Ergan could not hide his facial injury, he was covering up his drunken behavior by blaming others and damned be the consequences. Or maybe Ergan was setting up Danan and himself for a fall by making up an outlandish story. One motive was more sinister than the other, so he concluded that he would have to pay careful attention to Ergan and his activities for the next few weeks. Ergan might be playing a dangerous game of chess. He was also older than Jonah and probably had more experience in monastic politics. Jonah found this reasoning upsetting because he could not see what disparaging Danan accomplished, if anything.

One week after Jonah's interrogation, Danan spent some time whispering to him while they both lay in their beds. Danan began, "Did the abbot admonish you about not speaking to anyone else about your inquiry? I was admonished."

Jonah replied, "Yes, I was. And while I can understand why they have to admonish us, I sense there is something not right going on. I don't mind talking but remember the walls have ears."

Danan said, "I think Ergan spun a story about us that night since many of the questions the abbot and Prior Damien asked me were about the drunken things Ergan said to us and about the two girls."

Jonah said, "I agree. Other than being drunk or stupid, I can't figure out why he would do that."

Danan said, "I think Ergan has had something against me even before we went out that night to The Charging Boar. I don't know about you but there have been rumors circulating accusing me of lewd conduct in the privies. I don't know where any of the rumors came from but some of the things Ergan said to us that night seemed similar to what the rumors say of me."

Jonah said, "I think we need to be careful and just avoid him whenever possible."

Danan fell silent. He then said, "Many of the questions Prior Damien asked me had to do with convents, girls, and soliciting sexual favors. Nothing happened that night and I am too shy to have solicited anything anyway. They also asked if I had had been passing along rumors disparaging you and Ergan. I never started any rumors. I hardly ever speak to anyone besides you and Pompey and I never told you two any rumors about anyone. The only rumors I know of are those about me. Why would anyone say bad things like that about me?" Jonah could hear Danan's voice faltering then faintly crying in his bed. Danan stopped talking and cried himself to sleep.

Jonah was confused more than ever. He could also not see why anyone would want to hurt Danan. He had a hard time falling asleep.

Thunderstorm

During the night, a storm brought a steady monotonous rain. Later, it turned into a major downpour lasting through most of the early morning. Sleeping soundly was difficult but eventually the storm passed and the skies settled into a calm cold. Above, the stars shone.

Jonah awoke suddenly when he felt a cold salty breeze tickling his face. He shifted his weight and looked around the moonlit room. Focusing his gaze, he noticed Danan standing quietly before the open shutters, transfixed by the rising moon.

Jonah whispered, "What are you doing? It's freezing in here."

Danan did not turn to look at him but replied after a long silence, "I am watching Selunia rise. Her lighted crescent is reflecting off the gentle water, perhaps smiling upon what looks like fish jumping out of the sea. They may be spawning or it might be a shoal." He fell silent.

Jonah asked, "What is Selunia?"

"Selunia is what you call the Moon. My mother called her the Deity of the Sea."

"Danan, don't say that around here or someone might hear you. What if the abbot finds out?" Jonah chided. "This place is full of ears, remember?" Jonah paused then asked, "Where is your mother from?"

Danan said, "My family is from Vassans across the Calla Sea in Borea. My father faithfully attended the Church of the Holy Cross but my mother grew up learning the Moods of Selunia and Solarus. She gave up her ways when she wed my father because she loved him very much. But she secretly continued to speak of her ways to me. When my father found out, he raged, and then later had me committed to the monastery to set me right and punish my mother.

"Selunia's beauty is different here in Callamar as she rises in the east over the Calla Sea and sets beyond the Aerieal Horns. I never had this view in Vassans as Selunia rises over the Boreal woods and sets beyond the Calla Sea." Danan sighed in remembrance then closed the shutters and went back to sleep.

Jonah covered himself again and fell asleep, but not long afterwards the tower bell began tolling. Jonah thought, *couldn't he be late just for once?* Groggily he stood up and prepared for prayers at dawn. Danan was usually a later riser than he was, and so Jonah went down to use the privy then returned to his room to remind Danan not to be late for prayers. Danan had just risen and set off to use the privy as Jonah headed to the chapel. Queuing up to enter the chapel, Jonah did not see Danan anywhere even as the brothers began filing in. After he was seated, he still could not find Danan anywhere but he did notice the Skuas hurrying into the chapel, late. During the entire morning service Danan never showed up, and as everyone was walking over to the refectory, Jonah still did not see Danan anywhere. Jonah headed off to the scriptorium alone. The sun was struggling to break through the clouds but probably would not succeed. With low daylight it would be a difficult day for scribing. It was not until later that afternoon that Danan made his way to the scriptorium and sat down in his usual seat next to Jonah.

Jonah whispered, "Where were you? You missed morning prayers. I was worried about you. What happened? Are you all right?"

Danan replied, "I just came from the infirmary or what passes for the infirmary. I had a problem in the privy this morning. I slipped on the wet floor and hurt my neck. I went straight to the infirmary where I rested until I felt good enough to come here. I'll be all right but my neck is sore."

Jonah noticed that Danan had tied his robe so that Jonah couldn't see Danan's neck at all. Jonah sensed that Danan wasn't telling him everything so Jonah decided that he would keep a close eye on Danan that afternoon. During evening meal, Jonah sat with Danan as they ate. Pompey walked over and sat next to Danan. He looked briefly at Jonah and nodded a greeting. Then, he asked Danan, "How are you feeling? I did not see you in morning prayers."

Danan repeated his story to Pompey. The three of them continued their meal until another storm began dropping a cold incessant rain.

After most of the brothers had finished eating, Danan told Jonah and Pompey that he was going to the kitchen to find a few more bread rolls then head back up to their room. Jonah waited for Danan to return and told Pompey he would catch up with him later. Pompey assented. Danan emerged from the kitchen with a bread roll in his mouth. Jonah spotted him and shuffled off to join him. Jonah commented, "It's going to be another long stormy night and we might not get much sleep."

Danan lay down on his bed and gingerly pulled his blanket over his body. Jonah could hear Danan crying as he drifted off to sleep. Not long thereafter, Jonah tried going to sleep despite the storm raging outside. Unlike last night, this storm brought lightning and thunder loud enough to drown his thoughts.

Sometime after Jonah had fallen asleep, Danan got out of his bed trying not to make a sound but the thunder and rain covered all other sounds. He pulled from his robe a small folded letter which he then carefully slipped underneath Jonah's pillow. Jonah readjusted his body but then exhaled and fell still. Danan stood up and walked quietly to the door. With tears in his eyes, he took one last look at Jonah then whispered, "Thank you for being my friend." Then, he quietly slipped out the door and moved stealthily down the hall.

Lockdown

The storm ended in the early morning before dawn. Somehow, Jonah managed to fall asleep and slept until he felt more refreshed than he had been in a while. Jonah awoke. He was greeted by bright sunlight streaming through the shutters. Was he still dreaming? He could not recall hearing the morning bell toll. Or maybe it had tolled and he just slept right through it. He couldn't remember so he turned to Danan only to find that Danan was not in his bed. Jonah thought, *well that's a first*. Jonah got out of bed and put on his robe then went to his door and opened it. He looked out into the hallway and saw Prior Lund patrolling the hallway. When Prior Lund looked his way, he came quickly over to Jonah saying, "Everyone is being confined to their quarters right now. We are all awaiting further direction from Abbot August. Please be patient and remain inside your room."

Now Jonah was getting worried. *What's going on? Where's Danan? What happened to morning prayers? Did the bell ring? Why did the bell not ring?* His thoughts became a web of angst verging on panic. His eyes raced around his room, at the closed shutters, at Danan's empty bed. Then, he noticed something peeking out from underneath his pillow. He lifted up his pillow and sitting there was a small folded piece of paper with his name written on it. He froze for a time before slowly picking up the paper. With trepidation, he unfolded it and found it was a letter addressed to him from Danan. As he carefully read the letter, his face went from confusion to shock to horror.

Jonah,

Yesterday I learned that it had been Ergan and Borse spreading all of the rumors and complaints about you and me. Today in the privy, the Skuas cornered me and beat me up. I also heard them say they were going to blame you for beating me up. They really want to get to you, too, and I fear they may try, very soon, to beat you up as well. They seem bent on hurting you but to what purpose or end, I know not.

I feel this situation has to end and I have decided that I will be the one to end it. I am sorry it has come to this but I see no better alternative. Tomorrow, Ergan, Borse, and I will be dead. I want to thank both you and Pompey for being my only friends in this place. I don't fit in and I have no family here in Callamar. Below, I am leaving you one last thing in memory of myself, read it and please remember me fondly. Fare well.

Danan

As Jonah put the letter down, tears welled up in his eyes. For a long time, he lay crying, gasping for breath. He read the letter again in disbelief and could not gain any control over himself. He was devastated and now alone. After what seemed an eternity, he gained some measure of control and realized that he could not let anyone else know of the letter much less read it. He folded it back up again and tucked it into the most secret pocket inside his robe. He realized that he would always have to always keep it on his person and not allow anyone else to learn of its existence. He continued to lie there numb and devastated until he heard a knock upon his door.

Jonah slowly got up, wiped his face and eyes as clean as he could get them, and slowly opened the door. It was Prior Lund. Beyond the prior, Jonah could see many of the brethren slowly making their way out of their rooms, down the hallway, and towards the stairs. "The abbot has summoned everyone downstairs to the refectory where he will address everyone together in a short time." Prior Lund then left and knocked on the next door.

Jonah stepped out into the hallway and caught up to Pompey as he got to the stairs. The two of them eventually arrived at the refectory where the priors were gathering and telling the brethren to make haste and sit down as the abbot was ready to make an announcement. Soon the abbot arrived and took up a position where everyone could see and hear him.

The abbot began solemnly, "Late last night, three brethren – Ergan, Borse, and Danan – had to leave the monastery. They will not be returning. The duties these brethren performed within the scriptorium will be reassigned to other scribes as soon as possible. We will work on recruiting new scribes to help ease the workload in the near future. There will be no morning services or vespers today, but we ask that everyone pray for a safe journey for our three brethren."

The entire refectory was quiet with a growing sense of incredulity. No reasons were given as to why anyone had to leave so suddenly and where they would have had to go on such short notice.

Jonah whispered to Pompey, "That makes no sense at all. Danan would have told me himself if he had to go anywhere suddenly."

"I agree. This is all just skua spittle. I can also tell there is not going to be any inquiry, as they have already made up their minds about what happened. What exactly that is, they are not going to tell us. This means that we will not be interrogated which also means that I am going to have to conduct my own inquiry if we're going to find out what really happened. I'll let you know what I find out later."

Pompey left and began making subtle inquiries, approaching all of his contacts and using favors he had accumulated over the years. The story that emerged resulted from a combination of rumors and whispers between Pompey and his sources.

After a few days, Pompey knocked on Jonah's door. Pompey suggested that Jonah sit down. Pompey began, "Nothing I have to say is good, so please bear with me as I try to explain what I discovered and please do not tell anyone else. This is for your ears only."

Jonah sat down on his bed then looked at Pompey, "All right, I am sitting down and ready."

"There's no good way to say this so I will just say it straight; Danan, Ergan, and Borse are all dead. Brother Kason told me himself. He works in the infirmary and saw all of their bodies. They were then taken away from the monastery quickly and quietly, to where he did not know. Ergan and Borse both had their throats slit while lying in their beds and Danan was found outside in a pool of blood just below the bell tower, as if he had jumped or was pushed off of the roof. Please don't tell anyone else as I promised Kason I wouldn't tell anyone what he told me." Pompey could see that Jonah was looking and feeling devastated by what he was learning.

Some tears welled up in Jonah's eyes as he managed to squeak out a few choked-up words, "But why? Why are they all dead?"

Pompey speculated, "Well, I am of the mind that those bruises Danan received in the privy that day he missed morning prayers were not from falling down, as he told us, but were from a fight he had with the Skuas. I am guessing he may have taken some kind of revenge on them, though I've never thought of Danan as a vindictive person. The details of what happened I can't figure out. Do you have any thing you might be able to add to the picture? Did Danan drop any hints as to what he may have been planning to do that night he disappeared?"

Jonah scratched his head then swallowed. "No, he never said anything to me that sounded fatalistic or vengeful. He was moving around very gingerly that night after he said he got hurt in the privy. In spite of the thunderstorm, I fell asleep and slept most of the night. If he got up during the night, I never heard him leave, and you know how stealthy he can be when he wants to be."

Jonah reasoned that everything Pompey was saying sounded consistent with Danan's letter. Jonah now realized that he might be the only one who truly knew what had happened that night. Danan had ended what he called "this situation" himself and in so doing, may have removed what appeared to be a threat to Jonah's well-being and reputation. In a sense, Danan may have saved him from a beating by the Skuas. Was this also Danan's way of escaping from all of the problems he had endured since his first day at the monastery? Jonah thought that he and Pompey had been doing their best to make Danan feel welcome. But now, he was no longer sure. What was it that Ergan and Borse were doing to disrupt all of his and Pompey's efforts to make Danan feel at home in the monastery? He guessed that now he would never know.

Pompey opined, "What I think I do know is that the Abbot and the priors are using their authority to keep everyone ignorant of what really happened, which means they are all colluding to lie to us. And I think they will never admit to what happened, since it makes all of them look incompetent. I honestly don't know what to do or how to feel other than I feel very bad about not being able to help out Danan in his time of need."

"I need to absorb all of this. Let's talk again later this week," Jonah said as he prepared to go to sleep.

"All right, try to get some sleep."

Jonah went to lie down and fall asleep but a thought came to his mind. He remembered that Danan kept a diary in one of his desk drawers. Jonah got up to check if it was there and to his surprise, he could not find it. He looked everywhere but eventually gave up. He realized that he may have missed an opportunity to learn more about what may have really happened. He wondered if someone had sneaked into his room and removed it while he was in the refectory with everyone else. Jonah cursed himself for not thinking about the diary earlier. If someone else had the diary, then they might learn what had really happened. Jonah could only hope that Danan had destroyed it or hidden it. Jonah sighed then went back to sleep.

Master Po

A week's worth of prayers, vespers, and scribing had passed. One morning as Abbot August was concluding morning prayers, he announced a new policy change. The abbot announced that a special guest had arrived at Saint Dominic's and would be staying in the chapel for the next fortnight or so. This guest was a man named Master Po and he would be instructing them in the ways of discipline. Abbot August added, "And this monastery is very much in need of discipline. Whatever duties you have scheduled for this afternoon are henceforth cancelled or will be rescheduled. Upon the ringing of a new afternoon bell, you will all gather in the ascetic garden for your first indoctrination. Dismissed."

All of the brethren filed out of the chapel and wandered over to the refectory discussing what was happening and wondering who this Master Po could be. Rumors ran rampant but nothing seemed to make sense, yet. In the early afternoon, the bell tower rang out anew. In twos and threes, the brethren descended upon the ascetic garden. The edges of the garden featured many plants, flowers, and fruit trees, ranged around an open space large enough to accommodate all of the brethren, though it was not designed as a meeting place. The brothers and priors looked confused and disorganized as two men awaited their arrival, Abbot August and Master Po.

Master Po took up a position in front of everyone and looked coldly into each one of their eyes. Master Po's height was above average, a little short of six feet. He was wearing a light beige-colored robe with a black sash wrapped around his waist. He had white hair on both his face and head with matching bushy eyebrows. Some of his locks came down to his neckline and his moustache did not merge with his beard. He had tanned skin with eyes that appeared more narrow than most others' with crow's feet extending towards his ears, which had somewhat larger than normal lobes. Jonah had never seen a face like his before. Master Po was originally from the Land of Chin but had lived the majority of his life in Callalande.

After a long pause, a look of disgust overcame Master Po. "Every day you walk into the chapel and easily find your places if the pews are aligned and the nooks neatly spaced for you, but let you loose into the garden and you lose your sense of order. All of you, line up in front of me as if this were the chapel. Hurry up," Master Po said as he clapped his hands twice. The brothers took some time but they eventually organized themselves into rows of ten with a few columns behind until everyone had a place. The priors aligned themselves at the ends of each row, making the first few rows twelve across instead of ten.

Master Po waited for silence then said, "Now go back over by the chapel wall and file in again quickly to form this same configuration." Master Po clapped his hands twice, with more emphasis this time.

All of the brethren scurried back by the chapel wall and waited. When they heard Master Po's two claps, they all moved back as quickly as possible to their previous positions. Everything had gone more smoothly the second time, though everyone could see he was not impressed.

Everyone stood quietly at attention. Master Po began speaking, pointing at each person in turn. "I am Master Po. I am here to teach every one of you the Way of the Staff. In order to build discipline, we must all be able to work together with common purpose and commitment." Lying on the ground in front of Master Po was a short stick or pole made of wood. He slowly closed his eyes, wedged his foot under the stick and with a barely noticeable motion, launched the stick straight up into the air and caught it as it arrived at chest level with his fist, bringing it to a sudden halt. He stood absolutely motionless. With a huge breath through his nose and with both hands, he twirled the stick in front of him like a spinning blade. Then as quickly as he started, he stopped, with the stick tucked under his arm, holding it as if it were a knight's lance. He performed a few very impressive moves such as a thrust, a parry, and a sweep. He paused then returned to his original position with the stick horizontally in front of him. He slowly opened his eyes and spoke, "This is a small demonstration of the Way of the Staff. This is what I will teach all of you in the weeks to come. Return to me tomorrow at this exact place ready to begin. Return to your meditations and commit your bodies and your minds to discipline and your spirits will soar more freely than you have ever known before." And with that he took his leave. The abbot dismissed the monks to their remaining duties for that afternoon.

For the past week, Jonah had found it difficult to concentrate on his scribing. The sorrow he felt from Danan's death was taking a toll on him. Becoming more aloof helped him lessen the stress a little but he knew his production numbers were affected and he didn't know how to motivate himself. When Master Po introduced him to the Way of the Staff, he recognized that this represented something very new to him and maybe a way to relieve some stress.

So the next day, when the afternoon bell tolled, Jonah arrived early, stood at attention, and was ready to begin. As everyone else assembled in the garden, he stood anxiously, ready to see what Master Po had in store for them today.

Master Po looked out over the assembled brethren in silence for a time. He spoke, "Before you can learn the Way of the Staff, you must learn the Way of the Body. You must learn how the body can move. You must become one with your body as it moves. Therefore, you must learn the Kata of the Body. You will learn the motions as I demonstrate them. Then we will perform the kata together until everyone has learned it. Once you have learned the Kata of the Body, you will learn the Kata of the Staff. Now watch me perform the Kata of the Body slowly."

Master Po stood before everyone and faced them. He closed his eyes and began. Over the next few moments, he began moving slowly, shifting his body around left and right, altering his stance, rocking back and forth, spinning slowly in circles, balancing on one leg and back to two legs. He made deliberate motions that seemed to make his body flow smoothly, effortlessly, at times. He never once appeared close to losing his balance as he moved his arms slowly then quickly. He turned his wrists in many different ways, keeping his fingers straight and sometimes closing them into a fist. Finally, he drew to a stop, held his position, and opened his eyes.

"Now we will do this kata together slowly. If you cannot do it slowly, you cannot do it quickly. Follow me." Master Po turned his back to the brethren and slowly began the kata again. The brethren slowly, clumsily attempted to copy the master's motions with varying levels of failure. As time went on, they repeated the kata several more times until Master Po stopped and turned around. "We will continue tomorrow and every morrow until you have completed the kata without error. Only then will we continue." And with that, Master Po took his leave.

For at least two weeks, every afternoon everyone practiced and repeated the Kata of the Body. As time went on, even the slow learners' movements synchronized with those of the other brethren and even of Master Po. Finally, Master Po was able to turn around and watch the brethren perform the kata without his guidance. He spoke as they moved together, "Your mind guides your body and your body guides your mind. The two move together. They are inseparable. When you can feel the two moving together in harmony, we will take the next step."

Solitaire

The need for candles in the monastery and scriptorium was great, especially in the winter. Winter daylight hours for scribing were very limited and the scriptorium's special lighting system also had its limitations. So candles were always kept on hand. Within the cloisters, candles were the primary source of lighting when sunlight was unavailable. As a result, candle making had always been an important craft, primarily assigned to the ascetic monks. One corner of the stables was designated as their workshop. Tallow was acquired from local suppliers. While their efforts to supply candles year round were appreciated, it wasn't enough.

Over time, the monastery needed to supplement its candle supply from one or more local workshops. Candle workshops were contracted to produce occasional bulk orders of the basic candle designs, such as sticks, tapers, and votives. This task fell to Prior Lund, and he did his best to stockpile surplus candles and remain within the monastery's budget.

Each monk within the monastery received a weekly ration of candles for personal use within the cloisters. If they used up their candles, they had to wait for their next allotment. Amongst the brethren, candles were a currency that could be traded for favors or other items.

After the fallout from Danan's death, many of the brethren within the monastery were none the wiser about what had really happened, but most of them did not truly believe three brothers would just up and leave without saying goodbye. Many were suspicious of Jonah and thought he may have had something to do with the strange disappearances. So over time, rumors emerged regarding how Jonah must have had something to do with the timing of their absence. After all, Danan was his roommate, so he must be responsible in some way, in a bad way, in the most horrible way. Jonah now felt that everyone, except Pompey, was staring at him accusingly and a return to normalcy might be impossible.

Abbot August had no love for Jonah, anyway, and the negative rumors circulating gave him an excuse to confine Jonah to his quarters when not performing his scriptorial duties. Jonah was even instructed that he should eat in the kitchen rather than in the refectory so the brethren did not have to look at him. He was also told to be the last person into the chapel for prayers and the first person out. The abbot and the priors all told him it was all for the greater good and that it would not be long before he could ease up on his involuntary penance.

Jonah became frustrated with his confinement, so he approached Pompey with a request. Jonah wanted to work in the dormitory during the night making a copy of Callamar's laws and tax codes for himself. For that he would need time, writing supplies, and candles, more candles than he would be personally allotted on a weekly basis. Pompey, feeling that Jonah was being treated unfairly essentially by everyone, thought that working in his room was a good idea. He even acquired some extra candles from the scriptorium supply and passed them along to Jonah – under the table, of course.

So Jonah spent the next several months out of sight and out of mind. When he began to emerge from his seclusion, Jonah found it surprising that many of the brethren seemed to have forgotten about his supposed involvement with the monastery disappearances.

Jonah also found that working with Master Po during the short daylight hours allowed him to learn some discipline and a new way to defend himself. Master Po was satisfied with Jonah's progress in the Way of the Staff. While he still had a long way to go to master the Kata, Master Po began to see potential in him. Master Po suggested to Jonah that he begin to help some of the other brethren on polishing up their katas so that they could all take the next steps together. "One of the best ways to know if you have mastered a skill is to be able to successfully teach it to someone else," Master Po explained. And with that, Jonah became an unofficial assistant to Master Po.

With the help of Pompey, Jonah was able to acquire writing supplies and candles for his room. When he was ready, Jonah began scribing his own copy of Callamar's laws and regulations. He spent many nights as the fall became winter making a copy of his own book of laws. He was in no hurry to finish and tried to squeeze as many laws as he could onto a single page.

Over time, the abbot lifted some of the restrictions placed on Jonah and left it up to him as to whether or not to continue as he had been or go back to spending more time amongst the brethren. Jonah was also very thankful to Pompey for all of his help and consideration and realized that Pompey was the only person he could consider a friend.

Winter

Winter in Callamar could be brutally cold. Winter storms frequently made landfall from the sea and blanketed all of Callalande with thick snow. Borea's forests were also blanketed with snow and once the northern lands received their snow from the sea, it stayed around until the spring melt arrived. Creatures and plants that could not hibernate or migrate faced freezing to death. Animals with thick pelts could survive as long as they could find food, though they primarily relied on their fatty layers built up during the summer and fall. Farming generally halted, and farm animals were herded into barns and shelters and fed supplies of hay and feed. Most city functions slowed down but did not stop entirely. Traffic along most city streets was halted; however, the main streets were regularly cleared of the snow. There was enough residual heat from the streets to melt some of the snow into a gooey slush that created a muddy mess or hardened into dirty ice. However, winter was the season when military preparedness slackened so by the Duke's orders, soldiers were required to spend time shoveling snow off of the main public roads. This effort allowed the troops to stay physically fit and also meant that some measure of commerce could continue into the winter months which kept the economy moving and allowed for the dispersal of food supplies and firewood to the residents of Callamar.

The winter snows blanketed the roofs, walls, and stones of Saint Dominic's. The fireplaces within the refectory generally kept the interior of the dormitory lukewarm and comfortable. The rooms on the outer sides of the dormitory tended to get colder because of their exposure to the elements. So while Jonah was able to listen to the soothing breakers along the shoreline, his room felt like an icebox. Pompey on the other hand had a more comfortable interior room and never let Jonah forget that that was the case. Jonah did his best to seal off his window from the cold but the monastery stones functioned like a storage cellar, keeping the cold. Since he had neither fireplace nor stove, Jonah would have had to leave his door open so he could share some of the heat seeping from the refectory's fireplace. But he dared not risk others' seeing him working on his law book at night. So he shut his door and stayed cold during the winter. After a while, he came to like eating in the kitchen because it was always warm there. He got used to wearing two robes together along with extra undergarments. He also doubled up on socks and mittens that Pompey had acquired for him.

At long last, the spring arrived and with it, the thaw and more daylight. And while he was slowly being released from the abbot's restrictions, he decided to remain out of sight for the most part. It gave him more time to work on his law book and also to make his plans for a possible future beyond the monastery walls. During the growing springtime light his room began to heat up as the winter cold finally disappeared.

Late one night, Jonah was working on his book by candlelight when suddenly from somewhere without, he heard a voice call out his name, "Jonah." He quickly turned his head towards his door. Confused, he was about to ask, *who is there?*

PART 3

Derelicts

The main road passes through Callamar and crosses the Lycus River as a stone bridge with three arches that sits closer to the eastern edge of Callamar. The road then turns north-eastward, heading off towards Fallmouth at the mouth of the Snowfall River flowing into the Sea of Calla. Before leaving Callamar, the main road features several shops and services for travelers and local residents. Outside of Callamar, the landscape slowly gives way to farms and orchards which supply food to Callamar throughout most of the year. Every caravan coming from northern Callalande eventually passes through this part of town. The larger merchant shops and markets lie west of the Lycus River. While there are shops and businesses on the east side of Callamar, many of them lie derelict.

Many years ago when Duke Olan was transforming Callamar into an economic powerhouse, the Duke's brother, King Edmund III, issued an edict calling for volunteer conscripts to bolster the ranks of Korgynslande so that a military campaign could be waged to secure the southern forests of Korgynslande from the robber syndicates of Kraagen.

The Korgyns' intelligence network discovered that many goods and products moving south by land from Scullsbergen were not arriving at their expected destinations but instead were ending up on the black markets of Vassans, Zaroas, and other major cities. The campaign lasted for many years, with a great many soldiers losing their lives in the struggle. However, the southern forests were eventually swept clear of the robbers' roosts, severely compromising their ability to operate.

Back in Callalande, many families lost their heirs and loved ones, and over the years many a family home or business went bankrupt. One might have expected vagrants or squatters to move in and occupy these vacant buildings. Instead, many of the east side properties and estates lay fallow and unoccupied. Some of Callamar's stray animal population found its way into these buildings and conquered them. Soon empty buildings became dens of feral dogs while others became cotes to winter doves or harassing skuas.

After Anya and May left The Charging Boar, they stayed a night at The Barracks Inn, not far away. Throughout the night, they could hear the barking of dogs to the north. Some of the barks sounded like territorial statements such as, *this is my place, keep away.* Other barks sounded hostile and aggressive towards intruders, *oh you want some of this, don't you?* Many of the dogs foraged at night competing with other scavengers for Callamar's refuse and perhaps the occasional rabbit.

"They certainly don't sound like hunting dogs," Anya said as she was trying to get some sleep. It helped that they were sleeping on real beds instead of forest leaves.

"I can't imagine Callamar having any rabbit problems with all of those dogs around," May replied.

"You played right into his hands, that Pompey guy, didn't you? You said 'rabbits' and he spun it right back at you as a dramatic pickup line begging for our sympathies. And who was that drunk bastard anyway trying to use me? I should have taught him a lesson or two." Anya stewed.

"Controlling your emotions did us good tonight and we did not get into any trouble, though we did get kicked out of the tavern, but we were leaving anyway," May rationalized.

"And now you want to go pluck some feathers off some unsuspecting birds for some cute monk boy with a little coin because he was nice to you. You do know that birds fly, right? How are we going to catch birds without harming or killing them, without a trapping license, in a place we know nothing about? And your traps are for rabbits, not birds. Or maybe, that monk boy Jonah cast a spell on you, secretly saying, 'Bring me quills, May. I need quills.'" Anya nudged her sarcastically.

"Noooo, he didn't cast any spell on me, but I do have experience handling fowl. You do remember my farm had ducks and chickens, don't you?" May retorted.

"Ooooh, ducks and chickens, that'll do it. I think you're fond of him and want to see him again. What if he never shows up at The Charging Boar again? Are you going to sneak into a monastery housing a hundred monks because you 'know where he lives?' How will it look if we get caught and accused of being nighthawks or burglars? Yeah, I'm glad you thought this one through very well. And aren't those dogs ever going to shut up?" Anya complained snarkily.

"Let's get some sleep. I would like to walk in the daytime for once instead of having to sneak through the forest all night long," May replied.

Later that morning, the girls left the inn and began walking along the eastern road towards Fallmouth. The road curved to the north-east, passing by several derelict buildings. One such building may have been a tavern or inn at some time in the past but had since fallen into disrepair. Many dogs sat outside the building like sentinels barking aggressively, baring their teeth. The dogs had learned not to stray too far from their sanctum. In the past, many caravans hauling goods passed by this dog-infested mansion with guards in tow for protection. Sometimes the guards swung their swords or shot arrows at the dogs for practice or fun, killing many. Now the dogs were harder to kill.

As Anya and May passed the mansion of dogs, the dogs eyed them menacingly. May stopped and examined the estate from afar wondering if anyone in Callamar had made any effort to clear out the dogs. She thought, *I will inquire about this later*. But first, May wanted to harvest quills. Jonah from The Charging Boar had been the first man who had treated her kindly. May thought, *isn't that worth remembering*? To May, getting quills seemed easy as she did know how to handle birds. Growing up on a farm, she helped raise chickens and ducks both for eggs and eating. Dealing with derelicts would have to wait for another day.

Fallmouth

Fields and orchards bordered Callamar. The northern lands of Callalande, Borea, and Apollande were home to hardy apple trees called boreal apples. The trees produced apples from the late spring until the early autumn then lay dormant for the long winter. The small apples remained green and red no matter how long they stayed on the tree. The apples' sweet, tart flavor was popular with the local folk. Once planted, the trees took some years before reaching maturity but yielded several harvests throughout the year.

Another tree was the Calla cherry which grew its bounty once a year but also went dormant in the winter. Each year when the spring thaw arrived, many of the orchards surrounding Callamar burst into bloom creating a patchwork quilt of white and pink beauty that sometimes foreigners and Korgynslanders traveled to experience. Open fields were typically planted with barley and rye. Many of these grains were sold within Callamar but sometimes they were exported to Borea or stored as winter caches within Callamar's granaries.

As Anya and May followed the road to Fallmouth, they passed a patchwork of fields and orchards and numerous vegetable gardens. No doubt, this was where Ma's turnips, beets, and carrots came from. Carts loaded down with sacks of grains and vegetables, buckets of apples and cherries, made daily trips into Callamar. There were also carts carrying salted fish, buckets of shellfish, and the occasional hides and furs.

When Anya and May arrived in Fallmouth, the autumn harvests were in full swing. Farm laborers and cotters could be seen across the landscape harvesting fields and stacking sheaves of grain. Others were digging up tubers into piles to be picked up by carts and hauled away. The town was not very large but did host several fishing piers as well as docks for major ships. The main road split in the center of town on the west bank of the Snowfall River. The eastern branch wound its way into Borea and Northcamp. The north branch meandered towards the northern pass and eventually into the Duchy of Apollande. The pass also hosted caravan traffic throughout the year but not in the winter. Anya and May paused before turning north onto the Pass Road, leaving Fallmouth behind.

It was here that Anya and May got their first glimpse of the sea. There were many buildings in the way with fields and orchards blocking the view southward. But it was there, a thick blue line on the horizon with several boats off in the distance. It was a sight to see, a flat and shimmering vastness that felt intimidating yet alluring at the same time. They had lived all of their lives in Borea where forests were abundant, and the only water they knew of was in small lakes, creeks, and streams, water coming from somewhere and going somewhere else.

"Is that the sea? It looks so big and scary. And those white things look so small." Anya and May looked for a while then decided that they would have to come back here when they were done obtaining quills.

Anya and May also passed by Fallmouth's famous kitchen, The Calla Crab Inn, which featured their famous seafood stew and sourdough rolls. The stew was a delicious blend of codfish, crab, mussels, squid, and vegetables, reminiscent of a bouillabaisse but with a northern twist to the spices. But The Calla Crab Inn was a little pricey for the girls so they left town heading north. Soon, Anya and May spotted two manor houses on either side of the road with nearby cottages. As they spied the robust harvest activity, they picked up their pace to avoid being noticed. Over time, the farms began to thin out and the forest, once distant, began encroaching upon the road. Interspersed between many farms were small lakes and watering holes, perfect for raising northern livestock such as cattle, sheep, and goats. The cattle preferred the warmer climes of the south but the sheep and goats flaunted woolier coats, helping them survive the harsher winters.

May finally began to spot what she had been looking for, pheasants. She could see them at the edges of the woods eating wild grains. By this time, the pheasants had already finished raising their springtime broods and were fattening themselves up for the winter.

"Over there Anya. That's what I've been looking for. You see them?" May said as she pointed towards the edge of the woods.

Anya said, "Yes, I can see them. And all we have to do is catch a few of them and we're in business, right?"

"That's right. Let's move into the woods before it gets too dark and set up our camp. From there we can scout the birds and I'll figure out how best to set up my traps," May said as Anya rolled her eyes.

The woods where they set up their camp formed a narrow strip between the road and the west bank of the Snowfall River. The east side held thicker, more extensive forests stretching all the way to the Rowan River and Borea. This forest remained mostly untouched, though further south near the ferry, farmsteads were being carved out of the woods.

To May, the forest along the Snowfall River seemed ideal for their purpose. Pheasant hunting was regulated and they had not bothered to get a permit in Callamar for the season as they had no intention of killing any birds. Thus far they had not seen any other people in the woods, and the traffic along the road was not as heavy as the main road further south, so May hoped they would avoid detection.

The Wolf Hunter

For years, the wolf hunter plagued the forests of Callalande and Borea. He often hijacked carts filled with furs, killing the driver and traders, so he could resell the furs in Northcamp. He was very hard to recognize, even up close, as he sometimes wore a headdress made from a grey wolf's head and a body-length cape, camouflaged with forest greens and twigs. He was highly feared and everyone was advised to keep him far away or be aware of his whereabouts.

He originally got his name from being the best hunter of wolves in the northern forests of Borea. As his interests did not conflict with Nimrod's interests, they left each other alone. When the wolves of the boreal north began thinning out from overhunting, he crossed the Rowan River and began poaching in the wilds of Callalande. Not surprisingly, he did not give a rat's tush about the Duke's conservation policies or about obtaining a permit for trapping in Callalande. He became a scourge upon the land, and when officials discovered his presence and the destruction he wrought, the Duke recruited a military task force to hunt him down dead or alive. The task force failed time and again to catch him, and for years the wolf hunter remained many steps ahead of his pursuers. The only time the wolf hunter left Callalande was to sell his furs in Northcamp where he always received top coin, regardless of the condition the furs were in. In addition, the Duke set a bounty of 200 golds for his capture or death.

Anya and May had been catching, plucking, and releasing pheasants for several days and they were preparing to head back into Callamar with a good number of pheasant quills to sell to Jonah or to others, if they could not find him. On their last night they were tired and intended to sleep near their campfire. They made plans to go back into town the next day. But that night, a strong cold wind descended upon their camp from the north, chilling them to the bone. Anya's leeward shelter was doing its best to divert the winds but was not working very well. If there had been any moisture in the air, the winds could easily have become a sleet storm. For much of the night, the fire faltered, so the girls huddled together to conserve their warmth, cowering behind the ineffectual leeward shelter. By morning, the winds had died down a little but the cold remained unbearable. That was when the wolf hunter struck.

The wolf hunter crept stealthily upon the girls sleeping in a fetal hug. The howling winds masked his approach. When he reached striking range, he drew his serrated dagger and plunged it deep into Anya's back. Anya wrenched awake and screamed. The hunter pulled his dagger out and readied another strike when Anya rolled around and landed a fist onto his face. His headdress took some of the blow but she managed to scratch one of his eyes. His dagger plunged again into her side and her blood spewed everywhere. Anya reached for her dagger and flailed, barely missing the hunter. In great pain, she turned over then crouched and launched herself at the hunter, knocking him down as a third dagger pierced her torso, missing her heart.

Anya's screaming awakened May. With her ears ringing and the wind howling, May saw Anya launching herself at something to her right. Anya was tackling what seemed to be a wolf. May quickly moved to Anya's side and plunged her knife into the mysterious wolf figure. She felt her knife crack a bone and heard a loud grunt from the figure. Anya bore down on the figure trying to pin it to the ground but she was losing her strength. May plunged a second knife into the figure writhing under Anya's weight, and this time she struck softer flesh. She quickly twisted her knife then plunged it in again for a third time, feeling the blade squeeze between two ribs, damaging its heart. Again and again, she struck when an arm flailed and slapped her across the face. But by then her damage had been fatal and the figure's resistance drained away. She sensed Anya's body going limp.

May thought she heard Anya's voice calling to her during the melee but it may have been the wind. When May felt certain the figure was no longer resisting, she tried helping Anya, but Anya did not move. May rolled Anya onto her back beside the wolf figure and caught the sight of blood gushing all over her body and the ground. Anya's face did not move; no voice escaped her mouth, and darkness crept over her eyes. May screamed in horror, in utter disbelief. The wind carried her keening through woods and leas. She tried to stop the bleeding, but by then, it was all in vain. Without a pulse or heartbeat, Anya lay there cold, unfeeling, unspeaking.

With that last plunge of the wolf hunter's knife deep into Anya's chest, Anya felt herself getting colder not from the wind but from deep within. Her blood drained quickly and her body chilled fast. With her remaining strength, she held the hunter down until her grip gave out. Her body fell limp, and darkness crept across her eyes. Final visions passed before her as she lay dying upon the ground. She felt Berthe taking her hand, making circles by a kitchen fire. She saw herself and May, curled asleep together, dreaming beside a fading fire.

May cried so hard no air filled her lungs. Looking at Anya, May gasped and took in more air then screamed all over again – all into the morning cold, the banshee wailed incessantly. Finally, her lungs gave out and she lay down cold, in agony.

May sat beside Anya all day, brushing her hair, waiting for her to open her eyes and for everything to be all right. But Anya did not wake up, and for the first time, May began to understand that she was now alone. And it frightened her. She had always depended on Anya to be there for her. They were a team, always moving forward, moving together – never questioning one another. But now, that was over. And the more she thought about her new reality, the angrier she became at people like the wolf hunter, Nimrod, the Baron, the trappers, the traders, the coin masters, and on and on. And now Anya had become the victim of a world that took what it wanted and damned be the rest. May began plotting her next move.

May began looking for a suitable plot of land beside the Snowfall River. She found a shelf by the river bank overlooking gentle rapids and began digging a grave. All afternoon she dug a deep hole. She carried Anya's body to the riverside and began cleaning her face as lovingly as she could. She picked some flowers and weaved them through some forest vines, making Anya a lovely tiara. She then placed it upon her head and kissed her goodbye. May kept most of Anya's gear for herself but left her clothes and shoes. She wanted to remember Anya as she dressed. And when she was finished, she gently laid her into the earth and began filling her grave. When she finished, she collected the flattest rock she could find and carved what she thought was a letter "A" upon the stone. Then she placed it upright near Anya's head and cried some more. Evening and sunset came. May went back to the campfire, dragged the wolf hunter's body out of her sight then tried to get some sleep.

The next day, May spent all morning by Anya's grave sleeping, thinking, crying, wondering what to do. After much time, she went over to the wolf hunter's body and began searching it, cursing him and his ilk. She found several interesting items and a folded piece of paper. She took out the paper she had taken off of the bounty hunter's body and compared the two side by side. Though she could not read them, they looked nearly identical. The two papers had to be the bounty for Anya and herself. And the wolf hunter must have been trying to collect on the bounty just as the bounty hunter had before. How many more hunters were there going to be? Was there no place safe to run, to hide, to be left alone? And now alone, how would she be able to fight them all off?

On the wolf hunter's body, she found a few more coin, two small dark-blue rocks, and a small hatchet for chopping wood. She removed his headdress and cape, cleared the cape of leaves and vines. She took the hatchet and chopped off his head. Waiting for the blood to drain, she then wrapped the head up in his cape and tied it into a vagabond's sack. She dragged the rest of the wolf hunter's body and threw it into the river. She went to the trees and found a long stick to make into a spear. She sharpened the spear at both ends then placed one end through the vagabond's sack and balanced the spear on a shoulder. May spent some time by Anya's grave speaking to her. "I'm sorry I could not save you. I tried and failed my friend, my Anya. I am going to return to Northcamp to see what I can do. I pray that I will not fail again. Amen." She loaded up her pack with as much as she could carry then set off, with the wolf hunter's head, to the east.

Pyre

May spent three days traversing the woods and leas of Callalande before crossing the Rowan River back into Borea. She thought she would never return there again, but here she was, less than a fortnight later. By her reckoning, she was approaching Northcamp from the north. She was also worried that she might encounter trappers and that she might have to fight them. But luckily, she never found any. At last, she came to the edge of Northcamp and was pretty sure she could see Ma's Kitchen off in the distance. But she was not here to see Ma and company.

May figured that she would make her move after the night bell rang, since most of the businesses would be closed for the night. She also figured that the early morning would be the best time to implement her plan. But before she set out, she would need a few more spears and a change of wardrobe. She found some more sticks and sharpened them at both ends. She pulled out her spare tunic and covered it with campfire ashes she had kept from the past few days' fires. She also took the ashes and blended them with water and smeared them over her face, hair, and arms. She took out the bounty hunter's special shoes and put them on. They fit her well. As she walked, she did not make much sound at all. She found a good identifiable location and cached her gear. She gathered her spears, the wolf hunter's head, daggers on both legs, throwing knives at her back, and short sword on her belt. She waited. The night bell rang. And for some time, the town slowly went to sleep. A few hangers-on occupied the taverns, but soon even they were gone.

First, May eyed the Bear's Den Inn where her boy spy had identified the room housing the green-caped goons. She hoped the boy's information was still actionable and assumed the goons were still occupying the same room. She approached the inn from the wood and spotted a back stairs. May waited, then approached and crept up the stairs, making sure she did not trip a creaky board. Step by step she ascended to the second floor then entered through the upper door. In the dark hallway she could barely see the rooms. As her eyes adjusted, she could see the doors and recognize their numbers. She crept along and found a room that looked like it had a number "8" on the door. She tested the door and found it unlocked. And why not? These were the Baron's men. What fear had they of anyone? The door squeaked. She could hear two men snoring inside. The window was wide open casting a faint illumination around the room. She spied their beds on opposite sides. On a chair by one table dangled a long green cape. She could see the Baron's crest faintly. One man was snoring more loudly than the other, so she approached the quiet one. With a cloth in one hand and short sword in the other, she covered his mouth and slit his throat in one quick action. She held down his head as he began to struggle and flail but she threw her weight upon his form, preventing him from getting up or rolling over. He tried to scream but could not make a sound as blood welled up into his throat. His struggling soon ended.

May refocused. The other man continued snoring. She slowly crept up to the other bed and slit his throat. May waited in the cold silence to see if there would be any response from the hallway or the floor below, but she heard nothing. May calmed her breathing to combat her nausea. She was grateful for the darkness as she did not have to see the men's dead faces staring back at her. She moved to complete her task by cutting off both of their heads. After she wrapped the heads into one of the green capes, she quietly left the room the way she had entered and quickly escaped into the woods where she grabbed her tools and headed to the trading house.

The cart ports of the trading house were brightly lit with torches, as many a trader did not trust the dark in Northcamp. Thieves could be anywhere. May spied Nimrod's horses tied to one of the ports. The main entrance was not illuminated. May kept to the shadows and stealthily worked her way to the main entrance. She quickly planted three of her spears in the ground then impaled each of the three heads onto one of the standing spears. The Baron's men each got a green cape to go with their heads. Then May began climbing the trading house to the roof. The climb was not easy but she made it quietly and entered through an open skylight leading to the rafters supporting the ceiling. She found her way to the ground then cracked open the main door. There was a latch but it had no lock on it since the door could not be opened from the outside. May grabbed a lantern from one of the sconces, lit it, and then systematically set fire to all of the cubicles and tents stacked with furs and hides, ready for loading and their journey to the coast. They would never take that ride.

Before long, the interior of the trading house was afire with flames licking their way up to the rafters. Soon the entire roof was ablaze. A few night owls in town began yelling, "Fire!" And soon several people came rushing out of the inn, the hostel, and the brothel. The entire east end was in chaos illuminated by the blazing pyre. May emerged from the trading house through the main gate, ashen pale with spear, standing next to the impaled heads lit eerily from behind. As several townsfolk approached the fire with buckets of water, she charged them and knocked them over, sweeping with her spear, spilling their buckets.

May stood there yelling obscenities, threats, curses at the top of her voice, and chasing away all who approached the burning house. Soon, everyone saw that the trading house was a lost cause. They turned their efforts to protecting the nearby buildings, while keeping clear of the screaming banshee dancing about the pyre.

Furiously ablaze, the trading house became a funeral pyre consuming the hides of myriad animals. All at once, a torrent of animal souls wafted up to the sky yelping and screeching as the house collapsed upon itself. The intense heat kept people at a distance watching their profits turn to ashes on the mourning winds. Several horses galloped away from the ports neighing in terror.

From out of the brothel, Nimrod emerged catching sight of the ghastly pyre. Dressed only in body-length underwear, he stared in dismay at the conflagration, powerless to act. But soon he spied an ashen figure guarding the house, a screaming banshee gloating over her impaled prey. He began moving straight for the banshee, yelling, "You are no ghost. I will kill you with my hands and watch you die slowly." And with that, he reached out and grabbed May by the neck. His iron grip began squeezing, choking the life from her, nearly snapping her spine. Several spectators began closing in on Nimrod hoping to get a glimpse of the fatal spectacle now at hand.

Screaming and yelling, May had not noticed Nimrod's approach. When she realized that he was upon her, she quickly reacted by sweeping his legs but he was too heavy and strong for her spear to budge. His hands locked around her neck in an inescapable vise. May dropped her spear and brought her hands up to his wrists trying to break his hold, but he was too strong. She tried to punch him in the face or gouge his eyes, but her arms were too short, only reaching to his shoulders. Her punches bounced off of his chest. He was truly a giant. She could feel her life escaping. Growing desperate, she reared back her leg and kicked his groin as hard as she could, but did not sense any result. She repeatedly smashed her foot into his groin until he grunted slightly and his grip weakened. She grabbed his wrists and dug her nails into his tendons then swung her feet up onto his chest and pushed away with all of her might. Nimrod's arms were now supporting her entire weight, and his groin was smashed. When his grip finally loosened, she flew backwards several yards onto the ground. Nimrod fell backwards in response to her flight.

May gasped loudly, filling her lungs with air and ashes. As she lay gasping, breathing again, she quickly stumbled to her feet, drew her sword, and massaged her neck. Nimrod got up and charged at her with renewed fury but this time she dodged his grasp while she sliced a gash into one of his arms. She dodged his second charge again and she cut open his knee. His third lunge landed his hand upon her tunic. He clasped her neck again, staring at her maniacally, and began to squeeze. Gasping for breath she started choking again. About to panic, she plunged her sword into his chest. She kept hitting the pommel hard with her palms but could not get it to punch through his ribs. She kicked his sliced-up knee. His vise-like grip left her nearly helpless; breath was leaving her body. Again, she grabbed his wrists for leverage and kicked the sword's pommel deeper past his ribs into his heart. She kicked again and again driving it still deeper until finally she could feel his grip slacken. Then, she pushed herself away a second time. Nimrod fell backwards again but this time with a sword embedded in his chest. He grabbed the sword and pulled it out, releasing a fatal gush of blood. He tried standing up again, but this time his strength faltered and he toppled over, his great weight now a burden. He fell down one last time, bleeding out, gasping on the ground, looking up at the banshee who was leering down at him, gloating as darkness fell over his eyes.

Standing over the fallen giant, May released a primal scream into the ashen air, a portent of doom to all who would interfere, claiming the giant as her own. No one approached her. Townsfolk looked upon her from afar, shocked, aghast at the destruction around her. She had become the slayer of hunters, the slayer of giants, and the freer of souls. She was the Banshee of Northcamp and in that moment, everyone feared her. And like a ghost, she vanished into the night.

Solitaire

May returned to her cache, packed up, and wandered into the forest, putting as much distance between her and Northcamp as possible before sunrise. She figured that by dawn, the townsfolk would rally their wits and courage and form a hunting party to track her down. The roads were the fastest ways into or out of town, so she guessed the townspeople would expect her to escape along either of the roads. Instead, she headed northwest into the forests known only to bears and wolves, what few remained. Autumn snows still lay on the ground, mostly in patches. She avoided the patches and covered her tracks as best as she could. She still had time to get back into Callalande before the winter snows claimed the land. Her journey was cold, and she subsisted on the few rabbits she caught. With no place to sell furs and Anya no longer with her, she wandered without purpose. All she appeared to have was a pocket full of pheasant quills with her market far away in Callamar. Over several days, she kept pushing herself to the northwest until something strange happened. The forests began thinning out. The tall conifer trees were replaced by shorter pines more rotund, boreal pinons. Forest foliage gave way to barren plains where horrid winds barreled down the great northern crags, katabats, freezing winds that felled the foolish and punished the prepared. Like most others, May had always assumed that the northern forests stretched up to the northern crags, and that everything would be covered with snow. But that's not what she found.

May continued to the north then west and met nary a soul as the cold became a nagging presence. For the most part, the land gently sloped from the base of the mountains, flattening out to the south. The clean clear air made it difficult to perceive the true vastness of the slopes. Little ice lay upon the ground. A few outcroppings of man-sized rocks offered the only protection from the winds.

Most of the rabbits and hares did not venture this far north. A few insects such as locusts and midges could be seen but most had died off or were laying their eggs in anticipation of the spring. The only sizable creatures she could see were a few arctic voles and pika. They did not scurry but moved about gingerly, rationing their precious strength. Only the hardiest fauna survived in this environment. Dried grasses left from the spring waved in the winds. Only small shrubs with moisture-retaining bark could keep from drying out. Several small spine-covered cacti could be found low to the ground and far apart. This land was a desert of cold, but May plowed on ahead as if she had some idea of what she was doing. Eventually she came upon a very small creek dribbling runoff from the mountains further north, a winding ribbon of color in a vast land of tans and greys. She bent down and filled all of her water skins.

She figured this might be the source of the Rowan River, its humble beginnings trickling from the mountains down to the Calla Sea far away. But she could not be sure. The water had a strange taste to it. She was pretty sure she had left Borea by now and was passing into Callalande. She wondered, *am I crossing a border or is this what no man's land looks like?*

Distance was illusory as May strove to make progress across the great desert. She tried trapping anything she could find with what bait she had left. The hares had not ventured beyond the forest's edge and the voles did not take her bait or were too small for her traps to catch. Only pika seemed large enough but they did not fall for her bait as if human food were a foreign concept to them. Several times she tried approaching one, but they always scurried down a strategically placed burrow under a nondescript rock.

She had an idea. She had been lugging around that special crossbow for a long time and decided to practice using it to shoot something from a distance. As she held it up and examined it with her hands, it felt kind of small. She practiced loading it, test firing the trigger mechanism and aimed it a few times before actually trying to hit something. She also did not want to waste her ammunition as she did not know how durable it was. She set up a target using some rags she had been carrying. Then, retreating some distance, she set herself up, aimed, and misfired. She twanged her finger with the crossbow string and jumped up screaming, cursing as pain shot down her fingers. Her shot missed by a huge margin. She spent a long time looking for the errant bolt, eventually finding it with a damaged tip. She tried setting herself up again for a shot but this time noticed a pika not far away, hiding in plain sight. She shifted her aim towards the pika but the rodent saw her and scurried off to safety. She thought, *maybe it would be better if I was shooting with the sun behind me.*

She changed her position and again looked for the pika. But the pika was gone. She then noticed a vole foraging around further away in front of her. As the vole was smaller than the pika, she began moving forward to get a better shot. She got as close as she could without alarming the vole; then, she crouched down and took aim. From above and behind her head came a gust of air from a diving hawk leaving eddies in its wake. The hawk swooped to ground level, deployed its claws, and plucked the vole right off the ground. The hawk screeched away in triumph and flew back to the forest with its prize. May stood up, shaking her fist into the air, yelling, "Thief, that was mine! Curse you." She gave up hunting for the day.

As night fell, May found a small rocky outcrop and set herself up on its south side. She arranged the leeward shelter to help protect her. By now the leeward shelter had seen lots of use and was in need of major repairs. She doubled up on her clothes then curled up as best she could and tried to get some sleep. She was not able to create a campfire as she could not find a single combustible tree or bush anywhere, just small grasses and shrubs which were really good only for kindling. She did not want to burn the spear which she had been using as a walking stick. She could see to the south a thin line representing the forest's edge and a few clouds that were not able to move north beyond the forest. The sun began setting and the sky darkened. The wind picked up into a steady cold breeze then died down.

Looking up May saw the stars, vast in number and more resplendent than she had seen before. Some were brighter while others were of varying colors. Some looked red, some blue; most looked white. She had lived all of her life in the forest or on a farm near the forest where weather changed frequently. The stars hardly ever came out and the moon was always hiding behind a tree or cloud. But here in this cold wasteland, neither tree nor cloud blocked the sky. The mountains were far away and the starry splendor was expansive, a revelation, as if something new and mysterious were being made known to her. She lay back taking it all in, craning her head in all directions, basking in her smallness. The Moon appeared as a waxing crescent following the sun through the western sky illuminating the land in a magical glow. The winds never picked up again that evening and May slept comfortably during the night, though she did twitch off and on as she remembered her fight at the pyre.

Lake

May woke up in a sweat as if she were reliving the pyre. Absent the Moon, the western horizon showed hints of dawn. She decided to continue westward, and west she traveled for another day. She found a small rocky outcrop and rested. Except for the mountains which kept stretching westward, everything looked the same. She saw no pika or voles. Her water was running low and she was getting hungry. She moved on without food all day and the next day until finally she took out her crossbow and was able to shoot a pika. She discovered that she had no way of cooking it so she dried the meat into a jerky.

May began losing track of the days she had spent in the desert. League after league, she continued across the desertscape. Gusts of wind swirled within her ears like fluttering banners. She slowly became confused about what she was hearing. Soon, she came to hear what she thought were footsteps behind her. Paranoid, she wondered, *is someone following me?* May stopped and looked around many times, looking but seeing nothing. May began to question her senses and thought her ears were playing tricks on her. She looked around and saw nothing. There was nowhere for anyone or anything to hide this deep into the desert. Were voles or pika scampering about beyond her vision, conspiring to drive her mad with their barely audible footsteps? She saw nothing. Were they avenging the killing of their kin? Or was it …?

"Anya?" May blurted out, "Is that you?"

May saw nothing as the wind filled her ears. She was hungry. *Not even a ghost could hide in this desert*, she thought. With the last of her reasoning, she considered she might be hearing her own footsteps. *But why would my own footsteps sound so far behind me?* May sat down and rested awhile before moving again. As she rested, the footsteps faded away. *Am I going mad? Is this what it's like to go mad? Would I even know that I'm going mad? If so, then how could I be mad if I can question whether or not I'm going mad?*

Towards evening one day as the sun was dipping low into the west, she saw a thin orange line appear on the horizon. As the sun set, the line disappeared. Thinking, *water*, she began moving towards the line but realized that it was getting dark and the winds were picking up. She made her shelter behind a rock and tried to eat some of the pika jerky she had made. It did not taste good at all, especially with the funny tasting water she was carrying around. Nothing surrounding her looked any closer. The thin orange line appeared every night just before sunset. She could not tell if she was making progress, but she was not giving up hope.

After a day or two more, May finally felt like she was getting closer to the water. But she had felt that way for the past several days. Her jerky was finished and she had only one water skin left and no idea how far she had to go. She was getting exhausted and her mind swirled with the winds. It was then that she had a brainstorm concerning why the animals moved around so slowly. Uncertain of food or water, they saved their strength. She began slowing her pace instead of speeding up. As she trudged on, the orange line across the horizon turned to a pale blue – reflecting the sky perhaps? She would have to get closer to be sure. She still thought she had a long way to go, but before she knew it, she was already there.

May stood atop a small rise; sloping downward from her was a vast lake spreading out for at least a league to the west, maybe more. As she stood at the eastern edge of this vast lake, it was unlike any lake she had ever seen before. The water had a turquoise hue and was crystal clear. It was easy to see through the shallows to the bottom, which was what gave the lake its turquoise color. The air had an odor of rotten eggs.

May walked down to the water's edge and stood on a sandy beach of fine silt mixed with small pebbles and broken shells. Several contour markings surrounded the lake. Each contour consisted of long-dead vegetation and skeletal fish, bones that had rotted away long ago. Everywhere surrounding the lake were dead fish, bleaching in the sun. It was a ghastly sight, an entire lake of death. Not far from where she stood was a series of smoothed rock formations with waves lapping gently against the rocks. She could feel the winds blowing across the lake spreading ripples towards the southern shore. The water was not deep but the smell of rotting eggs and death kept nagging at her. May was very thirsty. As she crouched down and reached her hand to the water, she heard a female voice behind her speak. May stood up and turned around to see the lone figure of a woman wearing a grey woolen robe fluttering in the wind nearly twenty yards away. "Did you survive leagues of cold and barren desolation only to die here on this shore?"

"No. Is this water not safe to drink? Have you been following me? What is this place and who are you?"

The woman replied, "The water is venom and no, I have not been following you. I call this place the Lake of Bones as you have clearly seen yourself. Perhaps the desolation has affected your judgment. No one in their right mind visits this place. There are larger skeletons of humans and animals scattered around the lake and millions of shells mixed and blowing with the sands. As for me, time will decide if I tell." She paused. "Are you alone?"

"Yes, I am alone. And yes, I crossed the desolation alone. I am thirsty. Do you have any clean water? I would be very grateful and of service to you if you did," May replied.

The woman hesitated then replied, "I have clean water in my abode if you wish to follow." She turned away and followed the north shore towards a large rock formation in the distance.

May followed the grey woman toward the rock formation. As May got closer, she could see that the rocks were larger than anything she had seen for the past week or so. The rocks appeared to be layered in various colors and textures, winding and naturally carved into a veritable maze of nooks and crannies. The rocks also rose to the height of a multilevel building with pockets of dried bushes and plants nestled within.

The grey woman brought her to the edge of the maze and told her to wait. May thought of her as the grey woman because of the robe she wore, but when May finally got a closer look at her face, she saw that she was a very beautiful woman with copper-colored skin and dark hair braided behind her head. The woman was a lot darker than any man or woman May had ever seen. The woman's eyes held a look of sadness she could not place but felt she understood. The woman had an accented and alluring voice that was very melodic with a hint of resignation.

The woman disappeared into the maze and, after a short time, reappeared carrying a small jug of water. The woman handed May the jug and then spoke, "Here is some water. Do not drink too fast, as it is very precious. The desert can steal your life away without your ever knowing, and bringing it back takes time. Drink slowly."

May accepted the jug of fresh, crisply cold water. She drank it slowly as the lady had instructed. It was the best water she had tasted in years. Over time, she could feel her body slowly being restored and her mind clearing up. The grey woman sat down and watched May drink the water with approval. She observed May closely, marveling that anyone could have survived walking from the east. When some color had returned to May's face, the grey woman spoke.

"No one ever comes to this place from the east. Most people come from the south, as that is where the road runs from Callalande to Apollande. When people arrive on the south shore, I have little time to reach them before they have drunk the water and perished. You look very big and strong and that may be the reason you survived. Who are you and where did you come from?" the grey woman asked.

Visitor

May began, "I've lost track of how long I've been wandering but I began walking from Northcamp in Borea at least seven days ago, maybe more. Have you heard of it?"

The woman said, "I have not heard of Northcamp. I have heard of Borea but I have never been there."

May thought, *good*. And she continued, "Northcamp is where all of the fur trappers take their furs and hides to sell them for coin. Then traders cart them off to markets in Borea, Callalande, and elsewhere. I have trapped mostly rabbits and sold their furs but I also worked in a kitchen feeding the townsfolk. I decided to head north and west from Borea to catch birds so I could acquire quills to sell them to scribes south in Callamar. I have not found much success in this desert and I ran out of water just before I found your lake. My name is May."

The woman replied. "I can see how being strong and armed would allow you to hunt wolves and live to tell about it. Do you always travel alone?"

May said with tears coming down her cheek, "No. I had a companion who was stronger than I, if you can believe that, but she was killed by another hunter. We were jumped in the night and I managed to defend myself and get away. I have been wandering in this desert since and ended up here."

The woman looked at May quizzically but did not seek any clarification to her story. "If you are looking for Callamar, then you are a long way off course. The road to the south eventually leads to Callamar, but it is a long journey on foot.

Puzzled, May asked, "So why are you living here? This place seems like nowhere. You are the first person I've seen in over a week."

The woman appeared to choose her words carefully, "I used to live in Callamar before I had to run away. I was accused of crimes I did not commit so I fled to the highlands northwest of Callamar where many goat herders live. I hid there for some time until my antagonists found me again and I had to flee. I could not go to Apollande as they would find me there, so I ended up here. Near this lake, nobody bothers me. I would rather not talk any further of those times."

The woman changed her tone, "You are welcome to stay for a while but I do not have much to offer. I live here on the edge of starvation. If you wish to stay, you will have to do some work to earn your keep."

May said bowing her head, "You have shown kindness to me so I would be glad to help you until I can figure out where I will go next. Thank you for your kindness." May looked around curiously. She had the impression that the woman was not here alone.

"Many of the nooks in this place stay comfortably warm throughout the night. I will show you where you can spend the night as I have no room in my abode. Tomorrow, I will show you where to get clean water." The woman took May's empty water jug and disappeared. She returned with the jug half-full and a few small carrots. She directed her to a cozy nook where she could sleep in privacy and comfort. "If the winds pick up, they will whistle and moan, but you will not get cold. Have a restful night and I will greet you in the morning." And with that she took her leave of May.

May was completely surprised by her experiences that day. Looking at the orange carrots, she realized that she hadn't seen much color at all for the past week or so. May thought, *where did she get these carrots from*? She lay down trying to sleep and concluded that she had probably cheated death yet again by not drinking the toxic water in the lake. If she was a cat then she had already lost several of her lives. She wondered, *how many more do I have left*?

This place seemed otherworldly to May, delicate and harsh and full of mystery. During the night, Anya visited May's dreams and the pyre burned furiously. Several times she awakened in a cold sweat, coughing, cheating death again at the hands of Nimrod before falling back to sleep. Awakened again, she rubbed her eyes swearing that she saw a shadowy figure looking at her from afar. *Is it a ghost*? She put it out of her mind and fell back to sleep.

As the day began, sunlight entered the maze from somewhere unseen setting the rocks aglow in shifting swirls of color. The cliffs surrounding her reflected oranges, browns, whites, and greys all mixed together in a mysterious glow. It all felt surreal as she got up and went to see if the woman had awoken yet. When May emerged from the maze, she was surprised to see that she had slept almost till midday.

"So the sleeper finally awakens," the woman said. "The desert takes a lot of life from those who accept its challenge. You look a bit restored. I can see a glow about you."

May replied, "I feel much better than yesterday."

"Very good. When you are ready, there is something I want to show you," the woman said.

Water

The woman brought May to a place just south of the maze. Upon the ground was a camouflaged netting spread over the ground. She lifted up the net and pulled it aside. Beneath was a small trough dug out of the ground with a layer of finely-silted clay or something similar lining the bottom of the trough. On the north side of the trough was a very shiny flat rock, probably a kind of sandstone smoothed until it was flat. Cemented onto the flat rock were many smaller flakes of reflective minerals. Covering the trough was an awning made of a thin leathery material; a collector which drained into a small ceramic jar sat at one end of the trough.

The woman began, "This is my water purifier. I use this device only when the wind is still or gently blowing. The trough gets filled with creek water, not lake water, and the sun vaporizes the water into the collector here above the trough which drips the purified water into a jar. When the jar is full, I take it back to my storage room and begin filling another jar. I can get one full jar every day. Adequate sunshine is not a problem most of the year. This shiny reflector can be adjusted throughout the day to reflect sunlight onto the water, helping it to vaporize faster. The shiny rocks are flakes of mica that can be found all over the desert. Every week or so, the trough needs to be cleaned, as the toxins left behind accumulate. They can be thrown out into the lake with the other toxins. Water needs to be hauled from the creek, which runs from the mountains down into the lake. I have two buckets for hauling water and a cistern around here somewhere where water can be stored before it is purified."

May looked down at the device, impressed but understanding only half of what the woman had said. "What do you need me to do with the purifier?"

The woman said, "Filling up the buckets with creek water and bringing them to the trough would be a good start. Let me show you the creek."

Both May and the woman walked along the rocky north shore of the lake and when they got to the western side of the maze, they could see a small creek running into the lake, a thin colorful snake winding its way back up to the mountains.

"The creek water contains fewer toxins than the lake water. It won't kill you but if you drink too much of it, you can get very sick. I have never followed the creek into the mountains to see where the water comes from. That is too much effort for me. If you are going to stay for some time, stocking up on drinkable water is the highest priority."

May spent the rest of the day hauling buckets of water to the trough and cistern. The creek was a slow trickle of runoff. It was like hauling water from Ma's well except filling the buckets took longer.

While May was filling the trough, she could hear the woman shouting as her voice echoed through the maze of walls. May guessed the woman was either going crazy out here in the desert all alone or maybe she was shouting at someone else. May could not tell.

As the sun was getting lower in the west, the woman came out to her and said it would be best to secure the purifier as the wind was picking up and daylight was fading. "You have done very well. In about half a day, you were able to make over one jar of water. You certainly can haul water with minimal effort."

The woman said it would be best to get to shelter as the wind became colder. "There is also something I need to tell you that I should have told you sooner." When they returned to her abode and May's nook, she stopped May and then called out, "Talean." And from out of the maze a small boy of perhaps seven or eight years gingerly walked and stood beside the woman. She put her arm around his shoulders and said, "This is my son, Talean, and he has something he wants to say to you and give to you, right Talean?" And the little boy nodded his head silently. "Talean, tell May here that you are sorry and give her back her sword, now."

A very faint voice came out of his mouth as he slowly approached May, "I'm sorry." And he handed to her the short sword that she had taken from the bounty hunter.

"We are both very sorry. He is used to collecting items that people leave behind by the lake. I told him not to touch anything that belongs to you. He doesn't meet very many people out here by the lake and is a little shy with strangers."

She accepted her sword and said, "Thank you Talean. No harm done."

Talean turned around then quickly stood behind his mother, peeking from behind her robe.

So that was who she was shouting at, May thought. It made sense now. He was a cute little boy. His hair was not as long as his mother's but braided in the back just the same. He wore a warm woolen shirt and pantaloons, very much like his mother's robe. His face was a little lighter in skin tone than his mother's copper but still darker than her own. And he brought a smile to her face as he disappeared back into his mother's abode.

The woman then said, "You may call me Reya. My real name is best left unknown. Talean and I have been cooking up a small pot of stew. Would you like to share it with us?"

"I would be delighted to share, thank you."

And the three of them sat themselves down on rounded stones. They ate their dinner and drank the newly jarred water. The stew was very simple containing small carrots, some turnip chunks, string beans, leeks, basil, and not surprisingly, no meat. Talean kept quiet but his eyes were fixed on May for most of the meal while his mother Reya and May talked into the night. May liked the stew and wondered where the lady had found all of the ingredients.

Secret Garden

For another day or two, May hauled water, purified it, adjusted the reflector, and eventually filled all of Reya's water storage jars. Reya was impressed with May's work and happy that all of the water jars were filled. "Tomorrow, Talean has agreed to show you around the garden where all of the food you have been eating comes from. But for now, why don't you take a rest since you have been doing a lot of work?"

Instead of resting, May decided to take a short walk along the lake towards the eastern shore to understand her surroundings a little better. She practiced walking leisurely so as not to use up her strength. She recognized that the lake's odor was worse on days with no winds. The winds consistently blew south off of the mountains and blew most of the smell southward, away from the maze. She found many skeletons along the shore. Most were of very small fish, nothing one would be proud of catching. There were thousands of very small crustaceans and several vole skeletons. There were also skeletons of birds like geese and ducks and one or two larger skeletons. One appeared to belong to a wolf, which she judged, by its dry brittle bones and distance from the water, to be very old. As the lakeshore began to turn southward, she found her first human skeleton. Wearing a few tattered remnants of what would have been clothing, it also looked like a very old skeleton, from before her time. She figured it would take an entire day to get to the south shore where she expected most of the human skeletons to lie. She turned around and headed back. Looking back towards the maze, she had a difficult time seeing it at all. It just seemed to blend in with the rest of the landscape. May thought, *no wonder no one ever bothers Reya and her son out here. They can't be seen.*

May returned to the maze when it was getting dark. She noticed that the days were getting shorter as they were now entering late autumn. Experiencing a lack of snow on her trek across the desert, she wondered how much snow the winter would actually bring to the maze.

The next day, Talean was watching May sleep. When May's eyes opened, Talean was there eagerly ready to take her to see the garden. May told him she would be ready shortly. May stowed her things then got up to see what was in store for her today. Outside Reya's abode Talean said, "Follow me." He began walking through twisting wind-carved passages then came upon what looked like a natural staircase leading upward several levels. May continued following Talean until suddenly, the narrow passages opened up into a large chamber below. There appeared to be a narrow ramp leading down to the bottom of the chamber. Everything looked green. She could see sunlight coming in from above, and in front of her she could see many neatly planted rows of crops and a wall of what looked like string beans. She was amazed that all of this was hidden away, protected, and nurtured.

Talean said, "This is the garden."

May spotted many short rows of carrots, leeks, squash, dill weed, and some small berries. Excepting the green beans, all of the plants appeared to be somewhat small struggling to grow. However, nothing looked dried up or in need of water.

Talean came down to the crop level and pointed at the ground saying sadly, "These are the carrots. They don't grow very big."

May pushed a finger into the soil; soon she hit hard dirt. "I used to work on a farm when I was younger. Carrots need deeper soil to get big. Maybe if you could dig more deeply, you could get bigger carrots."

Talean responded almost apologetically, "I did try to dig deeper but the ground was too hard for me."

"Where did you get this dirt?"

He said softly, "My mother and I brought it here with the buckets."

"You mean you brought all of this dirt in here with just those two buckets?" He nodded.

Talean turned to his green wall. "My string beans grow long enough that my mother has to cut them up to fit into the stew pot. And the berries don't grow very large but they taste very good." He showed her a few berries that were just starting to turn blue.

He then pointed to the squashes, "I don't like these too much but my mother likes them a lot."

May stifled a laugh, "I don't like them much either, but they are good for you."

Talean continued giving May the grand tour. He scrambled to the top of the maze like a spider climbing a wall. May had some difficulty following him but eventually reached him atop the maze of rocks. From this vantage, they had a commanding view of the surrounding area while remaining concealed from view. Looking at the garden from above, she could see just how fragile an oasis it was amidst the surrounding desolation.

Talean pointed to the east saying, "Over there, I first saw you coming to the lake."

May looked eastward and concluded that he must have very good eyesight, as she thought she would have just been a speck on the horizon, barely noticeable.

When May and Talean returned to Reya's abode, she asked, "What do you think of our little garden?"

May responded, "It is a jewel in a wasteland of rocks. Talean tells me you brought most of the soil from outside. How did you get it all in there and where do you get the water to keep it alive?"

Reya said, "There are several natural tanks and cisterns within the maze. Once in a while it rains and we can channel the water into the tanks. We then use that water in the garden. Other times, we have to use the purified water or water straight from the creek. Either way, the water is heavy and it takes a lot of effort to move it."

May said, "Give me a day or so and I will come up with a way to improve your garden. I noticed some of those crops do not grow naturally in this desert or I would have seen them on my way over here from Borea. If I may ask, how did you get them?"

Reya said, "I will only say that I have a benefactor, sworn to secrecy, who sends me deliveries once in a while from Callalande or Apollande."

May thought, *a merchant or trader perhaps? The mystery deepens.*

The next day May worked at making more purified water. When the jars were full again, she set off to survey the land surrounding the maze. She was looking for good soil. But that was hard to find. She first looked near the creek for something that would have more organics in it and fewer rocks and pebbles. By now she knew what the toxins looked like and could tell if the soil she sampled had any in them. Eventually, she found a patch of soil which looked good.

May came back to Reya and Talean and explained what she had in mind: First, May would dig up soil, carry it back in buckets, and make a large pile against the north wall of the maze. The second stage of the plan would involve hauling buckets over the top of the wall rather than around it. Going back and forth and up and down through the narrow passages was just too much work. So Talean would fill buckets outside the maze while May would pull up the buckets then walk across the top of the maze and lower them down to Reya, who would be in the garden and empty the buckets into a large pile of dirt. May would do most of the heavy lifting at this stage. The third stage would be to make a deeper soil patch where they could grow larger carrots and even turnips and beets. She asked them if they had any questions.

Reya said, "We do not have a rope long enough to pull the bucket to the top of the wall."

May said, "I have a long rope we can use." May went to her pack and found her long rope. She tested it and found it strong enough to do the job. "Digging up the ground will be the hard part as I do not have a shovel and you do not have any forest trees around here where I can get some long strong sticks. I do have a walking stick but that may not be enough to finish the job."

Reya thought for a while then said, "Along the south shore of the lake amidst the skeletons, I think there is an abandoned cart where a few old timbers still remain. You might want to take a walk to see if anything there is suitable to your needs."

And with that, they all agreed to implement May's plan. It would take some time to set it up but once started, it could be finished within a few days.

Early in the morning, the wind caromed through the maze, sighing and moaning. May had trouble sleeping with all of the noise, so she got up and wandered over to the lakeshore. The dawn had not arrived and a full moon was setting in the west. May found Reya standing on the lakeshore with her arms stretched upward, facing the moon. The groaning winds fluttered her robe like a castle banner. In the eerie moonlight, the winds picked up many of the hollow lake shells and dropped them upon each other, creating a high-pitched tinkling rattle of tiny hollow bones. Shivers raced down May's spine as the wind carried ghosts and spirits through her body all at once. Her body shuddered itchily as if a thousand tiny ants were crawling over her back, arms, and legs. She hastily retreated to her nook and tried going back to sleep, scratching her whole body as much as she could.

When May woke up later that morning, she decided to venture out to the south shore. She was seeking wooden timbers that she could carve into spears, shovels, or pry bars. She filled up her water skins and then set off. As before, she encountered many skeletons and shells lining the lakeshore. When she approached the southern part of the eastern shore, she saw what looked like a bear's skeleton by the edge of the water. Its claws had been removed but it was otherwise intact. She could not gauge the age of the skeleton but thought it to be very old, like all the others. Continuing, May eventually reached the human skeletons spread out over a large area.

A short distance from the southern shore, May discovered the remains of a horse cart. Its contents had long been plundered. All of the metal parts were gone. Exposure to the elements had turned most of the wood into brittle husks but she did find what she thought could be three useable pieces. She collected the pieces, bundled them up with her rope, and began pacing her way back to the maze.

On her way back, she spied something glinting in the distance, not far from the shore. She set down her bundle and went off to investigate. When she arrived, she found the skeleton of a child, perhaps a little girl, probably not much older than Talean, half buried in the ground. Leaning next to her skull was what appeared to be a small hairpiece with corroded tines decorated with a colorful, mysterious crest in a ceramic glaze. *This must be what I saw shining in the sun*, May thought. She found nothing else of interest. She picked up the hair piece and thought to herself someday she would figure out who this little girl was and how she came to be here, to die here. That itchy tingle shot down her spine again as she looked back at the skeleton one last time before leaving.

She grabbed her bundle of wood and slowly made her way back to the maze. She arrived a little after sunset and when she set down her package,

Reya and Talean had dinner waiting for her. Talean was curious about the things May had brought back. Reya said, "Come Talean, let's eat first. I am sure May will tell us about her journey to the south shore while we eat."

Talean did not say much during dinner but did ask one question. "May, would you tell me about your home, Borea?"

May was a little surprised but then she realized that Talean had probably never known anywhere else but here. So she sat back and began a long story. "All right. Borea is a land made mostly of forests. A forest has may trees all close to one another and they grow upwards very tall, taller than the maze." Talean listened very attentively as she continued through the night with stories of trees, animals, and villages full of people. The moon shone overhead bringing a crystal glow to the stories she told.

Over the next several days, May, Reya, and Talean began work on the garden. First, May took out her hand axe and knife and started carving up the timbers. Talean watched curiously as items he thought of as being junk were magically transformed into gardening tools. She smoothed out some hand grips and tested them for sturdiness and slivers. She had only enough wood to make two larger and three smaller shovels and spears. She then took the buckets and shovels and returned to the patch of soil she had scouted out earlier and began digging. The spear was used to loosen the upper layers then the shovel was used to dig up the soil underneath. She encountered and dug up lots of rocks embedded within the ground. Soon she began filling the buckets with dirt and hauling them over to the maze, making a big pile. When Talean showed up, May taught him how to dig up the ground with the tools she had made. She explained that the work would go slowly at first. All work was like this and patience was the key to completing any good project. Before long, they built up a large pile of dirt ready to be brought into the garden. Reya watched May and her son working together from afar. A small smile crossed her face.

The next day saw the three of them working together to bring the piled dirt into the garden. Talean's job was to fill the buckets with dirt. May climbed to the top of the maze and dangled a bucket from her rope over the side down to where Talean was. He filled up the empty bucket and tied it to May's rope. May then hoisted the bucket up and took it to the other side where Reya was waiting for her to lower the bucket. While May did this, Talean filled up the second bucket. Reya took the bucket from May and emptied the dirt into a designated area; then, May pulled up the empty bucket back to the top. They repeated this all morning and afternoon until the entire dirt pile had been moved into the garden. They were very tired that evening, especially May, and drank lots of water.

The next day they took a break from the garden as they had to replace the water they had drunk the previous day.

The next day, May and Talean chose a place in the garden where they would make the new carrot patch. They began loosening the dirt with the spears she had made. Once they cracked the surface, they used the shovels to dig out large clods of packed dirt making a big hole in the ground. Before the hole was filled with the new dirt they had hauled in, they filled the bottom of the patch with some of the tank water then covered it with dirt and added more water and dirt. By the time they were done with the carrot patch, it was sunset and time for dinner. Talean was very tired and almost finished his stew in one gulp. While he was tired, he seemed very happy and proud of his new carrot patch. And his mother was very proud, too.

Katabat

With the work on the garden finished and the water supply at maximum, May's work was done. She began considering when it might be best to leave for Callamar as she knew winter was approaching. May talked to Reya about this and Reya agreed. May stocked up on supplies such as full water skins and vegetables from the garden. However, she did not want to leave right away as she had made a new friend, Talean. He had known only his mother and strangers and finally he had someone else to talk to.

May waited for a good opportunity to breech a different subject. "What about returning to Callamar? How long have you been gone?"

"I think about that a lot. I left when Talean was a baby, so it has been many years. I wish it was safe for me to return but I can't know for sure," Reya replied

"And what about Talean? Wouldn't he be better off growing up in a town instead of out here all alone? I grew up as a child living on a farm with only my father. As I got older, he would not let me go into town with him and kept me locked in the house unless I was working in the garden or with the animals. I sometimes had to sneak out in order to see my friends at all. If I did not have the friends I did, I don't know how terrible my life would have been. I was going crazy. Maybe I still am crazy," May said.

"I want to go back but I am afraid. As you can see, my face stands out easily in Callamar," Reya said.

"When I return to Callamar, I have a plan to get a place that I can own myself. Maybe after I clean the place up, I can sneak you and Talean back into town and you can live with me in disguise. Does anyone there know of or about Talean?"

"I don't think anyone would know about Talean, except my benefactor. But…" and her voice tapered off.

"Let me get back into Callamar and establish myself there. When I get a place, even if I have to build it with my own hands, I will return here and bring the two of you back with me. I promise things will be better for you and Talean in Callamar. This place is one step from poison and one step from freezing. You have done well to survive here but one big storm could ruin everything." And with that, May gave Reya a big hug as they continued talking about a possible future for all of them in Callamar.

As the evening wore on, the winds began picking up until they reached a greater ferocity than May had experienced since arriving. The winds came off the mountains as a major storm mostly of wind, a katabat. The cold dry wind carried dirt and dust in great sleets across the landscape, sandblasting the maze and the lake. May was very concerned about the garden, as she remembered what can happen to a farm during a winter storm. Everything dies or hibernates. So she went off into the garden to inspect the crops. To her surprise the cold wind chilled the garden but the garden itself remained intact. The open roof was angled in such a way as to retain some heat. The maze itself was able to fend off the sub-freezing temperatures with the warmth stored in the rocks and the tanks. Maybe a plant or two froze but, overall, the maze really was an oasis in the middle of a wasteland.

May returned to her nook and tried to sleep. Channeled winds snaked their way through the maze, playing its cracks and windows like some primeval organ. Winds shrieked, whistled, and groaned all night long recalling some forgotten toccata. Over time, the winds died down and hushed, waiting for the next katabat to return for an encore. May finally fell asleep.

That morning when May woke up, she knew she had to tell Talean the words he did not want to hear. She looked around and found that Talean had been sleeping in his bed all morning. "Talean, may I speak with you?"

Talean already knew what she was going to say but he remained quiet, not looking at her or acknowledging her.

"When you first saw me walking in from the east, I was on my way back to Callalande and I was so thirsty that I was ready to drink the lake water. You and your mother saved me from dying. I was running away from my home in Borea. Ever since that day, I have been looking for a new home and I believed Callalande would be that home. Your home here is a nice place but I can't live here. I told your mother that I would try to build a nice place of my own in Callamar and that someday I will return here to take you and your mother away with me," May explained.

Talean remained silent.

"All of the stories I told you about animals and trees and people living together are true. And I want to show them all to you someday. You are my new friend and nothing will ever change that. I am promising to you now that I will bring you and your mother back with me to Callamar someday."

Talean slowly rolled over and looked at her with teary eyes then spoke very softly, "Do you promise?"

"Yes, I promise. And when you come back with me to Callamar, we will build a new carrot patch together in a new garden."

Talean sat up then reached for her and gave her a tight hug and cried on her shoulder. "I will wait for you. I don't have any friends except you." He hugged her for a long time then he let her go and lay back down in his bed.

May finished packing her belongings and gave Reya one more big hug and then she set off towards the west. She followed the north shore until it turned south. May stopped and turned around to take one last look at the maze. She could see Talean standing atop the maze watching her leave. She waved one last time to Talean then followed the lakeshore south until she disappeared into the horizon and was gone.

Goat Path

After three days of walking south from the lake, May found the road passing from Callalande to Apollande running from east to west. To the west, the road slowly descended into more desolation and mountains off in the distance. To the east, the road slowly ascended until she could no longer see the road. To the south east was a mountain range rising ever higher. May thought, *are those mountains along the western border of Callalande*? She decided to travel eastward along the road.

Traveling eastward, she came across a small hovel every league or so by the side of the road. Each hovel looked like it had seen use, as the ashes of fire pits lay nearby. The hovels were made of piled stones. Some were conically shaped while others were more like oddly shaped boxes. *These must be shelters used by travelers in case of cold weather or storms along the road*, May thought. As the sun began setting, she found a hovel and spent the night there. She ate some of the vegetables Reya had packed for her and as she munched on a small carrot and some green beans, she could not help but think about Talean and how he had grown them for her. During the night, she awoke several times sweating from her nightmares and dried herself off before the cold air could chill her.

The next morning, May continued eastward. The southern mountains she had sighted earlier were becoming more clearly visible. It was not long before she encountered a small crossroad. She could see it slowly winding its way into the mountains. Also, she could clearly see some coloration on the mountain slopes far away, possibly bushes or trees. She knew the road went into Callalande but she was not ready to make a big entrance down the main road announcing her presence. May remembered what Reya had told her about hiding amongst the goat herders of the highlands. She decided that she would brave the mountain path. It seemed logical to her that there would be a pass along the path so she would not have to do any serious mountain climbing and would just have to deal with trudging upwards.

May noticed many footprints and goat tracks following the crossroad so she dubbed it a goat path. Taking the goat path was not difficult at first, but over time, it began ascending several alluvial fans until the path got significantly steeper. She crossed what looked like several dry creeks or washes coming down off the fans. Soon the path turned into a number of switchbacks and the ascent became more difficult. She slowed her pace to conserve her strength and to avoid sweating. The weather began getting colder. The hovels along the goat path became fewer and farther in between. Not knowing when another hovel would show itself, May decided to spend the night at a lower elevation before attempting a final ascent to the pass.

By now, she was close enough to the mountains to find some scattered firewood, and for the first time in a long time, she made a campfire and warmed herself. During all of this time, the weather had remained clear. Towards night fall, she could see the faint outline of storm clouds spilling out over the mountain tops. The clouds filled the sky and smothered the stars and the moon. While the weather was shifting, she warmed herself by her little fire and listened to what sounded like voices in the wind.

The next morning found a thin layer of frost on the ground and each day brought less daylight for climbing. May continued ascending the mountains thinking that she could find another hovel if she got too cold. New clouds were piling up and spilling over the mountains. As she was nearly halfway to the pass, a light snow began falling.

Dismayed, she decided to keep moving, but soon the trail became more difficult to find. Before long, she became confused. She tried to spot hovels sticking out of the mountainside or at least a nice rock formation with shelters or caves. Wood became more plentiful but it was an effort to collect enough for a fire. Contact with the snow floating through the air made her even colder. She stopped to put on some extra clothes and began walking towards what she thought was the mountain pass she had seen earlier. Fog gradually covered the mountains until the only thing she could tell was that she was walking uphill. She kept moving forward slowly. At least the snow was not that heavy and not as deep as during her flight a few months ago. She realized the sun was setting. She could feel the winds pick up chilling her body. She kept moving on looking for some kind of shelter. Just as everything appeared to go dark, she spied a small pile of rocks ahead and heard a few clacking sounds off to one side. She quickly made her way up to the pile. As she hoped, it was a small hovel. However, when she looked inside, she found the hovel occupied.

She saw a bearded man attempting to start a fire by hitting two rocks together to make sparks.

"Oh, I didn't realize this place was occupied. Sorry for the intrusion."

"Ye startled me a bit, that's all. Please come en. I know et looks a wee bit crowded with me nanny goat here but she don't bite and once I light this here fire, ye won't care how crowded et es," the man chuckled.

May decided to get in and scrunch up against one of the walls. She crammed her pack into the remaining corner then proceeded to take out her flint and steel. The man took one look and said, "By all means, go ahead and get this here fire started." May took her flint and steel and made a few quick sparks; the kindling began smoking and a few flames crackled up as their fire pit lit up.

"Mighty nice gadget ye got there," the man said as he smiled and began adding wood to the fire. Soon, the entire hovel was heating up and May could see the man more clearly. He was a middle-aged man, probably near her father's age, with leathery skin showing some years of exposure to the elements. He looked a bit grizzled with a light-colored scruffy beard and a few white hairs accenting his ears. He had on dark plaid woolen clothes and deer or goat-hide shoes. His eyes were a kind of hazel with bushy eyebrows. Several creases lined his forehead.

The man asked, "What brings ye up this high enta the mountains? Usually all I find es goats or traders from Apollande. Ye looks like a young lass. Ye ain't a trader are ye?"

May replied, "No, I'm not a trader. I was climbing this mountain because I'm looking to visit the goat herders of Callalande. I was hoping to beat the winter snows, but it looks like I might be too late."

"Aye, the snows have begun, but these snows have been gentle thus far. When they abate, et won't be hard gettin' back o'er the pass. I came here lookin' for this here nanny as she strayed a wee too far from home. Would ye like a cup o'tea?" the man asked.

"Yes, I would love some tea." May reached over very carefully towards the nanny goat and gently patted her head and scratched behind her ears. The nanny seemed to like May's petting and scratching.

"Ye know some things about goats does ye?" The man watched the goat's reaction to May's attentions.

"I used to live on a farm with goats and pigs and fowl. I had to milk the goats every morning."

The man took out a small metallic kettle and two cups from his pack. He filled the kettle with water from his water skin and placed it over the fire. He pulled out a small tin can and a spoon and waited for the water to boil. Before long, he had whipped up a nice cup of tea and passed it along to May who thanked him. He said, "Tea es one o'life's simple pleasures. I never miss a chance ta enjoy et, even out here on the mountainside. Cheers ta ye." He lifted his cup to her and then savored his tea.

May had learned from her previous introduction to tea; this time she blew over the top and sipped it slowly. It tasted different from the tea Lady Danae had served her, but it also went straight down to her stomach and warmed her from the inside. She sighed contentedly.

After a short pause, the man said, "Me name es Svane and I've been livin' up en these mountains near half o'me life. Goats es me life and every one es part o'me family, even the ones that go astray." He reached over and patted his goat on the head. "Up here en the clouds, family means different than down en Callamar. Family can mean as many as thirty ta over a hundred souls all livin' together en a cirquen or there can be many families livin' together en a settlement, each with their own cirquen."

"My name is May. I've been wandering for weeks and I need to get back to Callamar but I wanted to see the highlands of Callalande before returning."

Svane looked at her carefully then said, "Et may be true that this es part o'Callalande but we prefer callin' our homeland Torslande. Et don't matter a bunch ta me but ta others, they es fightin' words. Torslande gets snowed en durin' the winter and ef ye go there, ye'll be snowed en till the spring. Ef ye don't want that, then ye should turn around and take the main road enta Callalande."

May asked, "If I go into Torslande, where might I stay until the spring? Will it cost me much coin to spend the winter there?"

They both talked on into the night and soon they grew tired and fell asleep.

Torslande

As the sky dawned grey, the lifting fog revealed the pass not far ahead. The snow on the ground was not thick but neither was it near melting. Svane had his nanny goat on a leash and May was putting her pack on, preparing to ascend.

"Ye're welcome ta follow me o'er the pass, or maybe ye be better ta follow the goat. I'm sure we could find ye a place ta stay at least for a night or two," Svane said as he began walking up the path.

"Thank you," May replied. She took a swig of water then slowly followed Svane. As May and Svane climbed the mountain, May could more accurately gauge Svane's size and height. He was a little bit taller than she and ruggedly muscled. Behind her, May could see clear blue skies far in the distance but could not see the Lake of Bones. Around midday as they squeezed between two steeply sloped peaks, the wasteland behind them fell out of view.

A winterland of snow spread out before her; trees and bushes dotted mountain leas and plains. Sloping down below, barely visible, the highlands of Torslande awaited. Many rocky outcrops broke through the snowy blanket harboring shrubs and grasses in their clefts. A few barren patches of ground remained beneath the larger evergreen trees.

Torslande is a high, hanging plateau along the eastern side of the northernmost extent of the Aerieal Horns. The northern tip of the horns eventually descends into the northern wastelands and the Apollande to Callalande road. Averaging around 10,000 feet above the plains of Callalande, Torslande is not conducive to farming and remains sparsely populated. The land is better suited to grazing by animals smaller than cattle. Tall trees are not very abundant and take longer to mature than their kin further down the mountain. Grasses and small bushes are the norm, with a variety of berries flourishing during the late spring and summer months. Just about everything hibernates or dies during the winter, which can last four months or longer.

Torslande is a land of large extended families that intermarry for personal and political reasons creating a complicated economic and power structure. Many a marriage contract forges an alliance or solidifies a trade agreement between cirquens. Each cirquen contributes two members to a General Council that meets several times each year in Torsberg, the unofficial capital. Torsberg is centrally located and at the top of the only road leading into and out of Torslande. Because this road is the only road large enough to accommodate horse carts, it is easy to regulate trade between Torsberg and the rest of Callalande. The southern families are mostly sheep herders who trade in wool and mutton products. The northern families are primarily goat herders who trade in cheese and hides. As one might imagine, the scarcity of arable land is a major topic of discussion and contention amongst the families. And since scarcity of land means scarcity of resources, they cannot afford to have unlimited immigration to such a small and fragile environment.

Perhaps the most sought-after resource comes from the southern boundary of Torslande. Silver and sapphires have been found and mined in the southern foothills. Decades ago, the Kingdom of Korgynslande made a bid to annex Torslande into Callalande. An eleventh-hour agreement between Callalande and Torslande averted war and preserved Torslande's autonomy only after Torslande agreed to provide a set quota of silver ingots and raw sapphires to Callalande.

Svane and May had been resting their cold feet for a time. "Unfortunately, a never-endin' stream o'traders and quacks steal their way enta the southern mountains, so Torslande has restricted the number o'traders allowed ta do business with Torslande. The General Council was created en Torsberg ta deal with issues o'business, sovereignty, and family territories. Et works, but as with all councils, there's lots o'talk, bickerin', and little action." Svane scrutinized May's reaction when he said "traders and quacks." Svane paused a moment. "We're not far away now. Soon we'll be home and ye can meet me family."

Far into the distance Svane and May could see what looked like a settlement or cirquen; smoke rose from several buildings and blended into the cloudy skies above.

The snow kept getting deeper and each step required a greater effort. By nightfall, they were almost there, and May could see several campfires lighting up the cirquen. Downhill walking was definitely easier than uphill climbing. A few times, May felt woozy from the altitude, and she had to rest and let her head clear up. The air was harder to breathe for her but Svane didn't seem affected.

May heard a child's voice cry out, "Papa! Papa es back with the nanny. Everyone, papa es back." Excited voices could be heard within the cirquen. "There's also someone walkin' with papa."

Svane picked up a small girl who was running towards him and whipped her around in a circle, saying, "How es me little sugar pie?" He turned around holding his girl in one arm while she laughed and waved the other. With a jocular laugh he announced, "Here, look at what our nanny goat has found up en the mountains and brought all the way home ta us." And May walked into the settlement being pulled by the nanny on the leash. May felt awkward as every family member stared at her. Awkward was becoming the new normal for May.

Svane explained, "The nanny and I found her climbin' the mountains. Her name es May. Please give her a warm welcome as she'll be our guest for these next few days till she clears her mind o'fog and snow."

The goat had nearly pulled May into the center of the cirquen when a middle-aged woman came up and offered to take the leash from her. She said with a surprised smile, "Greetin's May, I'm Edel. Svane es me husband and ye're welcome ta stay with our family."

May replied, "Thank you, you have a nice family and a warm hearth."

May looked at the surrounding buildings. There appeared to be eight stone buildings significantly larger than the hovels she had been using for the past few days. Beside one of the buildings appeared to be a horse cart, and beside it appeared to be a small stable, with perhaps some horses. The buildings were arranged in a circle around a central open space, like a wheel's hub. The hub was covered with a tentlike structure made of patchwork hides that kept the snow out. Several campfires lined the hub. The buildings completed roughly three-quarters of a circle, leaving space for goats to gather and huddle during storms. There were many goats milling about with some huddled together staying warm for the night.

With Svane and May's arrival, the cirquen became a hive of activity. Supper was being prepared while many of the goats were huddling together for the night. Many of the children had come up to May offering her simple greetings, marveling at her size. She was almost as large as Svane, which in their view was impressive. Edel directed her girls to prepare a place for May to sleep the night and to show May to her bed. After May had stowed her pack, she reemerged as supper was being served. Supper was the communal meal of the day. The events of the day were discussed followed by story time.

Before May went to sleep, she made sure to secure her pack to keep out curious eyes and hands. Once she had done all she could, she fell asleep on a comfortable straw mattress.

Cirquen

When May awoke the next day, she felt comfortably warm. Several curious onlookers, mostly children, greeted her as she wakened from the morning voices and cirquen activity. As May sat up in her bed, the children launched a battery of questions at her, all at the same time. She felt awkward being the center of attention but fielded questions such as, *where are ye from? What es yer family like? How did ye climb up the mountain?* And so forth. Some of her interrogators were from the other cirquen houses, here to see their new visitor. Edel came over to rescue May and shooed the children off, telling them to make sure the goats didn't stray too far from the hub.

As May slowly stood up, Edel asked, "Did ye have a good night's sleep?"

"Yes, I did, thank you."

"This place es always crazy busy so ye best get used ta et or et'll drive ye mad," Edel said with a laugh and smile.

Edel came over to May and offered her a bread roll, some goat's milk, and goat cheese. May thanked her. The goat cheese and milk had a sharp taste. The bread roll was not as moist as Berthe's rolls but it was freshly baked. As May ate, she noticed that several sacks of supplies had been stacked against the walls toward the back of the house. She must have been too tired to notice the smell of foodstuffs last night.

Edel said, "Anyone or anythin' that shows up new around here es greeted the same way. Ef ye es going ta leave soon, ye may have a hard time travelin' down the mountain road enta Callalande as et's mostly covered en snow. There's no cart traffic en the winter so we are on our own. Just as well, most o'the people comin' up here only care about coin. However, most of the goods we buy from Callalande have ta come up by the road or et don't come up at all."

"How do you make coin here in Torslande?"

"We make coin mostly by sellin' cheese, goats, wool, and sheep. A few people dig up some kind o'rocks close ta the southern mountains. Many people try ta travel up from Callalande ta dig up the rocks themselves but they are sent away when they're caught because they lack permission from the southern families ta dig en Torslande."

Edel looked out the front door then continued, "As for us, we make cheese. We have some customers en Callamar who want a special kind o'goat cheese. They send us blends o'spices that we mix en with the goat cheese then over time, et ages en our cellars and we sell et ta them en Callamar. Svane takes care o'the sellin' and travelin' ta Callamar while we make the cheese here most o'the year. It works well for our family. Svane bought and hauled back all o'the supplies and furniture ye see here en this room. I know ye already told the children, but where'd ye say ye was from?"

"I'm from Borea which is over to the east beyond Callalande's forests and the Rowan River. I grew up on a farm where we raised goats, pigs, chickens, and ducks. They were a handful but they gave us all the food we needed and we sold the extra food stuffs in town for coin. We also had a vegetable garden," May said.

"Ef ye es from Borea, then how'd ye end up here so far away from home?" Edel asked.

"That's a long story which I may tell if I stay longer than a day or two. Someone told me about Torslande and I wanted to see for myself what your homeland is like. I am grateful to your husband Svane for letting me stay a few days. I told him I would pay in coin if I had to stay but I am also willing to do some work, if that would be more useful."

"There'll be no coin needed ta stay en me house but ef ye decide ta stay longer than a few days, we may have ta put ye ta work," Edel said.

"Certainly, I know how to grow a garden. I can milk goats and keep pigs. I can also trap rabbits and prepare hides for selling."

Edel shot May a daggered look when she mentioned rabbits. "Here en Torslande, we don't kill or eat rabbits."

"Oh, I can also do manual labor. But I don't like cleaning up outhouses or goat pellets. How many people live in your cirquen here? And what is the difference between a cirquen and a settlement?" May asked.

"The cirquen es our family home. Some families live like us en stone buildin's but others live en yurts or small tents. Those families and their goats travel around more easily. Ef there are two or more cirquens nearby, then that es a settlement. Some larger settlements have erected buildin's that are jointly owned by the nearby families. Ta the south es Torsberg, which has several families. They also own several storage houses for when traders come up ta Torslande from Callalande. Torsberg es at the top o'the road where et enters Torslande. A checkpoint regulates and inspects all traffic enterin' and leavin'. I don't know much about the families ta the south. I grew up here en the north and I'm too busy ta move around with me family and all," Edel said.

"What do the children do most of the day? I can see outside several people keeping the house clean of pellets, milking goats, and tending goats. Most of the smaller children are playing or gathering around your house to get a good look at me," May said.

"En time the smaller children will learn the chores we do every day. But for now, they're free ta play and explore," Edel said.

May and Edel talked more until Edel said she had to take a turn at milking the goats. Edel took May to the building that was not occupied by a family. Instead, it served as a goat dairy. Inside there were several large milk pots that clearly looked like they had been made somewhere else, perhaps Callamar. Two women were milking the goats by hand and collecting the milk into small jugs. These jugs were then taken and poured into larger pots by some of the younger women.

"This es where we make the cheese. Once the milk es collected, we bring the milk ta a low boil and separate the curds from the whey. The curds get used ta make the cheese and the whey es saved for the families ta drink. We eat some cheese but most o'et gets mixed with the spices which we also store here. The curds are then placed enta separate pots which get stored underground en the cellar. They'll age there until the spring when we take them ta Torsberg for traders ta purchase or Svane sometimes takes them down enta Callamar himself. He'll sell the cheese then buy supplies and haul them back," Edel said.

May was impressed at the level of organization of their endeavor, a well-oiled cottage industry.

"Ef ye decide ta stay, this es where ye'd fit en best, me thinks," Edel said as she began her shift milking goats.

As May walked out of the cheese dairy, she noticed a small building that she had not noticed before next to the horse cart and stables. As she approached the building, she spied several chickens standing next to the front door. A smile appeared on May's face as she realized that they had a small coop. She wandered over to the coop and looked inside. She could see several hens nesting on hay in wooden boxes. *Ah, egg-laying hens*, she thought. *They must have plenty of eggs.* Just as she was turning around, she felt a sharp peck on her ankle. She looked down and saw that she was being attacked by a rooster. She put her foot out and gently shoved him away while she left the coop quickly. *Stupid rooster*! She thought. *I must not have heard him crowing in the morning.* May noted that the chickens kept to themselves and the goats probably knew better than to mess around with the rooster.

"I'm sorry May. That rooster attacks just about anythin' or anyone. Are you all right?" One of the younger girls asked May.

"No blood, no problem," May replied then smiled. "There isn't a rooster I can't handle."

From within the hub, May counted eight stone buildings; each had wooden branches supporting a thatched roof. Svane had said that everyone in the cirquen was his family. She had never seen any farm back home housing as many family members as she now beheld. She asked herself, *how are they all related to each other*? She was confused and resigned herself to learning only their names. Svane appeared to be the patron of the house she was visiting, with Edel, his matron. They appeared to have four children, one boy and three girls. The boy, Jans, was about twelve years while the oldest girl, Yana, was about ten years. The next youngest girl, Rowena, appeared to be about the same age as Yana. The youngest girl, Winter, was no more than six years and the smallest of the four. She was the one Svane had picked up and swung around when they had arrived last night. Jans, Yana, and Winter all had reddish-brown hair with fair skin, very similar to their mother; Rowena however, had black hair and a fair complexion.

The house appeared to be used mostly for sleeping, socializing, and storage, while cooking took place between the front doors and the hub. Privacy was a luxury no one had.

From the hub, every house looked the same. However, not every family looked the same. Some had younger children while others had older children, several about the same age as May. There were several elderly family members socializing and preparing the evening meal. Omnipresent within the cirquen were the goats and their constant bleating. Most of the goats slept and huddled in small covered pens built between the houses as shelter, especially during snowstorms. Several family members from other houses were in charge of the goatherds and had already taken most of the goats out to forage. The goats were good at digging up dried grasses buried beneath the snow. If they could reach the lowest tree branches, they would eat them as well.

Svane returned later that day with many goats in tow. He found May in the house entertaining the children. "I'm afraid the first large snowstorm has hit us hard here en Torslande. Ye might not be able ta make the walk down ta Callalande until the snows are cleared from the road. Has Edel showed ye around the place? Et's not very big but we are the only cirquen for several leagues around."

May responded, "If it looks like I may be snowed in, what would you suggest I do? I was telling Edel that I have several services I can offer in compensation for room and board. Edel also refused to accept my coin."

Svane said, "I take care o'the business and the goats and Edel takes care o'the house. Ef she said no ta yer coin then that es the final word. We can let ye stay as long as ye need ta stay and I'm sure the goat dairy would appreciate any help ye can offer them during the winter. However, I may have a task or two for ye later on that someone o'yer skills might be able ta handle. Most o'me family members here don't know much o'the world down below. Ye appears ta be well traveled and knowed en the ways o'coin and animals. I make trips down ta Callamar once sometimes twice a year ta deliver cheese and goats but sometimes I wonder ef there are better ways ta sell things for us here en Torslande.”

May said, “I actually don’t know much about Callamar except how to get tipsy in a tavern. When I return to Callamar, my plan is to find a place of my own and begin a small business making foods. I don’t want to have a tavern or kitchen, but I do want to make some kind of specialty foods I can sell each day. There is a place I know of where I think I can make this happen but it will take a lot of effort and time.”

“Anyone who can find their way around the forsaken lands can probably accomplish anythin’ they set their mind ta. I think ye can make yer dreams a success. Ye’re young and strong and resilient. I want ta ask, at supper time, I usually tell the children stories. Maybe ye might be kind enough ta share some new stories with us. The children like stories. Not just my children, but all o’the children,” Svane said.

May replied, “I would be happy to tell some stories to anyone who would care to listen.”

Later that night after supper, May told Svane’s family about how she caught large birds such as pheasants without killing them, taking only two feathers from their wings and letting them go. As she talked, a crowd slowly gathered until everyone in the cirquen was listening to May. Then, she pulled out two feathers to illustrate her story. She explained that you don’t have to kill a bird to get feathers and that the bird will regrow the feathers over time. For most of the night, she had an attentive audience.

That night before she prepared for sleep, May went before Svane and Edel. “I have decided that it would be best for me to stay the winter as I do not want to freeze myself up walking down the mountain road to Callamar. If I may, I would like to stay. I promise to make myself useful while working in the goat dairy and helping your family make goat cheese.”

Svane smiled as Edel said, “We’d love ta have ye stay with us.”

Dairy and Garden

The master cheese maker was an older woman named Nata who along with several other family matrons formed the core of their cheese dairy. Other family members milked and tended the goats. The cheese makers knew the secrets to creating the fine cheeses their customers down in Callamar relished.

During the winter months, May provided her services to the cheese dairy. At first she lifted and hauled around the heavy kitchen pots and jars. She also helped milk the goats. She even spent time teaching some of the younger children how to milk the goats. Some of the goats were milked for cheese-making while others were allowed to nurse their young kids. Some of the older goats were preserved as breeding stock while others were ultimately used as food. These goats were butchered to provide meat and to make rennet for the cheese dairy.

Over time, May learned how to boil the milk properly and how to separate the curds from the whey to make the cheese. May also had to learn which jugs of milk could be used for cirquen cheese or for their selling cheese. Each milk jug had a unique aroma which said much about what the goats were eating. Selecting the best-tasting milk made for the best cheeses, a skill which took time to master.

Wood was a necessary though scarce resource within Torslande. The cauldrons constantly needed wood fires to bring the milk to a simmer but not to a full boil. Wood was sparingly harvested from local trees by chopping off only a few branches and not felling the trees. Svane and some of the older boys used special harnesses that he had bought in Callamar, to climb trees and work securely above ground. They also used the harnesses to gather pine nuts, which they ate as a delicacy. In addition to spicy cheese, they made several pots infused with pine nuts. Svane always collected wood from remote parts of Torslande every time he ventured out of the cirquen. He was always bringing home firewood from anywhere he could find it or buy it.

Once separated, the curds went through a thickening process. May learned that rennet was the key to success. She had to wait some months before Nata would tell her where the rennet came from and how to make it. It was a messy process and did not smell very good, as they had to use butchered goat innards to make it. She never really learned the entire secret but she knew enough to make her own cheese someday.

Making cheese was more work than she had supposed, but she learned the entire process from animal to cheese. She also started liking the cheese and developed a pride in her work that she had never experienced before. She cared about the quality of the cheese she made and enjoyed watching others enjoy eating it. As May got to know the cheese-makers better, she told stories about the farm she had lived on, the animals she had raised, and the crops she had harvested.

One day May realized that the cirquen, warmed by the perpetual fires under the tent, created an environment that never cooled to freezing. Beside the houses were small patches of ground that were never covered in snow. She loosened up the soil with her spear and found that it might be possible to grow some vegetables. When she was not working in the dairy, she created an experimental garden patch where she tried planting some of the seeds from the squashes and green beans she had packed from Talean's garden. There was more than enough water to irrigate the patch. She brought a few rocks to shelter any potential seedlings that might sprout. With persistence she was able to get a few seedlings to survive. They grew very slowly and needed lots of care, but they did not die.

Edel's girls watched May's gardening endeavor with curiosity and interest. May explained her plan to the girls and showed them the seeds she was planting. With Edel's girls helping May in her garden, the plants got as much care as they could handle. The odds were long but the fragile garden slowly took hold.

Over time, May observed that Svane liked to take one of his children with him each time he took the goats out to forage. While the goats dug up grasses from under the snow, he built a small fire and made his pot of tea then shared it with his son or daughter. They would talk together drinking warm tea until it was time to go back home. Each of his children was dear to him and he built up his relationship with each one that way. Each child trusted him to be honest with him or her. He also took his wife Edel out on a "tea date" once in a while where they could talk privately about their children, their plans, the cirquen, and the future. They also discussed what to do about Rowena.

Years ago, Svane had rescued Rowena from a disaster where her real parents died in a horrible accident. Svane brought her back to the cirquen where she had lived with them since. Every day they could see the tragedy written on her face. She was very young at the time and did not fully understand what had happened to her and why her life had changed drastically. They had hoped to find her next of kin but were never able to figure out who she was and where she came from. And Rowena herself was too young to be of any help.

Svane was proud of his son Jans. He taught him as many things as he could about life in Torslande and also about the world down below in Callalande. At twelve years, Jans was beginning to have thoughts of his own about the world, how it worked, and his place in it. Svane was not sure where his son's passions would lead him, but he was ready for the day his son might want to leave and move to another settlement or leave Torslande entirely. Svane hoped his son would want to stay with the family but reflecting back upon on his own life decisions, he knew anything was possible.

Frequently, Svane found solace with his goats, his thoughts, and his tea. He spent time reminiscing about his younger days before coming to Torslande. He had many different occupations, one of which was longshoreman. In Callamar, he had labored long and hard to load and unload cargo ships, fishing ships, even warships, all day long. Imported and exported goods from all over the Sea of Calla and beyond passed through Callamar's port. Svane was big, tall, and strong, and hauling large sacks of goods around the wharfs made him stronger. One day, a delivery cart driver fell ill and Svane was recruited to replace him, as Svane possessed basic driving skills. Soon, he was delivering goods by horse cart all over Callamar, Fallmouth, and Torsberg.

Over time, Svane became familiar with the businesses in Callalande. He even traveled the road to Torsberg, delivering goods and getting to know the land and its people. That was when he met his wife, Edel. Edel was helping her father sell cheese in Torsberg's trading house when she caught his eye. He found her strong, beautiful, and possessing a real passion for life and her work. She saw Svane as big, tough, and rough around the edges, the product of a different world and way of life. Eventually, Svane grew tired of working for others and subsisting on a driver's wages. He began to recognize Torslande as an escape from Callamar's never-ending lust for coin. The demands of employers and customers pulled him in many directions at once; consequently, he never found enough time to enjoy his own life. Drinking himself drunk with his work buddies in taverns was never satisfying to him. He heard Torslande's call from afar, offering him a way to live life on his own terms.

As a non-native living in Torslande, he felt welcome and accepted as a responsible cirquen elder. He also knew that he did not want to make any decisions for his children but he did want them to have an appreciation for the simple life he led and had built for them. And as for his wife, he was committed to her. She had lived her whole life in Torslande and had given him a loving family and rarely ever questioned his judgment.

While drinking tea, he pondered, *who es May?* He saw a little bit of himself in her, a self that was not completely lost to time. He asked himself, *why was she climbin' the goat path enta Torslande, alone?* At first, Svane didn't believe May's story about wanting to see Torslande and its goat herders. He initially thought she might be a trader or entrepreneur but had since changed his mind. *Es she runnin' away from somethin'?* Historically, many strangers had found their way into Torslande for countless reasons. Frequently, they were running away from something and usually brought their problems with them. He could tell that May had not been completely truthful about her background. And like Rowena, May had tragedy, that could not be easily erased, etched all over her face. On many nights, he was awakened by May's crying or gasping in her sleep, as if she were choking on fire. He sensed that there might be many demons lurking deep within her mind. He found her nightmares scary at times and could not reconcile them with her polite demeanor and strong work ethic. He figured it would be best to let her be. *She'll talk when she's ready.*

He also sensed that May might just be the person he was looking for to help him discover who Rowena really was and where she had come from. But that would have to wait until the spring.

Feather

It took time for May to discover that Rowena was an adopted daughter who somehow came into Svane's care some years ago. Rowena was quiet compared to her siblings. She did her chores and played with the other children and helped care for her younger sister Winter. She was very courteous but always looked sad.

Some days after May told her stories about catching pheasants, Rowena came up to her and quietly asked to see the pheasant feathers again. May went to her pack and brought out a feather. It was striped brown and black with a gentle curve from quill to tip. Rowena took up the feather and ran her fingers along the shaft, merging its delicate barbs into a single vane structure. She admired its simplicity and elegance. She marveled that feathers could grant the miracle of living flight. A smile crossed her face.

May recognized that Rowena was enjoying the feather very much and told her that she could keep the feather as a gift. Rowena ecstatically accepted the feather as if she had been given a golden crown. She slept with her feather every night since then.

From that day on, Rowena could not get enough of May's presence. She smiled a little more often than before. May taught Rowena how to milk the goats and to help with the cheese making. She also taught her how to tend the squash and the green beans in the garden patch. May taught Rowena and her siblings how to climb trees and collect pine cones.

Rowena's fascination with May did not go unnoticed by Svane and Edel. To Edel, Rowena had transformed from a quiet little girl into a child eager to learn and help out. Her relationship with her siblings improved, and Edel could not figure out how that happened so suddenly. She did notice that once in a while, Rowena would take out her pheasant feather and play with it before putting it away. However it happened, Edel and Svane realized that something amazing had happened and felt a sigh of relief for Rowena and her road to recovery. May also sensed that Rowena was emerging from a shell. May wondered if it was the feather or was she simply Rowena's new friend as she had been to Talean.

As May grew closer to Rowena's siblings, she taught them how to milk goats, handle goats, gain their trust, and how to discipline them when they misbehaved. Wrestling goats without getting kicked or butted was one of May's specialties. She also used the goats to demonstrate hog tying.

May also taught them wrestling, with Jans particularly eager to learn. She showed Jans and others defensive moves her father had taught her, moves such as how to use a larger person's size against them.

Edel watched May's lessons with curiosity. Edel knew Svane would eventually teach all of the boys how to fist fight but would probably teach the girls only how to defend themselves. What May was teaching was something Edel had never seen before. May teaching the girls how to defend themselves was uncommon, but she let it happen.

Edel also noted that May had a strong work ethic. May's industry always seemed to keep her active. Edel thought, *doesn't May ever take a rest?*

Edel asked May, "Where ye come from, are all o'the women as big and strong as ye?"

May paused before answering. "In Borea, most of the women I knew were taller than many of the women I've seen in Callalande and Torslande. I think I am taller and bigger than most women in my hometown. Maybe living and working on a farm made me stronger. I grew to this height when I was around eleven years. I don't remember my mother so I don't know how tall she was. My father is taller than me so maybe I got my height from him."

Edel asked further, "How'd ye learn ta handle animals and wrestle like that?"

"It was mostly my father. I lived alone with him on a farm after my mother died. He taught me everything I know about crops and handling animals. He also taught me to take care of myself against men since he was always suspicious of their motives. He wanted me to be able to defend myself against aggressive men and boys. I have found that most boys and men don't like being shown up by a girl, so I try to be careful when I am around them. I won and lost many fights with boys when I was growing up."

Starry Nights

The weather had been overcast and snowy for most of May's time in Torslande. The mornings were cloudy, even foggy, but then the clouds lifted revealing the Aerieals, snowy and mysterious. Blue skies and clear nights were very rare. The moon seldom appeared except as a soft-white glow, lighting up a few clouds.

But maybe once a fortnight or two, the clouds cleared away and the stars and moon emerged upon the vault of night, the likes of which May had never seen. Even her days staring up at the skies from the desert below did not compare. The stars from Torslande seemed even brighter and closer to her. She could not imagine being any more impressed than those nights in the desert where every night was a revelation. But here in Torslande, she felt she could reach out and pluck the stars from the darkness like apples off of a tree.

And the moon shone so bright and clear that May saw dark patches stretching across the moon's face. She also thought she could see pocks at the edges of shadow and light. The brightness cast a white glow across the snowy landscape very different from the gloomy grey she experienced on most other days. The mountains reflecting the moon's light created a fantasy land of moon-white snow, shadows, and stars.

Again, May felt that something was being revealed to her. She could imagine Reya standing in front of her as she had done that morning along the lakeshore, arms reaching up to the moon and listening to the tinkling of tiny shells, the whispers of sad spirits echoing over the lake and crawling up her spine. The winds of Torslande sometimes sighed through tree boughs, serenading the frosty night.

When the night skies cleared, Edel's brother Jerrod, who lived in one of the other houses with his family, told stories about the stars. He took everyone outside the hub where it was colder. He used the sky as his canvas and his hands as brushes and painted the night with animals and heroes. On one such night, May heard Jerrod tell stories about an ancient hero from a place called Greece. This hero's name was Heracles and he performed many amazing deeds. Jerrod drew Heracles upon the sky and told everyone to remember his name and where his stars could be found above.

On other nights, he told stories about the two bears in the sky. The little bear was always walking around the northern star chasing his tail, the star that never moved. The larger bear always protected the smaller bear as a mother protects her children. Sometimes the sky would fill with glowing green lights that slowly danced like celestial trees swaying in the wind. Sometimes on those green nights, wolves called to the dancing sky and snow hares paused, taking in the green landscape. *Perhaps it was here*, May thought, *where the taboo of harming rabbits may have originated. Maybe they possess some kind of spiritual connection to the mystical lights above or the landscape itself.* She found it touching. Maybe there was something more to rabbits than she had known before. Or maybe rabbits were not much different from people, also looking for answers to the great mysteries of life.

Sometimes instead of story-telling, there would be music and singing. Some of the teenaged cousins and elder aunts showed off their singing voices to the family. They sang traditional songs and ballads of the highlands about love, loneliness, heroism, and shenanigans. One of the boys who had taken up playing the wooden flute accompanied the women's voices in some of their traditional songs. And in a burst of inspiration, one of the older girls had composed a song to accompany one of Uncle Jerrod's stories about the great celestial lion of the spring and summer. Everyone was proud of her singing and encouraged her to sing her lion song often. Her song went as such:

> Lion, lion, shining bright
> In the stars across the night.
> Lo, I spy thy starry crest
> Drifting nobly east to west.
>
> Vaulting o'er the vernal skies
> Dost thou pounce with hungry eyes?
> Crouching through the solstice June
> Dost thou stalk the rosy moon?
>
> The chasing Sun blinds thy crawl
> 'Ere the equinox in fall.
> Waking from thy wintry lair,
> Mark my time another year.
>
> Fearless, stately, silent, strong,
> Lion, lion, hear my song.

On some nights, the flute player and the singers would play and sing dancing music. The aunts and uncles especially loved to dance the traditional dances. The younger children giggled while watching the adults dance. Most of the time, the adults were serious and hard-working. But when they danced, they became happy and carefree. All of the uncles waited for a turn to dance with the new girl, May.

May had not heard much music before. Back in her hometown, a band of musicians would play drums, flutes, mandolins, and lyres to accompany dancing throughout the nights of solstice or harvest festivals. May recalled the music's hypnotic sway; after a brew or two, she danced with some of the local boys. She had felt too self-conscious to enjoy herself but she began noticing boys a little more than she had before.

But in any case, May was living with Svane and his children who were all younger than she was. As May got to know some of the other families socially, she began to meet both boys and girls closer to her own age, a new experience as she had been frequently denied these activities by her father.

Now, egged on by Rowena, May danced with one or two of her neighbors. Some were closer to May's age than Svane's children. Eventually Rowena and her siblings also danced with May. While May found many of the younger men interesting to dance with and talk to, she often found herself thinking of Jonah and his friend Pompey from Callamar more than she cared to admit. Was this the reason she wanted to go back to Callamar? Was Anya right about May making up excuses to go seeking quills in hopes of selling them to Jonah, seeing him again? Now, she realized that her own promise to sell Jonah quills was also the excuse driving her back to Callamar, guiding her to seek out Jonah, even if it meant sneaking into a monastery with a hundred monks.

Departure

Eventually the dreaded day of departure neared. For months, May had lived with Svane and his family, had gotten to know them, and made many friends. She also became used to working in the dairy every day and learning to make cheese. But now she had to refocus her attention on returning to Callamar and her plans.

The snows abated and the days grew longer until the spring equinox brought the first melts. In another month the ground became free of ice and the leas and forests began their spring blooming. The goats were greeted by a land of plentiful grazing. May's tiny garden patch began to grow faster. She and the children were thrilled to find tiny buds on the surviving squash plants and green beans.

One day Svane came up to May and offered to take her with him to Callamar on the cheese cart if she wanted to leave. May said that she would like that very much and began preparing for her departure. When the family found out, they became despondent, especially Rowena. Like Talean, Rowena did not want May to leave. Rowena begged her father to take her with them to Callamar, but he explained that it was too dangerous to drive the cart with three people aboard and all that cheese. He did promise her to revisit the discussion when he returned. Rowena was not satisfied but she was fighting a losing battle with her father. May promised to see her again when she was old enough to ride down the mountainside with her father. For now, Rowena would have to wait.

When the day of departure finally arrived, May was sad as were all of Svane's children. Edel had come to respect May but realized that May's heart was set on something else and she had to let her go. The horse cart and the horses were brought out of their stable and checked over for damages and weaknesses. When Svane was satisfied with its sturdiness, he allowed the cart to be loaded with several of the cheese pots brought up from the underground cellar. Some of the cheese was destined for Torsberg's trading house and the rest for Callamar. May packed up her few belongings, made her farewells, and gave each child and friend a big hug. She promised if she was ever in Torslande again, she would stop by to say hello and tell more stories. Edel and the other matrons of Svane's family told her that she and any future family of hers would always be welcome in their cirquen.

May boarded the horse cart; with a crack of the reins, the horses began their slow haul toward Torsberg. May waved farewell one more time to teary-eyed faces. May also shed a few tears until she could no longer see the cirquen.

The road was bumpy and full of ruts. The horses were out of shape but eventually they learned to work as a team again. Fortunately, all of the cheese pots had been secured with several ropes. Along with the pots, May noticed that Svane had brought along another very different set of ropes and some of their tree-climbing harnesses.

The bumpiness of the journey was compensated by the beautiful springtime bloom of the Torslande leas. The open grasslands were teeming with goat herds and flowers. The weather was beautiful with cloudy skies and gentle breezes during the days. The mountains provided a majestic snowy backdrop to the colorful leas and streams of the Torslande spring. At night, the temperatures dropped significantly but not to freezing. Once in a while, Svane stopped the cart to let the horses graze in the fresh grass and drink from the mountain runoff. Encountering familiar fellow travelers, he stopped to hear gossip and news from afar, stories he would recount once he returned to his hearth and home.

After three days, they could see Torsberg on the horizon. When they arrived, Svane found some of his expected customers eagerly awaiting his arrival in the trading house. Many a trader came up from Callamar seeking cheese, wool, and livestock to bring back to Callamar or Fallmouth and the trading house serviced all. Svane was able to sell about a third of his cheese pots, thus lightening the load for their eventual descent into Callalande.

"This here tradin' house es where we make our first coin." Smiling he whispered, "But the best coin comes when we get down enta Callamar and sell the spicy cheeses ye helped ta make o'er the winter." He continued, "We'll be leavin' en the mornin' but first I'll be treatin' ye ta the special mutton stew they serve here at The Smilin' Sheep Enn. They make some o'the best stews en all Torslande. Since some o'the stories ye told me concern taverns and enns, I figure ye're no stranger ta a good brew o'ale. Someday soon, I'll share a brew with me boy Jans but for now, ye're me guest o'honor."

"Thank you. As you know, taverns and I don't always get along, but with you as my chaperone, I might finally be able to eat and drink in peace," she laughed.

They left their horses and cart in a secure stable, owned by one of Svane's acquaintances, and headed off for the inn. As they entered, May received the usual curious and scrutinizing stares but she felt a definite shift in the atmosphere when Svane followed her into the room. Svane was met with familiar nods and greetings as they both worked their way to a private table near one of the walls, not far from the fireplace. Svane ordered their food and before long, they were eating stew and downing ale.

Svane began, "This es one o'me favorite places. I hope ye like et. There's somethin' I've been meanin' ta tell ye for some time."

May looked puzzled but continued eating her stew in silence.

"I had ta say no ta Rowena comin' along with us as this concerns her. Ye know that Rowena es not mine nor Edel's natural daughter. We adopted her when I found her abandoned and cryin' along the mountain road one day, on me way ta Torslande from Callamar. Edel and I've been carin' for her since that day. Edel has been a wonderful mother ta her but sometimes, I don't think we've been able ta do enough for her."

"How did you come to find her on the road?" May asked.

"I don't know for certain whether she was comin' ta or leavin' Torslande en a tradin' cart that somehow fell o'er the side o'the road. Below the road where I found her cryin' was a lot o'debris from a cart that had fallen down the mountainside. The mountain es very steep and I wanted ta go down ta investigate the crashed cart but the weather es always cold, the wind blows dangerously, and I had no way ta get down the mountain. The road doesn't switch back along that stretch, so I couldn't just take me cart down ta see the wreckage. You probably noticed all the extra ropes I've en the cart. I've collected those ropes o'er the years hopin' I'd build up the courage ta use them ta climb down the mountainside and investigate. As ye can see, I'm very big and heavy. While I may be strong, I'm no mountain climber. I'm a goat herder. I also don't want other people ta know how I found Rowena, so I never sought anyone's help. Then, I met ye and I got ta thinkin', maybe ye might be able ta help me. Ye've been nothing but bold and brave when et comes ta climbin' trees with the children. When I show ye where the cart fell down and ye sees how hard et es ta get down the mountain, I'll understand ef ye doesn't want ta help or take that risk. But ef ye would be able ta help me search the wreckage, I'd be most grateful and en yer debt."

"As you can see, I'm not very old but I'm not afraid of challenges. I'll certainly help you if I'm able."

Descent

The next morning, the fog was slowly burning off as the spring sun broke through the clouds. May and Svane secured and rebalanced their cargo before finally beginning their descent into Callalande. The road was wide enough to allow the passage of opposing traffic. Keeping one's horses and pack animals calm and unstressed was paramount. The road descended nearly 10,000 feet with very few places to stop and rest. There were many switchbacks in some places but also several long gentle stretches lasting for miles. With good weather, the trip could be completed in a day.

Eventually, Svane found the place where he believed he had found Rowena. He stopped the cart along the mountainside then secured the brakes and tied the wheels to the mountainside, calming the horses with eye blinders and a few well-earned carrots. May and Svane approached the road side and looked down the mountain. The height was dizzying. After staring for some time, May thought she could see the broken timbers of a horse cart smashed amongst some rocks way down below. The mountain near the road was steepest. Far below, the slope became gentler and climbable without a rope.

"It's a long way down there. Well near a hundred feet or more. What was your idea on how to get down there?" May asked curiously.

"Aye, I know. That's what's scared me most over the years. I've been makin' this here knotted rope for the descent but that never comforted me. So I thought ye or I could also use a harness that can be worn and lowered with the climber. If I wear the harness while I lower myself down using the rope and I slip, the harness can save me until I can get back up. That's why this would be better as a two-person operation," Svane responded.

"Do you think the rope and harness can hold your weight?" May asked.

"Aye, I tested the harness back home by hangin' from trees. What I don't know es ef I can pull myself back up the mountain after goin' down. I've always had trouble pulling meself up the pine trees back home."

"What if I go down instead of you? I'm not as heavy and you are stronger than I so you would have an easier time helping pull me back up the mountain," May offered.

"Are ye sure ye want ta do that?" Svane asked.

"It makes more sense to have you pulling me up rather than the other way around. Right now, the weather looks good. If we start now, we could be done by midday," May estimated.

May and Svane took out, uncoiled, and assessed the ropes they had. May fitted a harness onto herself. She realized that Svane had modified the cart to act as a secure anchor for their rope against any sudden failures. They secured the knotted rope to the cart then tossed it over the edge of the road and saw that it was long enough to reach the gentler slope below. Svane secured the harness rope to the cart and also used himself as an anchor. He would bear much of May's weight when lowering her while she used the knotted rope to lower herself down.

"All right, are you ready Svane?" He nodded. "Send me down," May instructed.

"All right, ye be careful and ef ye have any problems or get scared, yell ta me and I'll bring ye up right away. We don't need ta be heroes today," Svane said.

May nodded. She slowly worked her way over the edge and then disappeared down the side of the mountain. May soon realized how precarious her position was and almost changed her mind. Snow wedged into many clefts shaded from the sun made it difficult to find secure footholds. But May gathered her courage and slowly lowered herself down knot by knot until, before she knew it, she had reached the gentle slope. She now understood that apparent distances up or down could be very deceiving. A short distance could seem infinite when dangling from a rope. She also had a harder time seeing the debris from the mountainside than from the road. Soon she ran out of knotted rope but her harness rope was still long enough. She yelled up to Svane that she was going to remove the harness, as the mountain was not as steep anymore and lots of rocks provided secure hand and foot holds. Svane nervously monitored her progress from above.

Step by careful step May descended and soon spotted broken cart timbers along with the remains of cargo crates, cheese pots, and barrels. Next to one of the shattered pots she found a small, translucent blue stone similar to the two stones she had found on the wolf hunter. She held it up to the light then put it in her pocket. She also found the skeletal remains of a horse in harness.

Not far from the wreckage, May found two human skeletons twisted out of shape. She realized that this could be all that remained of Rowena's parents. Something around the neck of one of the skeletons glistened in the sun – a half-buried necklace. Bending down, May unclasped it and found it to be a locket. She was unable to open it and tucked it away in her pocket. Near the other skeleton she discovered, attached to a decaying leather belt, a tarnished brass buckle embellished with the initials "MB." A further search revealed a small locked box and a tiny key that appeared to fit the lock.

The shifting shadows and the moaning winds made her realize how long she had been searching the mountainside. As she worked her way back to the harness and knotted rope, she noticed something she had missed on the way down: a small leather satchel nestled under a bush. The remains of a blue and white ribbon had been sewn into its seams. Picking it up, she secured it to her belt and then put on her harness.

"Svane! I am ready to come back up!" Soon she felt the tension in the rope increase. She began to pull herself up. Now she understood the reason for Svane's fears, as going up required different muscles from those used for going down. Svane's strength made her exertion much easier to bear as she slowly, awkwardly ascended to the road. Her feet slipped once or twice on the icier ledges but the harness held firm. Eventually, she made it to the road and heaving herself up, she rolled onto the road, exhausted, with both the leather bag and lockbox by her side.

Breathing heavily from her exertion, she began to feel nauseous and dizzy.

"Are ye all right? Ye don't look very good right now," asked Svane.

"I'll be all right. I'm dizzy and … and I want to throw up," May replied.

"Make sure ye continue breathin' strongly and close yer eyes for a while," Svane said.

May closed her eyes and took deep breaths; eventually, she began to feel better again. She crawled to the cart then used the cart to help herself stand up. When she felt comfortable standing, she showed Svane the box and satchel she had retrieved. Neither Svane nor May had any idea what she had found, but they both agreed that examining the items should wait until they got down the mountain. Svane secured the two items along with the ropes in the cart. He readied the horses for travel and they slowly resumed their descent into Callalande.

"Ye did very well and I'm very proud o'ye for goin' down the rope. I think I'd have been sick had I gone down the mountainside. I got dizzy just watchin' ye go down," Svane said.

"I hope the bag and the box will help us solve Rowena's mystery," she said with a satisfied smile. "I'm going to close my eyes for a while." She did not tell Svane about the blue stone, necklace, or buckle, at least not yet.

Their cart continued descending mile after mile until at long last, they entered Callalande.

PART 4

Into Callamar

Leaving the northern foothills of the Aerieal Horns, the mountain road intersects the great northern road. Two buildings feature prominently at this intersection, the Northern Barracks and the Last Chance Inn and Tavern. The Northern Barracks house a contingent of the Duke's soldiers that guard all vehicles traveling north towards Torslande and the Apollande-to-Callalande road. The Last Chance Inn and Tavern is the last stop for food and supplies before attempting the ascent to Torslande or traveling the wastelands to Apollande. Going south, the great northern road soon meets up with then follows the Lycus River. The river meanders through wild grasslands before encountering the first of many creeks running down the Horns. Orchards, farms, and ranches checker the landscape with shades of pink, white, green, and gold. To the east, the grasslands sprout scattered trees that slowly merge into the northern fringes of the Duke's Forest. To the south, scattered farms coalesce into the small villages of Cherry Grove and Dolmen until they merge into the sprawl that comprises the northern limits of Callamar. The river passes through Callamar's modest neighborhoods before finishing its journey to the harbor and the sea.

The great northern road is wide enough to accommodate carts passing in both directions. Once out of the foothills, it is a two-day crawl down the gentle slopes into Callamar. Before reaching Callamar, the road passes a great reservoir. Decades ago, Callamarans built a large earthen dam fitted with three sluice gates. The dam was built to capture and preserve mountain runoff as a hedge against droughts, quenching a thirsty land. While Callalande never resembled the northern wastelands that May had crossed, one could not reliably know how often drought conditions might occur.

Generations before Duke Olan arrived, droughts motivated Callalande's leaders to design and construct the great dam and its irrigation networks. Or was it the rapid growth of the ever-thirsty orchards and farms demanding irrigation? Or was it the unbridled growth of an urban population and its burgeoning industries? In any case, the dam provided a reservoir and the reservoir provided water. For Callamarans, it was a large public works project that met the needs of the day, aesthetically pleasing enough so that people ventured north to the reservoir for relaxation and recreation. More fruit and crops were grown than could be consumed in all Callalande so Callamar and Fallmouth developed an export economy of fruit, fish, and other abundant food products under the governance of Duke Olan.

As Svane and May emerged from the mountain road, their progress increased as the road flattened. Some nights they had either to rest in a roadside hovel or to camp under their cart along pullouts near the river bends. The spring weather was quite comfortable with short cold rain squalls here and there, nothing a good cup of tea couldn't fix.

Frequently along the road south, Svane and May encountered carts, pulled by teams of four or more horses, fully laden with rocks. These carts had come from one of the large quarries established along the base of the Horns. Year after year, the carts brought a steady flow of rock and stone into Callamar that fed a growing demand for building materials of higher quality – higher than the brick ovens near the junkyard could provide. Many a cart laden with clay for brick making or pottery passed up Svane and May. Svane had to remain vigilant so as not to get run off the road.

Weary and relieved, Svane and May entered Callamar from the north, passing by several indoor marketplaces and outdoor bazaars. Entering from the north allowed for a good view of the Duke's Palisade built against the steepest base walls of the Aerieal Horns. Three of Callamar's largest structures were also visible from within the city. The Cathedral of the Holy Cross arose multiple levels above the streets with the bell tower rising another two levels above its rooftop. The offices and rooms of the clergy and novices overlooked the Lycus River as it bent from south to southeast within the city. The two towers and dome of the Temple of the Embracing Goddess as well as the Temple of the Dawn could be seen further to the southwest, as could the cylinder of Saint Dominic's Scriptorium.

The neighborhoods surrounding the Duke's Palisade were filled with the more prosperous of Callamar's citizens. Government officials, wealthy merchants, retired dignitaries, and the older established families all had large manors or estates there. Beyond these neighborhoods emerged luxe markets that provided gourmet foods and masterly crafted goods. Within these markets Svane found customers for his spicy goat cheese.

Svane and May wound their way through Callamar's wider streets, but as they got closer to their destination, Svane turned into a narrow back alley and then pulled up alongside the rear entrance to The Spicy Hunk where Svane and May secured the cart. Svane was greeted by a man who seemed excited to see him.

"Svane! What a surprise! It is good to see you early in the spring," the man said.

"I'm doin' well and good ta see ye, too. I've brought ye the first o'this year's cheeses."

The man came over to their cart. "May, this es Gaius. He's the proprietor o'this fine establishment, The Spicy Hunk. Gaius, this es May, the newest member o'me family and dairy assistant. She helped make this season's batch o'cheese."

Gaius took out his cheese corer and tasted a small sample. "Young woman, this cheese is excellent. I think it will need only another month in the cellar before I sell it for top coin. Svane brings us the most sought-after goat cheese in my whole emporium. And this year, your efforts are much appreciated. I think this year's formula which we tweaked from last year has made us an even better batch of cheese. Congratulations on your efforts." As Gaius praised them both, he whistled to several of his workers to collect the cheese pots and take them into his extensive cellar.

The Spicy Hunk featured gourmet cheeses imported from all over Callalande, Borea, Korgynslande, Apollande, and Torslande, even from as far away as Kraagen. Cheddars, edams, soft cheeses, goat cheeses, moldy cheeses, and much more could all be found and bought within his emporium. His clientele had the taste buds and the coin to afford what he stocked.

Svane and Gaius went inside the office to complete their business while May stood aside a little and watched Svane play the role of businessman.

Firstly, she noticed a change in his tone of voice as he switched into full business mode. May found it curious to watch how he dealt differently with his customers. Svane was very congenial and mindful of his manners, different from how Ma talked to her suppliers back in Northcamp. Svane was receiving his coin from Gaius with what appeared to be a satisfied smile and a commitment to provide more pots before the summer's end. Gaius instructed his workers to provide Svane with two pots containing spices along with several empty pots equal in number to what they had just offloaded from Svane's cart.

As Svane was concluding his business, May wandered around the emporium never having imagined that there could be so many varieties of cheese in the world. They came in all kinds of packaging from ceramic pots, clay pots, cloth-wrapped bricks, wax covered bricks and wheels, and even glass jars. She even noticed a special machine capable of cutting off chunks of cheese to exactly the same size. May thought, *what a place*! When Svane had concluded his business, he told May that he was ready to leave. He bade Gaius a friendly goodbye until the summer's end and then they drove away to their next stop, The Cheese Larder.

The Cheese Larder was located towards the east side of town but nearer to the western side of the Lycus River. The Cheese Larder was not as large as The Spicy Hunk but did have clientele that preferred the taste and texture of nuts and dried fruits with their cheese. This was where Svane sold the pots that contained the pine-nut cheese they hauled down the mountain. Svane introduced May to Alyna as his business assistant, as Alyna was the proprietor of The Cheese Larder. May seemed equally impressed by her cheese shop but noticed that she also featured dried fruits and nuts for sale. Svane conducted his business similarly and took stock of some replacement pots as well as a pot filled with assorted nuts for filling the next orders for his summer delivery.

As Svane concluded his business, he told May that this winter and spring had been good for both of his customers and he received the full payments he was expecting. He told May that they would need to find a place to stay the night before making his rounds for supplies to haul back up to Torslande.

With the profits from Svane's cheese deliveries, he was able to get a modestly priced room at one of the inns close to one of the larger market plazas in the city. Svane did not tell May how much coin he had received but she could tell he made a good many golds and silvers.

Once Svane and May settled into their room and secured their cart and horses in the barn, they began examining the items that May had retrieved from the crash site. As May took up the leather bag, its seams burst open spilling several items across the tabletop: a small leather rollup, a few hair ribbons, several pieces of shriveled fruit, and a small tattered doll stuffed with straw.

Visibly anxious, May untied and unrolled the leather rollup onto the tabletop. May and Svane were astonished. The flattened roll contained a large collection of feathers! There were feathers of all sizes, shapes, and colors tucked into various pockets. May had no idea what birds the feathers came from but they were all there, neatly organized. May was astounded by the collection and now understood why Rowena had taken so eagerly to the feather she had given her. Tears came to May's eyes as she realized she was looking at part of a little girl's life that had been suddenly and violently stolen away and lost. Svane was equally surprised by what they had discovered.

Svane took the small key and fitted it into the keyhole of the wooden lockbox. Svane slowly turned the key, encountering some rusty resistance; he was careful not the break the key while turning it. He jiggled the key until finally he heard a squeaky click. The box opened. Inside were a host of letters and papers. Some looked like official documents possessing cracked wax seals. Svane couldn't make heads or tails of the words. Svane looked at May, "Unless ye can read these, –"

May moved her head side to side.

"– we'll have ta hire someone ta read them for us."

"I also found these." May pulled the locket, the buckle, and the blue stone out of her pockets and set them onto the table.

Svane picked up the stone and examined it in the lantern light. "I thought I saw ye pickin' up a few things down the mountainside. Where did ye find this?"

"I found it near some of the shattered pots."

Svane commented, "The buckle probably came off o'the man's belt and the stone might've come from one o'his pockets."

"I saw two skeletons and figured they were a man and a woman. I found the box in the cart wreckage and the bag further up the mountainside. What is that blue rock?"

Svane answered, "Et might be a rock called a sapphire. I've never seen one as large or as clear as this one before. There's a low-grade sapphire mine en the south o'Torslande but I've never been there."

May picked up the stone and looked at it in the light. "I've never seen anything like it before. It does look kind of pretty."

Svane turned his attention to the buckle. "This es not a cheap buckle. Hmmm, 'MB.' Et might be the man's initials or a monogram. And the locket, did ye look enside yet?"

May replied, "No I haven't been able to open it. I don't have the fingers for it."

"Let me see what I can do." Svane picked up the locket and scrutinized it then slowly slipped his thumbnail into a small crevasse in the locket's hinge and pulled out a locking pin; the locket slowly opened. Inside Svane found a very small portrait of a woman. "Ef ye found this on Rowena's mother then I would guess that this might be a picture o'Rowena's grandmother." From inside the locket slipped out a small tarnished key. Svane reassembled the locket, planning to give it to Rowena when he returned home.

Svane and May looked at the items in their entirety. "I think we need to find someone who can read these papers. We also need someone we can trust to keep them confidential," May said.

"We might be able ta take them enta a government office en the city somewhere and get someone ta read them ta us," Svane commented.

"I don't think that's a good idea. Call me crazy but I don't trust people I meet for the first time. They could tell us anything they want then confiscate the papers. I think I know someone who might be able to help us."

Street Fight

The next day, May told Svane that she wanted to show him what she was planning to do about finding a place to live in Callamar. May described to him the mansion with all of the feral dogs. May managed to find her way back to the main road on the east side of town that she and Anya had first taken into and out of Callamar. Eventually they were able to find the mansion and like before, it was infested with dogs.

May pointed, "That's the place I want to take over."

Svane took one look at the place and then looked back at May as if she had gone completely mad. "What're ye goin' ta do with a place like that and how're ye goin' ta take et away from all them dogs? Are ye goin' ta kill them all?"

May explained her plan to Svane. "I have been carrying around some wolf's bane ever since I left Borea. I figure I need to feed it to them then place a barrier of wolf's bane around the entire house so they will never want to come back inside."

Again, Svane looked at her like she was crazy, "And how're ye goin' ta accomplish that? Those dogs'll eat ye alive before they eat any o'yer wolf's bane. And them dogs don't look much like wolves anyway. Ye'd be better off burnin' the whole house ta the ground then rebuildin' et yerself."

"Now that's an idea I never thought of," May said.

"I'm pullin' yer leg. Ye might end up burnin' down half the city ef ye light that place up en flames. The city guard would arrest ye and hang ye from the palace wall."

"You're probably right. But I'm going to try ejecting the dogs one way or another."

Svane shook his head, but maybe May was crazy enough to actually pull it off. "En either case, ye need ta do some serious plannin'. Let's get back ta the enn."

Surrounding this house of dogs were a few buildings on the east side of Callamar. May and Svane could hear the clinking of a blacksmith's hammer coming from a small workshop next door to the dogs' house. She saw a young boy playing outside the blacksmith's shop with another, smaller boy. A little further down was a general store that looked neglected.

As May and Svane set off back towards the inn, May realized that they were being followed. Svane said, "Don't ye worry. I'll take care o'them ef they try ta do anythin' stupid. Let's just walk down the middle o'the street as ef we have no fear o'them."

May was carrying Anya's hunting knife under her tunic, easily accessible if needed. By the time they had walked a good distance further, four thugs were following them down the street. Most other people and residents of the neighborhood had withdrawn inside their houses. As they walked on, two burly looking men stepped into the street ahead of them, blocking their way.

The larger man, appearing to be the boss, spoke out to Svane, "Where'd ya think you're going in such a hurry with my coin? Why don't ya just hand it over to me and I will forget ya stole it from me."

"Listen up ye little punks, ye'd best be gettin' out o'me way or I'll clean up the road with all yer faces." Svane curled his fingers into two tightly packed fists and kept walking straight towards the boss. May was not sure what to do so she kept pace with Svane as he approached the boss without breaking his stride. The boss looked a little confused as Svane kept coming right at him.

"So that's how ya want it, then." The boss swung his arm back for a roundhouse punch at Svane's face. Svane quickly brought up his left arm to block the boss's punch then followed up with a wicked gut punch straight into the boss's stomach. The boss grunted then countered with a blow to Svane's ribs. The boss followed his rib punch with a quick spin and blow to Svane's back and legs. Svane was solid, sturdy, and hard to knock over, but that combination staggered him, almost knocking him down.

Svane counter spun, bringing his elbow straight into the side of the boss's face. The boss staggered as Svane followed with another gut punch then double fisted a blow to his back, knocking him to the ground. He gave the boss a quick rabbit punch and left him writhing in agony. The boss's henchman moved in to help his boss as he saw him trading blows with Svane. Before realizing what had happened, the henchman was hit head-on by a bull rush from May.

When May saw Svane and the boss trading punches, she used her quick reflexes to seize the initiative against the boss's henchman standing in front of her. The henchman was focused on Svane being the bigger threat and was surprised when May slammed her forehead into his jaw, knocking him to the ground. She got a few good blows to his face and head before he had a chance to recover and rebalance. By then he was flailing wildly and May was able to knock him out with a quick kick to the groin and a fist to the face.

As Svane was finishing off the boss, May turned around to see the four thugs behind them rushing forward. "Behind you, Svane," she called out as she quickly drew her knife, punching and slashing one of the charging thugs across his face, drawing blood. She dodged the second charging thug by crouching down low then sweeping his legs, tripping him to the ground. Svane turned around in time to catch one of his new assailants with a powerful blow squarely on his temple, knocking him out instantly. The last thug quickly realized that the fight had gone from 6 vs 2 to 2 vs 2. He turned around and ran away as fast as he could run. Svane picked up the man May had knocked to the ground and lifted his body up high then slammed his face into the ground, knocking him out. The man with the cut and bloodied face saw both Svane and May looking directly at him. As May and Svane got a good look at the young man in his late teens, he took off running.

The fight was over. May hogtied the boss and his thugs with some ropes she found by the side of the road. May dragged the thugs to the roadside while Svane dragged the boss's face through the dirt. Svane crouched down and spoke into his ear. "Didn't I tell ye I'd clean up the road with yer face? Believe me next time." Just for good measure, May picked their pockets before leaving.

Svane and May continued walking down the road. Svane was watching May cleaning off and sheathing her knife. With a jolly good laugh and a gentle hand to her shoulder, Svane said, "And I thought et was I who was protectin' ye. Ye had me back covered the whole time. Ye are truly full o'surprises, me lass. Maybe ye really can clear that house o'dogs after all. How about a cup o'tea when we get back ta the enn?"

May smiled and replied, "Of course."

May realized that Svane was much stronger than she had thought and was also a good street fighter. Her confidence grew as she could trust him by her side. He must also be keeping many interesting stories and secrets. They continued on to the inn without further ado.

Nighthawk

Later that night, May and Svane took off from the inn and walked towards the monastery. Svane was carrying two of their knotted ropes, one with a small grappling hook attached to one end.

"I still think this es a bad idea," Svane warned. "We might get caught or we might end up hunted by the night watch. They might even recognize us as the gang that replaced their favorite east side thugs and declare us a menace ta Callamar. We might even rot en jail. That would be a good story ta tell me family back home."

"We won't get caught. I just have to talk to him."

Now Svane felt obligated to help May in return for her climbing down the mountainside. He convinced himself that they both needed the documents read so they could help Rowena. The reward outweighed the risk, so he followed May. He sighed, "Ye better be right."

They finally arrived at the monastery. It was completely surrounded by a wall, steep but climbable.

"We can climb the wall near one of those trees and observe what's going on. It looks like the rooms have shuttered windows and some of them are open. I recall he said he had a room overlooking the sea. With luck, I might be able to see which room he lives in," May said.

"Aye, let's get started," Svane replied.

Before they climbed the wall, Svane insisted that May put some camouflaging grease on her face, just in case something went wrong. May was wearing her stealth shoes and darker clothes with a hood. Using the half-moon's light, they watched the activities of the monastery for some time. May thought she saw someone come to one of the lighted windows; she tapped Svane on the shoulder and pointed to the window with the figure standing in it. "I think that may be the right window. I need the rope."

"All right, now ye be careful. If there be any problems, ye sprint back here as fast as ye can and we get away together, right?" Svane instructed.

"Right," and then May went down the outer wall using one of the knotted ropes Svane had let down from the top of the wall. She quickly crossed the open space to the dormitory wall. At the bottom of the wall were many bushes and small trees. The wall was built of variously shaped stones, so there were plenty of hand and foot holds for climbing. She easily climbed the wall but she could be spotted by someone looking in her direction.

When May reached the lighted window, she slowly brought her eyes up and over the sill and spied into the room. She saw that the monk in the room was indeed Jonah and he was sitting at his desk in his brown robe with his back to her. He was writing something. A smile crossed her face. *He looks cute at his desk*, she thought. She decided to get his attention.

In a voice somewhat louder than a whisper she called, "Jonah." He turned and looked to his door. He was about to speak when May said, "Over here by the window. It's May from The Charging Boar." Jonah turned his head to the window and then he saw the top of her head, black-striped with eyes reflecting the candlelight.

"What are you doing here? How did you climb up the wall? How …" Jonah got up and walked over to the window.

"Can I come in, please? My arms are getting tired," May said.

Jonah hesitated for a moment then he recognized her voice and remembered that night at The Charging Boar. "Yes, get in before someone sees you."

May quickly hoisted herself head-first through the window and almost fell onto the floor. She slowly stood up.

"What are you doing here? Are you crazy? If anyone sees you in here, there will be big trouble," Jonah said in a hushed voice.

"I'm sorry. I need to talk to you. You are the only person I know who might be able to help me and a friend of mine out with some difficulties we are having," May explained.

Jonah looked a little puzzled. "What do you want?"

"I have several documents that I am unable to read. I was hoping you could come visit me at the Marketplace Inn near the Lycus River in Callamar and read them to me."

Jonah shot her a suspicious glare. "You want me to read documents and you didn't bring them with you?"

May hesitated. "If I do get caught, I don't want to lose the papers or have them confiscated."

"I cannot just leave the monastery without triggering another interrogation. I would need to get a pass, and they're not going to let me leave to have dinner with the same woman I saw months ago much less visit the Marketplace Inn."

"All right, point taken. Maybe I could sneak you out without anyone seeing you, leave, and then sneak you back in? I have help, too."

Jonah was aware of how crazy all this sounded, but he was also curious. She was taking a big risk by sneaking into the monastery; therefore, the papers must be valuable to her. And what was he going to get out of all this besides being disciplined, interrogated, and labeled disloyal?

"I don't think I can help you. There's too much risk and I've been under the abbot's thumb for a long time. I just want things to return to normal again."

"What if I give you several feather quills for your services?" May offered.

Jonah paused a moment, remembering their conversation outside of the Boar that night. "How many quills do you have?"

"I think I have around twenty or so. They are pheasant quills."

Twenty quills! He thought. *She must really want to know what those papers say.* "Did you say twenty?"

"Yes and maybe a little silver to boot."

"Quills and silver?" he said. He thought, *this sounds too good to be true.* "Well, I don't know. Tonight is not good."

Grabbing the knotted rope slung around her shoulder she said, "How about tomorrow? I can sneak you out of your room using this knotted rope. When I leave, I will show you how it works. You can use it to climb down the wall and back up again."

"I have to admit that the idea sounds intriguing but I don't know how I'd explain having pheasant quills should anyone notice. Like I said, there's lots of trouble to be had if I get caught."

"All right. I can return to your window tomorrow after everyone else has gone to sleep and have you back in here before dawn. I will also pay you in full before sneaking you out of the building."

Jonah said, "I'll let you know tomorrow if I can do it or not. I have to make some plans if it is going to work out."

May felt fairly certain that Jonah would not tell anyone in the monastery about their meeting tonight as it would likely get him into trouble no matter how he spun the story. May reached into one of her many pockets and pulled out five silvers and set them down on his desk. "Take this as a down payment. Let me demonstrate how to go down the rope."

May set up the rope using the grappling hook and secured it inside of the window sill. "Watch me climb down and when I get to the bottom, release the hook and drop it down to me. Until tomorrow?" She gave him a quick smile and then turned to back out of the window. Jonah leaned out of the window and watched her climb down knot by knot. When she reached the bottom, the tension in the rope slackened. He then released the rope and let it fall down to her. May coiled up the rope and then sneaked her way back to the wall where Svane was waiting.

Jonah saw May work her way to the monastery wall and could see a vague figure sitting atop the wall waiting for her. May climbed the wall then disappeared over into the morning. He now realized that he had forgotten to ask her if her friend was the same girl whom he met with May all those months ago back at The Charging Boar. He was trying to imagine what documents May possessed and wondered why she didn't just hire someone else in the city. May was playing with fire and he was wary of getting burned.

Fire or no fire, he decided to play her game. He looked at the five silvers stacked on his desk. He quickly took them and hid them away. He straightened up his desk, blew out his candles, then lay down on his bed and began working out what he was going to do and say and to whom tomorrow. He fell asleep with the notion that no woman he had ever known had gone to such lengths just to talk to him.

May and Svane jumped off the wall and quickly stole away back to the main road and into the city.

"Are we far enough away yet?" May asked.

"Aye we are. What did yer acquaintance have ta say?" Svane replied.

May gave Svane a full account of their conversation and plans.

"Let me get this straight. First ye sneak enta the monastery ta talk ta this monk boy ye met some months ago without the letters ye wanted him ta read for ye and now ye want ta go back tomorrow and steal him out? We bring him back here ta the enn. He reads us the letters en the box then we sneak him back enta the monastery as ef nothin' happened. Does that sound right ta ye?" Svane finished.

May nodded, "Yes, that sounds about right."

"And ef ye were me girl, I'd probably have ta swat ye a few times ta get some sense enta that head o'yers. But ef I tried, ye'd probably beat me up and leave me hogtied on the floor. At least ye figured out a way ta spend some o'the coin ye picked off those thugs."

Svane said after thinking for some time, "What could make this plan o'yers work better would be ef we found another enn closer ta the monastery so we wouldn't have ta walk so far durin' the night."

"Good idea." May said.

"I need some tea," Svane said tersely as they made their way back to the inn.

Sneaking Away

May and Svane paid the reckoning at the Marketplace Inn then got into their cart and set off. Svane purchased various supplies to take back to Torslande. He bought some specialty hay for the nanny goats, some new ropes to supplement his present supply, some bags of tubers and beets, a few gifts and candy for the cirquen families, some new crockery and furniture for the cirquen, and a supply of teas for himself. By the time they were done, they had found an inn much closer to the monastery.

Svane said with a big grin, "All right, this place will cost us more than the last one. How much o'that pilfered coin ye got left?"

May dug into her pockets and came up with about twenty-two silvers. "I have to save some to pay Jonah." She handed twelve silvers over to Svane.

"This may get us through a night ef we choose not ta eat any supper. I'm sure that Jonah friend o'yers es goin' ta be hungry after all the readin' we ask him ta do, right?" Svane said.

May reached back into her pockets and brought out a gold coin and placed it on the table next to the silvers.

"Aye, now that's more like et," Svane said. "Me wonders how many golds that boss-guy really had," he chuckled. "But this will do nicely."

Svane found a place to stow his cart and secured all of his new cargo. He cracked his knuckles, pointed at and said to the owner, "Ef I find anythin' es missin' when I come back, I'm comin' after ye." And the owner assured him nothing would happen to his cart or cargo. Svane paid the owner his fee and left.

Inside their new room, May brought out the things she thought she would need to make this night work. She had an extra tunic with hood and pantaloons for Jonah to wear so he would not look like a monk on the run. She had the rope with grappling hook and the payments she had offered him, twenty feathers and ten silvers. She also had her dagger in case there were more thugs about.

By evening, many clouds smothered the moon and stars, helping her blend with the night. Svane gave his knotted ropes and a few extra shorter ropes to May. "Here, take these for yerself since ye seem ta be fond o'hogtyin'. Et's certainly better than hurtin' or killin'."

May said, "Thank you. I have an extra knife if you'd like to carry it."

Svane opened his hands then clenched them into fists back and forth a few times. "No thank ye. I already have two weapons. Ye see hands, weapons, hands again, weapons again, easily concealed."

Finally, Svane and May set out from the inn to the monastery. From atop the wall, May could see the open window of Jonah's room. However, this time a pair of monks were walking around the outer dormitory, in full view. They were talking about which flowers and bushes would need to be tended to in the morning after prayers. May made a mental note not to trample the flowers tonight. Eventually, the monks disappeared around a corner. May saw Jonah come to the window and look around. He waved at them then went back inside.

May climbed down the outer wall and sneaked across to the dormitory, avoiding the flowers, and then looked around one last time before climbing the dormitory wall. When she reached the window, she found Jonah waiting for her. She heaved herself up through the small window and then somersaulted into the room landing in a crouched position, before standing up.

Jonah had already made a copy of himself sleeping in his bed by rolling up some of his spare robes under his blankets.

May took out the spare clothes she was carrying and told him to change into them, as his robe would make him conspicuous. "Don't worry, the clothes are clean, and I will turn around while you change." She sat down on his bed and looked out the window at the cloudy night. Jonah changed quickly then put his robe under his blankets with the other garments. May pulled out the feathers and silvers and gave them to him. He quickly stowed them deep into one of his desk drawers. "All right, let's go," he said. May explained that they would leave the rope hanging until they returned. The rope appeared to blend in with the wall stones and would probably not be noticed. May went first down the rope and waited at the bottom for him. Jonah blew out the candle then went out the window. At first, he was scared, but then remembered how he used to climb trees when he was younger. He took the rope and very slowly knotted his way down to the bottom. May whispered, "Don't step on the flowers."

"Right," he said. They quickly scouted for wandering monks but saw none. They moved across the grounds to the wall where Svane took Jonah's hand and hoisted him up like a sack of turnips. May climbed up and over. The three walked casually over to the inn then sneaked Jonah in when no one was looking. They quickly found their room and shut the door behind them.

Documents

When Jonah entered May and Svane's room at the inn, it was cozier than any room in the monastery. May and Svane had set up a table for Jonah's use; now they sat down across from him and explained what they wanted him to do.

While Jonah waited, he made several mental notes. May's friend Anya was not in the room. He had never met Svane before but Svane kept smiling at him. Svane looked old enough to be May's father but didn't act like he was her father. There was a significant time-gap between seeing May at The Charging Boar and May's appearing at his window. May did not seem as big as he remembered her from the Boar. Of the three of them, he was the smallest.

Jonah recalled the interrogations he had experienced over the past few months and how the questioning usually progressed. He recalled figuring out what his interrogators were seeking from the questions they asked him and how they reacted to his answers. The subtleties of conversation, interview, and interrogation had now come to fascinate him. If he was going to satisfy his curiosity in regards to what May and Svane were looking for, he would have to elicit it out of them through astute observation and subtle innuendo. He was ready.

Svane noticed that Jonah was watching everything going on in the room since they had arrived. He suspected there was more to this boy than May was telling. A smile came to his face. "Greetin's! Let me introduce meself. Me name es Svane and this here es May but ye already knew her from before I met her. We've been travelin' from Torslande and have come into possession of several documents. I have a personal interest in these documents. May tells me ye're the best scribe en Callalande and also very knowledgeable o'things we can only dream o'."

While Jonah listened to Svane, May was watching Jonah intently. He appeared very calm and at ease.

When Svane finished, May brought out the lock box with the papers and slowly opened it. May explained, "This was how we found the documents inside this box. We did not steal the box. We also want to keep these matters and papers confidential. Please, organize and analyze the papers any way you wish and don't leave out any details." May stopped and slid the box over to Jonah to let him handle the papers as he saw fit. "Also, if you get hungry or thirsty, we have some food and drink for you. Just say the word and we can take a break."

Jonah replied, "I would like some water if you have some. I don't know if I am the best scribe but I am the fastest scribe."

Jonah carefully removed the papers from the box and unfolded them. There were about eight in all. He explained, "There appear to be two types of documents. There are three official permits with seals and the rest look like letters or lists. These two documents here look like official permits issued by Callamaran government officials. The first was issued at the southern gate near the Monastery of Saint Dominic's and dated around six years ago. It allows the holder to conduct import/export business in foodstuffs with Korgynslande. It was issued to Mikal Basan. The second permit, also for foodstuffs, was issued a few years before the first one and has the name Zenja Basan on it. There is a third permit but it is different. It was issued in Borea and limits the holder to trading in cheese and apples only. It has the name Zenja Alder and is dated around eight years ago." Jonah paused to see if there were any questions and to gauge their reactions.

Jonah resumed, "The remaining documents look like letters. I will read them to you one at a time." Jonah grouped the letters based on whom they were addressed to.

Jonah picked up the first letter and read it to himself. He was surprised to find that it was written by Abbot Eddo. He read the letter aloud to May and Svane:

"To Abbot John of Saint Ausgar's Monastery in Scullsbergen,
(Dated about six years ago)

Your Excellency,
I pray your time in Scullsbergen has transpired peacefully and brought you good health. I write to inform you of good news. The brothers of Saint Dominic's will carry and deliver the cheeses you ordered from Torslande to Scullsbergen within the next week. I hope you enjoy them as they are of excellent taste and flavor.
The recruitment effort for quality scribes has begun in earnest. Saint Dominic's wishes to thank you for your efforts as we will soon be receiving our first cohort of scribes. We remain optimistic that a new day is around the corner for a new and fruitful scriptorium.
May the Lord bless you and your brethren at Saint Ausgar.
(Signed) Abbot Eddo of Saint Dominic's Monastery"

Jonah paused to watch their reactions to the letter. Jonah found the letter puzzling, as he had previously read all of Abbot Eddo's letters and could not recall Saint Dominic's being mentioned as a way station for exporting cheese. He assumed that the cheese they made in-house was entirely consumed within Saint Dominic's.

Svane asked Jonah to repeat the part about cheese and Torslande.

"Thank ye," said Svane.

Jonah picked up the second letter, read it to himself, then read it to May and Svane: "This document has no heading or anyone's name mentioned in it. It appears to be a list of items or instructions."

- Cheese received. Customer satisfied.
- Return to C safehouse 2
- New package ready by solstice
- Take cart for pickup in person
- Bring back to D in south
- Await further instructions from F
  (Signed?) Black Sun
  (Symbol) Half of a black sun on the horizon.

Jonah finished and looked up at both Svane and May. Svane appeared confused. May looked thoughtful with a slight grimace.

Jonah picked up the third letter, read it to himself, then read it aloud:

To Black Sun,

Word is true. New deposit of high-quality blues found in southern T. Location secret. Difficult to extract but highly appraised. Traffic in blues is regulated. Suggest investigate discretely. Keegen is contact in T.

-F

When Jonah finished reading, Svane looked astonished and concerned. May shifted her body slightly when she heard "Black Sun" again. Svane asked Jonah to read the letter again and asked if there were any markings on it other than the writing. Jonah did not find any other writing, but when he held the paper almost flat near the lantern, he thought he could see something barely visible, though not legible, on the paper. Jonah said, "There might be something else on the paper. It could just be smudges left behind by dirty fingers."

"Thank ye," said Svane.

Jonah picked up the fourth letter, read it to himself, then spoke: "This letter appears to be written in suborean."

> To Mikal
>
> Baron needs a delivery soon. Production must increase. Pick up and return. Baron does not care about other priorities. Send word upon delivery.
>
> Black Sun

May frowned in concentration. This was the third mention of "Black Sun." Jonah thought, *she must know something about this Black Sun that she's not letting onto.* May was thinking, *is this Black Sun thing related to the tattoo on that bounty hunter?*

Jonah picked up the final letter and read it: "This appears to be a letter that was never finished and was probably never sent. It is unsigned."

> To Black Sun
>
> Instructions received. Heading up to T to collect shipment. Will return in about a fortnight and make way to safehouse in C.
>
> (Unsigned)

Jonah waited to see if May and Svane had any further instructions or comments. "I thought the mention of 'cheese' was odd; if 'cheese' is not literally cheese, it might be a code word for something else. There also appear to be several mentions of the term 'Black Sun.' I am not familiar with this term. It might be a secret organization or a code word for something else.

There's just … something about that term that makes me feel uneasy – as if it connotes something sinister. I also don't like the fact that you are in possession of a private letter between two abbots. It is a very old letter apparently dealing with monastery affairs. If I may, I would like to make a copy of the letter."

May and Svane looked at each other and both seemed to be inclined to grant Jonah his request. Svane said, "Sure, but we have no writin' supplies with us."

Jonah pulled out from under his clothes a small blank folded piece of paper and a very special quill that appeared to be cut off and filled with ink that did not spill. He did not have an ink pot with him, "That's all right. I'm usually prepared with my own supplies." Jonah adjusted the letter and unfolded his paper. He prepped his pen by letting the ink out a trickle then he began writing in haste. Before anyone knew it, Jonah was finished copying the letter. He let the ink dry then folded it up and put it away along with the quill.

"Wow! That was fast. I've never seen anything like that before." May's eyes lit up.

When everything was read and reported, Jonah hypothesized to May and Svane that they had probably stumbled upon a scheme or plot to smuggle "cheese" and/or "blues" into Korgynslande and Scullsbergen from Torslande. He figured there were not many reasons for smuggling. One was to conceal the movement of goods, legitimate or stolen, from other interested parties or business competition, or to avoid paying taxes on something seen as valuable by a government authority. Jonah wondered what, if anything, Abbot Eddo had to do with this business.

Svane told May he wanted her to go outside and check if anyone was loitering nearby. He really just wanted to get Jonah to himself for a few moments. Svane said, "Thank ye very much for yer help en this matter. I was unsure at first about ye but I now believe May was right en askin' ye ta help us instead o'some government office. What I really want ye ta know es that ever since I met her a few months ago she has never taken any interest en men or boys and we have a lot o'them back home where I live. However, these past two days she has had nothing but googly-eyes for ye. So I say this ta ye, ef ye want a good woman en yer life then she might be the one for ye. I believe she would be loyal ta ye and take care o'ye. I know ye live en a monastery but a chance like this comes along only once en a lifetime. I know this because et happened ta me. I took me chance and I never looked back. All right, let's get ye back ta yer monastery so ye can still get some sleep tonight."

"I will remember what you said. Thank you very much," Jonah said.

Jonah's analysis had not taken long and there was still plenty of time for Svane and May to get him back to the monastery before dawn. His analysis had created more questions than it answered. Svane and Jonah sneaked out of the inn and joined May outside as they walked quietly down the street toward the monastery. They were able to get to the wall and hoist Jonah over the top. They made sure no one had followed them to the monastery, though they had come across a few night owls out on the street. May was able to get him back to the wall and rope. Everything looked as they had left it.

May whispered to Jonah, "Before you go, I want to thank you for your help and for trusting me and Svane."

Jonah wasn't sure he really trusted them, but so far, nothing had gone wrong. "You're welcome. I must say, I cannot make this sneaking around a habit. Sooner or later, I will get caught. So maybe let's make this the last time."

May replied, "All right. No more sneaking."

By now, the clouds had cleared up and the moonlight lit up the dormitory wall. Jonah was about to start climbing the rope when May touched his shoulder and whispered nervously, "Please, have dinner with me at The Charging Boar in a fortnight or two. I will buy you dinner if you say yes."

Jonah turned to her, watching conflicting emotions cross her moonlit face and eyes. "I will have to get a pass." He paused. *What the heck, why not?* He thought, *Maybe I can get some answers out of her.* "All right. Next week I will put a candle in my window before the midnight if I can go in a fortnight or two candles, if I can go in two fortnights. It would have to be on a Saturday night and I cannot guarantee I can come alone. Monastery policy now requires that all monks go out in pairs or groups to avoid troubles with local people. Do you count as trouble with local people?"

May replied with a smile, "I'm not local trouble. I'm big-time trouble. I'll check every night for your candles."

Jonah thought, *why did I even ask?* He turned and slowly climbed up the rope to his room. He made it easily. He quickly changed back into his robe, then dropped the clothes down to May along with the hook and rope. May collected her things then went off to Svane waiting at the wall for her. They quickly jumped the wall and set off for the inn.

Analysis

May and Svane woke up later than usual. Svane sat silently, staring at the documents.

"Well May, I don't know how Jonah figured there might be smugglin' going on, but I'm more confused than ever. I think we should go back to the beginnin'. Our original intention was to identify Rowena's parents. Let's begin with that."

Svane reorganized the papers on the table top. "Ef the two human skeletons ye found on the mountainside are en fact Rowena's parents, then her father's name was likely Mikal Basan and he possessed a Callamaran permit ta trade en foodstuffs. I may not be a language expert like Jonah but I do know me alphabet. The monogram, "MB," on the belt buckle ye found supports our assumption but does not prove et."

"Then her mother must be Zenja Basan as indicated by the second permit."

"I agree. They both have the same surname and both traded en foodstuffs. This leads us ta conclude that Rowena's surname es Basan. That gives us a starting point for our investigation."

May sifted through the papers and found the one that had the "Black Sun" symbol written at the bottom. There it was, the same symbol she had noticed on the bounty hunter's neck just before she and Anya had buried him. She was starting to think that maybe keeping the short sword and crossbow might have been a liability, as someone might recognize them.

"Let's continue with what we know. Ye said that ye found a wrecked cart and a horse skeleton on the mountainside, correct?"

"Correct," May replied. "And now that I think about it, I saw only one horse skeleton and not two. The cart didn't look very large to me, though the timbers were scattered over a large area so I can't be sure."

"En me experience, people who drive carts up and down the mountain road are people who do business en Torslande. No one rides a cart ta Torslande without transportin' somethin'. Someone drivin' a one-horse cart would not be expectin' ta pick up or deliver a large load. As for myself, I need at least two horses ta handle all the cheese and goods I take up and down the mountain road."

"The wrecked pots and crates I saw on the mountainside didn't suggest they were hauling or expecting to haul a large load."

Svane leaned back in his chair for a while before speaking again. "Gettin' back ta her parents, what should we make o'the fourth document Jonah read, the one beginnin', 'To Mikal?' This seems a likely reference ta Mikal Basan. The letter suggests that Mikal works for the Black Sun as a delivery man. The letter was probably written by a Black Sun subordinate who delegates assignments, a taskmaster, so ta speak. Of course, I'm assumin' the Black Sun es an organization and not a code word, as Jonah suggested."

"And his delivery must have been high priority since Mikal was instructed to reply upon completion of the delivery," May added.

"Aye. I might be supposin' much, but the unfinished letter addressed 'To Black Sun,' might be the requested reply that was never sent. Because he, Mikal, fell o'er the mountainside."

"That unfinished response also mentioned that someone, perhaps Mikal, was 'heading up to T.' Jonah read 'T' several times last night. I assumed the writer or writers meant Torsberg or Torslande," May said.

"So ef there's a delivery man, what was he deliverin'? The only things mentioned en the letters were 'cheese' and 'blues.' The abbot's letter talks about deliverin' cheese from Torslande all the way ta Scullsbergen. But, he mentions brethren makin' the delivery and not someone named Mikal."

May thought, *where is Scullsbergen*? "There were certainly many broken pots in the wreckage on the mountainside. It seems likely that cheese was being delivered to someone. The items listed on the second letter suggest that someone was 'satisfied' with their cheese delivery." May added, "Probably not as excited as Gaius was to see us."

Svane chuckled, "Gaius es excited about anythin' related ta cheese."

"The third letter is the only one that mentions 'blues.' So what does 'blues' stand for, sapphires? The sapphire I found, if you are correct, looked pretty blue to me. Or perhaps it refers to blueberries." May recalled, "Nata talked much about blueberries and cream when she wasn't talking about cheese."

"I doubt that there are enough exported berries from Torslande ta fill a cart. And don't ye go makin' me hungry like that. The letter mentions that the blues are 'highly appraised' and 'regulated.' The government doesn't regulate anythin' that esn't valuable so I speculate that 'blues' refers ta sapphires and not blueberries. We should take the sapphire ye found and get et appraised at a jewelry workshop. Then we'll know just how valuable they are."

"I agree."

"Speakin' for meself, I've never sold cheese outside o'Callamar. I don't know what me clients do with their cheese after they buy et. Other cirquens also make and sell cheese. Everyone makes good coin but et's nothin' ta crow about. And furthermore, what's so special about writin' letters about cheese and what's all the chatter about safehouses? There doesn't appear ta be a connection between cheese and blues mentioned anywhere. Ef cheese es being delivered all o'er the place, then why do blues need ta be mentioned?"

Svane and May sat and pondered things for a while. "You're right. There's no connection between cheese and blues in the documents other than their being in the same locked box together. However, the only direct evidence connecting the two is what I found on the mountainside: broken cheese pots and one blue sapphire. It's very weak evidence but it's there."

"Perhaps. Low-grade sapphires have been traded for many years en Torslande. Everyone on the general council knows that. Ef high-grade sapphires have been discovered and are being traded, then that's news ta me. The topic o'valuable sapphires has never come up at council meetin's, and everyone en the south has a brother or cousin named Keegan. I follow rumors and gossip like everyone else and I've not heard o'anythin' related ta valuable sapphires being moved or sold. Anythin' anyone does en Torslande eventually gets found out no matter how much one tries ta keep et secret." Svane paused to think. "Ef the council doesn't know about the sapphires, then smugglin' might be goin' on out o'Torslande. Ef so, then I prefer this ta be none o'me business. I also don't like that this Black Sun gang or whatever they are might be secretly messin' around en Torslande's affairs. We'll need more information."

"What can we do to get more information? I am not good at talking subtle."

"Bein' a council member, I have access to some things others don't. I'll begin investigatin' rumors en the council meetin's or the cirquens. I might be able ta set up an informant en Torsberg as well. I know I can trust ye and ef ye can find out anythin' here en Callamar, we can share notes when I sell more cheese later this year. I recommend that we stay mum on this subject as we don't know much and we're stretchin' our speculation thin. I'll take the locket and buckle back with me ta give them ta Rowena at the appropriate time. I will leave the sapphire here with ye. Get et appraised but be careful. Ef the Black Sun es all around Callamar, then assume they have eyes and ears everywhere. Et would be best ta vet yer jeweler first before askin' him t'appraise the stone. However, vettin' might not be that easy ef ye don't know anyone en the jewel trade."

"All right. Let's look at this from the perspective of Rowena's parents if that's possible. We don't know the level of their involvement with the cheese and blues. All that we can assume is that they were in possession of the same documents we are looking at and likely knew what they all say just as we do now," May said. "It's likely that one or both of her parents knew about sapphires, as I found one in their wreckage. So did they deliver blues in addition to cheese? If they crashed over the mountainside as we found, at least one shipment of something was never delivered. Or worse, whatever was being delivered was hijacked. However, 'hijacked' makes no sense without further information."

"That's just yer survival instinct kickin' en. The Black Sun would probably want their shipment back and they would leave no stone unturned lookin' for et. I've never heard o'any rumors regardin' anyone lookin' for a lost little girl en Torsberg. I would guess an accident befell Rowena, maybe bad weather or falling rocks spooked the cart horse. Accidents happen frequently along the mountain road."

"Since you found Rowena when she was a little girl, she was probably too young to know of any of these things. If her parents worked for the Black Sun and just disappeared one day, then someone else would have had to replace them as couriers and delivery specialists," May speculated. "Ultimately, you will have to decide when and how to tell Rowena about what we have learned today. I don't envy you your task. Maybe returning her feather collection or the locket might trigger a memory."

"Agreed," Svane said. "I'll discuss everything with Edel; then, we will decide what and what not ta tell Rowena. I suspect Rowena knows they're dead and won't talk about et ta anyone. Ever since I found her, she has never said a word about the accident on the mountain road ta anyone, not even me."

May had additional thoughts about the Black Sun which she did not share with Svane. Her recent experience suggested that the Black Sun was alive and well enough. The bounty hunter Anya killed in Borea had a Black Sun tattoo on his neck. At least that was what May was calling it now. She had never seen the man before yet he found both Anya and May. That thought frightened May. *Who else is looking for me? Do they know my name?* The letters suggested that the Black Sun people had infested Callamar with safehouses, hiding away and perhaps moving illicit goods. *Are there more Black Sun people in Callalande, Korgynslande, and Apollande?* Reliable intelligence would be needed to plan for the future. She was not keen on living the rest of her life fearing a knife in her back. May put her hand in one of her pockets and clasped the key she picked off the Baron's son. *I need to find out what this key opens and soon.*

One last thought crossed May's mind. She dug into her pockets again and pulled out the two blue rocks she had pulled off of the wolf hunter. She did not let Svane see what she was doing. As she compared the two, they looked like the same kind of stone.

"All right, let's go get some lunch. I'm hungry," May said.

"Aye, I could use a cup o'tea meself right about now," Svane replied.

Wolf's Bane

May decided to implement her plan to remove the dogs from the derelict mansion. Svane was about ready to leave Callamar and head back to Torslande, as he had already stayed longer than he would have liked. However, Svane agreed to stay one more day to help May out with her plan. May had inventoried her wolf's bane that morning and decided to use some of it to make a perimeter of bane stations and some to spike several large chunks of raw meat. She managed to acquire some burlap bags which she filled with straw and wolf's bane. Then, she attached them to wooden stakes which she would pound into the ground near the entrances and backyard area. Over all, she made ten stakes. Next, May and Svane went to a meat market and bought several fatty steaks. She sliced them into strips then rubbed them down with some wolf's bane. She put all of the meat into a small burlap bag and declared herself ready. Svane fully expected to have to fight dogs the hard way. While May was buying meat, Svane was buying leather scraps to wrap around his fists and arms. He encouraged May to do the same.

"I don't entend ta let any mad dogs bite me and give me mad dog's disease. Ye'd be wise ta defend yerself also against bein' bit," Svane said.

May agreed and wrapped her arms and legs in leather. May and Svane collected the cart and horses, left the expensive inn and rode out to the east side along the main road. When they arrived at the dog mansion, the dogs were still there and keenly aware of their presence. May attached the burlap bag to her belt and began taking baby steps toward the mansion. She wanted to get a good idea of how many dogs were inside and outside. As they moved closer, the alpha dog and his toadies began to snarl at May's intrusion upon their territory. Svane provided flanking protection to May's left. The alpha and his two toadies were soon joined by several more dogs emerging from the mansion. All together Svane counted eight protectors. Five of the eight were abreast each other, barking furiously. May took some meat chunks out of her bag and tossed them to the three dogs in the back row. The dogs looked puzzled but scenting meat, they quickly devoured them whole. The front row of dogs now looked confused but no less vicious.

Alarmed by the barking dogs, several of the neighbors from down the road came out of their houses and shops to investigate. Svane and May now had an audience and were not disappointing their crowd.

May pulled out a few more chunks and tossed them to the front row of dogs, trying to get each dog to eat at least one chunk of meat. When all the meat from the first bag was gone, the eight dogs took up their positions again, now sounding even more aggressive. The alpha lunged at May as Svane interposed and received a bite on his leather-wrapped arm. Once the dog bit, Svane gave him a solid bop on the nose and a kick to the stomach. The alpha released his jaws and scooted away. The two toadies each charged May and Svane and were met with a similar result. The other dogs kept their distance but remained as fierce as the others had been.

The beaten-up alpha and his toadies regrouped further away and were soon barking again from a distance. May and Svane pressed forward a few footsteps then held their position.

Svane asked, "How long before this bane o'yers takes effect? I don't want ta do this all day long."

"I don't know. I've never used it before, but Lady Danae told me it gave them severe stomach cramps and more or less disabled them," she replied.

"They don't be lookin' disabled ta me," Svane said sarcastically.

"Let's give it some more time."

They waited and waited. Eventually, two of the dogs stopped barking. They began panting and making yelping sounds.

May pointed to some dogs. "There, those two look like they're being affected. Let's advance again a few more steps."

"Aye," Svane replied. As they advanced, the dogs continued barking but with less ferocity. Svane tried to provoke one into biting his leather arm again and when he succeeded, he again bopped him on the nose and kicked him. This time the dog looked more than distressed. The alpha was still in charge but May could tell he was weakening. May now provoked a fight with the alpha and bopped him on the nose several times. All of the dogs were losing the will to fight and appeared to be getting sick.

May brought out the bane-spiked stakes and began waving them in front of the dogs, leading her steps with them. Some of the dogs began retreating into the house. Soon all of the dogs had retreated.

"All right, now what do we do?" asked Svane.

"First I need to secure the front with stakes so when we chase or throw them out, they won't want to come back." May said.

May placed two stakes in the ground by the front gate and one near the main entrance. Now she and Svane opened the horse gate and assessed how many dogs were still healthy. They could see several dogs lying down, sick, barely able to move. Several new dogs began barking viciously. As May identified these new dogs, she tossed them one or two chunks of meat and watched them eat up. They encountered several more dogs in the courtyard and in the garden area. Each barking dog received some spiked meat and soon they were all suffering from stomach ailments. Svane guarded May while she placed the rest of her stakes. She placed some of her stakes near the gaps in the perimeter walls then tried to block off the gaps with some debris she found lying around. There was also dog poop everywhere. As many of the dogs lay there sick to their stomachs, May and Svane grabbed them by their necks and dragged them out of the compound. They tossed the dogs out one by one into the street, giving them a big whiff of the wolf's bane and then a good kick to boot. May hoped that the dogs would remember that it was she who had done the kicking and intimidating. May screeched loudly into their ears and bopped their noses but otherwise did not harm them. She wanted them traumatized and able to remember just enough to avoid crossing her in the future.

It took May and Svane all morning, but eventually, the stakes were in place and all of the dogs had been booted out of the complex. May found the alpha dog and his toadies resting together and hogtied them, leaving them on the street as examples to all of the other dogs. Quickly, they closed the gate and sealed off all of the entrances they could find. By the time midday arrived, May felt that she could declare that the first battle for the mansion had been won. Would there be any future battles?

May was appalled by the rank mess that had been left behind by all of the dogs. She found and unlatched the front door. As May and Svane emerged, they were greeted by many dumbfounded Callamarans, amazed at their accomplishment. A loud round of applause was followed by congratulations for their success. May waved at the crowd then chased a few of the sick dogs away from the house again until they were running away in all directions with their tails down.

May was exhausted and Svane not too much better off, but the mansion was conquered. Svane saw that May could probably handle the rest herself and said that it would be best if he began moving up the road back to Torslande.

"I didn't think yer plan would work but here I'm schooled again. Ye'll have more than enough work ta do tryin' ta get this place clean and livable again, but then that es everyone's work en life ain't et? And think o'the stories I'll tell everyone back home about our battle with the dogs and our fight en the street. Don't worry, I won't tell anyone about the monastery.

"And before I go, there's somethin' else I've ta tell ye. First, I'm not yer father but I might as well be, given what we both have been through. Second, that monk boy o'yers es a good boy. He has the knowin' o'many things that others don't understand. He knows right from wrong and he's a tad good lookin' too ef ye know what I mean. And ef ye don't find a way ta get yer arms around him and never let go, I'll be a bit disappointed. Third, I'll be back en the summer ta sell more cheese pots and I'll drop by ta see how ye're doin'. I'm very sure Rowena will want ta visit ye, too, so ye better have this place cleaned up by then." Svane waved a fare well.

"You will always be welcome in my place," May said and with that he was off. Svane mounted his cart and began rolling down the road back to Torslande.

As Svane disappeared down the road, a few of the sick dogs lingered until May charged at them like a banshee and kicked them if they didn't run away fast enough. As May returned to her conquest, she was greeted by some of her new neighbors come to congratulate her and to thank her for ejecting the dogs. They explained that the dogs had been a menace for years. It had not been safe for children to be about, and the dogs had even chased away some of their customers.

One of May's new neighbors had a shop just next door, a blacksmith by the name of Krane. He introduced himself and his wife Cherie and their son David. Krane said, "If you had told me about your plans, I would have come out and helped you get rid of the dogs. They were bad for business, as horses became spooked when the dogs came snooping around my shop. Let me know if you need anything." Krane was a big man, slightly shorter than May and very strong. He had huge biceps and forearms since he spent much of his time hammering iron.

"I need to buy some cleaning supplies. Do you know where I might get some?"

Cherie said, "I can take you down to Ruthie's store. She runs a general store where she stocks all manner of buckets, brooms, shovels, brushes, and soaps."

"Thank you, Cherie. First, I want to make sure that none of the dogs try to return. When they don't return, I'll come back right away to go to Ruthie's Store with you."

Cherie confirmed, "I'll be waiting."

May stood outside her place for some time to see if her wolf's bane stakes were keeping the dogs away. She had very little bane left, and she would have a hard time getting any more. When none of the dogs could be seen, she walked down to find Cherie ready to go shopping with her. Her son David also wanted to go.

"My name is May and I am new to Callamar. I've been here a few times before and I thought that if I chased the dogs away, I would be able to live here now. Do you know who the previous owners of the house were and where they are now?"

Cherie replied, "This is my son David. My husband Krane and I have been living here only a few years now, and that place has been full of dogs since I can remember. No one has had the courage to face them down until you came along. We have complained many times to the Duke's offices, and they tried to send some of their soldiers from the nearby barracks to solve the problem but the soldiers always gave up after getting bitten several times. Their attacks only seemed to make the dogs meaner, so they gave up."

They finally reached Ruthie's Store where Cherie introduced May to Ruthie. Cherie told Ruthie what May and her friend had accomplished and that May now needed cleaning supplies. Both Ruthie and Cherie gathered some brushes and soap and even offered to help her carry the items back to May's place. May asked Ruthie if she knew the previous owners of her place.

Ruthie said, "That place used to be a small specialty inn and kitchen. It was run by an elderly couple; their son was drafted into the army years ago. He was sent to fight somewhere far away and never returned. After the elderly couple passed away, the dogs moved in. As far as I know no one has claimed the place as their own. There have been many efforts to remove the dogs, but they always returned. Be wary of any dogs trying to return."

"Thank you for sharing and thank you for helping me with supplies." May and Cherie returned to the house and May showed her around, but the pungent smell drove Cherie outside into the fresh air.

After Cherie left, May took a full tour of the place and decided to clean out one room immediately so she could sleep there tonight. She found an old well in the backyard area. The well's rope was old and frayed, so she took out one of her new ropes and attached it to the well's bucket. Once she felt the bucket hit bottom, she hauled it up and tested the water. It looked and smelled fresh. The bucket itself was molded and mossy so she cleaned it up then began cleaning one of the rooms. She began collecting dog refuse, piling it onto a burlap tarp. She used her clean bucket to bring water to the room and used her soaps and hand brushes to scrub the walls and floor until they were spotless. By the time the evening came, she was exhausted but at least she had one clean room to live in while she finished her spring cleaning. She went to sleep tired but very satisfied by what she and Svane had accomplished this day.

House Cleaning

May spent the next several days cleaning up her new complex. As before, she deposited shovelfuls of refuse and debris onto the burlap tarp, clearing one room at a time.

The full property consisted of several buildings. The room she slept in was one of several workshops attached to a large barn. One workshop was large enough to hold stalls for horses and pens for smaller animals. The barn itself possessed a hay loft, animal pens, a coop, a water trough, and lots of storage space. Near the well and barn was a patch of land that could be used for more pens or a garden. Several dead fruit trees occupied this space. A nearby staircase led to a second floor featuring two interconnected workshops.

The main building consisted of three floors. The main floor and entrance had a floor space that could be used as an eating area for a kitchen or a small tavern. The kitchen next to the main floor was small but contained a fire pit, an enclosed brick oven, and several work tables. A long countertop with a built-in display cabinet appeared to separate the main floor from the kitchen. A small walkspace between the wall and countertop connected the two rooms. Next to the main floor was a small office space and several storage rooms. One room contained the remains of several crates, sacks, and barrels. From the kitchen a door led into the main courtyard between all of the buildings. Several private rooms along the ground floor supported the two upper floors. A staircase next to the kitchen door led down to a cold, dark cellar. There were two staircases leading to the second and third floors. The doors to the second floor rooms opened onto a long L-shaped walkway and six private rooms. On the third floor were more rooms. Perhaps these had been used by the family or special guests. There were also some small storage rooms and offices with broken furniture scattered all over the place. Separate from all other buildings were the privies and showers. This building was in vast disrepair, ready to collapse, and reeking of refuse. Two large tanks, desperately in need of repair, stood upon the roof holding rancid water.

Every room showed evidence of dog dens and occupation. Some rooms were locked or jammed shut. May put off examining these rooms until she finished cleaning the main building. May thought that what she really needed was a horse and cart to clear out all of the junk and take it away to the city dump. During her tour with Cherie, she had heard of an establishment where she might be able to hire a horse and cart.

May took a break from her cleaning and walked down to Krane's Blacksmith shop. May found Krane working and asked him where she could hire a horse cart in Callamar.

Krane said, "Down the road is a horse and cart business called Hire Haus. Not far from the local barracks down the road is a side street which leads to the city dump. There, many things are burned away from the city. The winds usually blow the smoke out to sea. The city dump sends carts out once a month or so to collect refuse lying in the street, but anyone can take a cart and unload their refuse for free."

"Thank you, Krane," May replied.

May walked further down the road and noticed that she was not far from The Charging Boar. Hire Haus was across the main road and was mostly there to service the fish market by allowing fisherman access to hirable carts so they could deliver their catches to the fish markets without having to own or maintain their own horses and carts. May went inside to inquire about hiring costs. She discovered that carts and horses could be hired on a daily, weekly or monthly basis. With daily fees anywhere from two to five silvers depending on the circumstances, horses were fed and watered by the cart house. Weekly and monthly hiring required the clients to provide feed and water to the horses at their own expense, no exceptions. Deposits were also required in the event of accidents and property damages, similar to insurance.

May returned home and made plans to gather all the junk she could pile into a cart for one or two trips to the dump on a single day to minimize her costs.

Once May finished cleaning as much of the refuse as she could, she began gathering anything related to dogs such as sleeping places, hair, and bones. She used a second burlap cloth for this other dog refuse. This process took several days. Once completed, she examined and sorted the broken furniture and kitchen fixtures into piles of refuse and items that might be repairable. Intact furniture she left in their rooms until she could decide how best to clean them up. Once she had the floors cleared, she began the long process of hauling buckets of water up to the rooms. She scrubbed the floors and walls with soap or cleaning abrasives; intact furniture was also scrubbed clean.

Although exhausted from cleaning and scrubbing, May walked to the monastery each night to check Jonah's window. For safety, she walked with a large stick and two knives strapped to her legs. After about four days, she finally saw what she wanted to see: two candles in the window. That meant two fortnights before she could see Jonah again. This would give her time to finish cleaning her place.

Room by room, May scrubbed the floors and walls, removed cobwebs from the ceilings, removed broken furniture, and refitted the stables. She managed to pile enough junk and refuse for two trips to the city dump. May walked down to the Hire Haus and hired a horse and cart for one day. She acquainted herself with her hired horse by presenting him with a carrot. Although her driving skills were rusty, she did her best to steer the horse safely. Fortunately, there was not much traffic along the road and she arrived at her place shortly thereafter.

May's courtyard had a turn-around for carts and horses but all of her refuse piles made it unusable. She now realized that she did not know how to make the horse turn around and back up through her front gate, so she unhitched the horse and brought him over to her stable for some fresh water and another carrot. Then, May turned the cart around and backed it into the courtyard herself. She filled the cart with the most foul-smelling garbage. When the cart was full, she brought the horse over. When the horse got a whiff of the cart, he protested and neighed many times before May could hitch him to the cart. With horse and cart ready, she locked her gate and took her haul over to the city dump. As she passed along the main road, many of her new neighbors waved to her in thanks.

The stench of burning rubbish showed her the way to the city dump, where she saw piles of garbage sorted throughout the junkyard. Off to one side, a furnace or kiln sent up plumes of black smoke. As she approached a small kiosk-like shed, a man came out to greet her and inventory what she had brought. He instructed her to drop off the dog refuse in one pile and to set the broken furniture over in the wood pile down near the kilns.

May inquired, "What do they make in the kilns?"

The junkyard man explained, "The men over there make bricks for the masons of Callamar. We also receive shipments of clay for the making of bricks. The brick-makers earn enough coin that we don't have to charge anyone for refuse services."

"Thank you." May proceeded as instructed. Once free of the junk, May went back to her place and did it all over again. Once she had delivered her second load to the dump, she returned to Hire Haus and paid her fee. When May returned, she breathed more easily and the absence of clutter made the courtyard look larger.

After admiring the results of her labor, May investigated the locked rooms on the third floor. At first she tried to pick the locks with crude sticks or pieces of metal. When that didn't work, she set off to ask her neighbor Krane for help. She found him hammering horseshoes when she asked him about locksmiths.

"There are several locksmiths in Callamar. I recommend a woman named Amber. She owns a shop in central Callamar called The Extra Key. She is highly skilled and has an honest reputation. Tell her I sent you." Krane smiled then went back to his hammering.

"Thank you, Krane." May wound her way through central Callamar's alleyways when eventually, she found a store with two faded keys painted on the front door.

May looked around for shady characters and could see no one obvious in the alley. She pushed in the front door and, like magic, it opened very quietly. As May's eyes adjusted to the darkened shop, she saw that many shelves were filled with all sorts of gismos, widgets, and do dads. Behind a counter were a myriad of small precision tools and parts scattered all over the place, carefully organized. She looked around and could see no one in the shop. On the far wall was a closed door. May noticed a small hand bell on the counter. May went over to the bell, picked it up, and gave it a ring. As if on cue, a small high-pitched voice from behind her spoke, "Greetings. What are you looking for?"

Startled by the sudden response, May turned around and spied a smallish woman sitting in the shadows. She was wearing a dark tunic and pantaloons while holding a small shot glass half-filled with an unknown liquid. "Oh, hello. I didn't see you sitting there. I'm –"

"Very few people do," the woman replied.

"– looking for a locksmith named Amber. Would that happen to be you? My name is May."

The lady did not respond to her question. May continued, "A blacksmith named Krane told me about your shop. He's my neighbor over on the east side and he recommended you."

"I know Krane. Why did he send you here?" the lady asked.

"I just acquired a house next to Krane's Blacksmith shop. Several rooms in the house are locked," May explained.

"So you are the one that chased away all of the dogs. Impressive."

"How did you know that?" May asked.

"Word travels quickly. Your neighbors think you're a hero; dogs, a pariah." The lady spoke bluntly. "I can pick most locks in this city, for a fee of course. The question is why do you want the lock picked? Why not break the doors down or remove them?"

"I don't want to destroy the doors if I don't have to. I've been cleaning up the place in hopes of opening a business someday. How much do you charge for your services?" May asked.

"If I open the door for you and there is nothing in the room but furniture, there will be no problems. But if I open the door and there is a body or skeleton in the room, then I am professionally obligated to report the finding to the Office of the Census. Since I don't like government paperwork, I will require you to sign a waiver saying that you assume all responsibility for hiring me to open your door to the unknown. Would you be willing to sign?"

"Sounds complicated but I will sign your waiver," May replied.

The lady took another sip of her drink. "My name is Amber and I will come by your place tomorrow morning to open your doors, provided you sign the paperwork. Agreed?"

May left The Extra Key a little confused. As she walked home, she realized that she had not considered the possibility that the locked room might contain a dead body.

A little later after May arrived home, Krane and Cherie knocked on May's front door. Surprised to see them, she invited them inside. "I am afraid I don't have much in the way of food to offer the two of you but I can fetch some water if you like," May asked.

Cherie spoke up, "Oh no, we're not looking to stay long. We just wanted to check up on you to see how you are progressing on your cleaning. Krane says you might have gone to visit Amber this afternoon."

May replied, "Yes, I did visit Amber. She told me that I will have to sign some papers regarding my taking responsibility for hiring her and all that."

Krane said, "She covers herself thoroughly from personal liability. I have done business with her before. She does get the job done. It looks like you have almost got this place cleaned up and smelling normal again. Again, thank you for chasing the dogs away."

May took Krane and Cherie on a short tour of the place now that the worst of the smells were gone. Cherie explained to May that Ruthie had told her that the couple that lived in the house had been buried in the pauper's cemetery along the road to the north. As they returned to the main floor, Cherie said, "Thank you for showing us around. It is a wonderful place. I'm sorry, but Krane and I do need to get going as I have not started supper, yet." Krane and Cherie politely took their leave.

Not long after May woke up the next morning, she heard a knock on her front door. May found a short woman dressed in a light-colored, hooded tunic with matching pantaloons carrying a small leather satchel strapped across her back and chest. May recognized her as Amber and invited her in. Once inside, Amber removed some paperwork from her satchel and explained to May how she wanted it signed. When Amber found out that May could not write, she spent some time teaching May how to sign her name with a quill. May's signature was very coarse but she did not care; she could sign her own name now. "I charge four silvers in advance. If the lock proves more difficult, then I charge double. I charge nothing and return your silvers if I can't open the lock." Once May completed the paperwork, May gave Amber four silvers then led her up to the third floor where the two doors awaited.

"Will it take long?" May asked.

"That depends on the lock and the condition it's in. In Callamar, locks frequently get rusty due to the pervasive salty air," Amber explained. "I am going to need a chair and a small table."

May went downstairs and retrieved a chair and table. Amber arranged her tools on the table while May stood back and watched Amber do her magic. Amber discovered that the locking mechanisms were heavily corroded, so she began by oiling the lock and probing with her tools and skeleton keys. Amber worked slowly taking care not to break anything. Eventually the lock opened and she swung the door open. A rusty squeaking came from the hinges.

Amber told May to be patient and immediately went to work on the second lock. The second lock was easier to open, taking half the time.

"Now we find out if you have skeletons in your closet." May and Amber opened the door and were greeted by a flood of light from the small uncovered windows. The window panes were not broken and a stale must pervaded the room. Amber stood back and told May not to enter the room. "We should cover our noses and mouths before going further. You can never know what foul humors lurk within."

May and Amber covered their faces with cloths and entered the rooms one at a time. The first room appeared to be a library containing many book shelves and a large desk against one wall. May thought excitedly, *Jonah will have to see this room.* The second room looked more like a bedroom with lots of decaying clothes and window coverings. The bed appeared to have collapsed and was probably not salvageable. Against one wall was a large wardrobe that appeared to be intact with a small footlocker by one side.

"Good, no one dead in either room. I recommend you air out the rooms for at least a week before working in them. If you want to lock the rooms again, you'll have to purchase new locks," Amber explained as she picked up all of her tools.

May was impressed with Amber's skill and professionalism so much so that she decided to risk asking her about the Baron's son's key she had been carrying around for a long time. "Amber, there is one more thing I would like to ask of you if I may."

"All right. You may ask."

May reached into her pocket and pulled out the small key and handed it to Amber. "I was wondering if you have any idea what kind of lock this key might open?"

Amber took the key and widened her eyes. She pulled out a jeweler's loupe and examined the key in detail. When she was done examining the key, Amber held it up to May and asked, "Where did you get this key?"

May hesitated, "I found it along the side of a road. I figured someone must have dropped it days before I found it."

Amber hesitated then pointed to the key. "It looks like a bank box key. Callamar has several banks in town which offer private bank boxes to their more wealthy customers. However, this key does not belong to any Callamaran bank. The keymaker put a small notch at the end of its teeth here indicating that it was made somewhere in Borea. It also opens a box numbered '218.' So I would guess that it belongs to a bank in Borea." Then Amber changed her tone and looked directly at May. "Whoever lost this key is really going to want it back. Don't show this key to anyone else whom you don't completely trust." Amber handed the key back to May then departed.

May understood the hint. "Thank you very much for all of your help," she said as she waved Amber goodbye.

Clet's Tunics

For the past month, May wandered through many of Callamar's market districts. She was looking for a tailor but could not find one in her neighborhood. She had been wanting new clothes for some time but lacked the tools and skills necessary to make her own. Her clothes had been loyal to her by enduring many elements – Ma's kitchen, vicious dogs, a funeral pyre, and a fist fight or two involving blood – and now, her house cleaning was shredding them to pieces. So, she committed her remaining coin taken from the street gang to purchasing several new tunics and pantaloons.

After many forays into central Callamar, May discovered Clet's Tunics, a tailor located near the Church of the Holy Cross northwest from the Central Market. As May entered the workshop, she was greeted by a large assortment of cloth bolts standing against a wall, organized by color. Left-over scraps, spools of thread, scissors, and needled cushions lay scattered throughout the shop.

As May surveyed the chaos, a man rambled into the shop through a backroom door, "How may I help you, young woman?"

"Are you Clet?" May asked.

"Yes, I am. Fastest tailor in Callamar."

"Hello. My name is May. I would like to order some new clothes. How long will it take for you to make me two new tunics with two pantaloons?"

"You've come to the right place for tunics. We specialize in tailoring several varieties of tunics, shirts, and pantaloons. We can fill most orders within two days. However, we don't make dresses. If you are interested, I can recommend a seamstress." Clet proceeded to pull out several tunics from a hidden shelf and arrange them along the countertop. "These are my demonstration models in four styles. Each style can be tailored with or without a hood."

May was impressed by what she saw. After a short inspection, she selected two styles featuring multiple concealed pockets. While the man was assisting May with her choices, he called out, "Lora! We have a guest in the shop."

Some moments later, a woman emerged from the backroom and proceeded to assist May and take her measurements. While May was getting measured, she heard children's laughter emerging from beyond the backroom door. Turning towards the door, May spied an older girl, perhaps around twelve years, stitching a blanket - or was it a quilt?

May asked Lora, "Do you also make quilts?"

Lora looked back towards her daughter stitching, saying, "She makes quilts and blankets for herself and her siblings. Josie, would you come into the shop for a moment, please?" Turning back to May she said softly, "For the right coin, she might be persuaded to make a blanket for you." Josie walked quietly into the shop and stood next to her mother. "This is my daughter, Josie."

"Hello Josie, I'm pleased to meet you. My name is May."

Josie looked up at May, responding slowly and quietly, "Hello."

"She is a little on the shy side but she makes nice blankets."

"Is that so? I live on Callamar's east side and will be in need of some warm blankets soon. How long would it take you to make a blanket for someone as tall as me?"

Josie looked up at her father who nodded back at her. She looked back at May and spoke softly and slowly, "I can make a … a blanket in a … week. If you want a quilt, … it will take longer."

Lora retrieved a blanket from a back shelf and began unfolding it.

Josie spoke, "I made a quilt for … for … but she didn't like it and –"

Lora interrupted, "Josie made a quilt for a woman whose daughter slept in a large bed. She wanted Josie to stitch a cherry tree on the topside. When she finished, the lady refused to pay for the quilt." Lora unfurled the quilt and let May have a look. The quilt was large. May took hold of the quilt and and saw that it reached from the floor to the top of her head.

"I will understand … if … if you don't like it … and …"

"It's nice. Is it warm?" May asked.

"Yes, it's warm. It's made of wool and … and it has extra wool … in the middle."

"How much do you want for it?" May was already sold on the quilt but she could hear Anya whispering in her ear to be wary and bargain her down.

"The lady told me she would give me … five golds. I would like … to … to get four golds."

Where had May heard that before, five golds? She fell silent, admiring the quilt. It certainly felt warm and itchy as she folded it over her arm. "I can give you one gold and ten silvers now and another gold when you make me a second blanket without the quilting."

Josie counter offered. "I can give you this quilt … and make you a new blanket … the same size … for four … four golds."

"Two blankets for four golds?" May asked. Josie nodded. May wasn't sure if she was getting a good deal or not. But to May, two blankets for the price of one seemed like a good deal. May pulled her coin out of her hidden pockets and placed them upon the counter, paying for everything in advance.

"All right, here's two golds for the quilt and two more for the second blanket. The rest pays for the tunics and pantaloons as soon as you can make them."

Clet, Lora, and Josie agreed to May's request. Clet said, "We'll prioritize your order. When you return in a few days, we can make some final adjustments to your tunics and pantaloons before you leave."

"Thank you. I look forward to wearing them." May left the shop and walked home. Good deal or not, May treated everything as a gift from the street gang's coin; and who better to benefit than Josie?

The Charging Boar

Two fortnights had passed and it was now Saturday night. May stood in front of The Charging Boar in her new clothes, waiting for Jonah. The sun had already set behind the Aerieals suffusing the sky with a chromatic glow. As she waited, several people entered the Boar including a pair of monks with walking sticks, but neither of these was Jonah. After what felt like a long time, she spied another pair of monks approaching. As they emerged from the darkness, she recognized one of them as Jonah and the other one as – Pompey?

Pompey spied May standing in the lamplight and began bowing and waving his arm in greetings. "A pleasure to meet you again. As I recall, an angel from a time ago now donning spring finery, perhaps awaiting a night owl?" Pompey reached for her hand and took it, kissing it lightly. "I present to you a famished Jonah eager to partake of a boar steak and now perhaps your enchanting company as well?"

Jonah was embarrassed. He had asked Pompey to ease up on his pomposity but his plea had only encouraged him. Jonah greeted May, "Good evening May. Good to see you again."

"Yes, it is good to see you, too, and also good to see you, Pompey," May replied.

Pompey waved his arm towards the front door, "Well, that decides it then. Shall we?"

Something about The Charging Boar made people feel that time stood still. Entering the front door, they saw a raucous group of diners chatting and merrymaking in front of a crackling fireplace. They squeezed their way over to an unoccupied corner table and claimed it for the night. Pompey allowed May and Jonah to seat themselves before he took a seat. He quickly turned and beckoned one of the serving girls.

The girl wound her way over. "I hope you folks are having a wonderful evening. Tonight we have boar steaks with vegetables on the side and dinner rolls or a tasty boar stew with vegetables and cheese rolls. We're also offering four different beers and ales."

Pompey spoke up and ordered for everyone with a wink, "Ah yes, she serves with a bright smile and unrivaled grace. We shall have three of your boar steaks with three golden ales and a bowl of boar rinds au jus."

Their serving girl smiled and pinched Pompey's cheek as she floated away to return with their food.

Pompey sat down grinning broadly. "I have no doubt that there has been some clandestine communication between the two of you. I am not so foolish as to suppose this meeting has anything to do with chance. But allow me to reassure you: your secret is safe with me so please speak freely. I shall be discretion itself."

Encouraged by his apparent sincerity, and a little amused by his pompous "charm," May related her recent adventures. "Svane the cheese monger gave me a ride from Torslande. He helped me chase away a pack of feral dogs from one of the abandoned buildings along the main road. In the month that I have been living there, I've been cleaning the place and none of the dogs has returned. The neighbors seem friendly, too – so far, so good."

"Hold on!" Pompey broke in with exuberance. "You expect us to believe that you – and your mysterious friend – chased off a pack of feral dogs without as much as a bite mark or injury? I've heard some tall tales, but this – "

"I assure you, it's perfectly true. Svane returned to his family a month ago none the worse for wear while I vanquished the dogs with a judicious application of wolf's bane."

Pompey turned to Jonah with raised eyebrows, "Now that's a good story, worth every step from the monastery." Smiling, Pompey turned back to May. "You are way beyond trapping rabbits now."

Jonah also expressed surprise and admiration. "Well done! As for me, I have been mostly reclusive since I saw you last year. The monastery brought in an expert to teach us monks of Saint Dominic's how to defend ourselves with a staff." Jonah pointed to both of their staffs in the corner against the wall. "Everywhere we go, we take the staffs with us for walking but also for self-defense. You never know what might be waiting in the night here in Callamar. I have grown fond of our sparring sessions in the garden."

Pointing at Jonah, Pompey added, "I can vouch for that. Jonah has become one of Master Po's best students. He even helps instruct some of the other monks."

Jonah came out and asked, "I was wondering, how did you meet this man Svane and how did you end up in – Torslande, was it? And what became of your friend Anya?"

May struggled a moment before answering. "I don't know how to be tactful so I will just say it. Anya died several months ago. She was killed by a trapper dressed in wolf skins. She fought him and pinned him down while I finished him off, but Anya … Anya didn't make it."

Jonah and Pompey could see that May was upset. They engulfed her in comforting hugs. And then her tears began to flow freely. Seeing May in distress, the serving girl quickly brought out a clean cloth and cleared her tears away.

May said, "I'm sorry. I've been alone for a long time. Thank you." She gave both Pompey and Jonah big hugs. "After Anya died, I wandered around for a long time and ended up in Torslande. Svane was kind enough to let me stay the winter with his family. I helped his family make goat cheese. When the snows thawed, he brought me down to Callamar."

Eventually, they went back to eating their boar steaks. Jonah and Pompey realized that there were two people missing from the last time they were all together, Anya and Danan. They eyed each other, agreeing to tell May about what had happened to Danan. They explained to May that Danan had died around the same time as Anya, though under very different circumstances. While the rest of the night felt more somber, reminiscing over dinner effectively lifted a bit of the sorrow that had burdened them for the past few months.

Jonah realized that on a personal level he had committed a kind of sin. He had judged May wrongly when he should have been more open minded and evaluated all of the facts, some of which he did not have. He now realized that putting what he had been learning at the monastery into practice was very hard. But the lessons he was learning today made him realize that the world was very complex and could not be broken down into simple black and white. There were very many shades of grey in between.

True to her word, May paid for their dinner. She gave their serving girl a gold coin. She also gave the girl a little extra and told her she would be back again soon and to take care of herself. The girl gave May a hug and the three diners made their way out through the front door and into the cool salty air blowing north across the city.

May said, "Thank you for a good evening." She gave both Pompey and Jonah another hug before walking off down the main road to her new home. Before she left, she turned to Jonah. "There is one more thing I would like to ask of you. I want to write a letter to an acquaintance of mine in Borea. Could you help me write it and mail it to Northcamp?"

"Maybe. I will have to get another pass to escape the monastery. I don't expect that to happen soon, since I had to make a concession to get this pass." Jonah then leaned forward and whispered in her ear, "In a fortnight, I will put candles in my window to let you know when I can come back to the Boar."

"All right, I will wait." May waved before turning and walking back home.

Midnight Walk

For a time, Jonah and Pompey walked without speaking. Jonah mulled over May's story about the feral dogs. Jonah thought, *May and Svane must have accomplished that after I left the hotel room. Wielding wolf's bane, they must have been a formidable duo.* Jonah broke their silence first. "Do you think she really cleared out a building full of feral dogs?"

"That story is so fantastic that it has to be true. She could not have made it up. Besides, why would she lie to us? I wonder if she could make the skuas disappear."

Jonah chuckled then asked, "What do you think about her story of how Anya died, a trapper dressed as a wolf killing Anya and May finishing him off? If she's killed one man, maybe there are others."

Pompey replied, "That story must also be true. How could anyone make that up?" Pompey went silent for some time. "If I recall correctly, the Callamar Complaints Department has been rife with stories about someone called 'the wolf hunter.' For the past few months, several people have visited the Office of Internal Security claiming to have killed the wolf hunter and asking to collect the bounty. But as far as I can tell, no one has been awarded the bounty because they have been unable to prove that they killed the wolf hunter. So they come back and complain again that they are still waiting for a bounty which has still never been awarded. Come to think of it, a report of a headless body found on the shore of the Snowfall River was filed last year in the fall. It was purported to be the wolf hunter but it could not be positively identified. I wonder. If May did kill him, she would be entitled to collect the bounty if she could prove it. I think the bounty is 200 golds."

Jonah exclaimed then whispered, "200 golds! I mean 200 golds. She could buy a nice house with that, though she already has a house, now. She could start her own business with that. Did you see how she paid for dinner with that gold coin?"

"Yes, I did." Pompey observed Jonah closely before continuing, "As I said, I'm aware that nothing tonight happened by chance. She's obviously crazy about you, and if you feel the same way, she's yours for the taking. All you have to do is take her in your arms and she's yours."

"Maybe you're right."

"Of course I'm right."

Was Pompey ever less than certain? "I'll admit I'm tempted, but while I'm living in the monastery –"

"You've been talking about leaving the monastery for months now –"

"Hold on –"

"– ever since we first encountered May and Anya. I thought you were foolish to even consider throwing away a promising career as a scribe, not to mention free bed and board. I also thought you were consumed with guilt over Danan and weren't thinking straight. But now that she's got coin, you've a real chance to escape monastic life and build a family. A chance like this only comes along once, maybe twice, in a lifetime. You're lucky you're still young."

"But she's killed a man – maybe more than one."

"Most of the world is like that: kill or be killed. Even in our safe little cocoon, we have to learn how to defend ourselves. Imagine what it's like for a girl alone out there on the streets. Or is that what's bothering you? You don't think a woman should be better than you at fighting or providing? She could probably protect you better with her fists than you could with that staff of yours."

Jonah and Pompey walked silently for a while. "I think you should find a way to help her write that letter. She gave you an open invitation to go visit her. It would give you a chance to talk to her alone without someone like me making you two feel awkward. And don't wait; do it as soon as you are able. I will cover for you if that's what you need to make this work."

"Thank you. I have given thought to leaving and I think I may have found a way. Since I have been copying many law codices for the past year, I've discovered that boys at eighteen years can sign contracts with the city to serve in the military or the night watch. Apparently, the city considers eighteen years the age when a man can consent without requiring permission from a family member or guardian. Of course, one becomes bound to the contract. I could make the argument that my contract, signed by my parents when I was fifteen years, with the monastery committing me to service until twenty-one years, is contrary to city law and should be nullified."

Pompey said, "You may be onto something there. What would you do? Be a scribe for the Duke's government offices?"

"No. I don't want to be a scribe anymore. It's killing my hands and wrists."

"Maybe you should go into business with May. The two of you could lead a mercenary outfit, hunt down fugitives, and collect bounties."

Jonah laughed, "Silly boy. But I will find a way to help her write that letter."

"Now that's what I want to hear."

They continued talking quietly all the way back to the monastery.

Secret Tasking

The next morning, Pompey met Jonah as they made their way to morning prayers.

While Pompey and Jonah were eating breakfast, Pompey whispered, "I am going to request permission from Archscribe Rene and Prior Lund to send you out on an errand to purchase some more writing supplies. That way you get out of the monastery during the day and not at night. You take the long route to the supply shops and just happen to pass by May's place and ask for directions (wink wink). You then help her write her letter and mail it for her. I don't care how long you take, but make sure you complete your secret mission. Understand?"

"I think so. I think I can make a thorough search for supplies, even get lost down a wrong street or two."

"Good. I will let you know when I am ready to give you that assignment." Jonah and Pompey then went to the scriptorium and began their daily work.

Pompey did not have a supervisory position but he did have the authority to place requests for writing supplies. Pompey might have gone himself on such an errand to purchase supplies, but he told Archscribe Rene that he was having ankle problems and would prefer not to go out himself. He suggested that he send Jonah to do his errand for him. Jonah walked faster than most others, and since Jonah was one of the best monks in the use of the staff, Jonah could handle himself on a simple daylight mission.

Archscribe Rene expressed skepticism concerning Pompey's request but did not deny any of the facts Pompey had put before him. The archscribe did not think the errand necessary and was aware that Abbot August did not want Jonah out and about, especially on his own. But Pompey was full of charm and persuasion and not to be denied. He casually mentioned that Jonah's route would take him past one of Callamar's pastry shops where he might pick up a few apple fritters if Rene would approve the request. And of course, no one else needed to know about the fritters. Pompey noticed a little glimmer in the archscribe's eyes when he said the word "fritters." The archscribe told Pompey that he would consider his request. "Come back tomorrow and I will give you my decision on this matter."

"Thank you, sire, I will come back tomorrow," Pompey replied.

After vespers that evening, Jonah looked happier than he had been for several months. Pompey wondered, *maybe The Charging Boar does make a difference*. Pompey told Jonah that he would know tomorrow if their plan had a chance of working.

Jonah thanked Pompey and went back to his room. When he got into bed, he lay there thinking about what Svane and May had requested of him. They had both asked him to read documents that they could not read themselves. And now May wanted him to write a letter for her. Were these services for which many Callamarans would be willing to pay? How many other people like himself in Callamar were already providing such services? Was this something he could do for a living? Would he need an office or a workroom to have such a business?

Jonah recalled his days back in school, how most of his life had been spent reading, writing, and learning. He remembered having the impression that the world was a place where everyone was literate. When he first arrived at the monastery, he was surrounded by scribes, skilled as he was. Over time, he found that the ascetic monks did not possess scriptorial skills like the scribes but they did possess many other skills, talents, and wisdom that he did not.

Since first meeting May, he realized that he had no idea what it was like to live life unable to read or write, to live life on the edge. His understanding of the world was changing rapidly. Was he really living in a "cocoon," as Pompey suggested? Beyond the monastery walls lived throngs who possessed neither reading nor writing skills. He wondered, *why is this the case?*

The next morning, Jonah and Pompey went through their usual routines, morning prayers, breakfast, scribing, katas, reflection, vespers, dinner, chores, and recreation. Sometime before vespers, Pompey found Jonah and told him that Archscribe Rene had approved his trip into the city for writing supplies and apple fritters. Pompey gave Jonah final instructions: "Be ready to go after breakfast tomorrow morning and make sure you take enough paper and quills to write May's letter. I will give you some coin tomorrow to buy the writing supplies, but buying fritters is the highest priority."

Jonah smiled. "Thank you, I will be ready tomorrow."

"You just make sure you accomplish your mission. Now go get some sleep tonight. You will need it." Pompey left.

Jonah went into his room and lay down to do his thinking before sleeping. He wondered why Pompey was helping him. Did Pompey really care that much about Jonah's future? Jonah had thought that Pompey harbored resentment against him for what had happened to Danan, but apparently he had forgiven him.

And what about May? Svane and Pompey seemed keen to see Jonah and May together. He had to admit to himself that she did have a cute smile and that he found her attractive. What most concerned him about May was that she had killed someone. Above all else, this behavior was most contrary to everything he had been taught back home in Scullsbergen and to what he had learned here at the monastery about service, forgiveness, peace, and "doing unto others." For his own peace of mind, he would have to visit this subject with her. Spending time alone with her would allow him to better assess her real character.

In her favor, she had chased the dogs out of her new house instead of killing them outright. That showed him that she respected life. Reassured by this thought, he finally fell asleep.

Letter

The next morning after prayers, Pompey met Jonah for breakfast. Pompey said, "You should leave now while everyone is having breakfast." Jonah and Pompey left the dining hall, working their way circuitously to the main entrance. Pompey gave Jonah the coin he had promised and reminded him of what he needed to do. "Just return to the main gate and you will be let in normally. Then bring everything you bought to me."

"All right, I'll do that," Jonah said as he left through the front gate.

Jonah left the monastery and started walking along the main road through Callamar. He knew it was a long walk to May's place past The Charging Boar so he built up a brisk pace and avoided traffic as best as he could. He enjoyed walking in the spring weather – at least until he neared the fish market where he was hit by the smell of dead fish and decaying fish parts. Even though the skuas took away most of the leftovers, the smell of fish innards and bones lingered.

At the usual supply shops he purchased a few quills and ink pots but there was not much paper available, and the price had gone up since the last time he had shopped. He bought a bit of paper, saving some coin for the fritters. Down a side street, he found a pastry shop called Scylla's Bakery. He bought as many fritters as he could find, about nine in all, and had the owner wrap them up for him. He pulled out a small net bag with a shoulder strap and carried them off after paying the owner. He hoped the fritters would earn himself and Pompey some favor with Archscribe Rene.

After shopping, Jonah crossed the stone bridge and entered a part of the city he had never visited before. He passed by the eastern barracks and the road to the naval docks. He could see several soldiers practicing defensive tactics with their shields and wooden swords. Once past the barracks, he could smell the city dump. *What a putrid assortment of smells*, he thought. He soon approached the edge of town. Off in the distance, he spied a colorful patchwork of orchards and farmsteads. He noticed a run-down building. All the doors and gates were closed. Jonah heard the clinking of a blacksmith's hammer nearby.

A voice reached out to him as he walked down the road. "You look like you might be lost. The monastery is on the other side of Callamar along the main road."

Jonah turned around to see an older woman standing on her porch. Jonah replied, "I am not lost. I am looking for someone called May. Would you know where I can find her?"

The woman gave him a curious look then pointed and laughed, "She lives in that old building over there. If she knows you, she'll let you in. If not, you'd best be ready to run."

"Thank you."

Jonah walked over to the old building. It looked like an inn that had not been used for years. Wary of dogs, he looked around and did not see or hear any. Jonah knocked on the front door. Nothing happened. Then he took his walking staff and banged it against the front door a few times.

No sounds came from behind the front door; instead, he heard the front gate to the courtyard slowly unlatching and opening. As he turned to face the gate, he saw May looking at him.

"Oh," she said. "I didn't know you were coming." She opened the gate a little wider and invited him inside. She seemed pleased by his sudden appearance. "This is a surprise. Please come inside. The place is still messy but cleaner than it used to be." May opened the gate wider and Jonah passed through.

"You are not the only person who can make a surprise entrance." Jonah looked around. "It looks larger from the inside."

May quit her cleaning and offered to show Jonah around. They toured the barn and workshops, the garden area, the first-floor rooms, and the main floor. May had managed to assemble a few pieces of unbroken furniture in the main floor area where she invited him to sit.

"I'm afraid I don't have much besides a few bread rolls and cheese. Please feel free to help yourself and I will get you some water."

Jonah smiled. "Thank you. Water would be nice."

May came back with a pitcher of water and some cups. "How did you find this place? I thought monks did not leave the monastery during the daytime."

Jonah replied, "It is not easy to leave the monastery at all, day or night. Let's just say the planets aligned and here I am."

"The planets?" May looked puzzled.

"I will explain that another time. Let's just say that I was lucky. I am on several missions right now. One is to purchase supplies for the monastery, another is to buy fritters for the archscribe, and –"

May interjected, "You have fritters? Are they apple fritters?"

Jonah smiled and said, "Yes and yes, but they are for the archscribe. They are the bribe I have to pay him for letting me out of the monastery today. However, I am sure he wouldn't miss one fritter."

May took the hint and went off to get a plate and knife as Jonah proceeded to open up the bag of wrapped fritters. Jonah placed one out on the plate. May's eyes lit up with child-like anticipation and cut it in half.

"Thank you. You are such a sweetie." May lifted up her half and took a bite, relishing the fritter. "I have not had an apple fritter in a long time." Her joy was palpable.

"I'm glad you like it."

As May and Jonah ate and talked, Jonah realized that he had never been alone with a woman before – at least not since he was a child. He rather liked the sensation. He also liked talking quietly and not having to yell across a table as he had done at The Charging Boar.

Eventually, Jonah explained, "So, I'm ready to help you write that letter you mentioned. Pompey set it all up and managed to get me out of the monastery without attracting undue attention."

May looked into his eyes while finishing her fritter. "That was very kind of him."

Excited, May brought her chair much closer to Jonah's. "I want to watch you write the letter. I've never watched anyone do writing before, except when you copied that letter last month. Guess what? I can sign my name, now. When you are done, I want to sign the letter myself. Please show me more."

"All right, let's get started." Jonah brought out some paper, quills, and ink from several of his hidden pockets. "First I'll show you how to make a pen out of a quill. Remember this?" He showed her one of the quills she had given him. "You take an ordinary bird's feather then you cut a notch in the quill, like this, so the feather can absorb ink." He dipped the quill into the ink. "Not too much you see? Then, when you scratch the paper, it leaves a mark." He demonstrated.

"Oh, I see. I want to send a letter to Lady Danae in Northcamp."

"Is that Danae, like the mother of Perseus?"

"The mother of …? No, I don't think she has any children of her own. She has a niece named Deanna."

Jonah smiled to himself and wrote "'Dear Lady Danae.' All right. What do you want to say to Lady Danae?"

May leaned closer, brushing his shoulder. "I want to tell her how Anya died but I don't think I can do it without crying."

"Just take your time."

May narrated the details of Anya's death – the trapper, the howling wind – and how she had buried Anya by the banks of the Snowfall River. She breathed deeply as she wiped a few tears from her eyes. She asked that Danae convey the sad news to Ma, Karl, and Berthe and to tell her how sorry she was to have left without saying goodbye. She did not mention anything about killing the greencoats or the trapper or Nimrod or burning down the trading house.

Jonah didn't say a word about the trapper or how he and Pompey had conjectured that May had killed the wolf hunter. Clearly, May did not want Lady Danae to know this, yet.

May attentively watched Jonah's hand moving the quill across the page, effortlessly forming letters. "You make it look so easy." Line by line her letter took shape before her eyes.

"All done. What's next?" May detailed the struggle with the feral dogs, explaining the key role that her wolf's bane had played. She made sure to invite Lady Danae to visit her and to bring her niece, Deanna, to tea so she could return her hospitality.

"What is her niece's name again?"

"Deanna – she's slightly younger than I am. I think she's Danae's ward. Anyway, she's studying with her to be an herbalist and an … apothecary." She pronounced each syllable carefully.

"Impressive!"

May asked if Lady Danae knew where she could find some more wolf's bane in Callamar.

Finally, she explained to Jonah that he should address the letter to Northcamp Apothecary, and not use Lady Danae's real name.

When Jonah had finished writing, she asked him to read the letter back to her. May was satisfied that all she had wanted to say was in her letter. She took the letter in her hands, amazed that everything she had just said to him was there in writing. It was like seeing magic before her eyes, she thought.

"All right, where do I sign the letter?" May asked.

"Right here at the bottom." May took the quill from his hand and slowly wrote out her name. May beamed with pride at her letter and thanked Jonah for his help.

"If she answers the letter, will you help me read her reply?"

Jonah said, "I can do that. But we'll need to find a more efficient way to communicate."

"If you lived here with me, there would be no more problems with communication." May said bluntly but before Jonah could respond, she continued, "You can have your own room and as much privacy as you want or need. I've overheard Pompey's talk about you wanting to leave the monastery. What could be better than right here?"

Jonah was not sure if he was hearing May correctly. "You want me to live here with you?"

"Yes! I am sure you would be able to find work in Callamar. Why wouldn't someone want to hire the fastest scribe in Callamar?"

Jonah spoke up, "It is … (sigh) … complicated. I can't just leave the monastery. By contract, I am obligated to serve in the monastery. Many people would be upset and come looking for me if I left."

"A contract?"

Jonah said, "I cannot promise anything right now, but I will think about it."

May gently touched his hand. "All right. Take your time. I enjoyed talking with you today."

"Right now, I have to go post your letter." Jonah said, "But, I would like to ask you something. When we talked at The Charging Boar a few nights ago, you said that you 'finished him off,' referring to the trapper that killed Anya. Does that mean you killed him?"

May looked puzzled but decided that she must be honest. "Yes. I had to kill him because he was going to kill me."

Jonah could see tears in her eyes as she said this. He embraced her and whispered, "We all do what we have to do to survive and protect those we love and care about." He released her and tried wiping away her tears.

"Pompey and I think the trapper you 'finished off' might have been someone called 'the wolf hunter.' Pompey told me that his body was found in the Snowfall River near Fallmouth with its head missing. It turns out that the Duke of Callalande had placed a bounty on the wolf hunter. Many people have tried to collect the bounty but no one has proved that they were the one who killed him. So if you really did kill the wolf hunter, then you might be able to collect the bounty."

May appeared surprised. "How much is the bounty?"

Jonah said, "Pompey told me that it was 200 golds."

May's eyes lit up. "How would I be able to prove it was he?"

Jonah said, "That I don't know. You might inquire about that yourself at one of the government offices. I could also ask Pompey if he knows how to find out."

May said, "I don't know. I would like to forget about that day and would rather not tell anyone else about it, either. I don't want to be known as the killer of the wolf hunter and I don't want fame. I just want to live peacefully now and start my own family, someday – or I could start my own kitchen business."

Jonah said, "I understand. If you don't want me to talk about this anymore, I will keep my mouth shut."

May took Jonah's hands in both of hers and thanked him.

Jonah then took the letter and began folding it into an envelope. He brought out some sealing wax and asked May if she would light a candle for him. Jonah took the candle and melted some wax onto the letter, sealing it. Jonah told her to press her thumb into the wet wax quickly so as not to get burned. Then he turned the letter over and addressed it to the Northcamp Apothecary.

Before Jonah left to go post May's letter, she had a parting gift for him. She went back into one of her storage rooms and gathered one of her knotted ropes. She gave it to Jonah saying, "This is for the day when Pompey isn't able to help you get out of the monastery."

Jonah thanked her. May opened the front door where he waved to her one last time before walking off down the main road. When he was finally out of sight, May closed and locked the front door behind her.

Jonah found a coach house and paid a postage fee for May's letter to arrive a week later and to be personally delivered. Jonah was happy to see some daylight left; he would probably be able to attend vespers without anyone having noticed his absence.

As Jonah walked back to the monastery, he thought of May. She was big and strong but also had a delicate touch, a gentle touch that he had not experienced before in his life. He liked it.

Return

As soon as Jonah reentered the monastery grounds, he made his way to the scriptorium. There he found Pompey working. He gave Pompey the quills, ink pots, paper, and left over coin. He also gave Pompey the special bag that smelled a lot like baked apples. "Take good care of these, as they are fresh, and we don't want any curious lookers poking their noses around."

"Very good," Pompey replied. "I will visit you later tonight after dinner."

Jonah went to visit the privies to freshen up a little before heading off to vespers. Jonah was half-heartedly into the day's prayers and while the chanting was beautiful as usual, he was so tired that he nearly fell over. After vespers ended he got a few strange looks from the brothers standing near him. Some asked him if he was feeling all right.

"Yes, I'm all right. I'm just very tired. I should probably go to bed early and get a good night's sleep." He realized that working during the night was negatively impacting his sleep. Walking several miles to and from May's place had further exhausted him.

After dinner, Jonah went back to his room. Opening his shutters, he could hear the waves breaking against the rocks below. He heard a light knock at his door. Sure enough, there was Pompey.

"I've been dying for this all day. So tell me, how did it go with your starry-eyed princess-in-distress from Borea? Did you compose her letter for her?"

"Yes I did. I went to her place, knocked on her door, and interrupted her cleaning. She showed me around the various buildings. We went into her main floor area and wrote out her letter which she signed herself."

"Did she flirt with you?"

Jonah interrupted, "Yes, she did. And before you ask, I enjoyed every moment of it. She is also fun to talk to and, as you already know, can be sensitive, especially concerning Anya."

"Did she ask you to move in with her?"

"How did you …? Yes, she did suggest that I move in with her to facilitate better communication."

"However, you've been communicating with her before. She wants you closer to make communication easier. I think it's time for you to ask the hard questions. Do you really want to leave the monastery? Because if you do, this may be the best chance you ever get."

"I have been thinking of accepting her offer. She told me I could have my own room and privacy and suggested that I look for work within Callamar."

"I guess I will have to figure a way to get out of my contract with the monastery. I will need to get an audience with the Callamaran government and probably also with the abbot. Of course, the abbot will have none of it, so it boils down to whether I can get a government official to agree with my interpretation of the law," Jonah said.

"Yes, that would be the main sticking point. It would be best to convince the government but if that fails, there is always the more dramatic gesture," Pompey suggested.

"What is that?" Jonah asked.

"You could just run away. Disappear into the night and never return." Pompey pointed towards the window. "Make your way to May's and then hide out there until you turn twenty-one years."

Jonah eyed Pompey sarcastically, "That sounds very tempting. But how long would it last before someone recognized and reported me? I can see the troops now, dragging me away with May getting into trouble for harboring a fugitive." He thought, *she did say she was big-time trouble.*

"All right. Obviously, we don't have to make any decisions tonight. But now that we have some concrete goals, we can focus our planning."

"Hold on. Why do you have to be involved in this? I can get into trouble all by myself, thank you. I don't want you to bear any responsibility or blame for this."

"If you do the planning, you will definitely get caught. I am the charmer, remember? Nothing happens that I do not allow to happen. Just wait while I find out about getting audiences with local officials, all right?"

"All right, and for what it's worth, May might have some special connections or favor with a noblewoman back in Borea."

"Interesting. All right. I have to go now, but I'll let you know what I've learned as soon as I can. Get some sleep. You almost fell over in vespers."

"Was it that obvious?" Jonah said, embarrassed.

"More than obvious. Good night." Pompey quietly closed the door.

Northcamp Revisited

Northcamp's trading house, once filled with robust trade, was now a burned-out husk, an unrisen phoenix, polluting the east end with foulness and decay. When the trading house burnt down, the fur and hides business had been dealt a major – though not a fatal – blow. The town council had decided against rebuilding the trading house in favor of establishing an outdoor market with knockdown stalls and huts. The trading businesses would no longer have permanent stalls and were required to operate on a first-come, first-served basis. The new market was now vulnerable to the weather, so large quantities of furs were stored in local warehouses, awaiting shipment.

Larger animals were increasingly difficult to find. Trappers had to range further afield, making hunting less profitable than it had been. In the absence of the larger predators such as bears and wolves, some of the smaller animals experienced a population boom and suddenly the forests were filled with rabbits, weasels, skunks, and other rodents. The traders in smaller furs benefitted at first, but the overabundance of these animals caused prices to drop drastically. The fur trade shifted into a subsistence mode with recovery uncertain. Most other businesses in Northcamp had taken a hard hit and would probably never rebound completely.

While the fur trade was reeling from its losses, many of the older residents were not sad to see it go into decline. Northcamp embarked on a modest return to the older forest town it once was and many of the ruffians left town to seek fortunes elsewhere.

In springtime, Northcamp was once again filled with singing birds, buzzing insects, and the aroma of wildflowers. One day, a covered coach arrived from the west and delivered its passengers and cargo to the Bear's Den

Inn. Once the passengers had disembarked with their luggage, the coach driver delivered a small sack of mail to one of Northcamp's municipal post offices. One letter from the batch he kept, carrying it down one of the side streets until he reached a white-fenced house covered in creeping greenery and spring flowers: the Northcamp Apothecary. The driver slipped through the white picket gate, walked up to the front door, and pulled on the hanging door bell. After a short time, Deanna peeked through the side-door window.

The driver greeted Deanna, "Good afternoon, young lady. Is this the Northcamp Apothecary?"

Deanna replied, "Yes, it is."

The driver said, "I have a letter for delivery to the Northcamp Apothecary from Callamar. Will you accept it?"

Deanna replied, "Yes, I can accept the letter on behalf of my lady. Thank you."

Deanna cracked the door open. The driver handed the letter to Deanna and then tipped his cap and went on his way.

Deanna closed and locked the front door then took the letter to Lady Danae who was sitting at her desk in her bed chamber. "My lady, a driver has just delivered a letter from Callamar."

Danae examined the letter. "It looks like it is from Callamar."

Deanna asked excitedly, "Is it from the Amber Academy in Callamar?"

Danae replied, "I do not know. It does not look to be. There is no name and only a partial return address upon it. Well, let us find out who it is from."

Danae found her letter opener and gently broke the letter's wax seal to reveal a beautifully written letter addressed to her. She read the entire letter all the way through before telling Deanna who it was from. Deanna could tell that it was not a happy letter since she could see her lady visibly upset at times.

Danae looked at Deanna then said to her, "I want you to promise me not to repeat what I am going to say to you. Otherwise, I will not read the letter to you."

Deanna replied, "I promise not to repeat to anyone what you will say to me now."

Danae continued, "Do you remember when we went out foraging for mushrooms and elderberries last fall with Anya and May?"

Deanna replied, "Yes, I remember. We had a big harvest that day."

"Well, this is a letter from May. She says she is now living on the east side of Callamar. She had to fight off a pack of feral dogs to get them to leave the building."

"What!?" Deanna laughed at the thought of May fighting with wild dogs. "How did she do that?"

"I do not know. She does say that she used the wolf's bane I gave her. Perhaps she will explain that to us someday."

"Wolf's bane? Interesting."

"May continues on with something sad to tell. When she and Anya were traveling near Fallmouth, they were attacked by a trapper and - I am very sorry to tell you – Anya was killed."

"Oh, no!" Deanna's face turned sad.

"On a more positive note, May has invited us to visit and to take tea with her should we ever travel to Callamar."

"Oh, can we please? We are going to make arrangements with the Amber Academy in Callamar soon, are we not?"

"Yes, of course. You will begin your studies in the fall. Let me see if I can coordinate our visits. Remember Deanna, politeness dictates that I respond to this letter promptly. I will read it to you before I send it. Now, were you not pickling in the kitchen?

Deanna smiled then scurried away to the kitchen where she was making pickled buttons before being interrupted.

Lady Danae next decided that she must first deliver the sad news about Anya to Ma's Kitchen before she could reply to May. She wanted to describe accurately how the bad news was delivered and how it was received. Danae knew that Ma always opened her kitchen at midday so she would have to wait at least until tomorrow morning before delivering the sad news.

The next day around midmorning, Lady Danae set off for Ma's kitchen. As she walked, breathing in the fresh morning air, she twirled a sunny yellow parasol to keep the direct sunshine from damaging her complexion. Men stepped aside to allow her passage, and as they did so, they invariably bowed and tipped their hats, saying, "A good day to you my lady." She in turn nodded acknowledgment. "A good day it is."

As she approached Ma's kitchen, she could smell the appetizing aroma of stew. The front door was closed so she walked around to the back door, which she found open. Ma and company were busy in the kitchen preparing for the day's crowd of hungry customers. Ma recognized Lady Danae standing in the doorway and immediately went to attend her.

"Greetings, my lady. How may I helps you this morning?" Ma wiped her hands on her apron.

"Hello, Ma, a nice day to you. I am here to deliver a message I received yesterday from May."

When Danae uttered the name "May," everyone in the kitchen stopped what they were doing and turned towards Danae. Ma fell silent, waiting. Danae took out the letter and began to read the part about Anya and how she had died and how May was sorry for leaving the kitchen so suddenly without saying goodbye.

Before Danae could finish reading the letter, Berthe's eyes began to well up with tears. Berthe covered her mouth and started walking towards the back door. Before she even got to the door, she was running and sobbing uncontrollably. She ran outside, up the stairs, into the hallway, and into her room. She slammed the door behind her and fell onto her bed crying and crying and crying – all morning long.

Danae, Ma, and Karl were surprised by Berthe's reaction. Ma said, "I guess I never knews how close Baker was to Anya and May."

Danae finished reading May's letter, apologizing for being the bearer of bad news.

Ma stated, "Don't you worries about bringing the bad news. We all liked them a lot. I'll goes upstairs and calms her down. Takes care and feels free to comes in for lunch or dinner anytime. Business has been a little slower lately, and I can gets you a private table if you likes."

"Thank you very much. I will come by again soon." Danae left the kitchen and walked back home.

When Danae returned home, she asked Deanna if she would be a dear and bring her some tea. Then she went into her chamber and sat down at her desk. She spent some time reflecting on what had happened, before slowly, methodically writing a letter to May. Deanna arrived with a fresh pot of tea. "Thank you, Deanna. I will be busy most of today and tonight."

Danae sat there writing, thinking, writing, and thinking until long into the night. All day and night, Deanna curiously monitored Danae's progress. Finally, Danae went to sleep exhausted without eating any dinner. Deanna thought, *what happened to my lady today?*

The Duke

Duke Olan's treks into his beloved Callamar usually began in the morning. The Duke always traveled with an entourage of officials, advisors, security, and cronies. He liked to see and visit all parts of his city and converse with the people who lived there. He did not like to listen to citizens complain within his offices or receiving hall; he preferred meeting and listening to people in their own element. They were more comfortable in their own shops and homes and talked more freely and honestly. He rarely had a chance to ride as far as the east side of Callamar. Today he decided to visit the eastern barracks along the main road and perform a surprise inspection.

During his inspection, he learned from the soldiers and officers stationed there that crime had dropped recently due to someone having broken up one of the local street gangs. The gang boss, Queel, and several of his toadies had been found along the side of the main road hogtied and severely beaten.

One of the Duke's executors retrieved some paperwork from his leather satchel and presented it to the Duke. The report described what witnesses had seen: a man and what some thought was a woman (while others claimed it was a man), were assaulted by a local gang as they walked down the main road. The two had made quick work of the gang, driving off two and hogtying the remaining four. Once the intended victims left, several of the townsfolk and travelers found the helpless gang members and further pummeled them. The gangsters were then stripped of any valuables they still possessed. They were later discovered lying in the gutter in their underwear by some of the daywatch's regular patrols. Untied, brought in, and questioned by the sergeants, they never recovered from their wounds.

Duke Olan expressed concern that no one had come forward to take credit for defeating the gang. He asked if there was a new gang in the area. Could this be the beginning of a new gang war?

Captain Corban Adeley, the commanding officer of the eastern barracks, opined that he did not think so. He said, "None of the local townsfolk were able to identify the two intended victims, nor did they know who eventually subdued the gang. They did comment that the townsfolk were happy that the gang was gone and that boss Queel had been an unwelcome scourge on the local businesses."

"Were these victims local vigilantes taking matters into their own hands?" the Duke asked.

Captain Adeley responded, "Our best guess is that they might have been. That could explain why no one has come forward with any identifying information. No one seemed willing to untie the gang while they were lying beside the road."

"I see. Now, tell me about what happened to the feral dogs further up the road. I assigned that task to your station and all I have heard for a long time is that your soldiers are scared of the dogs. The dogs all run away when your troops attack them and then they return after the soldiers leave. Hardly the mark of a competent operation, wouldn't you say?"

The captain, feeling the increased pressure, reported, "The dogs were definitely a problem but their numbers have been kept in check by local traders. Several sweeps were mounted to clear out the dogs but they smarted up and returned every time."

"So, now, just like magic, I am reading reports saying that all of the dogs are gone, vanished into the night, gone to who knows where. Explain this to me."

The captain explained honestly, "As much as I would like to claim credit for this success, my soldiers were not responsible. From what we have gathered, the local residents say that one day a man and a woman chased them all away and the dogs never came back."

"So, hocus-pocus and poof, they're all gone. Is that right? One man and one woman accomplished in one day what my trained soldiers could not accomplish in months. Are they the same two that took out the local gang?"

"Possibly, but no definitive connection has been made between the two events. They just came out of nowhere, got rid of the dogs, and then the man rode off. The woman has been living there for some time now. We are still investigating the reports. Word is that local business has picked up since the dogs left. There have been no complaints for weeks regarding the dogs or the east side gangs."

The Duke was annoyed that his soldiers looked incompetent, unable to fulfil the tasks they had been assigned. Apparently this girl now lived in the dog mansion. He was eager to question this girl for himself.

The Duke left the barracks promising to be back soon to inspect them again. He expected improvements the next time he returned or reprimands would be levied against all slackers. "Perhaps a day or two scrubbing down the docks will clarify your duties and responsibilities." The Duke and his entourage rode off down the main road. He arrived in front of a shop owned by someone named Ruthie. As he dismounted his horse, many local residents were surprised and honored to see Duke Olan visiting their neighborhood. He found Ruthie near the back of the shop and asked her how business was doing since the dogs had disappeared.

"Your Excellency, it is an honor to have you visit my humble shop. Since the dogs left, business has been better. Trading carts now stop by my shop more often, as well as by the other businesses nearby. Krane, the blacksmith, has been hammering all week long. We hardly heard him before the dogs left."

The Duke asked, "So how did all of the dogs disappear? Did someone kill them all?"

Ruthie replied, "Her name is May and she lives in the building where the dogs lived. One day she arrived in a cart, chased them all away, and they never came back. May is a very nice girl and everyone likes her. She's not in trouble is she? I wouldn't want to see anything bad happen to her. I will vouch for her if need be."

The Duke calmed her concerns, "That will not be necessary. You say a girl chased away all the dogs? How old is this May?"

"I don't know her age but she is young. I can't imagine her being more than eighteen years, but she is also very big and strong."

The Duke changed the subject as he browsed around her shop. He asked, "What are these things here?"

"Those are apple candies. They are very popular among children and their parents."

The Duke pulled out a silver coin and said, "Let me have some, please."

As the Duke emerged from Ruthie's shop, he popped one of the candies into his mouth then handed the bag to one of his soldiers for safekeeping and remounted his horse. The Duke then led them down the road to the person at the heart of all these stories. He looked forward to meeting this local hero.

The Duke's entourage stopped in front of May's house. No sound emerged from the large building. On cue, one of the Duke's footmen walked up to the front door and gave it a good knocking. He stepped back and waited. Nothing happened for a few moments. The man knocked again. Not long afterward, everyone noticed the front gate opening a crack; a girl looked out and over at them. A look of surprise crossed her face.

May, in her working clothes, opened the gate and said, "Greetings, fine sirs; what can I do for you?"

The footman turned and announced, "His Royal Excellency, Duke Olan, calls upon you this day for a short chat."

"Your Excellency wishes to speak with me? I am honored by your visit. I must apologize for my appearance, as I have been cleaning all morning." May was not sure if she was properly dressed to receive someone of the Duke's stature. "I can clean myself up and make myself more –"

The Duke had already dismounted and was walking up to her, saying, "That will not be necessary. I am Duke Olan of Callamar. It is my pleasure to make your acquaintance, May. That is your name, correct?"

May replied, "Yes, my name is May. I have been living in this place for about a month now. Would you and your men like to come into the courtyard where there is more shade?"

"No thank you. I will get to the point. I have heard reports that you have cleared out all of the feral dogs that used to be a scourge upon this neighborhood. Is this true?"

Memories of Lady Danae crossed her mind as May suddenly realized that she would have to be very careful with her words. She wished Jonah was here; *he would know the right things to say.* "Yes, that's true. I cleared out the dogs from this place with some help."

"Would you care to explain how you accomplished this feat when many before you have failed pathetically?" the Duke iterated.

May hesitated for a moment then spoke. "Wolf's bane and foolishness. Only someone with nothing to lose would choose to fight a pack of vicious dogs. I defeated the alpha dog and the others all ran away."

May could see some of the Duke's entourage nod their heads slightly.

"Your accent suggests that you are from Borea. Is that where you acquired your fearlessness and candor?"

"Yes, your Excellency, I am from Borea. I grew up on a farm so I know how to handle farm animals. I arrived here in Callamar not long ago. I can show you my season's permit if you would like to see it," May replied.

"Not necessary. Do you worry that someone will return to this place and reclaim the property?"

"Your Excellency, Ruthie from the shop down the road told me that the heirs to this property have passed away."

"Your bold actions have proved my soldiers incompetent and unimaginative." The Duke cued over one of his officials. "I have decided to investigate the history of this property. If it proves to be as you have claimed, with no remaining living heirs, then I will award this property and full citizenship to you as the one who has succeeded where so many have failed. I congratulate you on your success and welcome you into Callamar."

"Thank you, your Excellency. I will work hard to contribute to the success of Callamar."

"Very good. Is there something you would like to ask of me before I leave you to your chores?" May thought carefully.

"I met a monk at The Charging Boar some time ago." May told her story about Jonah and how he believed that his contract with the Monastery of Saint Dominic was unfair. He also felt that he was being treated unfairly in regards to a death that occurred within the monastery several months ago. One of the Duke's entourage whispered into his ear that they had passed The Charging Boar earlier on their route and that monks were known to frequent the tavern. The Duke nodded his head.

"The monk is a scribe and has read the laws of Callalande many times. If your government officers would give him an opportunity to explain his case, he may be willing to serve the city of Callamar instead."

"Is that ALL you wish to ask?" He chuckled a little. "I can see you do indeed have candor and fearlessness." He asked one of his entourage to take note of her request. "We shall see if anything can be done about the scribe Jonah but I make no promises."

"Thank you, your Excellency." May bowed to him with grateful tears in her eyes.

The Duke and his entourage turned and rode away. As they were passing The Charging Boar, the Duke stopped and looked at the building. The Duke beckoned his advisor over. "I would like to investigate incidents that have happened here." The Duke continued. "Furthermore, have you heard of any deaths or injuries at the monastery within the past year? I do not recall any incidents."

His advisor said, "We have no record of any recent injuries or deaths at the monastery."

The Duke asked to see a list of reports related to the monastery. "Send word to the abbot that I want to meet with him in the next week."

With that, the Duke and his entourage returned to the Palisade and readied themselves for the afternoon's work to come.

Nighthawk

May scarcely dared hope that the Duke might actually relieve Jonah's plight. She figured she should tell Jonah what happened as soon as possible.

Later at night, May walked down to the monastery along the main road. Fueled by adrenaline, she got to the monastery quickly and found her view of Jonah's window. She climbed the wall under the same tree as before, scouting for monks walking along the pathways under his window. Eventually, she saw Jonah's window light up. He came to the window and looked out over the rocks. She worked her way down the wall and across to his window then quickly scaled the dormitory wall as she had before. She saw Jonah sitting at his desk, staring at a paper. She wondered, *what is he thinking about*?

May hoisted herself through the window then somersaulted into his room with a thud. Jonah turned to see May sprawled out on his floor. She began rubbing the knee she had hit against one of the bed legs.

"What the …?" Jonah whispered, "What are you doing here? Are you crazy?"

May whispered back, "I have something to tell you that can't wait. I'll leave soon so I don't get you into trouble"

Jonah had to think fast. "I am expecting Pompey at any moment now. You will have to hide lest someone see you."

And then there was a knock at the door.

"Hide," Jonah whispered.

May quickly rolled under his bed tucking her knees back, as she was longer than the cot he called his bed.

Jonah cracked open the door. Pompey stood just outside the doorway. Jonah did not see anyone else in the hallway. Jonah grabbed Pompey by the robe and pulled him into the room quickly, quietly closing the door behind him. Jonah spun around and put his finger over his lips saying, "Shhhh."

Pompey moved to the center of the room and whispered, "What's going on? I just came to give you an update on –"

"Be quiet. Someone might hear you."

Then a whisper came from under Jonah's bed, "He's talking about me." May squeezed out from under the bed and stood up.

Startled, Pompey looked at May and Jonah, then broke out in laughter. He muffled his mouth with his hand. Unable to control himself, he fell over clutching his stomach trying not to laugh too loudly.

"Get up. It can't be that funny though I admit it does look ridiculous," Jonah said.

"It's … it's …" Pompey continued laughing and rolling on the floor.

May smiled and began laughing, too, mostly at Pompey as he looked ridiculous rolling around on the floor. After a while, everyone stopped laughing.

"All right. Now that everyone's calmed down, what was it that you wanted to tell me, us?" Jonah asked.

May began, "Today, the Duke and his entourage visited me and –"

Startled again, Pompey asked, "The Duke came to YOUR place?"

"I suspect it had something to do with the dogs. He asked me questions about how I had chased them off. He also asked me if I had any questions for him so I took the opportunity to ask him if he would be willing to give Jonah an audience in regards to his contract. He told me he would try."

"Well, I'm not sure what to think about that. The government of Callamar takes its own sweet time when addressing requests or complaints. Even if the Duke promised to help, I would not expect you to hear anything about it for months," Pompey said.

Jonah realized he was going to have to tread carefully. He was concerned that the abbot not get wind of his intentions before he had a chance to present his case. He was aware that some in the monastery might go to any lengths to keep him there. On the other hand, he was touched by May's attempt to help him.

"May, I sincerely thank you for making this request on my behalf. But we have to be careful. One word in the wrong ear could lead to disaster."

"Oh. I didn't think … still, the Duke seemed genuinely interested, especially when I suggested that if you were free from your obligations to the monastery, you might offer your services to the city, maybe even to the Duke's court. He told someone in his entourage to write down my request so at least it's on paper somewhere."

Pompey interjected, "Jonah, you should immediately submit **your own** request for an audience with the Duke, while it's fresh in his mind. You don't want the Duke to mention anything to the abbot in the meantime, so the sooner you get your audience, the better. Two requests are better than one."

"That's true."

"I'm just going to say this: Jonah, you'll never be happy while you're living under the monastery's yoke. This is your chance to live life on your terms – to make your own living in whatever way you choose, to build a family, to come and go as you please."

May blushed at the unspoken implications, but she was greatly cheered to hear Pompey's words of encouragement and support for her plan.

May smiled her gratitude. "Pompey, you are such a sweetie."

"At your service," he said as he bowed.

"Jonah, do you have the rope I gave you?" May asked.

"A rope?" Pompey exclaimed, "Wow, you smuggled a rope in right past me. Endless surprises!"

Asking Pompey to extinguish the candle, Jonah retrieved the knotted rope he had hidden underneath one of his robes, secured it to the window, and heaved the rope over the sill to the ground below. May took the rope and lowered herself to the ground. In no time she had crossed the walkway to the wall. She waved one last time then jumped the wall and left as quickly as she had arrived.

Pompey relit the candle saying, "So that's how you communicate. She comes like a ghost in the night. I'm sorry I interrupted your quality time."

Jonah coiled the rope then put it away. "She gave me this rope thinking that I would use it to escape and visit her. I do intend to use it that way but, of course, I have to limit our secret trysts."

"It's not a tryst if there's no kissing involved. It's more like an apple-fritter handoff."

"Call it what you want," Jonah laughed then fell silent. "The Duke has to be a busy man. Do you think he would have ANY interest in the hopes of a scribe indirectly serving the City of Callamar?"

"I would guess not. He would probably tell you to wait until you turn twenty-one years before leaving the monastery. So we will have to think of something important enough to curry his attention. Let me put something together and show it to you before requesting an audience."

"We could tell them about Danan and the Skuas," Jonah said glumly.

"Yes, there's that. That could be our last resort. Hopefully, we won't have to use it."

"All right. Let's see where things go. I need some sleep or I will fall over again during morning prayers," Jonah said.

"I'll let myself out. Wishing you pleasant dreams of May or is it June already?"

"Get you and your puns out of here now," Jonah snarked.

Pompey left quietly chuckling to himself as he closed the door.

Questions

Jonah went about his daily duties, waiting patiently to see if any of the seeds he and Pompey had sown would take hold. He was able to complete his own copy of the Laws of Callalande over the next few nights. He spent some extra time with Master Po working out some of the kinks in his katas. Jonah had begun seeing Master Po as a kind of mentor and noticed that Po rarely ever spoke about himself. As Jonah wrapped up his practice for the day, he turned to Master Po and asked, "Master Po, pardon my curiosity, but do you live in Callamar?"

Master Po was not expecting a personal question. Packing up his bag, Master Po ignored Jonah until he was ready to leave. "Yes, I live in Callamar. I live north of the city," Master Po answered.

Jonah risked another question of Master Po, "I have lived only in this monastery ever since I came to Callamar years ago and have visited The Charging Boar like everyone else. Do you know of any other places to go or things to do in Callamar that might be of interest to a woman?"

Master Po berated Jonah with a stern stare. "As a monk you ask me that?" He reconsidered, "Perhaps you are expecting a visit from a relative? The Lantern Festival takes place during the first full moon after the summer solstice. It is held next to the Temple of the Dawn, beside the Lycus River. I must go now. Tell no one what I have said. If you do, I will deny it and break some of your bones with my staff, understand?"

"Yes, master, very clearly, master," he replied apologetically. Master Po turned and left quickly with a smile across his face.

Jonah went back to the scriptorium and resumed work on the codices.

Before long, Pompey came up to him and quietly informed him that he had filed a request for an audience with the Duke. "It could take a long time before anyone responds," Pompey explained.

Jonah said, "Thank you, Pompey."

"No problem. My contacts will inform me if anything develops. Try to get some sleep tonight; you look exhausted."

Inquiry

The ringing of the bell tower woke Jonah, as it did most mornings. He ate breakfast and prepared to go to the scriptorium and begin his work for the day. The days were growing longer as they approached the summer solstice. More light meant more work could be done.

As Jonah worked, a brother entered the scriptorium shuffling quickly, immediately seeking out Archscribe Rene. Pompey came over to Jonah's desk to tell him that something was going on within the chapel; no one was being allowed in or out. Archscribe Rene stepped out of his office and announced, "Brethren scribes! Duke Olan of Callamar has ordered everyone within the monastery to proceed immediately to your rooms where you will remain until further instructions are received. We will lock the library and yield the scriptorium to the Duke's guards. Let's move quickly."

All of the scribes locked up the library and evacuated to the dormitory. Several of the Duke's guards escorted brethren to the dormitory. Jonah had flashbacks of the lockdown after Danan's death.

Jonah saw Pompey coming towards him, "I know we requested a hearing with the Duke but this feels a little overdone. Do you think we said too much?"

"I can't imagine so. I guess we'll just have to ride out the storm and see where this leads. Maybe it has nothing to do with our requests," Jonah replied.

"I hope so," Pompey said.

A voice rang throughout the courtyard instructing everyone to move quickly to their rooms. Jonah, Pompey, and others headed into the refectory together then climbed the stairs to their rooms before separating.

"Just remember, remain calm and answer their questions truthfully, but don't give them any more details than they ask for. They might not be that smart." Pompey whispered, "And remember, we've been through interrogation before so this is nothing new to us."

"Right, I'll do that. We'll talk again after this thing blows over," Jonah said.

By this time, the Duke's guards were everywhere. Jonah went directly to his room in the dormitory but did make one stop by sneaking into the privies before getting to his room. Guards stood in every hallway junction, staircase, and common room. Jonah began speculating on what was going on. He sensed something was not adding up. This was more than just a requested hearing. He searched his memory for a time within the past few years when the Duke's guards had entered the monastery. Was the Duke here himself? If so, it would be the first time he had ever visited while Jonah had lived here.

Earlier, Duke Olan rode through Callamar to the monastery with his favorites. He also led an entourage of magistrates, inquisitors, accountants, scribes, and a contingent of his elite troops. The Duke's presence marked a change in his unwritten policy granting self-governance to the monastery. The Duke was making it clear that he was the ultimate authority in Callalande.

Duke Olan gained entry to the monastery near mid-morning and sought to secure the abbot's cooperation before beginning his inquiry. The Duke's troops found Abbot August in his rectory. As the Duke entered the abbot's chambers, Abbot August protested angrily, "What is the meaning of this invasion? You are in violation of *Unam Sanctum* and have no authority within the Monastery of Saint Dominic or the Church of the Holy Cross."

"I am Duke Olan, brother to King Edmund III of Korgynslande. I have sole authority over all matters, public and private, within the province of Callalande of the Kingdom of Korgynslande. I am also responsible for the well-being of all citizens and residents within Callalande, as you are already aware."

"I remind you that all kings and nobles must yield to the direct authority of the Pope as per Pope Boniface VIII's bull of 1302. The Pope of the Church of the Holy Cross has dominion over all kings and churches. King Edmund is no different from any other king."

Duke Olan laughed, "So your Pope unilaterally declares himself ruler of all that is seen and unseen and everyone must just accept it as so? And which pope is that, the Pope of the Vatican or the Pope in Avignon? Your church can't decide –"

Abbot August interrupted Duke Olan, "There is only one Pope. He is seated within the Holy See of the Vatican and is answerable only to the Lord. All others are pretenders and heretics. Your disobedience and insolence may result in your excommunication and/or eternal damnation. As you know, kings have been excommunicated, including Phillip of France, only to return to the Church and beg for restitution."

Duke Olan explained, "Neither Pope nor any other religious official has any dominion over Korgynslande or Callalande. I grant self-governance to all religious orders as a courtesy within Callamar and Callalande. An inquiry will occur today. It will work better for everyone if you and your priors –"

"I will have nothing to do with any inquiry. You have no authority here. I command you to take your leave at once."

"– cooperate with my guards." Duke Olan grew stern. "You command nothing. You will remain confined to your quarters and summarily summoned at an appropriate time of my choosing. You are dismissed."

With the abbot confined to his quarters, the chief magistrate informed Prior Damien, the Prior of Security, that the Duke's inquiry could last as little as a day if everyone cooperated and everything went smoothly. Like Abbot August, Prior Damien demonstrated no inclination to cooperate and demanded to speak to the abbot privately. The chief magistrate told Prior Damien, "The abbot had been confined to his quarters. The sooner you cooperate, the sooner we will leave the monastery."

Duke Olan assigned the questioning of witnesses to his inquisitors. The Duke intended to observe every action and hear every word and gesture made by all sides with interest and scrutiny. Inquisitor Bjorn would lead the Duke's inquiry by first questioning the priors and the archscribe. Duke Olan had given Bjorn a list of questions that he wanted answered. The Duke explained, in no subtle terms, that the primary goal of the inquiry was to determine if any deaths had occurred within the monastery and if so, why had they not been reported in a timely manner. Most other violations of the Duke's policies could be treated as forgivable, but unreported deaths and their causes were very important to the Duke. He considered a person's death a solemn occurrence, holding that the dead should be treated with some measure of dignity. And while death was expected to come to all, intentional killing such as murder was not to be tolerated.

The Duke took his seat and nodded for proceedings to begin. In turn, each prior would be summoned to the abbot's office beginning with

Archscribe Rene. Rene was brought in and asked to swear an oath on a Bible that his testimony would be truthful.

Inquisitor Bjorn began, "How is the coin received from completed-city contracts accounted for?"

Archscribe Rene explained, "I do not handle coin received from city contracts. Prior Tallis is responsible for the accounting of all monastery funds."

Inquisitor Bjorn asked, "How much of the contracted coin is spent on the brethren who fulfill city contracts?"

Archscribe Rene explained, "Prior Tallis is responsible for dispersing monastery funds. I am allowed to request funds only for supplies and maintenance of the library and scriptorium."

"How are scribes assigned to work on city contracts?"

The archscribe stated, "I am responsible for assigning specific scribes to specific tasks. Naturally, the most difficult tasks fall to the most skilled scribes. I track their progress and make sure deadlines are met."

"How do monks become scribes?"

The archscribe stated, "At Saint Dominic's, all scribes are monks but not all monks are scribes. Young men who possess superior penmanship – that is, who write clearly, quickly, and accurately – are recruited to join the monastery as scribes and are naturally expected to conform to the rule of monastic life. Others devote their lives to being monks and come to the monastery with other gifts."

"How are scribes compensated for their services?"

The archscribe stated, "The monastic rule stipulates that all brethren share equally in the fruits of their collective labor. All within these walls have a place to sleep, solitude for contemplation, fellowship, and guidance. They receive nourishment for their bodies and sustenance for their souls."

"How exactly are scribes recruited here at Saint Dominic's?"

The archscribe stated, "The monastery recruits scribes primarily through but not limited to parochial schools within major cities as scribing requires a very specific set of skills. Families heeding the call sign a contract pledging their sons' services until the age of twenty-one years."

"I assume that all recruits understand what the monastic rule entails. How do you make these expectations clear?"

The archscribe stated, "All who wish to be scribes must sign a contract. If they are under the age of majority, which we hold to be twenty-one years, a parent or guardian must sign. The contract delineates the conduct expected of the recruits at all times. The recruits promise to remain in the monastery at least until their twenty-first year. At that time, they may choose to return to the vicissitudes of worldly life – though few choose that path."

"So of this contract that binds a scribe's service until the age of twenty-one years, is it signed by the recruit himself or is it signed by one of his family members – father or uncle?"

The archscribe stated, "– or guardian. I believe it is signed by the scribe's parents or in some cases, a legal guardian."

"So the recruit himself never signs his own contract of service?"

The archscribe stated, "I believe that is correct, though I am not the keeper of the contracts and I cannot confirm that without reviewing the contracts."

"How do you determine the age of a recruit?"

The archscribe was caught off guard, "Determine? Why would we question the word of those who wish to serve the Lord?"

"In addition, how do you verify that the signatures on contracts are authentic?"

The archscribe's anger and indignation were increasingly apparent, but he controlled his voice, "In my experience, families are proud to offer their sons to the Lord. Contracts are signed for all to witness, in the presence of the Lord. Who would violate such a sacred trust – to what end?"

Seeing his consternation, Inquisitor Bjorn changed his tactics. "Do you recall the scribes known as Brothers Danan, Ergan, and Borse?"

The archscribe hesitated, "I … I remember hearing those names."

"Are they no longer living amongst the brethren at the Monastery of Saint Dominic?"

The archscribe answered, "Yes."

"What became of them?"

The archscribes's silence lasted several long moments.

"Did you hear the question?"

The archscribe answered, "No – that is, yes. But I can't answer. I do not know what became of them. I was told they had left the monastery."

"By whom were you told this?"

The archscribe stalled, playing with his fingers. He put his head down into his hands and quietly said, "I … I believe I was told … that is, we all were informed … by the abbot."

As Archscribe Rene finished his testimony, he was escorted directly to the scriptorium where he was told to await further instructions.

Prior Tallis was the next to testify. He took an oath on the Bible and then sat down.

Inquisitor Bjorn began, "Prior Tallis, are you responsible for accountancy within the monastery?"

Prior Tallis responded, "I am responsible for the collection and dispersement of all funds within the monastery. Some funds I am authorized to disperse myself and others require authorization from the abbot."

"How is the coin received from completed city contracts accounted for?"

Prior Tallis responded, "All coin received from city contracts is placed into the monastery's general treasury and recorded as credits in the monastery's general ledger."

"Does the monastery have any sources of revenue other than city contracts?"

Prior Tallis responded, "Yes, we have other sources of coin, but they are small fish compared to the city contracts. The monastery also receives many donations such as foodstuffs."

"Please give me some examples of how funds are dispersed."

Prior Tallis responded, "I disperse funds by purchasing supplies for many of the monastery's needs. Much of the time, the monastery is self-sufficient in terms of foodstuffs. The winters in Callamar can be unpredictable and brutal so sometimes I purchase supplies to bolster our food stocks for the winter.

The monastery also receives many donations from generous merchants and residents. These gifts are entered into a separate ledger. The bulk of the expenses come from supplies purchased for the needs of the scriptorium such as ink, paper, and quills."

"How much coin is left over from the city contracts after monastery maintenance and supplies have been purchased?"

Prior Tallis explained, "I would need to access my ledgers to answer the question accurately." Prior Tallis was escorted to his ledgers, accompanied by one of the Duke's accountants, Jon. When they returned with the prior's ledgers, Jon performed a quick audit and found there to be a significant surplus of funds.

Prior Tallis confirmed, "That is correct."

"What other expenses was this surplus used for?"

Prior Tallis explained, "Some of the coin was sent to the Bishop of Callamar seated in the Cathedral of the Holy Cross while some was sent to the Monastery of Saint Ausgar in Scullsbergen." Jon nodded in confirmation then raised his hand at Inquisitor Bjorn.

"Proceed, Jon."

The accountant stated, "The ledgers indicate that there were a number of unspecified items purchased by Abbot August and Prior Damien. Another curious ledger entry indicates an unusually large payment made out for cleaning services in the late fall, last year."

Inquisitor Bjorn turned back to Prior Tallis, "What was this large payment for cleaning services for and who received the coin?"

Prior Tallis explained, "I was instructed to make the funds available for cleaning services, but I do not know where they were sent or who had received them. I remember around that time, the monastery hired Master Po to begin training monks in the techniques of self-defense. I recall that ledger item being distinct from the cleaning services ledger entry." Jon nodded in confirmation.

"Who instructed you to make the funds available?"

Prior Tallis hesitated.

"I remind you that you are under oath to speak truthfully."

Prior Tallis continued to hesitate then closed his eyes and stated, "The abbot instructed me."

Inquisitor Bjorn changed his subject. "Do you recall the scribes known as Brothers Danan, Ergan, and Borse?"

Prior Tallis stated, "Yes, I do."

"Are they no longer living amongst the brethren at the Monastery of Saint Dominic?"

Prior Tallis stated, "They are no longer living within the monastery."

"What became of them?"

Prior Tallis stated, "I don't know. I was told that they had to leave and would not be returning."

"Who told you they left?"

Prior Tallis stated, "Abbot August told me they left. He never elaborated."

"Are you aware of any deaths occurring within the past year within the Monastery of Saint Dominic?"

Here Prior Tallis hesitated then answered, "I have no direct knowledge of any deaths within the monastery."

"I remind you again that you are under oath to speak truthfully."

Prior Tallis stated, "I don't know anything about any deaths. I recall only that there were rumors circulating within the monastery that the three brothers, whom you named, were dead, but I never gave those rumors much credence. Neither the abbot nor the priors ever substantiated anything related to those rumors. Prior Damien is responsible for Security and inquiries within the monastery, so I believed the abbot when he said that the brethren you named had left the monastery."

When Prior Tallis finished his testimony, he was escorted directly to the scriptorium where he was told to await further instructions.

Prior Damien was summoned next. Once he was seated in front of the tribunal, he refused to take any oath and explained, "I do not recognize the Duke's authority over monastery matters and I refuse to answer any questions."

Inquisitor Bjorn decided to go straight to the heart of the matter. "Did you know or were you familiar with a scribe named Brother Danan?"

Prior Damien remained silent.

"Refusal to testify for the Duke's inquiry is punishable by fines or imprisonment or both regardless of whether you recognize the Duke's authority."

Prior Damien remained silent.

"Is Brother Danan no longer living amongst the brethren at the Monastery of Saint Dominic?"

Prior Damien remained silent.

"What became of Brother Danan?"

Prior Damien remained silent.

"Has anyone died within the walls of the monastery within the past year?"

Prior Damien remained silent, but he was clearly becoming agitated.

"Where are Brother Danan's present whereabouts?"

Prior Damien continued his silence.

"Are you familiar with two scribes named Brother Ergan and Brother Borse?"

Prior Damien continued his silence.

"Where are their present whereabouts?"

Prior Damien continued his silence.

Finally, the Duke instructed his Captain of the Guard to detain Prior Damien for refusal to cooperate. He addressed the prior directly, "As Prior of Security, it is your responsibility to ensure the safety and security of all brethren within the monastery. If it is determined that monks died within this monastery within the past year, during your tenure, you shall be held responsible. All deaths, natural, accidental, or malicious must be reported in a timely manner to my government offices."

Prior Damien then spoke squarely to the Duke and his tribunal, "You have no authority here within this monastery and no authority over me. The Lord will judge you accordingly."

The Duke said, "You are dismissed."

The Captain of the Guard and his deputy escorted Prior Damien to a secure room and awaited further instructions.

Prior Lund was summoned next. After he had taken his oath to answer all questions truthfully, Inquisitor Bjorn asked, "Prior Lund, what are your responsibilities within the monastery?"

Prior Lund responded, "I am responsible for the well-being of the brethren."

"What does your understanding of the term 'well-being' entail?"

Prior Lund responded, "It means several things to me. I ensure that our food stores are equitably distributed and that foodstuffs are adequately stocked should adverse conditions arise. I ensure that the monastery does not turn into an icebox. While it is understood that monastic life is one of spartan and meager comforts, no one should have to freeze during the cold winter nights. I am responsible for issuing recreational passes in accordance with the monastic rule. Monks and scribes may be awarded time off for good behavior and work well done. It helps maintain the work quality at an acceptable level. I also monitor and help stock the infirmary with medicines. I am usually the first to hear when problems arise within the monastery."

"I see. So then it would be you who knows where Brothers Danan, Ergan, and Borse have all traveled to after they left the monastery suddenly several months ago?"

Prior Lund responded, "All monastery matters fall under the jurisdiction of the abbot. The abbot made it clear to me that he is the ultimate authority within the monastery and all queries should be directed to his attention."

"How do you define the term 'monastery matters'?"

Prior Lund responded, "'Monastery matters' is a loose term generally referring to all events and occurrences that take place or have taken place within the walls of Saint Dominic's to the abbot, the priors, or the brethren."

"Today, the abbot is not in charge of the monastery; rather the Duke has authority over monastery matters. Do you know where Brothers Danan, Ergan, and Borse went after they left the monastery last year?"

Prior Lund responded, "I cannot answer your question as I have no authority to answer."

"I remind you that you are under oath to speak truthfully."

Prior Lund sat back silently.

"If you wish to be dragged off to jail for refusing to cooperate, that is your prerogative. If the Duke wishes to shut down the monastery, he will do so. I advise you to answer the question."

At last Prior Lund spoke, "The abbot told all of the brethren that Brothers Danan, Ergan, and Borse had all left the monastery very suddenly and that they were being looked after by the Church. I do not know anything other than what I have been told."

"Did no report reach your ears that the three missing brothers had in fact died?"

Prior Lund replied, "I am aware that there were rumors to that effect."

"Did you take steps to find out if those rumors were true?"

Prior Lund replied, "I did attempt to investigate but the abbot instructed me to cease my inquiries. I never found out if the rumors were true."

"Did it bother you that the abbot told you to cease your investigation?"

Prior Lund replied, "Yes, but the abbot has the final authority on monastery matters. It is not my place to question his decisions or his authority."

"Was it your decision to hire Master Po?"

Prior Lund responded, "Not directly, but I did recommend establishing order and discipline within the monastery. Abbot August liked the idea and felt that Master Po might bring a fresh perspective to training the body to quiet the mind."

"Were you in any way responsible for the hiring of any cleaners around the time of the disappearance of Brothers Danan, Ergan, and Borse?"

Prior Lund responded, "I heard about the cleaners after they had left. I was not informed by the abbot as to why they were hired. I spent most of that day trying to maintain a lockdown in the dormitory to make sure brethren remained in their rooms until summoned by the abbot."

Inquisitor Bjorn decided that Prior Lund had given all of his relevant testimony. Prior Lund was escorted directly to the scriptorium where he was told to await further instructions.

Prior Lund was the last of the priors to be questioned. Duke Olan now had a difficult decision to make. If he brought Abbot August in for questioning, the abbot might become insolent as Prior Damien had and turn the inquiry into a battle of wills. The Duke decided to question the abbot back in his Palisade where he could preserve a measure of the abbot's dignity. The Duke ordered his Captain of the Guard to escort both Abbot August and Prior Damien to his Palisade. The Duke continued the inquiry with some of the brethren who were closest to the individual disappearances.

Brother Kason was brought before the inquiry and took his oath. Inquisitor Bjorn sat down and Inquisitor Piotyr took over the questioning. "What are your responsibilities here within the monastery?"

Brother Kason explained, "I have several responsibilities. I help plant and harvest vegetables within the garden plots. I help make candles in the stables, but my special duty is in the infirmary. It is my honor to help injured or ill brethren recover from wounds or sickness."

"What do you remember about the disappearance of Brothers Danan, Ergan, and Borse in the fall of last year?"

Brother Kason fell silent and became very agitated.

"I remind you that you are under oath to speak truthfully."

Brother Kason fidgeted with his hands, stalling. He let out a sigh of resignation before finally speaking up. "Duke Olan, before I say more, I wish to place myself in your personal protection. I swear fealty to you and promise to reveal all I know. In return, I ask that you protect me from the wrath of those whose confidence I now betray. For revealing what I know will certainly place my life in danger."

An air of astonishment grew within the chamber. The Duke accepted Brother Kason's pledge of fealty and promised the requested protection.

Brother Kason continued in a strained voice, "On Saint Anders Mass last, shortly after compline, I was summoned to attend one of the brethren, whose body had been discovered on the pathway below the bell tower. It was Danan. To my sorrow, I was too late to administer last rites or receive his confession, as his soul had but then departed his body. It appeared to me that he had fallen from the tower and landed where he was found. I assumed that Prior Damien required my assistance in washing the body and laying it out in the chapel, according to our custom. But Abbot August was anxious to remove and conceal the body from the rest of the brethren and asked that we remove the body quickly and clean away all traces of blood. After we had completed these tasks – "

Inquisitor Piotyr interrupted, "Brother Kason, would you please clarify who you mean by 'we.'"

Brother Kason responded, "By 'we,' I mean Prior Damien and myself."

"Thank you, please continue."

Brother Kason continued, "I was further instructed by Abbot August to assist a small group of women who were engaged in a similar task within the cloisters. The bodies of Brothers Ergan and Borse were carried past me on palls, both in a dreadful state, by the same women."

Inquisitor Piotyr interrupted again, "Brother Kason, how did you know there were women in the monastery?"

Brother Kason responded, "They wore dark robes concealing their identities, but I heard their voices and I could tell that they were women and not brethren."

"Thank you, please continue."

Brother Kason continued, "By my candlelight, I could discern that the throats of Ergan and Borse had been slit and the bedclothes were stained scarlet. I do not know where the bodies were taken, but I had the opportunity to observe a bloody kitchen knife on the bedside table in Borse's cloister."

"Did you observe any knife wounds on Danan's body?"

Brother Kason responded, "I did not see any knife wounds on Danan's body but I was able to observe only his head and neck when moving his body." Brother Kason paused for a moment in thought then continued before Inquisitor Piotyr could ask another question. "The day before Danan's body was found, I personally treated him in the infirmary for several bruises on his torso and neck. Danan told me that he had fallen down in the privy before morning prayers, but his injuries were not consistent with falling down."

"If I heard you correctly, you directly observed all three brothers, Danan, Ergan, and Borse, to be deceased?" Brother Kason began to cry quietly. "Why are you crying?"

Brother Kason stifled his crying and wiped away his tears. "Yes, I saw all three brothers deceased. Every day, I think about what happened and wonder if I could have done anything differently to help Danan. I still don't understand why these deaths occurred."

"To your knowledge, did Abbot August know that the aforementioned brothers were all deceased on that day when you were instructed to assist?"

Brother Kason responded, "He knew for certain that Danan was deceased. I don't have any direct knowledge of what he knew or did not know about Ergan and Borse. I assume he did since he instructed me to assist the women."

Inquisitor Piotyr brought a small cup of water to Kason and changed his questioning. "When the abbot convened all of the brethren the next day, did he tell everyone that Danan was deceased?"

Brother Kason responded after drinking the water, "Thank you. Abbot August informed everyone present that Ergan, Borse, and Danan, had had to leave the monastery suddenly and that they would not be returning. He also said that their duties would be reassigned. He never said anyone was deceased."

"What did you think about Abbot August's statements to the brethren that day?"

Brother Kason responded, "Death is a sensitive subject, so naturally the abbot wished to protect the brethren from knowledge of the brothers' tragic deaths. While I don't condone withholding the truth, however unpleasant, I understand the motives that prompted his prevarication. I was admonished not to say anything about what I saw or did."

When Brother Kason finished his testimony, he returned to his room and was told to await further instructions. The room filled with murmurs after he left.

Brother Lars, one of the Skuas, was summoned next to testify. After the oath was administered, Inquisitor Piotyr asked, "What was your relationship with Brother Ergan?"

Brother Lars responded, "Ergan was my friend. We worked together as scribes in the scriptorium. We spent time together as a group. Ergan called our group the Skuas."

"Do you know anything of Brother Ergan's current whereabouts?"

Brother Lars responded, "I don't know where he is or what may have happened to him. The abbot told us that he left the monastery, but I have heard others speculate that he is … deceased." Lars choked a little as he said, "deceased." He regained his composure and continued, "All I know for sure is that I have not heard anything definitive from him or about him since he disappeared."

Inquisitor Piotyr brought a small glass of water over to Lars. "Did Ergan say anything to you about planning to leave the monastery before he disappeared?"

Brother Lars took a small drink of water before he responded, "Ergan said nothing to me about any plans to leave the monastery in the fall. As far as I can recall, he never once talked about leaving the monastery. He anticipated taking his final vows and hoped to someday become the archscribe or a prior."

"Do you have any knowledge of whether Brother Ergan is deceased?"

Brother Lars responded, "I don't know. All of the stories I've heard are conflicting. By now, I would have thought that something more definitive would have been made known to us, the brethren. Thus far, that has not happened and I expect it never will." Lars choked up again, "He was my friend. He would have said something to me – not just disappear."

"Did you ever witness Brother Ergan get into any physical altercations with anyone before he disappeared last year?"

Lars took a little longer to answer this question. "Ergan and Danan might not have liked one another and they may have gotten into a fight in the privy. I did not witness anything happen between them, but afterward, Ergan did show me some bruises he said that he received from Danan."

Brother Lars was asked the same questions with regard to Brother Borse. Inquisitor Piotyr received essentially the same answers. Lars returned to his room after being told to await further instructions.

Brother Kraig's testimony was similar to that of Lars. He explained that Ergan had called their group the Skuas as a kind of joke. The name caught on and they had been known as the Skuas ever since. Ergan also felt that all the work he had done for the monastery over the years went underappreciated.

And finally, the knock came, the knock that Jonah had been anticipating. He was escorted through the hallways to the abbot's office and directed to the interrogation seat where he took his oath and sat down. Inquisitor Piotyr asked Jonah about his relationship to Brothers Danan, Ergan, and Borse. Jonah began a long narrative about how Danan was his roommate until that fateful day and how Ergan and Borse were bullies who picked on Danan after Abbot Eddo left the monastery and Abbot August arrived. He recounted the incident at The Charging Boar for the Duke and his tribunal. He knew that story so well by now that he could recite it without pause or hesitation.

Jonah continued, "I cannot think of any reason why Danan would have left the monastery without telling me. Danan was my friend. Yes, he was homesick, but he was not stupid enough to leave without permission."

Jonah had already thought long and hard about whether or not he was going to tell anyone about the letter Danan had left for him. Ultimately, Jonah decided that the letter was private. He kept it in a secret pocket next to his heart. No one else needed to know about it.

Jonah continued, "Danan went to sleep that night just as I did. He never said a word about leaving. When I woke up the next morning, he was gone and the monastery was on lockdown. I did my best to investigate, but to this day I don't know everything that happened."

"Was Abbot August or Prior Damien aware of your investigation?"

Jonah stated, "Oh, no. They would have shut me down and sanctioned me if they were aware of any investigation going on behind their backs."

"What did you discover through your investigation?"

Jonah stated in a sorrowful tone, "I don't know many of the details and probably never will, but I am confident that Danan is dead, along with Ergan and Borse."

Jonah could see that the Duke was listening intently. Jonah thought, *is the Duke aware of my request for an audience?* As the Duke listened, he thought, *so this is the scribe Jonah.*

Jonah's questioning continued but nothing new was revealed.

Duke Olan's inquiry lasted well into the evening. Many additional testimonials were taken, including Pompey's. The inquisitors had much work ahead in compiling a comprehensive report to be submitted to the Duke. Likewise, the magistrates would write their own reports and conclusions on the testimonials. Eventually, the Duke would have to make a final determination with regard to the inquisitors' and tribunal's findings.

After carefully considering all of the evidence that had been presented and after weighing the veracity of various witnesses, the Duke preliminarily concluded that Brother Danan had likely killed Ergan and Borse before jumping to his own death. That a sincere Catholic would commit such grave sins suggested that he had suffered extreme provocation. Since the one responsible was deceased, the Duke could foresee nothing to be gained by placing public blame on Danan, nor by adding to the suffering of his family or friends.

The only matter that appeared to need serious determination was how much responsibility should be placed upon those in charge of the monastery for not reporting the deaths in a timely manner. Some bigger questions also needed addressing, such as how much oversight did the Duke's government need to place over the internal affairs of religious orders? A formalized policy needed to be drafted, debated, ratified, and proclaimed.

Another ethical question arose to confront the Duke: is it better to suppress unpleasant truths to protect the people's feelings or do those people have the right to know the truth even if as a result they suffer? The Duke sided with the latter. It was frequently stated that "the truth will set you free." *Pain and freedom appear to walk together.* The Duke promised the monastery staff and brethren that he would return with a week's time and report the inquiry's findings to one and all.

While many of these issues raised and questions asked were debates for another day, there was one more matter that Duke Olan wanted to explore, and he insisted that his tribunal and inquisitors indulge him.

The Duke's Offer

Jonah was summoned once more before the Duke's inquiry. As Jonah entered the chamber a second time, he was clearly exhausted.

The Duke himself spoke directly to Jonah, "Brother Jonah, it is my understanding that you wish to make a case for nullifying your contract with the monastery and subsequently serving the City of Callamar. You have my attention."

Jonah was expecting to be asked more questions about Danan, but suddenly he realized that this was the opportunity he had been waiting for. He took a deep breath, calmed his mind, and spoke. "Thank you, your Excellency. For some years I have been fulfilling scriptorial contracts by copying legal codices for the City of Callamar and in doing so, I have noticed that young men of age eighteen years or more can sign contracts on their own with the government of Callamar to serve either in the military or in the local night watch. I figure if a man can be responsible for his own commitment to public service at eighteen years, why would I not be able to sign such a contract pledging my service to the City of Callamar instead of having to serve here in this monastery until my twenty-first year, especially since I never signed my current contract myself. However, I do not wish to serve in the military or in the night watch or as a scribe for the City of Callamar. I am in my eighteenth year. Is there some other capacity in which I might be able to serve the City of Callamar?"

"There are few positions in Callamar for which someone of your age might qualify besides those which you have mentioned. Why not just wait until you turn twenty-one years to leave the monastery?"

Jonah fell silent before responding. "Before your Excellency and everyone else gathered here today, I swear I had nothing to do with the deaths of Danan, Ergan, and Borse. Yet, in the months since that day, I have been treated as if I were guilty of all three deaths. I was and still am scorned by many brethren. Abbot August sequestered me in my room for much of that time 'for my own good.' While I have felt much regret over Danan's death, I am not guilty of anything. I feel that I can no longer work effectively under these conditions. The only solace I feel is when I am training with Master Po. Leaving the monastery would be the best way for me to relieve the stress I am living under. I think that if my own family had known about such mysterious disappearances, they might never have signed the contract that brought me here in the first place."

"I see." The Duke sat back in his chair and thought for a moment. He then asked, "I understand that you are one of the best and fastest scribes here in the monastery. Is that true?"

"I am certainly the fastest scribe, and I can speak and write several languages."

Then, one of the Duke's entourage asked the Duke for permission to speak. "There may be an alternative to what Jonah proposes. The city needs teachers skilled in penmanship and language. However, becoming a teacher requires some training. Jonah would have to leave the monastery and find somewhere else to live."

The Duke interjected, "Interesting. Jonah, does becoming a school teacher sound like something you might be interested in doing? If so, I would be willing to release you from your contract with the monastery and allow you to sign a new contract as soon as you leave. Let me know by tomorrow afternoon. I will send one of my education officials tomorrow afternoon to release you from the monastery and deliver you to a temporary boarding facility until you are able to find something more permanent." Duke Olan then dismissed Jonah from the inquiry saying that he looked forward to receiving his response.

"Thank you, your Excellency. I will have my response ready for you tomorrow afternoon." Jonah bowed and smiled.

Walking to his room, Jonah began to realize what had just happened. The Duke was offering Jonah a way out of the monastery, HIM of all people. This was something he had to tell Pompey. Jonah went straight to Pompey's room and knocked on his door. Pompey opened his door expecting to see a guard summoning him back to the inquiry but his face turned into a smile when he saw Jonah standing there. "Are they gone?" Pompey asked.

"Yes. They're all leaving, I think. Can I come in?" Jonah replied.

"Sorry, of course, come in," Pompey said.

"The most interesting thing just happened. I was summoned a second time before the inquiry and the Duke spoke to me himself. He offered to release me from the monastery if I accepted an offer to become a school teacher for the City of Callamar," Jonah explained.

Pompey's face lit up, "That's wonderful! You did it! You managed to get out of the monastery. How did you come up with that idea?"

"I didn't. One of the Duke's officials suggested it. I have until tomorrow afternoon to accept the offer," Jonah said.

Pompey grabbed Jonah's shoulders and shook him excitedly saying, "And of course you're going to accept it, right? This is what we've been working for all this time. And May is going to be just as happy as you are." Pompey glowed with excitement.

Jonah was confused. Everything was happening so fast. He realized that if he accepted the Duke's offer, this was going to be his last night in the monastery.

"Why are you looking sad?" Pompey asked.

"I am thinking that I might not be able to see or talk to you much anymore, if at all."

"Hogwash! We'll still be able to see each other once in a while. This is your big chance to begin a new life away from all of this misery. And no one knows what misery will befall us as a result of this inquiry. I expect things to become hectic for a while until everything is sorted out. You need to get some sleep soon or you are going to fall over."

Jonah went to his room and looked around at all of his things. He still had the bag that he brought with him to the monastery those many years ago. He began packing all of his possessions into the bag and found he had a hard time fitting everything in. When the time came for him to leave, he would be fully loaded down.

Jonah went to the window and opened the shutters. The moon was behind the monastery but still lighting the shoreline. He could see the whitecaps of breakers rolling into the shore, sounding on the rocks below. He realized that this was the last time he was going to see the view from his window. He took one last look across the Sea of Calla, then closed the shutters and went to bed.

Jonah looked up at the ceiling, thinking. He knew he would have to act normal tomorrow all day until he was summoned to the front door. Mentally, he plotted a path to the front door that would pass by the fewest rooms and offices. He imagined what May's face would look like when he came knocking on her door tomorrow.

A New Life

Jonah heard the bells tolling and awoke. He prepared himself for morning prayers as usual. He met Pompey in the hallway and walked down with him to the chapel. Jonah had not slept well. He quietly yawned as prayers were starting later than usual. Prior Lund entered the chapel, preparing to lead the morning's service. Abbot August and Prior Damien were nowhere to be seen. Jonah thought, *what happened to the abbot and Prior Damien*? There was an unnatural quiet and air of anxiety within the chapel as the service finished quickly. Whispers circulated concerning yesterday's inquiry. Jonah and Pompey walked to the refectory for breakfast as everyone eyed each other suspiciously. Jonah felt more eyes looking his way again. *This is not something I need right now*, he thought.

Pompey whispered, "There's been lots of confusion this morning. Don't worry about anything. Soon all of this will be behind you. I'll quash any ill feelings directed at you when you depart. I am so happy for you. I will always value and honor your friendship. You may have escaped the monastery but you have not escaped me. Friendship is forever. I am Danan's friend and will always be yours."

Jonah replied with a tear in his eye, "Thank you Pompey. Yes, of course we will always be friends. When you get a chance to take some leave, you can stop by and see me at May's place. And of course, there is always The Charging Boar."

After breakfast, Jonah went back to his room to wait. He was prepared to tell anyone who asked that he was not feeling well and needed to rest. Jonah had all of his possessions packed and ready to go. He waited and waited and waited. As the sun fell low over the Horns, he was becoming concerned. He thought, *Is there a problem?* As the last sunlight was dimming over the Horns, there came a knock on his door. It was Pompey.

"Hurry up, Jonah. Someone at the front gate is asking for you. He does not look like one of the Duke's officials we saw yesterday." Jonah picked up all of his things and the two of them took the quiet route to the gate. When Jonah got there, the official was waiting next to a horse cart.

The official introduced himself to Jonah as Education Secretary Gwyon and apologized for being late as he had had difficulty procuring a cart. Jonah introduced himself.

"All right, the first order of business is for me to ask you if you are prepared to sign a contract pledging your services to the City of Callamar for the position of school teacher. This constitutes agreeing to the Duke's offer which I understand you received yesterday," Gwyon explained.

"Yes I am. I am prepared to make that commitment and sign your papers," Jonah replied.

"I'm glad to hear that. We can take care of the paper signing later. Right now, I must give you and your friend here a copy of this document. This document is an order from Duke Olan releasing you of your obligation to serve out your contract with the monastery. It is signed by Duke Olan. Here is one copy for your personal records and here is one for the monastery's records. I am giving this to you, – I'm sorry, I didn't catch your name."

"Pompey."

"Of course, Pompey. Please deliver this copy of the Duke's order to the individual responsible for contracts and records."

"Thank you. I will deliver this to the archscribe," Pompey replied.

"Very good. Jonah, you are now officially released from your services to the monastery. I am going to take you to a temporary boarding house we have set up for school employees until they are able to find lodging. Please put your belongings in the cart and we can get you there before it gets dark."

"Thank you," Jonah said as he loaded up his possessions. Before Jonah climbed into the cart, he turned around and gave Pompey a big bear hug. "Tell Master Po where I am and thank him for everything."

"I will, good luck and I will contact you soon," Pompey said.

Jonah climbed into the cart and settled in. The cart driver cracked the reins and they set off down the main road into Callamar. As the cart rode out of sight of the front gate, Jonah asked Secretary Gwyon if he would take him to a different place along the main road instead of to the boarding house as he thought he might already have a place to stay in Callamar. The Secretary agreed and told the driver to heed Jonah's directions. In almost no time they arrived in front of an old building.

"Are you sure this is your destination? It looks like it's deserted," the driver said.

"Yes, this is my destination. Let me see if anyone is home."

As Jonah walked to the front door, he could see a weak flicker of light coming from one of the front windows. He breathed deeply then knocked. He heard approaching footsteps. The front door opened and there stood May looking surprised and pleased. "Are you all right? Did something happen to you?"

"I'm fine. Do you have a place where I can stay for a few days?" Jonah asked.

"What's wrong? Are you a fugitive now?" May asked.

"I'll tell you everything soon enough, but my ride here needs to move along, with or without me."

"Of course, you can stay as long as you need to stay."

Jonah grabbed his belongings from the cart. Secretary Gwyon said to Jonah, "Here is the paperwork that you will need to present to Headmistress Agnes on Monday. Make sure you are on time. Agnes is our best trainer but she is also a no-nonsense kind of person. There may be some confusion as you are essentially appearing out of nowhere. Don't let that intimidate you. All your paperwork is in order and you can sign your contract on Monday when you begin training. Good luck. I will be in touch. Do you have any questions?"

"No. Thank you for everything," Jonah said.

The driver turned the cart around and hurried back along the main road into Callamar, racing the darkness.

Jonah turned to May, his hands full of paperwork. "Hello, May. Fancy meeting you here on a night like tonight."

May opened the door wider, "You need a place to stay tonight?" May asked.

"Yes, I'm in need of a place to stay. Let me explain. The Duke raided the monastery yesterday with his troops. With Pompey's help and your rope, I narrowly escaped with my life. I need a place to hide until things calm down. Hopefully, they won't find me here."

May eyed him quizzically. "You are starting to sound like Pompey. You will need more practice before you sound convincing. What really happened?"

Jonah set his belongings down near her front room table and sat down in one of the chairs. "This will be a long story." May brought a jug of water and two cups and then sat down ready to listen.

Jonah told her what happened yesterday. He explained how the Duke had made him an offer which he had accepted. He showed May the papers Secretary Gwyon had given him just now. "I'm to report Monday to begin training as a school teacher. I was told that I'm free of the monastery and will be working for the City of Callamar soon. I have no place to stay unless you can take me in as your guest. I am willing to compensate you once I begin earning a steady income."

"Don't be a silly boy. I've already invited you to live here with me and I am true to my word. I have several clean rooms from which you can choose. You can search through all of the furniture tomorrow to see if you can find something of use. I am so happy you are here. You and Pompey made me think that it would be months before anything would happen."

"I thought so, too. There was no time to think anything through. Everything happened all at once and now I'm here. Would you like to show me the rooms you have?"

"Of course I will. There are lots of rooms. You can have a ground level room or you can be higher up. Some windows face the rising sun, but there is no bell tower. Come, I will show you." May took his hand and almost dragged him up the stairs.

May gave Jonah a grand tour of the residence rooms, the privies, the barn, and the workshops. Eventually Jonah settled on one of the upstairs rooms with a view of the rising sun. The room also had a view of the main road below and of the farmlands and orchards to the east. It also happened to be right next to May's room. When he finally settled into the room, there was a cot with no blankets and a chair with no desk and not much else. May gave Jonah a few candles and a warm woolen blanket. He thanked May for everything she had done for him as they bade each other good night. Jonah thought he would have had time tonight to gather some furnishings from May's used furniture emporium downstairs but exhaustion from his long ordeal caught up with him.

May was happy that Jonah, with the Duke's help, had managed to escape the monastery and was now living in her place. While she wondered how much her own efforts had helped Jonah escape, she now thought, *that doesn't matter anymore. He's here with me, now.* She was in a better position to win over his heart as he seemed genuinely interested in her company despite her complicated life and history. She would have to be careful, discrete, and nurturing all at the same time. She recalled Svane telling her to get her "arms around him and never let go." That was what she intended to do.

The next morning, Jonah was greeted by bright light streaming into his room. It was not a tolling bell, but it did wake him up. He rolled onto his side away from the light and went back to sleep, managing to sleep until near midday. May did not try to wake him but he could hear her making noises in the kitchen and in some of the nearby rooms. Jonah finally got out of bed and groggily headed downstairs to the privy and then tried to find some water to wash his face. Eventually, he made his way to the kitchen where he found May busy scouring many of the kitchen utensils from years of caked-on dirt, grease, and tarnish.

May greeted Jonah as he walked in, "Good morning, sweetie. How are you feeling today?"

"I must have been exhausted from yesterday. I feel like I got hit by a charging boar."

May laughed. "There's a little bread and some cheese and water, but if you want some milk, you will have to milk the cow."

"You have a cow? Wait a moment …" Jonah realized May was teasing. He looked around, "Wow, you've really been working on the kitchen."

"And I am almost finished cleaning the pots and utensils." May saw Jonah was wearing one of his robes. "If you are going to live here, you are going to have to get some new clothes. I don't want anyone thinking I am running a half-way house for recovering monks."

Jonah chuckled. "All right, we will have to wear matching robes or I will have to find some work clothes like yours. Do you have any fresh fruit or vegetables? In the monastery, we usually had only what we could grow or what people were willing to donate to us. We usually received lots of apples and stale bread. There are vegetable patches all over the monastery grounds;

every nook and cranny has something growing in it. Sometimes we bought turnips and carrots to supplement our vegetable and fish stews – mostly fish, but sometimes something unknown that swam in the sea. After all, we were close to the harbor and received lots of fish that were never sold."

"You seem to know a lot about food. Did you also work in the kitchen?" May asked.

"In the kitchen? No. I learned about the food we ate from the other monks. Sometimes we would make bets to see who could correctly guess what we were eating on any particular night. The cook would then settle the bet and the loser had to clean the privies or the hallway floors in the winner's stead. Sometimes, even the cook didn't know everything that went into the stew."

May winced. "Why do people donate food to the monastery?"

"The monastery blesses all people who donate food or provide services to the monastery. Many people in Callamar believe that the monastery's blessing provides good luck."

"Why don't we visit the Central Market across the river? They have all kinds of things there. That way I can show you off to all of my neighbors. I don't say this in jest, but you will need to be recognized in this neighborhood as a resident. If we walk together, they will know you are with me," May suggested.

"All right. I have a few days before I have to report to training. Let's also find the training school so I will know how to walk there come Monday."

"I know a place where we can get you some new clothes, hopefully before you have to begin your training."

Jonah and May prepared to venture out into Callamar's markets together for the first time. Jonah borrowed one of May's tunics and pantaloons for their excursion. As they walked through May's neighborhood, she made sure to wave to everyone and show off her new boyfriend. They followed the main road southwest past Ruthie's Store; then, they took a smaller road veering west. This road crossed a narrow bridge that was only wide enough for foot traffic. Jonah's school was located along the same road they had been walking on since crossing the river, two blocks past the road heading north into the Central Market. It had not taken them long to get to the school so Jonah figured it would be an easy walk there and back from home. From the school, they wound their way back into Callamar's central marketing district and passed many interesting buildings.

May first took Jonah to Clet's Tunics so he could order some tailored clothes. May and Jonah spent much time fussing over the choices. Jonah insisted on lots of pockets as May picked out the fabrics and styles. After placing a rush order for his new clothes, they passed Lux Aeterna, a candle workshop that produced wax and tallow candles. May purchased several of their cheapest candles but noticed they featured many colorful, slow-burning candles for extra coin.

Next, they headed over to the Central Market's Food Bazaar. They both agreed not to buy any fish today. They found many farmers and merchants selling their produce. They selected some carrots, turnips, and celery. They also bought some ground-up flour, a few sourdough loaves, an apple fritter, dried beans and lentils, and a little salt. After they got most of the things they needed, they wandered around, passing by a carpenter's workshop. They entered into the shop and inquired about new furniture like beds, simple writing desks, tables, and reading chairs.

May explained to Jonah, "Before you order yourself a new writing desk, I want you to look inside the third-floor rooms back home."

"All right," Jonah replied.

Jonah was amazed by how much there was to see and do in the marketplace. And May was by his side. What could be better? The problem, as Jonah saw it, was that the marketplace was based on coin. And if one had the coin, one reaped the benefits. If not –

Northeast from the Central Market, they passed an interesting temple with a small red-paper banner announcing the date of the Lantern Festival. Jonah remembered what Master Po had told him and wondered if Master Po would attend the festival. At least he had found where the festival would be held.

When they returned to May's place, they sorted through all of their purchases. Then, they cooked dinner together. They made a simple stew with water and shared the apple fritter for dessert.

Teacher Training

Jonah's first day of teacher training came soon enough. May admired his new clothes and wished him well. As he set off ready to begin his new life, she looked at him with pride.

Jonah made it to the school training building relatively quickly. As he entered the building, he spied an open door leading into an office. Inside was a long countertop reaching up to his elbows. Behind the counter a woman sat at a desk. When she noticed Jonah standing at the counter, she addressed him, "Can I help you with something?"

"Yes, I am here to begin teacher training today. My name is Jonah Bergan," he said.

After examining some papers on her desk, she asked, "Are you sure you came to the right office? I don't have any paperwork for anyone new today."

"Are you sure? I have some paperwork here." He handed her the small stack of papers that Education Secretary Gwyon had given him. "Secretary Gwyon gave me these papers to show to you. He said that there would be more papers for me to sign when I arrived here on Monday. It is Monday, isn't it?" Jonah said.

"Of course it's Monday but I don't have any papers for you." The woman slowly got up and walked over to the counter to examine the papers Jonah was waving at her. "These papers seem to be in order but I don't see the ones we need. Who told you the papers would be here?" she asked.

"Secretary Gwyon told me they would be here for me to sign when I arrived on Monday, today," Jonah said. He continued explaining to the woman that he was supposed to begin training today.

"We do have a new class that started last week, but I don't believe I saw your name on the new trainee's roster."

Jonah quickly realized that he hadn't a clue as to how things were supposed to work in a school or in a school office. "Has class begun for today?"

"No, that class does not begin until the headmistress arrives and calls the class to order."

"How is the class usually called to order?" Jonah asked.

"The school bell rings around midmorning and roll call is taken."

"Which classroom would that be?" Jonah asked.

"The class meets in room 104 but you cannot enter the class without the headmistress's permission and proper paperwork."

"So I can't enter the class until I meet with the headmistress. Is she due to arrive soon?" Jonah asked.

"The headmistress should arrive soon."

"I guess I will have to wait for the headmistress to arrive," Jonah commented.

"Yes. Please have a seat until the headmistress arrives."

Jonah thought that the headmistress probably possessed all the paperwork necessary for his enrollment. Jonah sat down and began looking around the office. The office was right next to the main school entrance with the main hallway going deeper into the building. While Jonah waited, he saw only one other person enter the building; a woman passed by the office quickly on her way to somewhere down the hall. Jonah heard a bell ring and asked, "Is that the school bell?"

"Yes, that is the bell."

"I have not seen anyone enter the office since I arrived," Jonah commented.

"The headmistress must have entered the building through the back door."

By now, Jonah was getting frustrated. "Thank you for your help." Jonah stood up, exited the office, and walked down the hallway to find room 104. The woman poked her head out of the office, warning him that he had to see the headmistress before going into the training room. Jonah ignored her, found room 104, and entered the room.

Inside was a woman wearing a black dress standing in the front of the room. *She must be the headmistress*, Jonah thought. Four other people were sitting at desks facing the headmistress. Everyone in the classroom was surprised by Jonah's entry. The headmistress spoke to Jonah in an authoritarian voice, "May I help you? This room is restricted."

"Sorry for the interruption, but I am here to begin teacher training. I was told by Secretary Gwyon that I was to begin training on Monday, today. Here is the paperwork that Secretary Gwyon gave me." Jonah held out his paperwork, handing it to the headmistress.

The headmistress took the paperwork and looked it over carefully. "These papers look legitimate. Did you speak to Elise down the hall about your enrollment papers?"

"Is Elise the woman in the office down the hall?" And just as he said that, there was a knock on the door and Elise entered the room.

"I am sorry for interrupting you, Headmistress Agnes, but this man walked down the hallway to your room without any paperwork from Main Department."

Now Headmistress Agnes was getting frustrated. She searched her bag but couldn't find any paperwork. "Elise, would you go into my office and check my desk and mail box to see if there is anything new from Main Department?"

"Right away, headmistress," Elise said as she went back down the hall.

Jonah thought, *she couldn't do that while I was waiting?*

Headmistress Agnes turned to Jonah saying, "I'm sorry, I did not get your name."

"My name is Jonah Bergan and I am supposed to begin training today."

"This is very unusual as candidates are not allowed to enroll without my approval," the headmistress explained.

Jonah explained, "I am sorry for the inconvenience. I was told to show up here on Monday and present to you the paperwork you are now holding and that my other paperwork would already be here ready for me to sign."

Headmistress Agnes said pointedly, "Let's not waste any more time. Please sit down over there and pay attention while Elise figures out what happened to your paperwork."

And with that, Jonah began his training. The other trainees in the class were confused and annoyed by what they had witnessed and kept eying Jonah suspiciously. *Maybe it's my lot in life to be eyed suspiciously,* he thought.

Headmistress Agnes continued with her instruction until, finally, the school bell rang signaling a lunch break. Elise entered the classroom with a thick letter addressed to Headmistress Agnes from Education Secretary Gwyon.

Headmistress Agnes opened the letter and found several documents signed by Secretary Gwyon and Duke Olan himself. She asked Jonah, "Is your name Jonah Bergan?"

"Yes, that is my name," he said, thinking to himself, *as I told you before.*

"Take the quill here on my desk and sign your name to this document. By signing, you are pledging your commitment to serve the City of Callamar as a teacher in Duke Olan's sponsored schools. Your pay and benefits are itemized on the second page of your contract."

Jonah took the quill and signed his name at the bottom of the contract and everything became official.

Headmistress Agnes said, "As I told you before, I usually approve new candidates myself but for some reason, the Duke has approved your contract, somewhat hastily, I might add. Do not for a moment think that this class is a mere formality. I will be watching and documenting your progress closely. Welcome to Callamar's teacher training program."

After a short lunch break during which Jonah signed his contract, Jonah settled into the class. Over time he learned the names of the other teacher trainees. Holly and Tera were learning to become primary school teachers while Helene, Kunge, and he were to become secondary teachers.

Over the course of several weeks, Jonah did his best to absorb everything that was taught to him. He found it very challenging and began harboring anxiety and self-doubt; he wondered if he could succeed in the classroom as he realized that his experiences with children had so far been minimal. On many days, Jonah thought back to his time in school. He grew up attending a parochial school administered and taught by clergy members of the Church of the Holy Cross. The more he recalled, the more he realized that his classes had been designed to develop skills that would one day help him serve the Church or Korgynslande's government. In his naiveté, he daydreamed of careers working in the business, academic, or legal sectors of Scullsbergen. Perhaps that was why he found it shocking when his parents committed him to the monastery to serve as a scribe. Only now was he able to view those events as linked together in his past. He now understood that his future had been carefully planned in advance for years and all of his daydreams were delusions.

But with the help of the Duke and others, he had escaped that fate and was now training to teach in Callamar. Was he now becoming a servant of the Duke, trained to mould the futures of children by exploiting their naiveté? Until now, Jonah had never heard of a Duke-sponsored school. He had now grown wiser and his intuition was telling him that this Duke-sponsored school system was different, in no small way, due to the efforts of Headmistress Agnes. He viewed her differently when compared to the clergy members he recalled and the priors who ran the monastery. All of Jonah's previous authority figures had lectured him on how he needed to behave, then expected him to figure everything out on his own. While Agnes had her own priorities and agenda, she worked with him and his cohorts, drawing out their gifts and skills. Then, she wove her own knowledge and experience into theirs, building up their competence and confidence.

One of the things that made Headmistress Agnes different was her policy of getting to know her cohorts. Agnes did not like the word "cohort" due to its military connotations, but she used it anyway. During the weeks of training, she met with every one of her cohorts for one-on-one conferences several times to gauge how they were progressing and to give them encouragement when needed. Over time, Jonah had many conferences with Agnes. Jonah learned from Agnes how the different school systems in Callalande worked and how he would fit into his role as a teacher of reading and writing. Jonah soon learned that Agnes was as honest and frank as anyone he'd ever met.

"As I told you before, your situation is unique in that I know relatively little about you. Ordinarily, I work closely with my cohorts, assessing their skills and abilities before they are admitted to our training program. Because of the sudden and irregular manner by which you were 'recommended' to me, I have had to use some initiative to fill in the gaps, so to speak. I understand that you served as a scribe at Saint Dominic's Monastery and that you were released from you duties there by Duke Olan himself. How have your experiences as a scribe prepared you to be a teacher?"

Jonah was unsure whether he could trust Headmistress Agnes, yet. Jonah's experiences of being committed to the monastery, enduring several interrogations, and suffering through Danan's death had eroded his willingness to trust people, especially authority figures. Only those he considered his friends had earned his trust.

Jonah gave Agnes a redacted version of his experiences at the monastery and why he left. He conveyed to Agnes that he did have many fond memories of school and had enjoyed learning back before he moved into the monastery. Over several weeks, Agnes methodically calmed his concerns and reassured him that he could be a successful teacher. He slowly began to trust Agnes and her confidence in him.

"I will be frank with you. Being a first-year teacher can be a most frustrating experience. Many a teacher will come to realize that they can leave the teaching profession and apply their skills to make more coin elsewhere. That is true. But consider this: within the world are many streams. Some streams lead to riches and power while others lead to comfort and complacency and still others lead to ruin and misery. The stream that is teaching can lead to a life of purpose and contentment; sometimes it can lead to frustration. Many a teacher takes pride in their work and is satisfied with their commitment to building a more educated society. What I am saying is this: if you give the teaching profession a chance, you may be surprised at the benefits you receive. There is more to life than coin alone."

Jonah stated, "I will give teaching a chance to make a positive impression on me. I would like to ask, how are children placed in schools and where will I fit in?"

Agnes continued, "The main criteria used to determine a student's school placement is age. All children twelve years or younger become enrolled in primary school. Primary school classrooms usually contain a mixture of boys and girls. Primary students are required to take and pass a number of classes satisfying a course of study qualifying them to graduate and become secondary students. Teachers of primary students teach one class of students for a year in all subjects. Too much change for younger students can lead to unnecessary stress in their lives. You will not be teaching primary students. Children older than twelve years are considered secondary students with very few exceptions. Not all graduated students move on to secondary school."

Jonah asked, "Do primary teachers teach how to read and write?"

"Primary teachers mostly teach the alphabet and how to read simple words and sentences. Students may learn how to use a slate and chalk to write a few words and numbers and maybe learn simple arithmetic. But that is about all."

Jonah said, "I see."

"The majority of secondary school students are boys. Some girls are admitted, too, but that is uncommon. The Duke-sponsored school system runs on taxes collected within Callamar. Tax funds are allocated to cover much of the schools' expenses, which can vary from year to year. So families of secondary students end up paying for some of their own school supplies. Where funds are limited, families usually choose to send only their boys to school. Unfortunately, this is the reality that many families face. All students in your classes will have purchased their own paper, ink, and quills. So classes are essentially limited to those who are able to buy school supplies. The school tries its best to supplement your supplies, but as you can imagine, you will use them up rather quickly."

Jonah said, "Yes, we burned through supplies at a fast rate within the scriptorium."

"As you will soon become aware, we can teach only a limited number of subjects based upon our budget and personnel. For example, topics such as music, art, and recreation are not taught here; however, Callamar has many craftsmen and artisans who offer apprenticeships. Our core mission revolves around three pillars of achievement. The first pillar is literacy. We would prefer that all students become literate. That is a huge challenge and we do the best we can. That is part of your specific tasking as a reading and writing teacher. The second pillar is numeracy. We would like all students to complete arithmetic and geometry but that is also a major challenge and part of the tasking of our mathematics instructors. The third pillar is citizenship. Students are taught how to be good citizens and to become civic minded. This involves becoming aware of the laws of Callalande and having a respect for law enforcement. Getting students to understand how a city works and why laws are important is the tasking for our legal instructors. Once in a while, we can offer advanced topics such as engineering, literature, history, foreign languages, astronomy, and others. But many of those subjects are reserved for the university or specialty schools within Callamar.

"Since you will be part of the first pillar, literacy, your role is very crucial. The other two pillars require students to be able to read and write. The Duke-sponsored school system needs good teachers. That is my tasking. I train and educate good teachers, which is what I expect you will become. You already have the literacy skills needed for success. You just need to acquire good teaching skills, which is what I will give to you."

Black Sun

While Jonah was using the last of his free time to prepare for his first day of training, he did not notice several figures skulking in the east-side shadows, surveilling his comings and goings from May's Place.

These secretive figures were seven members of the Black Sun. Four were initiates, intimidating but lacking experience. Two were conditional members still proving their loyalty and worth to the organization. The seventh was their leader, Rogan, a seasoned professional. Rogan specialized in smuggling and intelligence but was never assigned to apprehend individuals. That was work for the covert strike team. Rogan's current assignment involved the training of his initiates in gathering intelligence regarding persons of interest to the Black Sun, such as the "Banshee of Northcamp."

For months, Baron Wesselman had experienced a series of calamities: two clearly identifiable henchmen decapitated, the wolf hunter missing – presumed dead, a smoldering trading house, and a son running hog-wild around Northern Borea making a mess while trying to fix something he wouldn't talk about. While the Baron did not own the trading house, he made much coin there through trade, intimidation, and extortion. His incurred costs were mounting and the Baron was losing patience with his henchmen and his son. So the Baron reached out to the Black Sun to assist him with several matters.

Baron Wesselman's requirements were communicated to Rogan in Callamar. The Baron had no patience for ghost stories and wanted a positive identification of the so-called "Banshee" as soon as possible.

Rogan established a new safe house in Callamar. As he began training his group, they spotted May almost by accident, walking through Callamar's Central Market. She piqued their curiosity because of her tall stature, strong build, and Borean accent. According to the Baron's son, there were supposed to be two girls traveling together. Instead, they found a young man walking with her through town; they tracked the two back to May's place.

Rogan was having difficulty reckoning why he had received two separate taskings from his Black-Sun handler regarding the Baron and the Baron's son, Willem. They both seemed to be looking for similar persons, but they were two separate taskings. To Rogan, something wasn't passing the smell test.

In either case, Rogan saw this development as a good opportunity to apprehend the boy and girl and interrogate them. Reporting back to the Black Sun in Borea, awaiting instructions, and deploying the strike team would take some time, perhaps a fortnight. Rogan was already in Callamar, ambitious, and confident in his unarmed combat skills. He figured that it wouldn't be difficult to apprehend the two and save some valuable time. He might suffer some cuts and bruises, but he had six associates and concluded that seven versus two were favorable odds. However, Rogan noted that sometimes May carried a knife and therefore was probably the more dangerous of the two. Rogan presumed her boyfriend did not pose much of a threat so he planned to secure the boy first; then, he could use him as leverage when he interrogated the girl. If she proved to be the Banshee, Rogan would smuggle them both back into Borea. If not, well, they were expendable loose ends.

Over several days, Rogan's team mapped out Jonah and May's daily routines. They drew up a plan where they would apprehend them on an early Wednesday morning. They procured a closed-cabin-horse-drawn coach in which they would secure Jonah and May, then smuggle them across the Rowan River into Borea.

Wednesday morning began like any other morning for blacksmith Krane. He arose early and began preparing his shop for work. He had several orders for horseshoes needed by midday. Krane walked outside of his shop and looked down the main road in both directions. That's when he noticed something unusual: a horse-drawn coach parked in front of May's place, unusually close to the main gate. In fact, it was blocking the main gate. A few tough-looking men stood in a semicircle around the coach and the front door. Krane thought, *this doesn't look good.* Krane could hear a female voice screaming from somewhere inside May's place. He slowly approached one of the men and asked, "Hello. If I may ask, is there a problem I can help you with?"

A black-clad man turned toward Krane, "Mind your own business!" The man grabbed Krane's arm then twisted it around behind his back, driving a pain up his arm and through his shoulder. The man then pushed Krane away from the coach and back towards his own house. As he shoved Krane into his shop, he said, "Shut your mouth if you know what's good for you." The man then drew a long knife. "If you don't shut up, I'll cut your throat and the throats of everyone in your family. Understand?"

Krane nodded his head. When the man left, Krane stood up and went to find his wife and son. When he found them, he told them, "Sneak out the back and run down the main road to the eastern barracks as fast as you can. Tell Captain Adeley we need help right away!" Krane then went back into his shop and took his biggest hammer with him out into the street.

Earlier that morning, Jonah was awakened by the sunlight streaming into his window and illuminating his bed. Jonah got up and dressed quickly. As he stepped out of his door onto the second-floor walkway, he was assailed by two masked figures dressed in black. The figures tried to grapple him from behind. As soon as he realized what was happening, his self-defense training kicked in; he immediately stomped on one of his attacker's feet. He charged toward the walkway railing, trying to pull one of his assailants with him over the side and down to the ground. He was not successful. He tried to break his assailant's hold by letting his legs go limp, slipping down and tumbling away. This worked. Now free of their holds, he sprang up quickly and ran down the stairs to the ground floor. As he ran towards the kitchen, he could hear May screaming curses at someone. He also heard May yelling his name, begging him to wake up.

However, before Jonah could get to the kitchen, one of his assailants leaped over the second-floor railing and landed in front of him. In one motion, Jonah slid and tumbled around his assailant's legs and sprang up behind him, running into the kitchen. He could see May exchanging blows with two assailants, avoiding their attempts to grapple her. As she did everything she could to elude them, Jonah rushed past her for the main door where he had left his walking staff the previous night. He grabbed the staff and began striking May's attackers. All of his training and katas came back to him and he inflicted several stunning blows to their heads and torsos. May and Jonah made quick work of the two thugs attacking May. The two men chasing Jonah emerged from the kitchen. Jonah and May were ready for them. Jonah's pursuers saw that Jonah and May had evened the odds, so they drew some nasty-looking daggers. May dodged their slashing daggers or blocked them with her kitchen utensils. Jonah parried several dagger thrusts before counterattacking with a few well-placed whacks to their knees and ears. Jonah's adrenaline kicked in and his months of practice with Master Po put him into a centered state, allowing him to anticipate his opponent's attacks and counter them successfully. May's other assailant was attacked by Jonah who was able to seize his dagger. Seeing this, May charged forward and flattened the miscreant against a wall, pummeling him mercilessly until he slipped to the ground, out cold.

May turned to Jonah to check that he was all right. "Are there any more of them? They just came out of nowhere."

"We need to get out of here." Jonah headed for the front door and opened it. Outside, May and Jonah found themselves confronted by three of the burlier, more experienced Black Sun thugs. May and Jonah moved away from the front door along the side of the building, taking up a defensive posture. One of the men aimed a small black crossbow at May while the other two wielded short swords. May recognized their black leather outfits.

The man aiming the crossbow spoke. "Surrender now or you will die."

Jonah positioned his staff defiantly. Out of the corner of his eye, he could see Krane approaching, hammer raised high and ready to strike.

May blurted out, "Who are you to violate my house?! Leave us now before I carve you up into dogfood!"

The words had no sooner been spoken when Krane's hammer came down hard on one of the sword-wielding men. The man Krane hit had already turned to face Krane upon detecting his approach. Krane's blow hit him squarely on his sword shoulder. May feigned a lunge at the crossbow-holder, trying to induce him to fire while she dodged. The man did not fire so May launched herself forward causing the man to shoot. The bolt missed her arm and passed through her tunic sleeve, striking the outside wall of May's place. May's rush missed her target as the man dodged and kicked her knee from behind. May fell to the ground but quickly sprang up behind him. He turned and dropped his crossbow quickly then engaged May in an unarmed melee trading blow for blow. As time wore on, May sensed she was fighting a losing battle with this Black Sun man. So, she repositioned herself into a defensive stance, waiting for an opportunity to counterpunch her foe.

Meanwhile, Jonah had been trying without much success to separate his attacker from his sword. With May rushed forward, he began yielding ground, keeping the slashing sword away from him. The melee lasted for several moments, with wounds inflicted on both sides. Krane received a sword cut to his off arm and his back when he could not pivot fast enough to block a slash from his adversary's sword. Krane landed another hammer blow to the man's arm. The man reeled to the side before he could regain his balance.

As the fight wore on, several crossbow bolts whizzed into the fray striking the three black-suited men. Confusion ensued as three more bolts struck the thugs in the chest or back and they all went down to the ground. Jonah pressed his advantage, giving his assailant a solid whack to the head, knocking him out. May kicked the crossbow man firmly in the groin and finished him with a strong fist to the temple. Krane's assailant toppled over and hit the ground with a thud.

Jonah recognized their change in fortune and yelled to the armed horsemen who had come to their rescue. He pointed to the open front door. "There are four more inside the kitchen, if you would be so kind."

Duke Olan and his entourage along with Captain Adeley and several armed troops had been riding up the main road from the eastern barracks when they saw the fracas and intervened. They engaged the Black Sun assailants with their heavy crossbows and brought the fighting to an end. The Duke instructed Captain Adeley to round up all of the assailants and to tend to the wounds suffered by Jonah, May, and Krane. Captain Adeley instructed his medic to treat their wounds starting with Krane. The Duke wanted all of the black-outfitted men, dead or alive, loaded into their own horse-drawn coach, saving the leader for questioning.

Once order was established, Duke Olan addressed the three victims, "I see we were in time to help the three of you out. Have you suffered any serious wounds?" The Duke offered Krane free medical services at the General Hospital where he could spend a day or two recovering from his wounds. Jonah did not appear to have any open wounds though there would doubtless be some bruising. May had some severe bruising on her body and face but would make a full recovery in several days.

The Duke spoke directly to Krane before the medic escorted him to the hospital, "I want you to know that your son is a hero. His quick and decisive action informed us of your plight and facilitated our intervention. You should be very proud of him."

"Thank you, your Excellency. I am very proud of him. He is a beautiful boy," Krane said as the Duke patted him on his good shoulder.

Next, the Duke turned his attentions to Jonah and May. "Well this is a surprise, the two of you fighting together and protecting each other in melee combat. I commend you on your success. Your neighbor also acted valiantly."

May said, "Thank you, your Excellency. I don't know where these men came from. They broke into my house and tried to kidnap me and my friend Jonah. We managed to fight them off for a while, but your timely arrival saved our lives." May bowed courteously, as did Jonah.

The Duke responded, "We will need to figure out why you were attacked. Let us ask what appears to be the ringleader of these thugs right now. Captain, wake up this man right here."

Captain Adeley dragged Rogan up onto his knees then slapped him a few times before he finally woke up. The captain then asked the man, "What is the meaning of this attack on the people of Callamar? Explain yourself."

The black-suited man spoke as he pointed at May, "She is wanted by Baron Wesselman of Borea for crimes committed in Northcamp and Wesseltown. I have an edict in my pocket." The captain reached into one of the man's front pockets and pulled out a piece of paper and handed it to Duke Olan.

Duke Olan took the paper, unfolded it and read it to himself. He put the paper aside and spoke, "Do you have a permit to operate as a bounty hunter within Callalande?"

The man said, "No, your Excellency. But she is a fugitive."

"This edict lists two girls, neither by name. You are way out of line and a threat to Callamar and its citizens. What is she accused of, anyway? Your sham edict says only crimes against the Baron's family. This could mean anyone or anything. WHERE is the due process in your country? Here in Callamar, you must have a specific charge supported by evidence or sworn testimony and a writ signed by a judge before anyone can be arrested or extradited. You cannot just go up to anyone and seize them without due process."

The man managed to squeak out a few more words, "She has killed four men back in Northcamp, including the wolf hunter and Nimrod the Giant."

The Duke laughed, "Nimrod the Giant? Are you serious? Does she look like the kind of person who could kill Nimrod? And let's just say she did kill Nimrod by some miracle, it would have to be in self-defense as I don't know of any man or woman foolish enough to attack Nimrod unprovoked. Did that thought cross your mind?"

The man knelt there silently. The Duke told the captain to take him away, along with all of his thugs, to the jails in the eastern barracks and await his return. Captain Adeley worked to remove all of the bodies while the Duke walked back over to Jonah and May. "You heard the man. Is there any truth to what he had to say?"

May said, "May I talk to you and your officials privately. There is a table inside the front door where we can all sit down."

The Duke looked her in the eye skeptically and then spoke, "All right. Lead me to your table. You will have but a few moments to explain yourself." The Duke gave a cue and four of his officials led him into the main floor of May's place. May sat down at the table while Jonah remained outside. Once the Duke sat down, May began:

"Your Excellency, I don't know what the man is talking about when he claims I killed Nim …, or whatever his name is, but I do think I recognize the name of the wolf hunter. Last autumn, a trapper dressed like a wolf attacked me along the Snowfall River and tried to kill me. I was lucky enough to be able to defend myself. At the time, I did not know he was the wolf hunter. I threw his body into the river hoping never to see it again. Later, I learned that there was a bounty placed on him for 200 golds. I have no way of proving that I killed him, though I did take some of his possessions including his wood axe."

The Duke sat back in his chair, pondering. "One cannot be faulted for self-defense, and the wolf hunter was a scourge upon the land. I was the one who offered the reward. You are lucky to be alive. If by some miracle you are the one who slew Nimrod, the world is a better place for it. However, that is a Borean matter. If you can prove you slew the wolf hunter, I will definitely award you the bounty."

Secretly, the Duke was not sure what to think about May's story as it was clearly self-serving. And while the Black Sun leader Rogan, was a shady character, there might be an iota of truth in what he said. "For now, I encourage you to recover from your wounds. It appears you are well respected within your community, as your neighbor Krane risked his life to help you fend off your attackers. I recommend you go visit him in the hospital and personally thank him and his son." With that he stood up and took his leave.

Before the Duke's entourage mounted and galloped off, the Duke received much thanks from the local residents. Krane's wife Cherie and son David had arrived onto the scene shortly thereafter. She thanked the Duke humbly for saving her husband and then took David to go see him in the hospital.

Jonah stood along May's outer wall, watching everything that was happening and trying to remain calm. He had experienced many things this morning and learned some things about May he had not known before. He wondered about what had happened back in Borea. *And who is Nimrod?* Jonah walked back into the house and found May sitting at her table with her head on her arms, crying. He pulled up a chair next to her and put his arm around her shoulders. He ran his fingers through her sweaty hair and gently rubbed her head. May stopped crying but did not look up.

Jonah leaned towards her and gently whispered into her ear, "Those men were all Black Sun weren't they?"

May slowly nodded.

Jonah continued, "I saw a tattoo on their leader's neck. It looked just like one of the symbols from the letters you asked me to read back in that inn with Svane."

May slowly lifted her head, "You remembered that? Yes, you're right. Oh, my! You're going to be late for classes! We can talk about this later."

Jonah realized that she was right. "Yes, I do have class today. Why don't you meet me in front of the school after my classes end? Then, we can both go over to the hospital together and see how Krane is doing and thank him for his help."

May said, "That sounds like a good idea." She gave Jonah a big hug and kissed him on his cheek then went off to go wash herself. Jonah went upstairs to his room and quickly changed into some cleaner clothes.

Before Jonah left, May came up to him with her healing salve and put a little of the ointment onto the scrapes clearly visible on his face. "This will help your wounds heal a little faster. I will see you after your classes." May gave him another kiss on his forehead.

Jonah took off walking briskly. As he mulled over the events of the morning, he was satisfied that all of his training with Master Po had paid off. He also felt a warm glow remembering that May had kissed him twice this morning.

When Jonah arrived at school, classes had already begun. He opened the classroom door quietly and tried to sneak in; however, everyone instantly turned to him. Headmistress Agnes spoke sarcastically, "Nice of you to join us today. If you think I am going to tolerate –"

Jonah interrupted, "I am sorry for being late. I have no excuses other than to say that I was jumped by several thugs this morning who tried to kill me. But, alas, they failed, as I whacked them several times with my trusty walking stick. Here is my homework, late but completed. Don't bother to report my mishap to the authorities as Duke Olan already knows about what happened." Jonah sat down at his desk as the headmistress just stared at him incredulously. She noticed his facial scrapes and bruises and his bloody walking stick. She scowled and resumed teaching the class.

After a long day of classes, Jonah walked out of the school building and waved to his departing classmates. Waiting in front of the school entrance, May came up to him and gave him a bear hug. "How were classes today?"

Jonah said, "I was a little late but I think Headmistress Agnes understood."

Jonah and May then took off towards the General Hospital where Krane was being treated for his wounds. May showed Jonah a small bag of sugar pastries, with diced apples on top, that she was bringing for Krane.

As Jonah looked at May, he saw that several black and blue bruises had manifested upon her face and arms. "How are you feeling? It looks like the boss man hit you pretty hard."

"Yes, he did. I was slowly losing the fight against him until the Duke arrived. He hit me in the ribs a few times and it hurts when I breathe too hard. At least he did not hit me with his crossbow. Thank you for fighting with me and protecting me. You are very skilled with your staff." May smiled and gave him another hug.

When they arrived at the hospital, the sky was still light. A triage nurse was waiting at the entrance and greeted May and Jonah, "How may I be of assistance to the two of you?"

May spoke up, "Good day. We are here to visit a friend of ours who arrived here this morning. His name is Krane." While they waited, May looked around the lobby and noticed several people waiting, seated on some of the chairs.

The nurse made a quick check of her admission records. "Here we go. Krane was admitted this morning and is currently resting in the Main Hall, bed number 22. He is currently allowed visitors but only for a short time. Our doors close to visitors at sunset. You must first wash your hands thoroughly and wear one of these masks, which you may purchase for a copper each.”

May pulled out two coppers and took two masks. She gave Jonah a mask after they washed their hands in the nearby basins. They found Krane’s wife Cherie sitting in a chair beside Krane holding his hand. They also noticed Krane’s son David standing next to his bed. When May and Jonah arrived and stood at the foot of Krane’s bed, Cherie recognized them and thanked them for visiting.

“We came by to thank you for everything the three of you did for us this morning. It was very brave and selfless of you to help us fight off those horrible thugs. Jonah and I brought the three of you some apple pastries. Please accept them as a small token of our appreciation. How are you feeling?”

David’s eyes perked up when May said “pastries.” Cherie spoke up first, “Thank you. The doctors treated his cuts this morning and they said he was going to heal just fine but it might be a day or two before he can go home.”

Krane spoke up. “Thank you for coming to see us. I am sorry I could not get into the fight any faster, but I am a little slow when it comes to running.”

Jonah spoke up, “You did great! I saw you running to help us and I tried to distract the thugs so you could surprise them, but that one thug turned around before you could knock him out.”

“Thank you. Those guys really were thugs and goons. You two fight well together, like a team. Where did you learn to swing your stick around like that? They never touched you!”

“I had some training at the monastery under a mentor called Master Po. He taught me everything I know and I am grateful for it. And you young man,” Jonah turned to David, “the Duke himself commended you as a hero for your swift and brave action this morning. I am also very proud of you. Congratulations.”

“Thank you, Jonah. I ran as fast as I could to the barracks and that’s when I saw the Duke sitting on his horse. I knew he was the Duke because he came to visit May’s house not long ago.”

Krane and his family continued talking with May and Jonah until one of the nurses came by to tell them that visiting time was ending for the day. May and Jonah said their good byes to Krane and decided to walk back home with Cherie and David. It was a long day and everyone was exhausted but satisfied that the Duke had the situation in hand and that Krane was expected to make a full recovery.

Rowena

Local gossip attributed the Black Sun's attack on Jonah and May to the usual band of thugs and ne'er-do-wells. East-side residents dared hope that this fight signaled a victory over thuggery. Only Jonah, May, and the Duke knew the truth. For years neighbors told the story of the valiant Duke and his brave troops riding into their midst and saving the day. And when Krane came home from the hospital, he basked in his share of glory as well. May and Jonah, more than happy to deflect attention from themselves, heaped praise on their rescuers.

During the next few weeks, May and Jonah settled into a comfortable routine. Jonah left early with his walking staff and returned in the late afternoon. He was making good progress with his studies and had advanced to working with real teachers and real students. Technically, he was in class as an observer but practically, he assisted the teacher and worked with the students. He was also starting to make some coin. Since May was not charging Jonah rent, he was able to afford some food and clothing. He also planned to buy a new writing desk for his room and a comfortable reading chair.

May had finished white washing all of the buildings and scouring the kitchen clean. The buildings now shone bright in the sunlight. May turned her attention to the old wall and fences surrounding the property, which were in a sad state of disrepair. May considered bringing in a contractor to rebuild the walls and to add new secured gates. May also wanted a new privy with a reliable showering system.

One day while Jonah was in school and May was pondering what to fix next, a familiar horse cart came rolling down the main road and stopped in front of May's gate. She immediately recognized Svane atop the driver's seat reining in the horses to a stop. May rushed to the gate, opened it wide, and ran to give Svane a big hug.

"I didn't think I'd merit such a big welcome but here I am with a surprise for ye," Svane said. As she released him from her bear hug, she noticed Svane had a passenger. Rowena greeted May with a large smile and big hug. May noticed that Rowena was wearing the locket that May had found on the mountainside. May welcomed both to her home. May also directed Svane to bring his cart in through the front gate to the barn where he could find some fresh hay and water for his horses.

Svane explained to May that he and Rowena had already delivered their cheese pots to his usual customers. "For the past month, Rowena has been relentless on comin' ta visit ye here en Callamar, especially when ye didn't return ta Torslande. Et looks like ye've done a lot o'work on this place since the last time I saw et. This certainly looks like a lot o'place for one person ta be livin' en."

May smiled and replied, "Actually, I'm not living here alone."

"Oh, so ye've made a friend here en Callamar or maybe ye've a tenant rentin' a room from ye?" Svane asked.

"You will meet him when he gets back from school," May replied with a giggle and smile.

"Him? This sounds intriguin' ta say the least, a school boy?" Svane and Rowena did not have to wait long to satisfy their curiosity. Soon they heard footsteps approaching and saw Jonah come in.

Svane spoke, "Well, I'll be a billy's brother. This es a big surprise!" A huge smile appeared upon Svane's face. "Greetin's, young Jonah. Ye must be the mystery tenant stayin' here en May's place." Turning towards May, "How'd ye steal him out o'the monastery all by yerself?"

"That is a long story but you're right – he's living here now. He has one of the upstairs rooms. And both of you are welcome to stay with me in

Callamar for as long as you like. The rooms are a little bare but there might still be some salvageable furniture you can use."

After chit-chatting for some time, the four friends decided to walk down to The Charging Boar. Inside, they chose to try the boar stew with cheese rolls and three golden ales with a half-tankard of pale beer for Rowena. Rowena wanted to try the ale but Svane nixed that idea quickly. "Ye're not old enough yet ta drink ale, but soon enough ye can have a sip or two."

May and Jonah told Svane and Rowena how Jonah had been able to escape the monastery with the intervention of the Duke himself and that Jonah was now training to become a school teacher for one of the Duke-sponsored schools within Callamar.

Svane commented, "Impressive, rubbin' elbows with the Duke!"

Rowena was enjoying listening to the big people talk and tell stories. She also looked about curiously at the many other people eating and socializing in the tavern. Rowena then reached for a boar rind, examined it, and popped it into her mouth. Very quickly she regretted chomping down on the rind and discretely spit it out.

Jonah chuckled.

Rowena drank some beer then deflected by asking, "May, how did you meet Jonah?"

May began to explain, but Jonah cut her off. "I met May for the very first time right here in this place. She was sitting right over there by that window making funny eyes at me and my friend Pompey, so my friend went over to her and introduced himself and –"

"Nooo! You were looking at me first," May interjected.

"– invited her to come over and sit with us. This place has great sentimental value," Jonah finished.

"Jonah is not remembering things correctly, but we both like this place for the same reasons."

Rowena laughed, "That sounds funny; the two of you sneaking looks at each other."

May was relieved that Jonah had not told them about Anya. Eventually, May and Svane began discussing Rowena's situation. Svane explained that he had first spoken to Edel, then they revealed to Rowena the recovered items they found along the mountainside. Svane returned Rowena's feather collection. When she recognized the collection, he then knew for sure that it was Rowena's parents or guardians that had perished years ago. What Rowena said later, Svane and Edel were not ready for. Rowena told them that she wanted to live with May in Callamar if May agreed. Svane discouraged her. He told Rowena that May was still very young and not ready for the responsibility, emotional or financial, of taking care of a ten-year-old girl.

"Svane is right. May would have to assume guardianship of Rowena in Callamar. Rowena would also have to enroll in primary school, as she is not yet twelve years. May's place is more than large enough to accommodate all of Rowena's needs," Jonah explained then decided to shut up.

Rowena had always been blunt but now she outdid herself. "May, I want to stay with you here in Callamar. Can I stay, please? I can help you keep house. I know how to cook and I can help you in the garden. I took care of the garden you left behind in Torslande. The squash and beans grew well –"

"Rowena, yer mother and I have told ye May es young and not ready ta be a mother ta ye. She has ta live her own life."

"We can be friends! And I can help her with babies! I have been helping mama with Winter for a long time. I know how to hold babies, how to feed them, burp them, change them – Mama doesn't need any help with Winter so much now, so now I can help May with her babies."

May had flushed crimson. "Whoa! Slow down there, Rowena. There are no babies – nor do I expect there to be any for quite some time."

Jonah had also blushed. He quietly ate his dinner, glad to remain unobserved. Apparently both Svane and Rowena were assuming that May would be married soon – to **him**. *Would that be so bad*? As he listened to the conversation about May's future, he realized that he had been assuming that he would be part of it. Whoever May was – whatever she may have done – he couldn't imagine a future without her.

"Rowena, that es not for ye ta decide, young girl. We've heard yer opinion and we know yer wishes. Now let May and me discuss the matter quietly –"

Rowena opened her mouth. Svane cut her off, "– **alone**. Then we'll let ye know what we've decided."

Rowena folded her arms defiantly, pouting.

The four friends finished their meals then strolled out under the moonlight. Walking next to May, Jonah broke his long silence. "In a few nights the moon will be waxing to full. I was thinking we should go to the Lantern Festival. There will be lots of good food and we can watch all of the lanterns drift down the river to the sea. What do you think?"

"That sounds lovely! You're such a sweetie. Yes! Let's go!"

Rowena giggled, "I want to go, too! Papa, can we stay for the Lantern Festival?"

Jonah thought Rowena could profit from a swift kick but held his tongue. Svane sighed, realizing that Rowena's boldness and willfulness were increasingly unchecked. It would not be fair to leave such a headstrong child with young, inexperienced May. On the other hand, if May could handle a pack of feral dogs, she would certainly have no trouble with Rowena. Perhaps it would be best to leave Rowena with May for only a short time – say a month or two. He could return for Rowena before the snows fell. And in the meantime, both girls would have a better understanding of what such a relationship would involve.

"Ef ye'd like ta go ta the Lantern Festival, et's all right with me."

Lantern Festival

The day of the Lantern Festival finally arrived. Although Jonah did not have any classes, he woke up at his usual time, when the sun shone on his face. He dressed quickly and went downstairs. He found the kitchen a hive of activity: May and Rowena frying eggs and ham, and Svane boiling water over the fire.

As he stepped into the kitchen, Rowena immediately handed Jonah a plate of ham and eggs on toast hot off the skillet. "Papa will make you some tea if you like."

"Wow! Perfect timing," May said sarcastically.

"Thank you, Rowena." Turning to Svane, "Yes, please. I would like some tea." He smiled at May. "Good morning May."

"Aye, she's ready. Good and hot," Svane said as he poured Jonah a cup of tea and handed it to him.

Rowena served eggs and ham with toast to everyone before seating herself. May supposed Rowena was showing off her cooking skills. May was not disappointed.

"Mama taught me how to make eggs and lamb but today I used ham. I hope all of you like it," Rowena said.

As they slowly ate breakfast, Jonah spoke up, "This is very good Rowena. Thank you very much for cooking breakfast."

"I'm glad you like it," Rowena smiled. As they were finishing their breakfast, there was a double knock on the front door. May stood up, turned, and moved towards the door while Jonah assumed a defensive position. Svane observed May and Jonah with curiosity as May cracked open the door. She found an older man in the uniform of a carriage driver. May opened the door wider saying, "May I help you?"

"Hello miss, I have a letter for someone named May from the Northcamp Apothecary in Borea. Would you know if she lives here?"

May's concern suddenly turned to excitement as she said, "I am May and, yes, I know the Northcamp Apothecary!"

"Then this letter is for you. Have a nice day." The driver handed her the letter, tipped his cap, and bowed.

May's face lit up as she took the letter from his hand. "Thank you very much," she said to the driver as she gently closed the door. She wanted to read the letter right then and there, but she realized that there might be things in the letter that she wouldn't want Svane or Rowena to know about, yet. So she told the others that it was from a friend back in Northcamp. Of course, Jonah knew exactly who the letter was from. May tucked the letter into a tunic pocket and then began clearing the table of dishes. Rowena helped May.

Svane leaned over and whispered to Jonah, "We should go help the girls with the dishes." As Svane and Jonah began drawing water and washing dishes, they discussed plans for going to the Lantern Festival later in the day.

Jonah said, "I don't know much about this festival other than that Master Po recommended it to me when I was living in the monastery. We should probably arrive in the late afternoon well before sunset. I expect that the releasing of the lanterns is timed with the rising of the full moon to the east.

Svane asked, "Who es this Master Po?"

"He's the man who taught me how to use my staff as a defensive weapon. I trained with him for several months at the monastery.

Jonah dropped his voice to a whisper, "Several days ago, May and I were attacked by what appeared to be seven members of the Black Sun." Svane looked surprised. "We fought them off with the help of our neighbor when the fight spilled out into the street. At the end of the fight, Duke Olan rode in with some troops and mopped up the Black Sun goons. He carted them all off to the nearby barracks down the main road."

Jonah continued, "While the goons were all members of the Black Sun, I don't think this attack had anything to do with the documents we read some time ago. It seems to have been more about something that might have happened to May back in Borea. In either case, our neighbors have great respect for May and her willingness to protect herself and the east side neighborhood. She has become a living legend, partly thanks to you for helping her clear out the dogs that used to live here."

"There's always some kind o'goat bleatin' and buttin' goin' on en Borea, so I wouldn't be surprised ef someone holds a grudge against her. And et sounds like ye and May can both fight together against a common foe, much better than fightin' and arguin' against each other en yer own house, heh, heh. Aye, that was quite a fight against all o'them vicious dogs. But et was May and her wolf's bane that carried the day. I did me best ta keep the dogs off o'her."

"Did you get any more information about the Black Sun or the monastery?"

"Not yet, though I managed ta pull a favor ta set up an informant who will try ta collect some intelligence on the movement o'goods en Torsberg. Et will take some time for et ta bear fruit, but when I learn more, I'll share my information with ye. But understand this, we have ta keep any information we get secret as my informant es en a very delicate position up en Torslande. I've also tried ta get my customers ta keep an eye out for mysterious characters en the cheese trade," Svane explained.

When everyone finished their cleaning in the kitchen, May came up to Jonah and whispered, "I want to read my letter. Will you come up to my room and help me read it?"

Jonah told her he would be upstairs in a few moments. When Jonah entered and closed her door, May had already broken the wax seal and was admiring Lady Danae's handwriting. "She writes so beautifully."

"Yes. That is very beautiful handwriting. Pay careful attention as I read." Jonah took Lady Danae's letter and began to read it to May, pointing to the words as he read them:

Dearest May,

It is with great sadness that Deanna and I learned of the passing of your dear friend Anya. I met Anya only once, but on that day I recognized how dear of a friend she was to you. And although she is now gone, your friendship with Anya will never end. As long as you remember her as she was and keep her close to your heart, she will always remain by your side to help you and guide you for the rest of your life. Death is not an end but a new phase of life. It is not a day to dread but a mystery to be explored.

Your friends at Ma's Kitchen were also saddened by Anya's passing. Berthe took the sad news very hard. Perhaps a gentle letter of condolence may help her cope with her sadness.

Deanna and I are intrigued by your acquisition of a residence in Callamar. We are looking forward to visiting you in your new place someday soon. I will send you word before we arrive. I look forward to having a chat over tea. I will also bring some wolf's bane.

Soon, Deanna will be enrolling in the Amber Academy for Herbal Medicine. She is excited about beginning school in Callamar and also by the prospect of seeing you once again. She remembers fondly the two of you foraging for elderberries and buttons last fall.

We wish you all prosperity on your new venture in Callamar. Until we meet again, may Selunia keep you safe and Solarus grant you strength.

Faithfully yours,

Lady Danae of Northcamp

Jonah put down the letter, realizing that May was in tears. "Oh Jonah, no one has ever written a letter to me before in my life. That was wonderful. Will you please read it to me again?"

Jonah read May's letter to her five more times. By then, she had committed it to memory.

When Rowena finished working in the kitchen, she went to fetch some water from the well to clean herself. Afterward, she noticed that May and Jonah had seemingly disappeared. She found Svane in the main room drinking the last of his tea when she asked, "Papa, have you seen May or Jonah?"

"I've not seen them since she went upstairs ta her room," Svane said.

"Oh, did they sneak off alone to her room? And what are they doing all alone upstairs?" she giggled.

"Now Rowena, I'm sure they both went upstairs ta read the new letter that she just received today. We shouldn't speculate on personal matters ef ye know what I mean."

"What is a letter?" Rowena asked.

"Et's a message that someone sends t'another person. The message es placed onta a piece o'paper using symbols written by the person sendin' the message. The receiver o'the letter es then able ta read the message by followin' the symbols. That's how people can talk ta each other over long distances without havin' ta see each other." It was at this point that Svane realized that no one in his family except himself knew how to read or write. He also now realized that if he allowed Rowena to stay with May in Callamar, she would probably have to go to school and consequently, learn how to read and write.

The four friends began preparing for their walk into Callamar for the Lantern Festival. The sky had been partially cloudy all day, but the four friends dressed lightly in anticipation of a warm evening. Jonah brought his walking stick along. "Make sure you secure your pocket coin as there might be pickpockets and thieves about," Jonah reminded everyone.

They secured the doors, windows, and gate before walking down to the footbridge. When they got to the Central Market, they turned north then cut back east until they arrived at the Temple of the Dawn near the bank of the Lycus River. Many colorful festival lanterns created a magical glow. As they approached the temple, they could hear the sounds of music from small groups of musicians scattered throughout the festival grounds. Some musicians were playing traditional tunes on stringed instruments. Others chanted recitations and prayers of the nearby temple echoing piety, longing, sadness, and hope. Ahead, crowds entered along the road. There were no ticket sellers, as the festival was free, but there was a table near the temple entrance soliciting alms and donations. Near the main entrance and at several other key locations, several members of the city's night watch provided security.

Rowena had a look of wonder on her face. Music and singing filled the air along with the smells of fresh foods. Booths offered bowls of noodles and rice, sweet rice wrapped in leaves, skewered meats and vegetables, jellied candies, mooncakes, crisply fried wontons, and apple and cherry fritters. Special tables offered an opportunity to create floating lanterns decorated with colorful papers and flowers. Merchants sold incense sticks which could be added to lanterns, taken home, or used within the temple.

May made a beeline for the apple fritters and in no time was munching away heartily. Svane's eyes lit up when he found a tea vendor displaying an assortment of exotic teas. Rowena savored the skewered meats and sweet rice as she walked around, taking in the entire scene. Jonah was not sure what he would find in the mass of humanity, but he eventually encountered a calligrapher who scribed prayers and wishes onto small scrolls of paper in a language he had never seen before.

Jonah asked, "What are the scrolls used for?"

The calligrapher replied in a nasal-like accent, "People usually place them into the floating lanterns as they are cast into the river. The Moon goddess will grant them if they please her. They may also be placed with offerings within the temple."

Jonah asked the man to write up a small scroll for him. As Jonah worked his way back to May, a hand fell upon his shoulder and a familiar voice rang into his ear, "I see you have taken my advice. Are you having a good time?" Jonah turned around and instantly recognized Master Po.

"Master Po! Yes, I am having a good time. I am here with several friends of mine," Jonah said.

Master Po explained, "In the monastery, I am Master Po, but here today, I am Po Weiping. That is my given name and I use it when I am with family and friends."

"But yes, of course. Do you see that big tall girl over there making a lantern? Her name is May." Jonah pointed his finger across the throng at May, "She is the girl I wanted to bring here. She is my girlfriend."

"She looks big, strong, and attractive. Perhaps you were wise to leave the monastery for her. The two of you must fight well together, as you successfully beat up those dark thugs who jumped you some days ago."

"How did you know about that?" Jonah asked.

"Gossip travels fast within Callamar. If you seek to be anonymous, you will find that very difficult, especially if you use the Way of the Staff to defend yourself in public."

"Yes, we fought together. Everything you taught me at the monastery helped me protect myself and May. For that I am grateful to you."

"I heard from Pompey that you are training to become a school teacher. Is this true?"

"Yes, it is. I am expecting to teach secondary school and teach children how to read and write in the near future," Jonah said.

"Someday, I will retire from teaching the Way of the Staff. Perhaps someday you might be able to teach others in the Way of the Staff. I will have to teach you several more advanced techniques before you can become Master Jonah. When you are ready, you may seek me out north of Callamar in the village of Cherry Grove. I can see my family is almost ready to launch their lanterns. I must leave you now but I look forward to seeing you again someday." And with that, Po Weiping moved off towards the river's edge.

Jonah moved through the crowds of people and found Rowena and May making a lantern. They were decorating it with colorful paper and several summer leaves and flowers. In the center was a small votive candle which would be lit before they launched the lantern onto the river. While munching on several chunks of cheddar cheese, Svane watched the girls diligently working together on their lantern.

"Enjoying your cheese?" Jonah asked as he caught up with Svane.

"Aye, I eat goat cheese all the time back home. These cheddars make for a nice change and I eat them here en Callamar when I can. I may have a new customer when I return en the fall," Svane heartily replied.

"I'm impressed that you can have fun and do business all at the same time," Jonah commented. "It looks like the girls have almost finished their lantern."

"Aye, they have. They seem ta work well tagether," Svane commented.

As the sun slowly dipped behind the Aerials, the sky began darkening. Many festival lanterns glowed in the twilight. As the sky grew darker, the faint glow of the full Moon to the east could be seen. For most of the festival goers, the Moon represented one of the few certainties in life – dependable, reliable, and eternal. The Moon always returned to its full glory once a month, year after year, generation after generation. And while the Moon had many moods, she was the constant in their lives – the marker and mistress of time itself.

As the Moon rose above the eastern horizon, people gathered along the riverbank and began to launch their lanterns into the river along with their hopes and prayers. The waters began carrying the lanterns slowly downriver on their voyage to the sea. Adorned with hundreds of undulating beacons, the river became an otherworldly glow. Other lanterns were released from penitents renewing their yearly vows. As the throng thinned, Rowena and May carried their lantern to the riverside and lit their candle. They were about to launch their lantern when Jonah came up to them and placed his little scroll against one of the flowers.

May asked, "What is that?"

Jonah whispered into her ear, "Just a little something for Anya and Danan."

Looking across the water into the moon, Jonah realized that this simple act of remembrance would be considered heresy by the Church. If Danan had indeed killed himself, he was a sinner and destined to burn for all eternity. But the Church – or its earthly representative, the monastery – had driven Danan to this extremity; as far as Jonah was concerned, it was responsible for his death. And Jonah could no longer blindly accept the Church's "truth." He would rather rely on his own judgment than risk error by relying on others.

Svane came up to watch the launching. May and Rowena released their lantern and watched it drift and bob away slowly down the river, adding to the spectacle of lights already floating away. Rowena seemed giddy watching her lantern drift away. At this moment, Jonah reached into his tunic and pulled out a piece of paper from one of his most secret pockets. He unfolded the paper explaining that he had a letter from Danan. He read aloud:

Selunia

Selunia reveal to me
Thy moods that move the restless sea
That stirring up incessant waves,
Batter shoreline clefts and caves.
Thy sounding breakers placate me.

Selunia thy ancient face
Waxes full with soothing grace.
With teardrops welled within my eyes,
Sorrowful I watch thee rise.
Heal my scars, my soul assuage.

Selunia please hear my cry,
My sorrows spilled across the sky.
Forsaken on this foreign shore,
Comfort me forevermore.
Judge not my deeds but piety.

Selunia my muse, my bane,
Raise me from this mortal plane.
And if no space remains above,
Deem me worthy of thy love.
Let me not have lived in vain.

As Jonah read Danan's poem, he thought he could feel Selunia receive Danan's prayer. A cool breeze stirred as if Selunia herself were acknowledging the penitent voices, their prayers, and their hopes for the future. Slowly the lanterns drifted down the river and out to sea.

Jonah refolded the letter and returned it to his pocket. He turned to May as she watched the lanterns disappear around the final river bend. Jonah put his arm around her and began gently rubbing her back. May turned to him and looked into his eyes. As they slowly leaned closer to each other, Jonah reached up to May and she down to him, their lips slowly meeting. They embraced each other as they kissed, releasing a torrent of longing and passion as the Moon bathed them in a romantic glow.

Rowena's jaw dropped at the sight of May and Jonah kissing in the moonlight; she turned away to give them a modicum of privacy. Svane smiled, leading Rowena back to the festival. He whispered, "We'd best leave them alone for a while."

The crowd was thinning as festival-goers headed home. An older lady dressed in festival finery came up to May and Jonah, rubbed both of them on their arms, bringing her hands together and speaking excitedly, though neither of them could understand what she was saying. She held up a small mooncake and offered it to them. May and Jonah each took a small piece of the mooncake and fed it to the other. They bowed respectfully and thanked the mysterious lady. The lady smiled broadly as she patted their backs and walked away into the crowd. May and Jonah finished their mooncake and walked arm in arm back to the festival. They found Svane and Rowena at the cheese booth savoring a few small samples.

The four friends made a few final purchases; then, holding hands, Jonah and May led the other two back to May's home. May and Jonah embraced gently then separated for the night.

Chief Assessor

The next morning, Jonah had just left the house when May and Svane heard a knock on the front door. May went to the door and opened it. Standing in the doorway was an official-looking man with two assistants and two bodyguards. May asked, "May I help you?"

"My name is Talus. I am the chief assessor for the province of Callalande. Duke Olan sent me to resolve some issues concerning this property. Are you May?" the chief assessor said.

"Yes I am," May replied.

"May I come in?" the chief assessor asked.

May opened the door and allowed the five men to enter. She made sure to keep all of the men in front of her. She showed them to the table as she cleared the remaining dishes and cups. "Forgive my mess. Please have a seat."

Svane was in the kitchen cleaning his tea pot and cups.

The chief assessor began, "Miss May, we are here on behalf of the City of Callamar and at the Duke's direction to report to you our findings concerning the past history of this property where you now reside."

"Would you and your men like some water to drink?" May asked.

The chief assessor continued, "No thank you; we have a number of findings to report to you. First, this property belonged to Michael and Aeolia Glomb. They were the proprietors of the East Orchard Inn and Kitchen for many years. They had one son who was recruited into the army. He served along the southern border of Korgynslande many years ago. According to our records, he was killed in action and left no family behind. The couple Michael and Aeolia also had no kin registered as living in Callamar and there appears to be no next of kin listed under the ownership documents for this property. As far as we can tell, all potential claimants to this property are deceased. No claims have been filed since their passing. The assessor's office has no objection to your making a claim to this property. Therefore, the Duke has instructed us to offer you the deed to this property, contingent upon your sealing an agreement with the City of Callamar to pay quarterly taxes on the property itself and on any business located on the premises. Taxes are assessed based on the type of business operated and when the appropriate paperwork has been filed and a business license issued."

Chief Assessor Talus handed May the deed to the property with several "X" marks where she was to sign her name. It was a lot to look at, and she needed Jonah to help her make sense of what was happening. Svane overheard everything from the kitchen.

The chief assessor continued, "If you file your property deed within the next week, the city works department can schedule a work order to be performed on your property during the next quarter. I will describe what that entails in the next order of business. Business paperwork can be filed at a later time when you are ready or never, should you choose not to open a business. You may obtain advice from the Assessor's Office or from any barrister specializing in business law located throughout the city should you have any questions or concerns."

The chief assessor continued, "The next order of business is that the property cited in the deed you have been awarded shows that it extends a good distance beyond the existing walls. The duke is generously offering the services of the City Works Department to tear down and rebuild your outer wall so you can more properly access the land that you now own. City Works can begin work on this project as soon as you file your deed with the Assessor's Office. Labor costs, along with the price of standard materials, will be covered by City Works. If you wish to upgrade your materials, you will have to bear the cost yourself."

"Now, onto the third item. Within Callalande, the Duke has authorized a bounty in the sum of 200 golds to be paid in full to the slayer of Torqual, the wolf hunter. The wolf hunter was found dead and headless on the shores of the Snowfall River just north of Fallmouth. The presentation to me and my officers of any three of the following listed items will constitute proof of your having slain Torqual, the wolf hunter, and you will be awarded the bounty of 200 golds."

May interrupted, "I have to go upstairs to collect the items if I am to prove anything today."

The chief assessor continued, "All right. We will wait."

May excused herself and rushed up to her room where she found the items amongst her curios she had taken from the wolf hunter's body. As she came back down into the kitchen, she heard Svane asking, "The wolf hunter?"

"Yes, let's hope these things belonged to him."

May sat down at the table and placed four items in front of her along with the wood-cutting axe she had taken from him: a small whistle, a small leather pouch containing a rounded curved piece of glass, a small translucent rectangular stone or crystal of a yellowish-brown color, and a small necklace made from four canine teeth sharpened to fine points.

The Chief assessor pulled out his list of items determined to have been owned by the wolf hunter and began, "First item on the list is a grey wolf headdress known to have been worn by the wolf hunter."

May replied, "I did not keep that item, though the wolf hunter did wear one when he tried to attack me. I thought he was a wolf until I unmasked him."

The chief assessor nodded, "I see. All right, second item on the list is an oculus. The oculus can be used as a magnifying glass or reading glass or as a fire starter."

May reached for the small pouch and opened it up to reveal a small rounded piece of glass. She handed the item to the assessor.

"Fascinating." He placed the glass up to his list and noticed the writing on the paper became enlarged, making it easier for him to read. He then put the glass up to his eye and found he could see things a little sharper when holding it a certain distance from his eye. "Wow, I guess this must be an oculus." One of his assistants took up the oculus, experimented, and concurred with the chief assessor.

May smiled.

The chief assessor nodded, "All right, one correct item. Third item on the list is a whistle that makes no sound."

May replied, "A whistle that makes no sound? How can that be?" May reached down for the whistle and then put it up to her mouth and blew. No sound came out of the whistle. She tried again and could not make a sound. She handed it to the assessor; he tried the same thing and could not make a sound, either. The assessor handed the item to one of his assistants and asked him to blow into the whistle. Again, there was no result.

Rowena walked into the kitchen, "What are you doing in here?" She realized that May and Svane had company. "Oh, I'm sorry." Svane gently grabbed her by the shoulders and quietly whispered to her, "May es busy right now."

The assessor asked all of his assistants and bodyguards if they had heard anything at all and all of them shook their heads. The assessor nodded, "All right, a whistle that makes no sound, two correct items. Fourth item on the list is a serrated hunting knife."

May replied, "He did have a knife but I did not keep that item, either, since I ... since I have two of my own."

The chief assessor nodded, "All right. Fifth item on the list is a sunstone shaped like a tilted rectangular box."

May looked down at the items and picked up the yellowish crystal. "This must be a sunstone as it looks yellow like the sun." She handed the item to the assessor who took the item, placed it onto his list of items, and looked through it. As he did so, the words on the paper could be seen in duplicate. As he turned the crystal the words circled around each other. His assistant concurred with the assessor's observation after moving the crystal around on the paper for a while. "Very interesting, it's shaped like a tilted rectangular box, it's yellow, and it duplicates the words. All right, a sunstone. Three correct items."

The chief assessor smiled, "May you have met the threshold of proof as outlined in the Duke's instructions and I will award you the bounty. However, please indulge me for a moment as you still have items remaining on the table. The sixth item on the list is a necklace of sharpened wolf's teeth."

May could barely contain her excitement. She picked up the necklace and saw that the teeth were definitely sharpened to fine points. She handed the necklace to the assessor who then tested the sharpness of the teeth with his finger and agreed – no need for concurrence.

The chief assessor nodded, "All right, four correct items. Seventh item on the list is a small wood axe used for chopping wood. That must be the last item on the table. Five correct items. Assistants, do you concur that May is in compliance with the orders issued by Duke Olan?" The assessor's assistants agreed. "May, you have done better than the minimum of three correct items and as such, your case is considered impervious to challenge. Congratulations!" The assessor wrote a few things onto his paperwork and told May she could sign on the line below her name. May took his quill and signed her name. One of the assessor's assistants co-signed the document as a witness. Then each of the guards dug into a satchel bag each was carrying, pulled out a large purse of coin, and plunked them both onto the table top.

The chief assessor announced, "All of the paperwork is in order. On behalf of the City of Callamar and Duke Olan's government, I want to thank you for ridding Callalande of that vile scourge Torqual, also known as the wolf hunter. In accordance with the Duke's decree, a bounty of 200 golds is being paid to you in full on this day. That concludes all of the business we have scheduled for today. Do not forget to file your deed within one week's time. I want to wish you a good day and, again, Callamar thanks you for your service."

The chief assessor and his entourage then let themselves out through the front door and rode off down the main road.

"And I thought I got paid well for me cheese on this trip. Ye just hit pay dirt, so ta speak. Ye would do well ta hide yer golds where no one else will know where they're hidden. There are now eight, soon ta be nine, people who know that there are 200 golds ta be found somewhere within this place o'yers. Ye need ta be cautious or take them ta the bank and secure them there."

"What were you two doing just before I walked into the kitchen?" Rowena asked.

Svane and May looked at each other blankly. Svane asked Rowena, "Why do ye ask?"

"I thought I heard papa's boiling kettle whistling in the kitchen. I went to the kitchen, but when I got there, I heard nothing."

May thought for a moment, picked up the whistle off of the table then blew into it. Rowena put her hands to her ears. "That's it. Stop it, please."

May looked at Rowena as Svane laughed. May said, "I think this must be a wolf whistle which means Rowena might have some wolf's blood in her."

Rowena was not amused but she was puzzled. "May I see the whistle?" Rowena took the whistle and blew into it. She could hear a faint high-pitched sound and she could feel vibrations on her lips from the whistle. She immediately took the whistle out of her mouth and rubbed her lips to get rid of the funny sensation. "This is definitely what I heard and I am not a wolf."

Svane took Rowena in his arms and said, "Don't ye worry about that. I think et must be because ye're still a child that ye can hear things the rest o'us adults can't hear at all. Sometimes the simplest explanation es usually the right one."

Svane continued, "So today, May es a triple fortune winner. First, she won the deed ta this property. Second, she'll be gettin' a new wall and some extra land. Third, she won a bounty for riddin' Callalande of the wolf hunter. The day es young. Makes me wonder what else could be en store. Maybe Selunia heard your prayers last night and witnessed your moment with Jonah." Svane smiled.

May blushed a little saying, "I made no prayers last night, though Jonah did place a little scroll into the lantern. Rowena and I only launched our lantern into the river and watched it drift away."

"Sometimes et's the humblest o'people that're granted wishes and prayers, especially those who give ta others and ask for nothin' en return," Svane turned to Rowena. "And with that, I'm en a position ta grant another wish. Rowena, are ye still interested en stayin' with May here en Callamar?"

"Oh papa, yes! I want to stay here with May. Will you let me stay here with you May?" Rowena pleaded.

May replied, "Your papa and I talked about you this morning and came to an agreement. You can stay here with me in Callamar for two months until the fall when your papa will return to Callamar with more cheese to sell. At that time we will decide if you should stay longer or return to Torslande. While you are here, you will have to follow my rules and you will also have to respect and listen to Jonah. Also, other people may come to live here in the future. How would you feel about that?"

Rowena answered very excitedly, "I will agree to follow your rules and I will be very nice and respectful to everyone else who lives here with you."

With that, Svane agreed to allow Rowena to stay in Callamar with May until the fall when he would return. Rowena gave her papa a very big hug and promised to be a good girl.

Paperwork

Jonah finished reading the property deed. "It looks like all you have to do is sign and deliver the papers to the Assessor's Office and this property is yours. When you sign the papers, you become responsible for property taxes, not much at all compared to your windfall earlier today. As a property owner, you are being granted citizenship In Korgynslande and all of the benefits thereof. Wow!"

"Would you recommend going to the office tomorrow?" May asked.

"I recommend I go with you to the Assessor's Office in the morning so I can hear what the secretary has to say about filing out the paperwork and what constitutes an acceptable signature. We should also stop by the Census Office and find out if Rowena can stay as a visitor until the fall. Having legal papers for Rowena could be important. You also will need to find a bed for her. I have to admit, when Pompey and I were speculating as to whether you would successfully collect the wolf hunter's bounty, I didn't think you would actually get it. But now, you are in a better position to begin that business you've been talking about. Pompey thinks you could even become a professional bounty hunter!" Jonah said.

"Not on your life, though if we have to keep defending ourselves against goons and thugs, we may have to build a store of bigger weapons. Maybe you and Svane can collect more information on those Black Sun goons and pass it along to the Duke's intelligence agents or whatever they're called," May said.

"You mean Svane and I become spies? That has all the makings of a disaster. Come to think of it, I might have access to some interesting paperwork if I can ..." Jonah's voice trailed off as he started thinking quietly to himself.

Svane said, "I don't want ta be part o'any spy outfit. All I want es ta figure out how them sapphires fit enta the big picture and whether or not there es some corruption back en Torslande. There's nothin' illegal about makin' honest coin, though sapphire smugglin' would be problematic. Maybe that kind o'intelligence needs gatherin'."

May interjected, "All right, while you and Svane toy with dreams of spying, Rowena and I want to get dinner started. And I also need to figure out what to do with all this coin here. As Svane said we need to hide it or bank it. Jonah, you seemed to be good at hiding things back in the monastery. Maybe you can suggest what to do with the coin."

"A large bank might be the most secure place to keep it, but they will also take a percentage of the coin as a 'fee' for keeping it safe and secure, sometimes as much as twenty percent. For now, make sure you have one hand on it while you sleep. I'm sure we can find a location where no one would think of looking," Jonah said.

The next day, Jonah and May went to the Assessor's Office in the morning so Jonah could go straight to school afterward. Jonah and May found a surprisingly short queue. Soon they were at the office window where May explained that she was there to file the paperwork of ownership for her newly acquired property. Jonah also asked the secretary about the proper protocols for signing. The secretary explained that before May signed her name, he would call a clerk from the back office to sign as a witness, and Jonah could also sign as a witness. The secretary checked over all of the paperwork and in almost no time they were done. The secretary then gave May a copy of the taxes and explained what she needed to do. Before long, they were out the door. Jonah told May that she should take her copy of the deed home and put it in a safe place. He would now go to classes and see her later. "If Svane leaves before I get home, tell him goodbye and that I will talk to him when he returns in the fall," Jonah said.

As May walked back home, she realized that she was truly going home; she was now a property owner and had the deed to prove it. She was also now a citizen of Korgynslande. Furthermore, she was working on a new relationship with Jonah and she was going to be responsible for the safety and welfare of Rowena. She smiled broadly and radiated joy as she walked down the street. Her happiness was tainted only by the thought that Anya was not here to share her joy.

When May finally arrived home, Svane was in the process of double checking his cart and securing all of the empty pots to be hauled back up to Torslande. "Are you leaving?"

"Aye, I've already stayed longer than I should've and I know when I return home without Rowena, everyone es goin' ta ask what happened. I'll probably have ta bring everyone down here ta visit ye and Rowena next time. Just make sure ye take good care o'her. I know ye're strong and good en a fight, but none o'that matters when ye've a young girl livin' with ye. Ef things get rough, just remind yerself I'll be comin' back en the fall," Svane said.

Svane said his goodbyes. He gave Rowena a big hug and told her he would be back in the fall so she had better be a good girl or he would find out about her misbehaving.

Svane filled some of the pots with water from May's well for the horses in case he could not find any water along the trail. He also loaded up some of May's hay. One never knew for sure if snows would make the roads impassable. May opened up the gate as Svane brought his cart out onto the main road to head back to Torslande. For the second time, May watched Svane ride off to the north.

May then spoke, "Rowena, do you know which room you might –?"

"I want to be next to you," Rowena said quickly.

"Oh, all right. You'll be to the north of me since Jonah is in the room to the south," May replied.

"Are you and Jonah going to live together in the same room now?" Rowena giggled.

"And why would I do that?" May asked.

"Because you were kissing him in the moonlight for such a long time," Rowena said.

"Does that mean we have to marry? And I wasn't kissing Jonah for that long," May objected.

Rowena stated bluntly, "During the festival, papa told me not to look at you two, so I counted to 100 and then I turned around to see you two were still kissing. Then I turned around and started counting again –"

"Oh all right, so it was a little longer that I thought it was but I still have to make sure he's the right boy for me."

"It seems to me that you already know he's the right boy." Rowena giggled and kept teasing May about Jonah but eventually they got around to looking at the room next to May's. Although it contained some furniture, it looked rather spartan. "Would you like to add more things? A chair or sofa, perhaps?"

"You know where I lived with papa and mama in Torslande. I shared everything with everyone. I had nothing of my own and I slept on the floor. The feather you gave me was the only thing I could call my own. This room will be more than good enough. Do you still have nightmares?"

"What kinds of nightmares?" May asked.

"The kind where you wake up screaming and crying, saying something about a fire."

May realized that her nightmares about the fire in Northcamp must have been obvious to everyone in Svane's family. She had to hope that her ramblings had not been intelligible.

"Yes, I do. Please don't mention them to anyone else. I am hoping that in time, they will go away and leave me sleeping in peace at night."

"All right, no talking about bad dreams," Rowena said as she opened the door to her new room.

Rowena's room was a small rectangle with a small window in the eastern wall and a door opening out onto the second floor walkway. There was one more room just north of hers which was currently unoccupied and closer to one of the staircases.

"With this room, you will certainly have privacy if you choose to. One rule: if you find a door closed you must always knock on the door and wait for permission to enter," May explained.

"All right, knock first then wait for permission," Rowena repeated.

Preparing for sleep, May put the bags of gold close to her bed and covered them with some dirty clothes. She closed her eyes and tried to sleep, but she had too much to think about. With her new wealth, she had many options open to her. She could start a business but what sort of business? The possibilities seemed endless. She missed Anya sorely and wished she were here to share in May's success – after all, Anya had made it possible for May to collect the bounty. In fact, without Anya, May probably would not have survived. May was not religious in a strict sense; she had not been raised in a specific faith. Throughout her adventures she had encountered many different religious and spiritual beliefs and ideas that appeared, at times, both contradictory and complimentary. But throughout everything, she had always felt Anya watching over her, protecting her, and providing for her. *Is she watching me now?*

Maybe Anya had led her to Jonah – though she hadn't been his biggest fan when she was alive. The memory of Jonah's kiss and embrace warmed her; she couldn't wait to kiss him again. In fact, she couldn't imagine a future without him, not because he could read and write better than anyone she knew. She planned to learn to read and write, too. But she knew that deep down he was a good person, someone she could rely on, someone who could truly be a partner, someone who wanted for her what she wanted for herself.

Knowing her past – well, some of it – Jonah understood and accepted her. Her conscience, if that's what it was, troubled her when she remembered some of the things she had done – her deeply buried anger over Anya's death and her need for revenge. But her acts of violence didn't have to define her, she decided. She could not alter the past, but she could resolve to do good in the days ahead. She could start by giving Rowena a loving home and a promising future. She could make sure that Rowena went to school and learned how to read and write while she was still young. Above all, she could be an example to Rowena of a strong, independent woman who acted selflessly to make others happy while making herself happy, too. She finally drifted off to sleep, waking only occasionally to reassure herself that the bags of gold were still beside her. *I will have to deal with this gold, soon.*

Jonah was also having trouble sleeping. He was preparing to pledge himself to May, but he had to admit that he was worried about what he might be getting into. He did not believe that the recent attack by the Black Sun had been merely random. And who was this Baron and why was he looking for May – maybe even looking for him, now, too? He reluctantly realized that committing to life with May would almost certainly mean committing to fighting her enemies alongside her even if he didn't understand who they were. He was going to need additional training from Master Po. Sticks versus goons was one thing; sticks versus swords was something else. And he resolved to do whatever was needed to gather information about these mysterious enemies. This might involve working with the Duke and others who held power in Callamar – merchants, guilds, the monastery.

He would need a secret workspace and a safe repository for all of the data he acquired. He would speak to May about secretly building a vault somewhere on her property, maybe within the walls of this building. And how would he gather knowledge? Of course – through people he already knew and trusted. Pompey had access to Saint Dominic's Library and would readily agree to pass along information about the monastery and scriptorium. He would make an ideal spy! They already knew that there was some connection between **someone** in the monastery and the Black Sun organization. And how did the sapphires fit in? His head was still buzzing with his calculations and plans long after he had fallen asleep.

Commitments

Several weeks had passed since Svane had left and Rowena had taken up residence next to May in her new room. Jonah had slowly come to know Rowena and to appreciate her cooking, especially her breakfasts. Eating hot, delicious meals every morning instead of stale bread and cheese made for a welcome change. There was definitely something to be said for eating a hot breakfast as Rowena's cooking helped him get through and finish his teacher training. Nothing to brag about but Jonah was getting passing marks. He was also getting hands-on experience teaching older children and young teenagers how to learn. Eventually he learned some of the common strategies for teaching reading and writing skills. Headmistress Agnes watched him like a hawk until he finally was able to handle a classroom full of children for a few days a week.

Eventually, Jonah passed all of his courses, and soon he and his cohorts had satisfied Headmistress Agnes' requirements and were eligible to receive their certificates of completion. Agnes arranged a small ceremony to which all of the candidates could invite their friends and family. Jonah invited both May and Rowena to attend the ceremony and, surprisingly, Pompey found a way to escape the monastery and attend, as well.

After the ceremony, Pompey found a brief moment where he could talk privately to Jonah. "A few days after you left, the Duke returned to the monastery and gave everyone a short summary of the inquiry's findings. In his own words, the Duke said that he was certain that Danan, Ergan, and Borse were all dead though the circumstances of their deaths remained uncertain. He passed along his condolences to everyone. He also made a donation of several young apple trees for planting within the ascetic garden in their honor and remembrance. The Duke also declared Abbot August and Prior Damien –"

"What are you two whispering about over here?" May interrupted.

"– personae non gratae within Callalande."

Shocked, Jonah said, "The Duke did all of that? I mean boarsteaks sounds good to me."

May eyed Jonah suspiciously. "I sense conspiracy –"

Pompey said, "I recommend we parade over to The Charging Boar. I was telling Jonah that I am the newly appointed Archscribe of Saint Dominic's!" Pompey patted himself on the back as Jonah smiled and May looked confused. "With the departure of the abbot and Prior Damien, Prior Lund was promoted to Security and Archscribe Rene is now Prior Rene. Prior Lund has been acting as the abbot until the Church appoints a new abbot."

"Congratulations Pompey! That sounds wonderful! You will make a great archscribe."

As Pompey embodied pomp and circumstance itself, he strode forth with Jonah and company to The Charging Boar. While eating their dinners, Jonah and May were surprised by how proud Pompey was of Jonah's accomplishments. Rowena was discovering Pompey to be funny and entertaining but also very weird.

When Pompey found the opportunity, he turned to Rowena and introduced himself with a bow, "Young Rowena, you must be May's new ward. My name is Pompey, master of pomp and scribe of arches, at your service." Pompey then winked and whispered, "I need you to spy on May and Jonah for me. I mean, I need you to protect May and Jonah from the ubiquitous criminal elements infesting this magnificent city. Agreed?"

Unsure of what Pompey was asking, Rowena replied, "Um, I'm only ten."

"Perfect! No one will ever suspect you." Pompey laughed then wandered off to refill his ale. Rowena leaned towards May. "Is Pompey always like that?"

May sighed. "All the time."

May had finally finished cleaning her place to her satisfaction and whitewashing all of the rooms and exterior walls. The City Works Department scheduled May's outer wall extension and repairs for the middle of the fall. Rowena enthusiastically helped May begin experimenting in her kitchen. She hoped that when her papa returned, she would be able to convince him to let her stay at least through the winter in Callamar.

When May had cleaned up the third-floor rooms, she invited Jonah to see the dilapidated study. He immediately saw a potential library or office.

As May and Jonah were spending more quality time together, their relationship slowly grew. May waited a long month for Jonah to come to her room. Every night she plotted and considered and left her door open ever wider, but he didn't take the hint. She finally decided that if they were to have a future together, **she** was going to have to make the first move. So one night, while Jonah was planning his strategy for embarking on his new career, he was startled to find May in his room … sitting on his bed … waiting for him. She was apparently dressed for bed wearing a new robe, her hair loose around her shoulders, and barefoot. Her eyes shone with desire and apprehension.

Jonah asked casually, "How was your day? Aren't you cold?"

"I want you to promise me something," she purred seductively.

"You want me to –?"

"I want you to promise me that you will do everything in your power to teach everyone who lives under this roof now and in the future – beginning with me and Rowena – how to read and write."

"Is that what you –?"

"If you make me this promise, I in turn promise to be your loving and loyal companion forever. I will be your woman, a partner you can depend on, a mother to your children. Do we have a deal?"

Jonah struggled for composure realizing that she was proposing to him. He smiled, took a deep breath, and took her hand. "I promise to teach you and Rowena to read and write. And I promise to be your faithful companion, husband, and helpmeet, from this day forward. And I promise to teach reading and writing to our children and our children's children." Jonah took May into his arms and began kissing her. At some point, her robe had fallen to the floor. May couldn't quite understand what he was saying anymore. He seemed to be saying something about defeating the Black Sun and slaying demons but honestly, she wished he would stop nattering on and concentrate on what he was doing, which she was rather enjoying. Strangely, once she got her hands on him, she didn't transform into a murderous monster – other than having killed that bounty hunter and assassinated those greencoats and slayed the giant Nimrod – but he need never know about THAT.

They made love throughout the night secure in the knowledge that they would be stronger together and that their bond would help others gain power and knowledge, not only Rowena, not only Jonah's future pupils, but their own children and their children's children. Throwing out discretion and come what may, they consummated their commitments.

ACKNOWLEDGMENTS

I wish to thank my former teaching colleague and friend, Kathy Starrenburg. Kathy spent many weeks patiently editing my novel and without her expertise in grammar, style, and history, my book would be little more than word salad.

I also wish to thank my friend Michael Morris whose generous and invaluable commentary helped me organize many of the plots and storylines.

Finally, I would like to thank my family: my parents Aida and Marvin and my siblings, Brian, Natasha, Nathan, and Estrellita. All have contributed in many ways to the stories and experiences that went into many of the characters and the world in which they live.

MAPS AND FLOOR PLANS

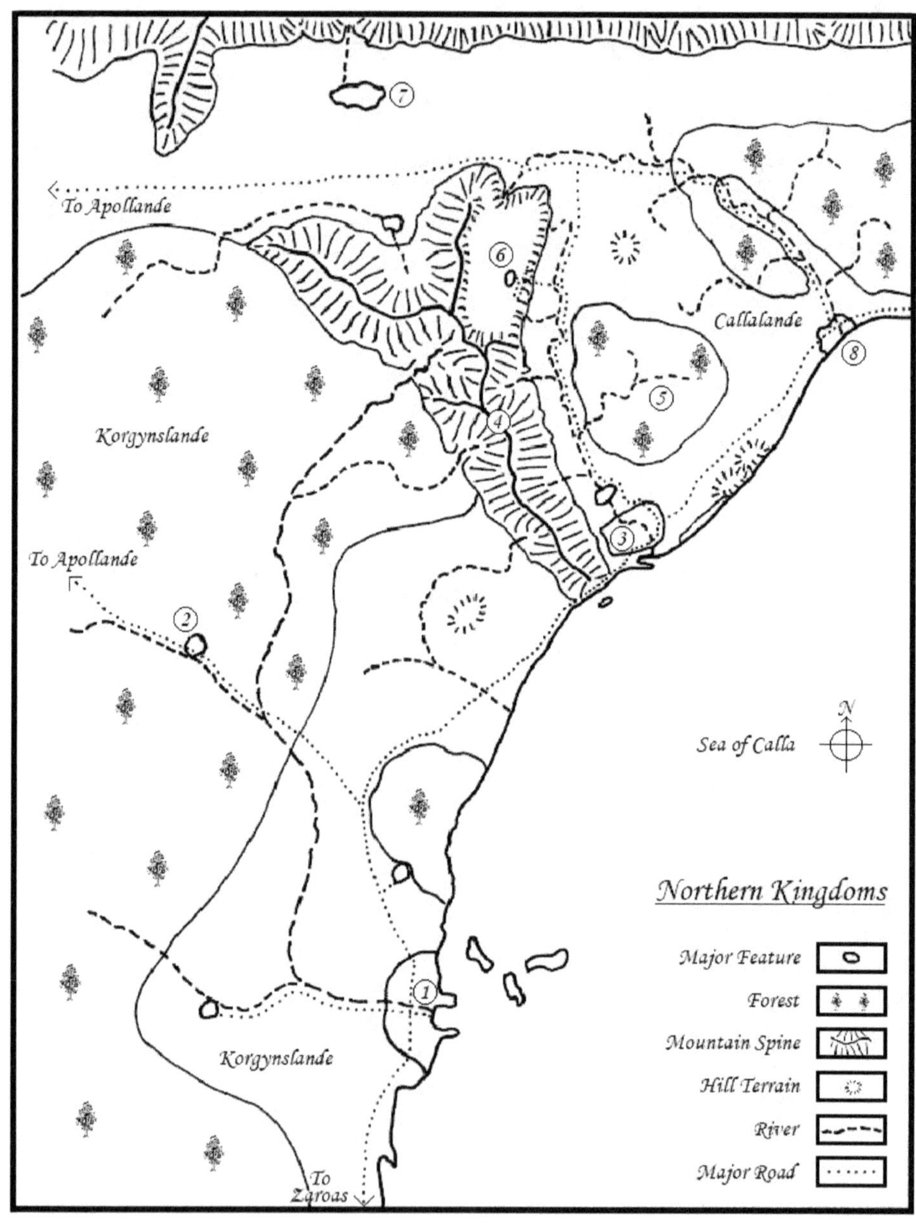
To Apollande
To Apollande
Korgynslande
Korgynslande
Callalande
Sea of Calla
N
Northern Kingdoms
Major Feature
Forest
Mountain Spine
Hill Terrain
River
Major Road
To Zaroas

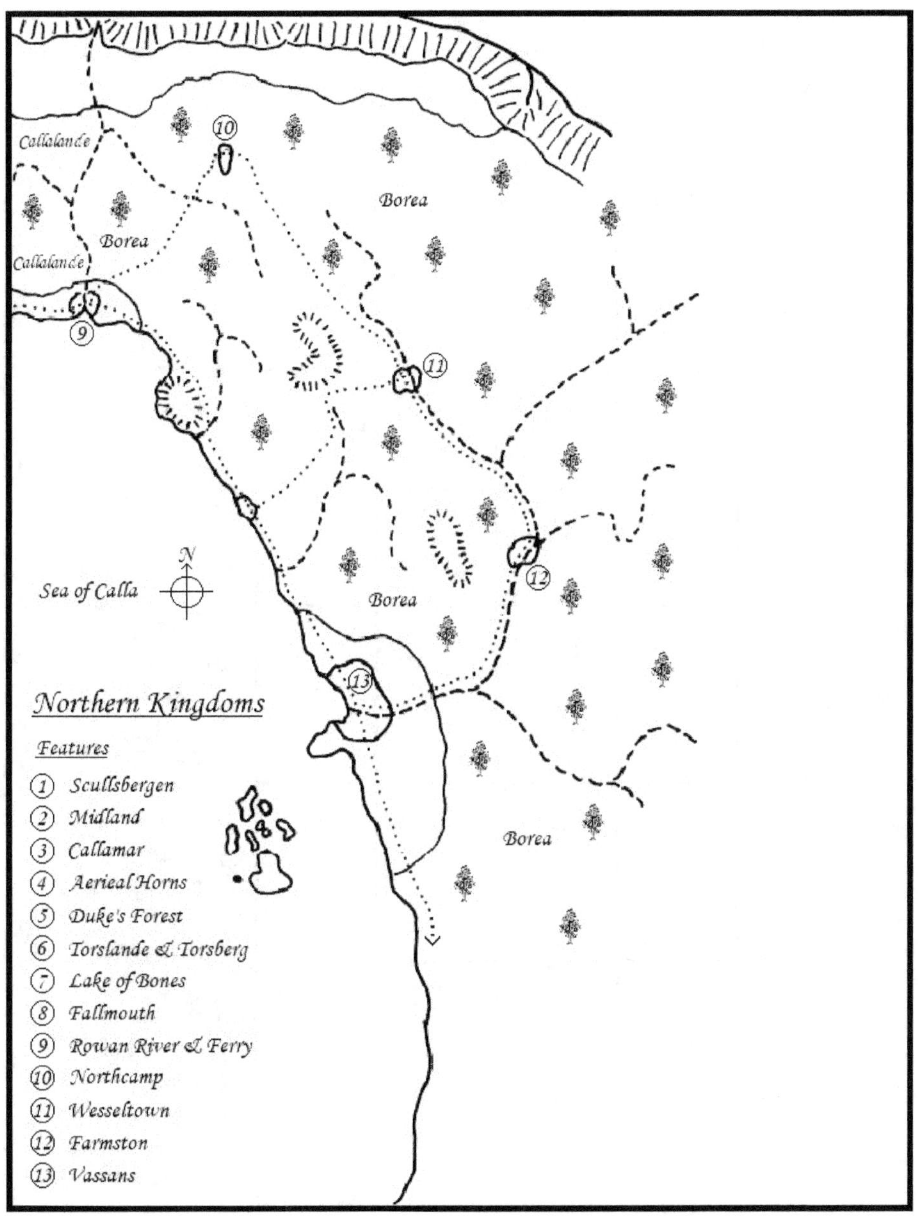
Callalande
Borea
Callalande
Borea
Borea
Borea
Borea
Sea of Calla
N
Northern Kingdoms
Features
1 Scullsbergen
2 Midland
3 Callamar
4 Aerieal Horns
5 Duke's Forest
6 Torslande & Torsberg
7 Lake of Bones
8 Fallmouth
9 Rowan River & Ferry
10 Northcamp
11 Wesseltown
12 Farmston
13 Vassans

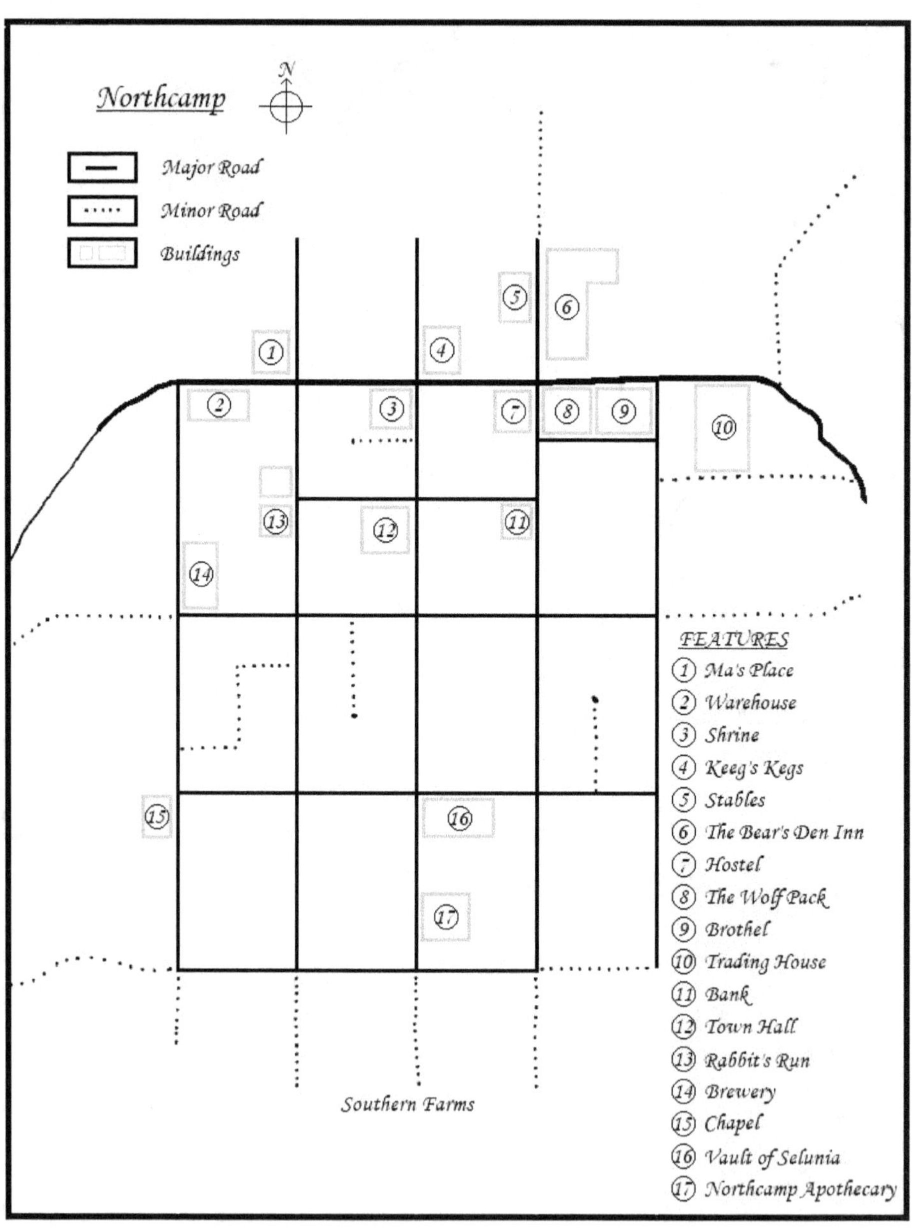

Northcamp
N
Major Road
Minor Road
Buildings
1
2
3
4
5
6
7
8
9
10
11
12
13
14
15
16
17
Southern Farms
FEATURES
1 Ma's Place
2 Warehouse
3 Shrine
4 Keeg's Kegs
5 Stables
6 The Bear's Den Inn
7 Hostel
8 The Wolf Pack
9 Brothel
10 Trading House
11 Bank
12 Town Hall
13 Rabbit's Run
14 Brewery
15 Chapel
16 Vault of Selunia
17 Northcamp Apothecary

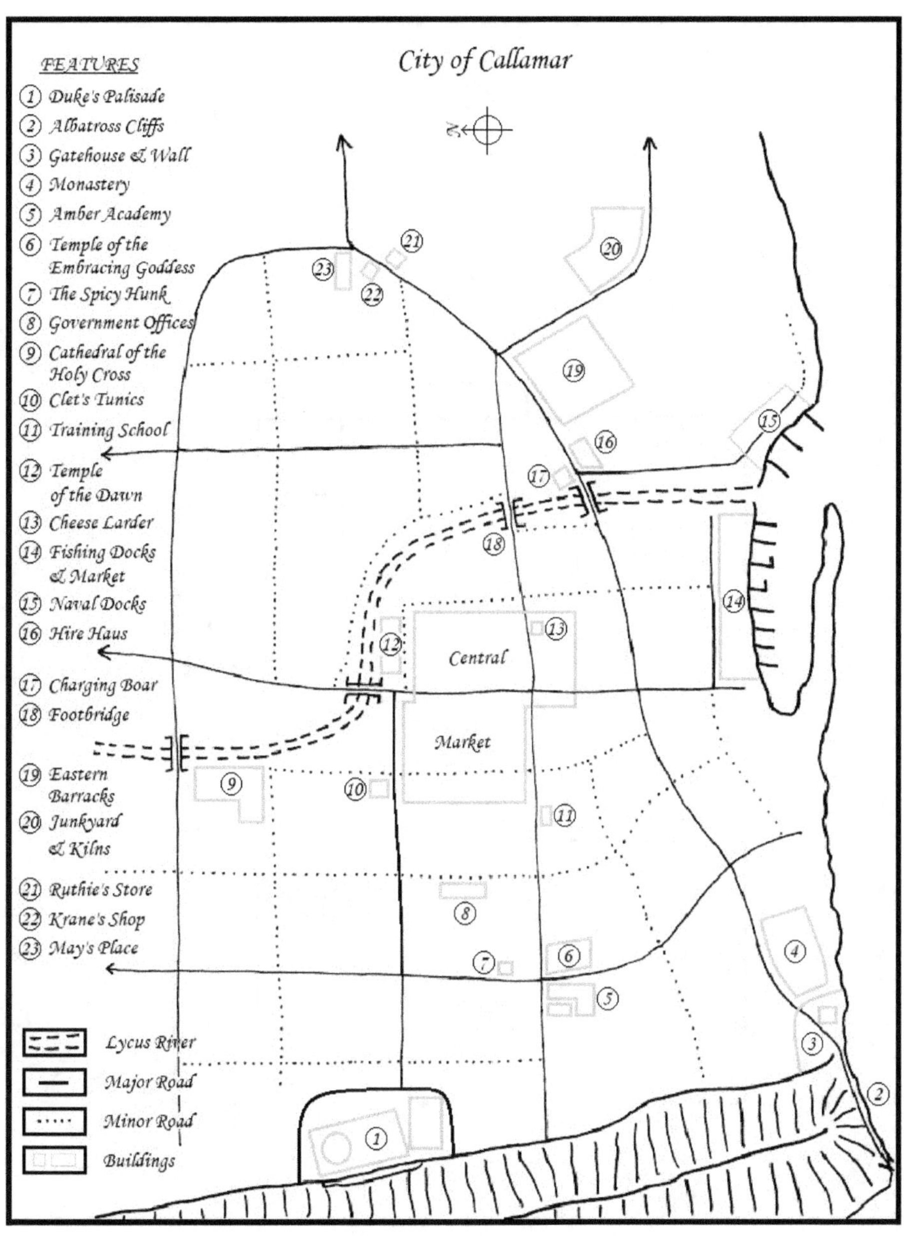
City of Callamar
FEATURES
1 Duke's Palisade
2 Albatross Cliffs
3 Gatehouse & Wall
4 Monastery
5 Amber Academy
6 Temple of the Embracing Goddess
7 The Spicy Hunk
8 Government Offices
9 Cathedral of the Holy Cross
10 Clet's Tunics
11 Training School
12 Temple of the Dawn
13 Cheese Larder
14 Fishing Docks & Market
15 Naval Docks
16 Hire Haus
17 Charging Boar
18 Footbridge
19 Eastern Barracks
20 Junkyard & Kilns
21 Ruthie's Store
22 Krane's Shop
23 May's Place
Lycus River
Major Road
Minor Road
Buildings
Central
Market

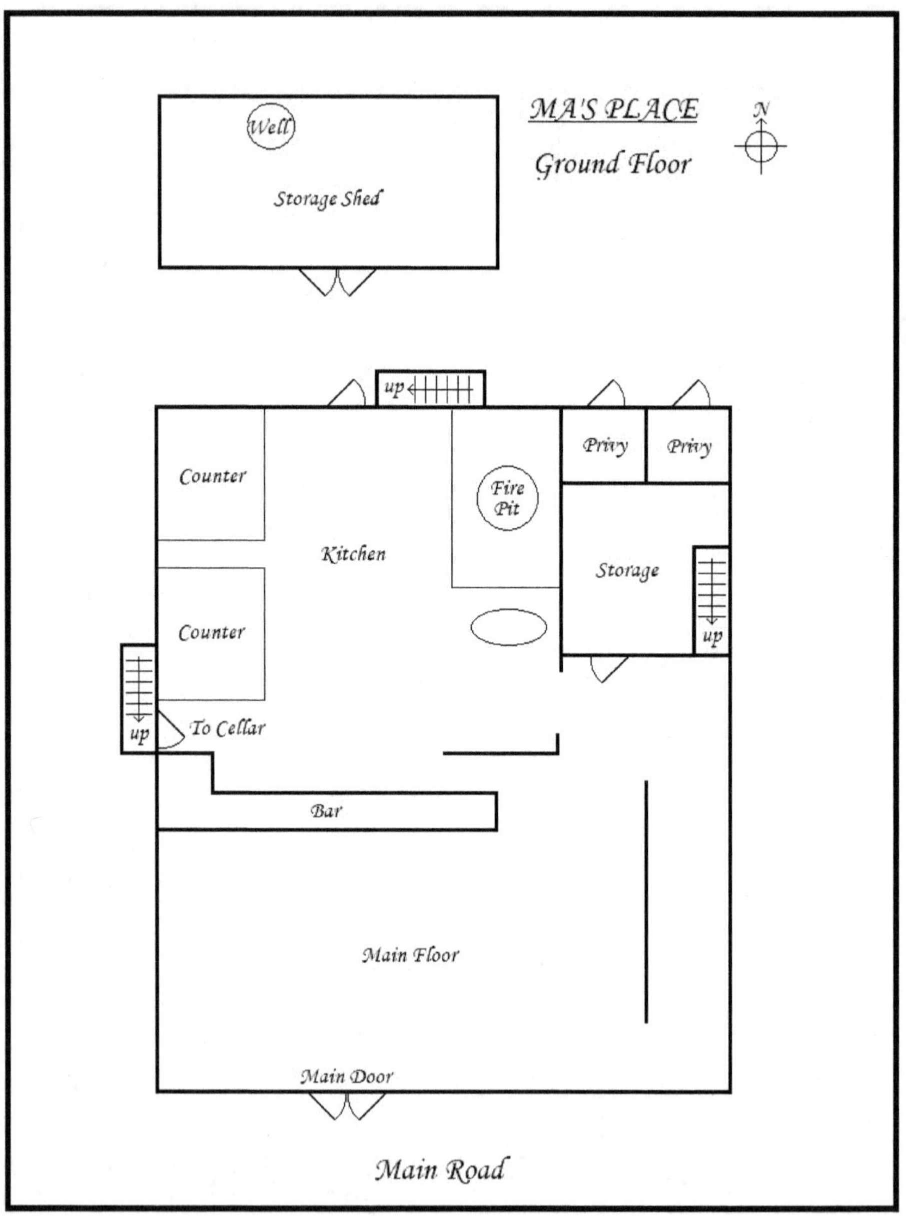
Well
Storage Shed
MA'S PLACE
Ground Floor
N
up
Counter
Kitchen
Fire Pit
Privy
Privy
Storage
up
Counter
up
To Cellar
Bar
Main Floor
Main Door
Main Road

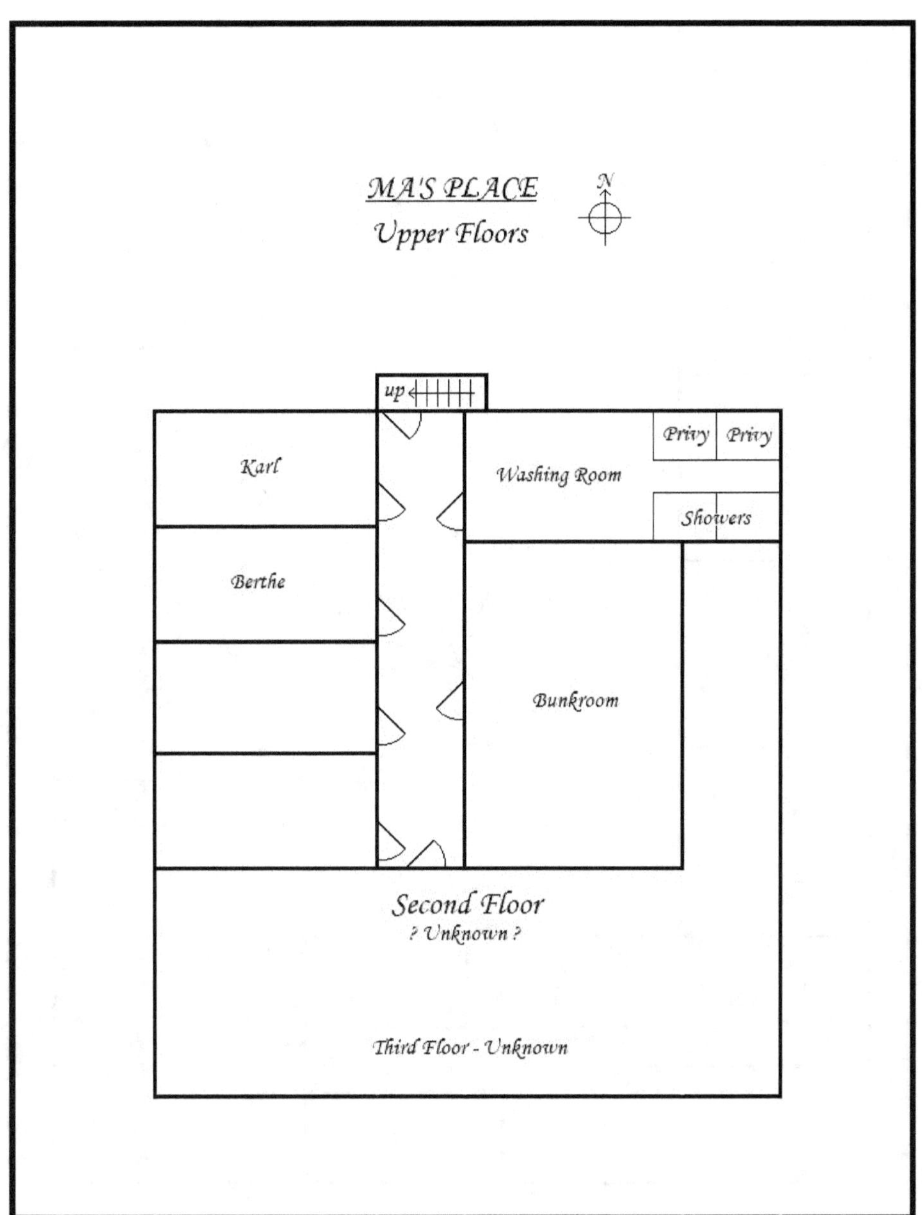

MA'S PLACE
Upper Floors
N
up
Karl
Berthe
Washing Room
Privy
Privy
Showers
Bunkroom
Second Floor
? Unknown ?
Third Floor - Unknown

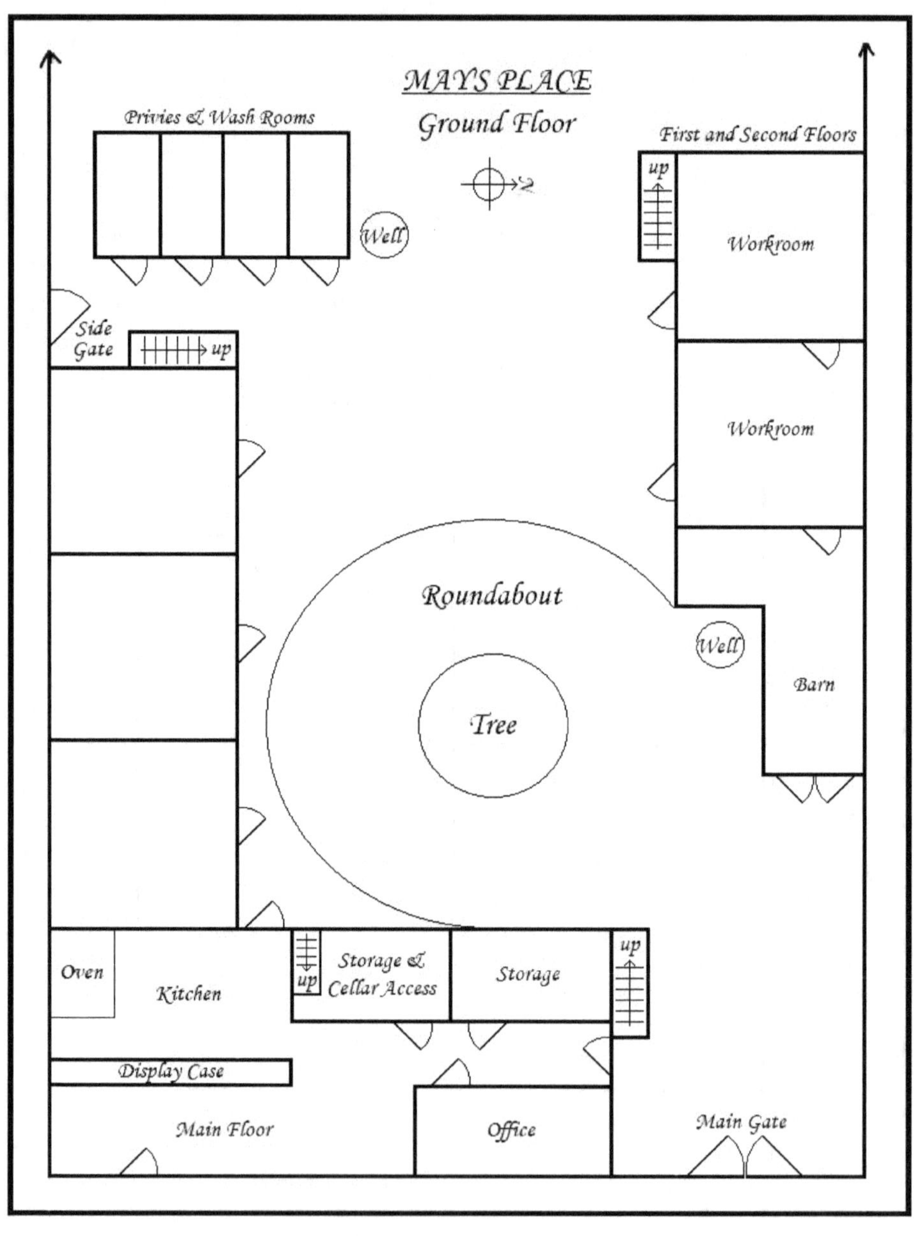
MAY'S PLACE
Ground Floor
First and Second Floors
Privies & Wash Rooms
Well
up
Workroom
Workroom
Side Gate
up
Roundabout
Well
Barn
Tree
Oven
Kitchen
up
Storage & Cellar Access
Storage
up
Display Case
Main Floor
Office
Main Gate

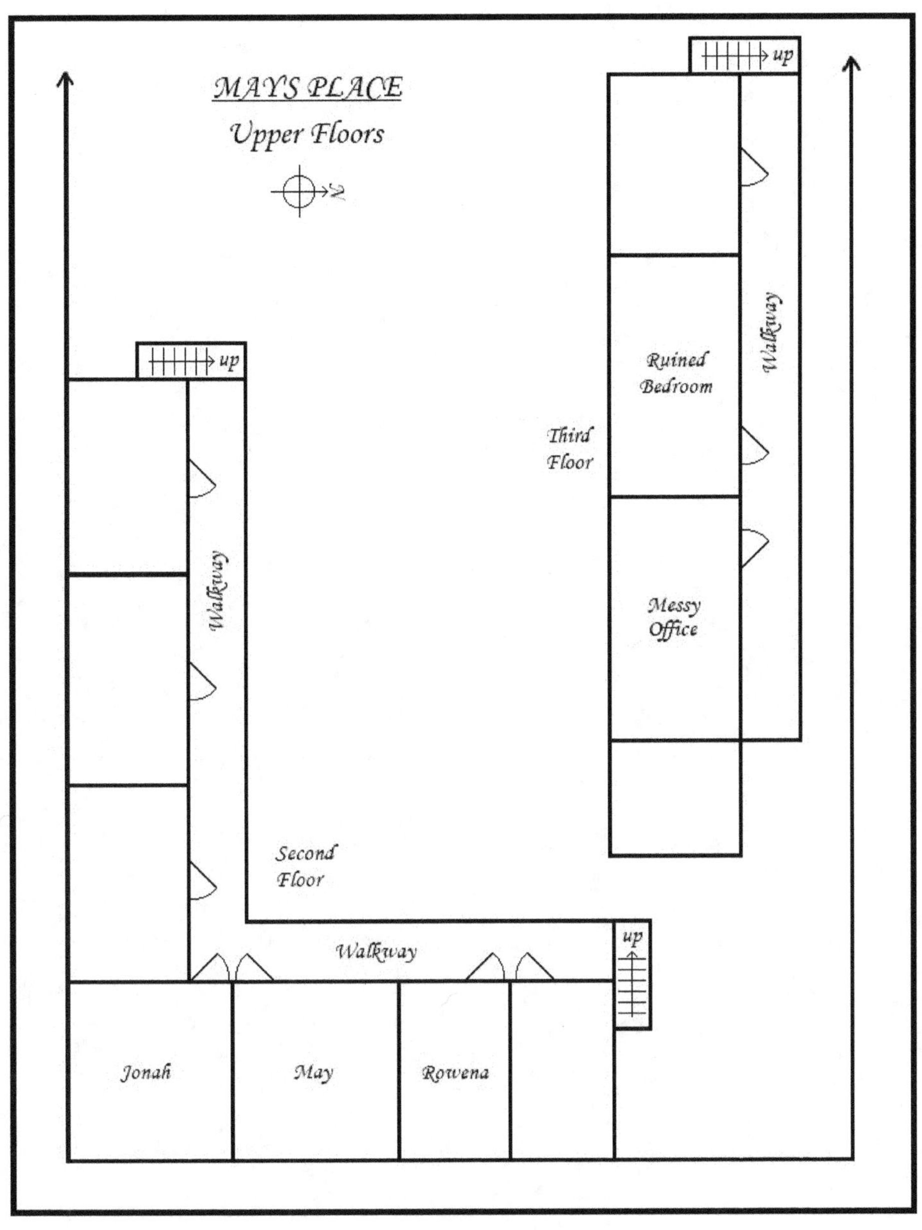

MAY'S PLACE
Upper Floors
N
up
Walkway
Ruined
Bedroom
Third
Floor
Messy
Office
Walkway
Second
Floor
up
Walkway
up
Jonah
May
Rowena